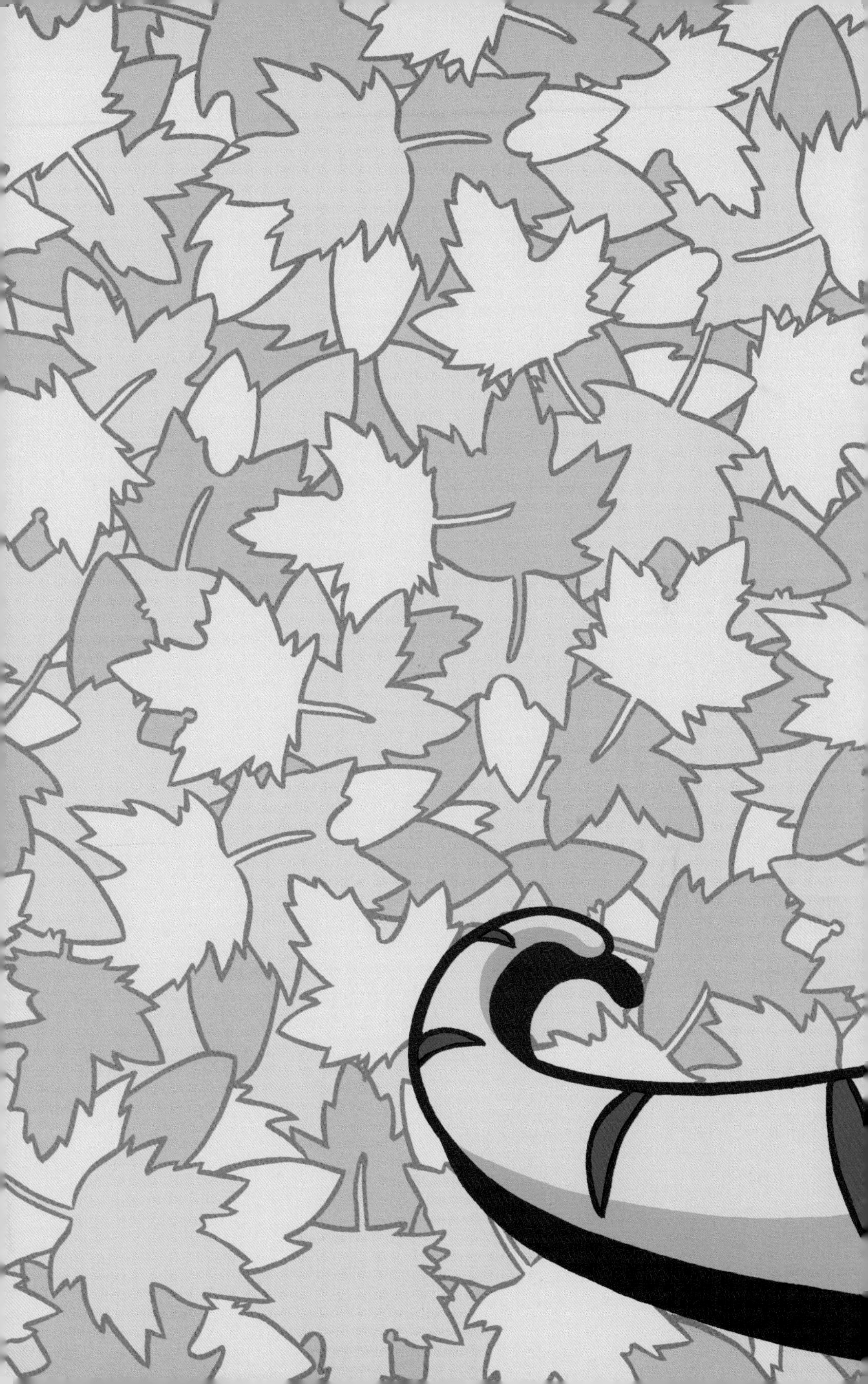

JELLABY

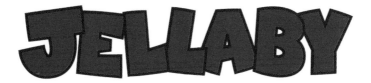

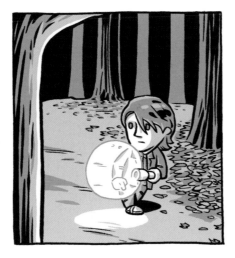

JELLABY

by
KEAN SOO

HYPERION BOOKS
FOR CHILDREN
New York

ACKNOWLEDGMENTS:

SPECIAL THANKS TO CALISTA BRILL, ROBERTA PRESSEL, JUDY HANSEN, HOPE LARSON, DAVID & NICOLAS SEIGNERET, BEN HU, JASON TURNER, CLIO CHIANG, KAZU KIBUISHI, AND OF COURSE, ALL MY FRIENDS AND FAMILY FOR THEIR LOVE AND SUPPORT

AND A VERY SPECIAL THANK-YOU TO THE CANADA COUNCIL FOR THE ARTS FOR THEIR SUPPORT OF THIS WORK

Published by Hyperion Books for Children, an imprint of Disney Book Group.

For information address Hyperion Books for Children, 114 Fifth Avenue, New York, New York, 10011-5690.

Printed in Singapore

First Edition
3 5 7 9 10 8 6 4 2

Library of Congress Cataloging-in-Publication Data on file.

Hardcover edition:
ISBN-13: 978-1-4231-0337-0
ISBN-10: 1-4231-0337-8

Paperback edition:
ISBN-13: 978-1-4231-0303-5
ISBN-10: 1-4231-0303-3

Visit www.hyperionbooksforchildren.com

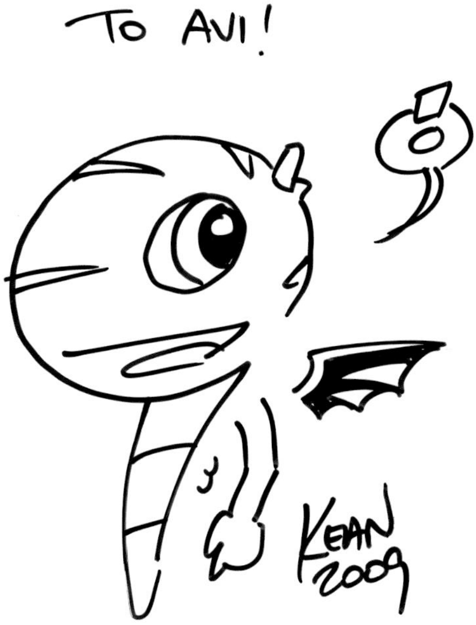
TO AVI!
KEAN
2009

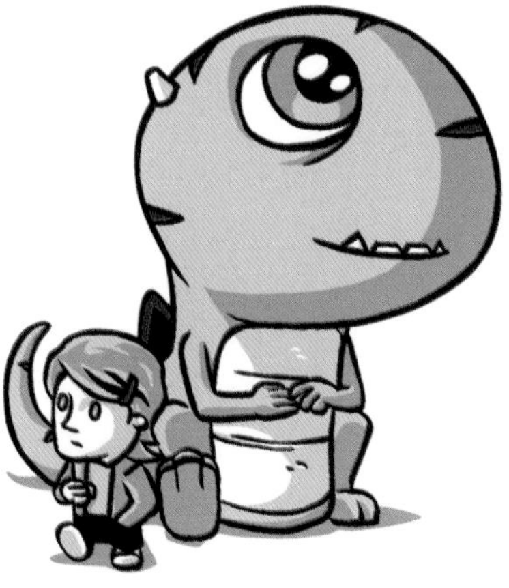

CHAPTER ONE

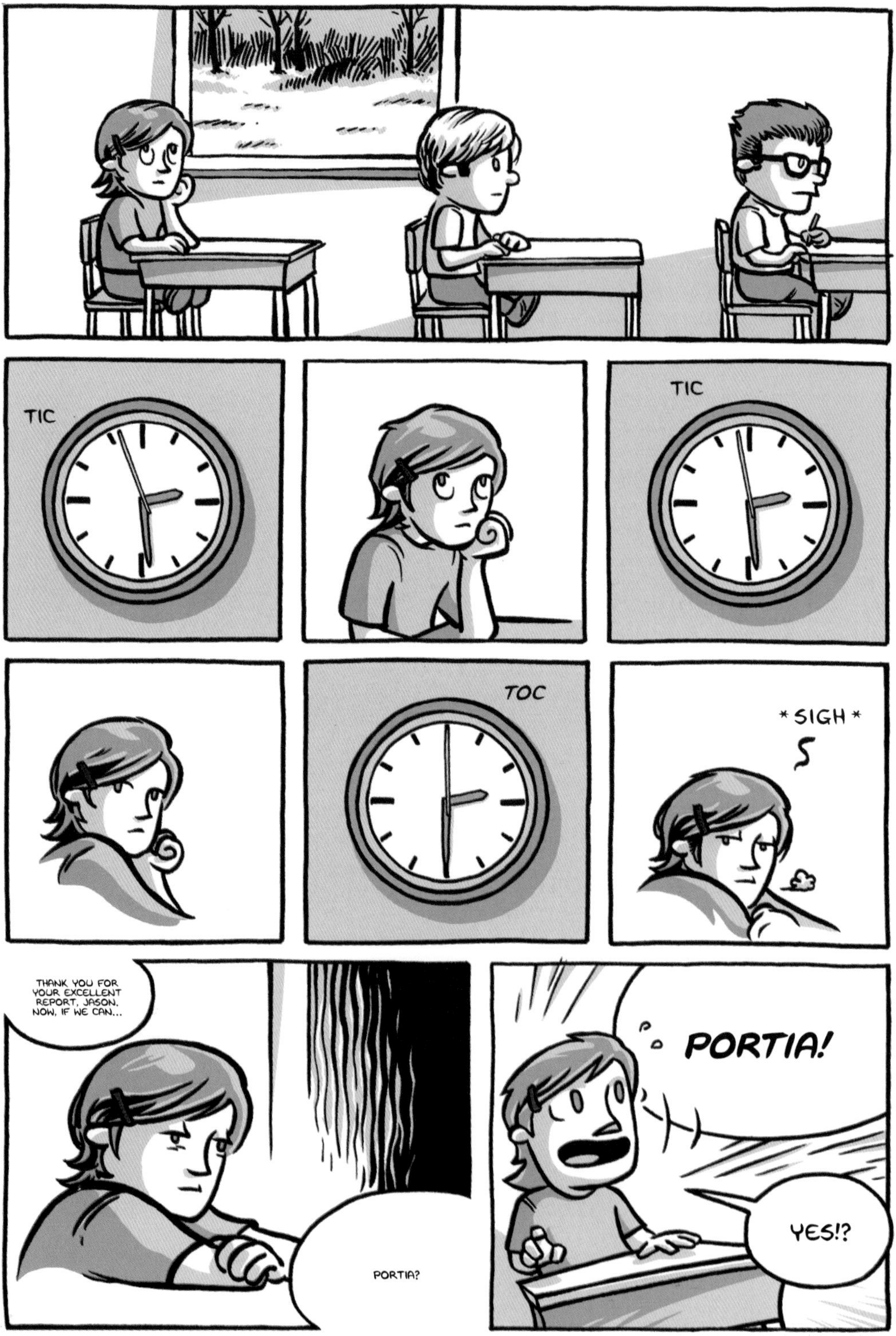
TIC
TIC
TOC
SIGH
THANK YOU FOR YOUR EXCELLENT REPORT, JASON. NOW, IF WE CAN...
PORTIA?
PORTIA!
YES!?

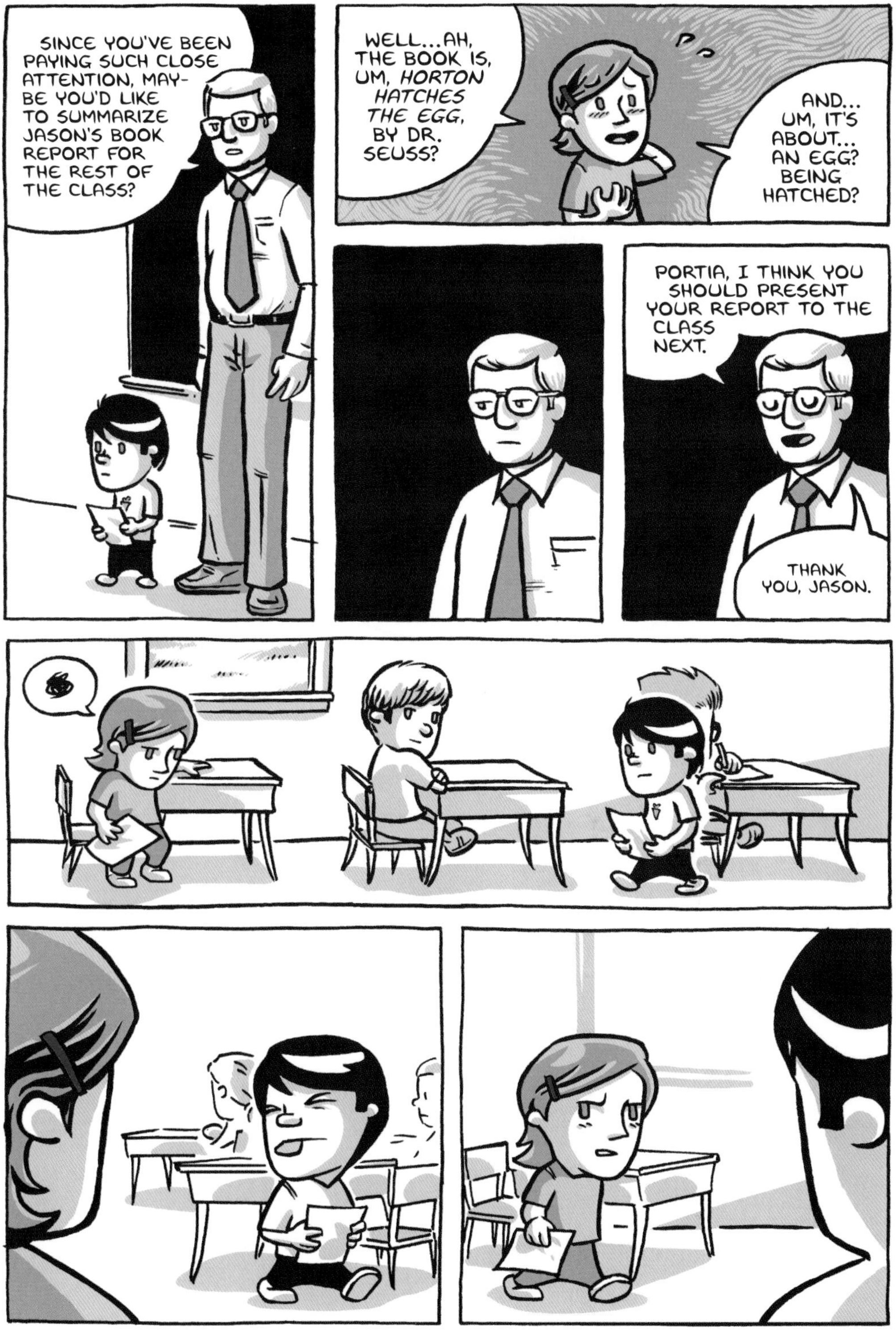
SINCE YOU'VE BEEN PAYING SUCH CLOSE ATTENTION, MAYBE YOU'D LIKE TO SUMMARIZE JASON'S BOOK REPORT FOR THE REST OF THE CLASS?
WELL...AH, THE BOOK IS, UM, *HORTON HATCHES THE EGG*, BY DR. SEUSS?
AND... UM, IT'S ABOUT... AN EGG? BEING HATCHED?
PORTIA, I THINK YOU SHOULD PRESENT YOUR REPORT TO THE CLASS NEXT.
THANK YOU, JASON.

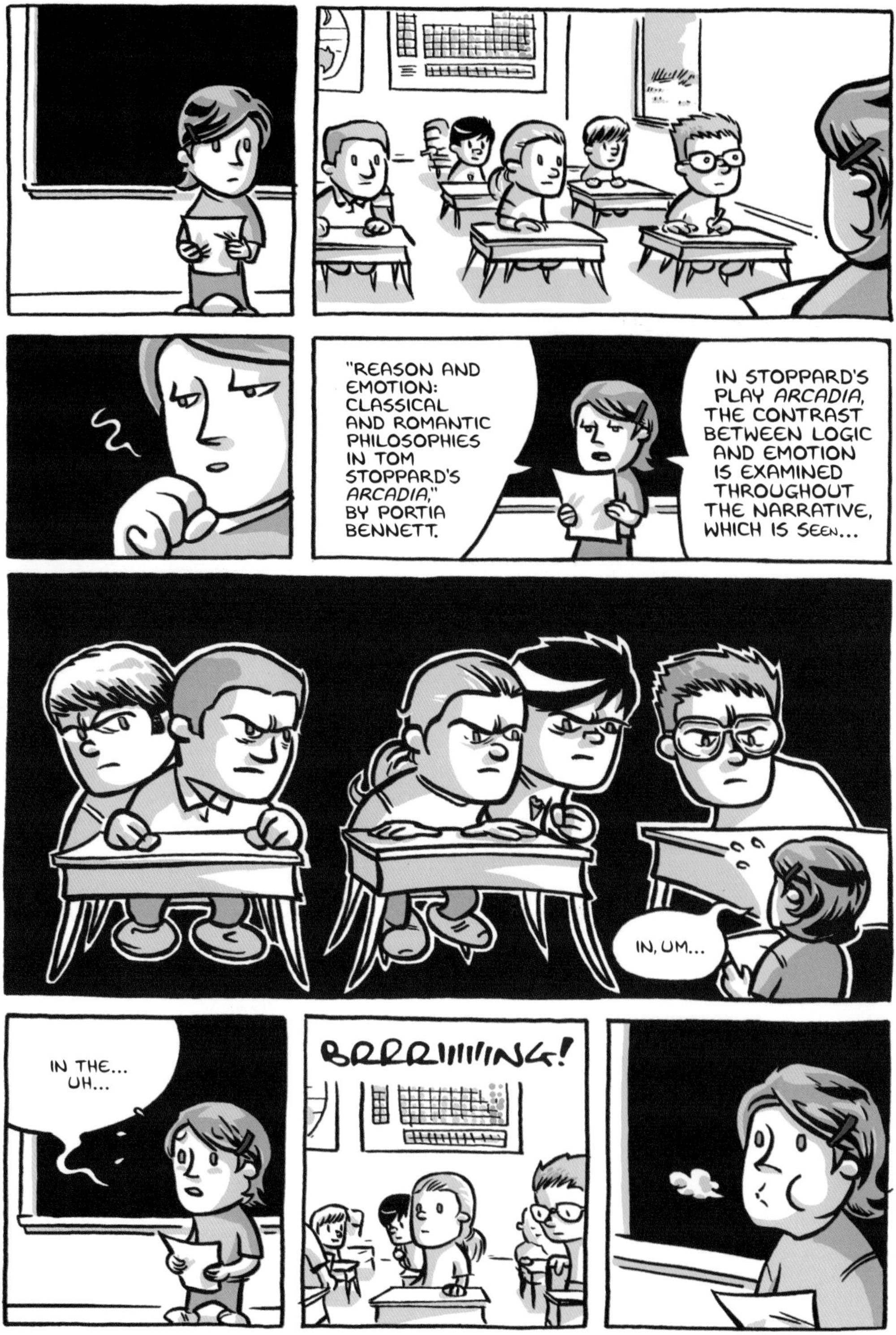
"REASON AND EMOTION: CLASSICAL AND ROMANTIC PHILOSOPHIES IN TOM STOPPARD'S *ARCADIA*," BY PORTIA BENNETT.
IN STOPPARD'S PLAY *ARCADIA*, THE CONTRAST BETWEEN LOGIC AND EMOTION IS EXAMINED THROUGHOUT THE NARRATIVE, WHICH IS SEEN...
IN, UM...
IN THE... UH...
BRRRIIIIING!

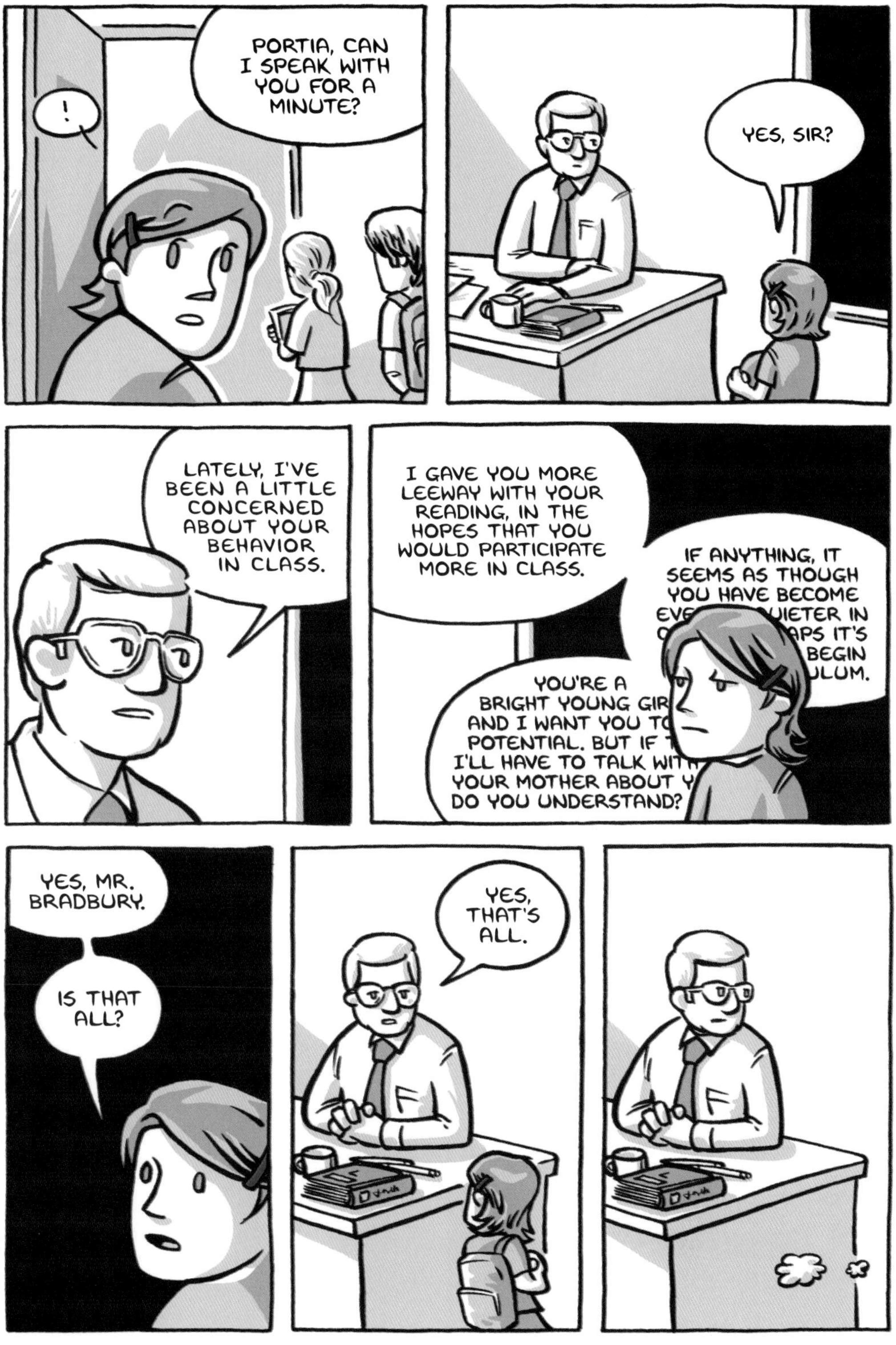
PORTIA, CAN I SPEAK WITH YOU FOR A MINUTE?
!
YES, SIR?
LATELY, I'VE BEEN A LITTLE CONCERNED ABOUT YOUR BEHAVIOR IN CLASS.
I GAVE YOU MORE LEEWAY WITH YOUR READING, IN THE HOPES THAT YOU WOULD PARTICIPATE MORE IN CLASS.
IF ANYTHING, IT SEEMS AS THOUGH YOU HAVE BECOME
YOU'RE A BRIGHT YOUNG
AND I WANT YOU
POTENTIAL. BUT IF
I'LL HAVE TO TALK
YOUR MOTHER ABOUT
DO YOU UNDERSTAND?
YES, MR. BRADBURY.
IS THAT ALL?
YES, THAT'S ALL.

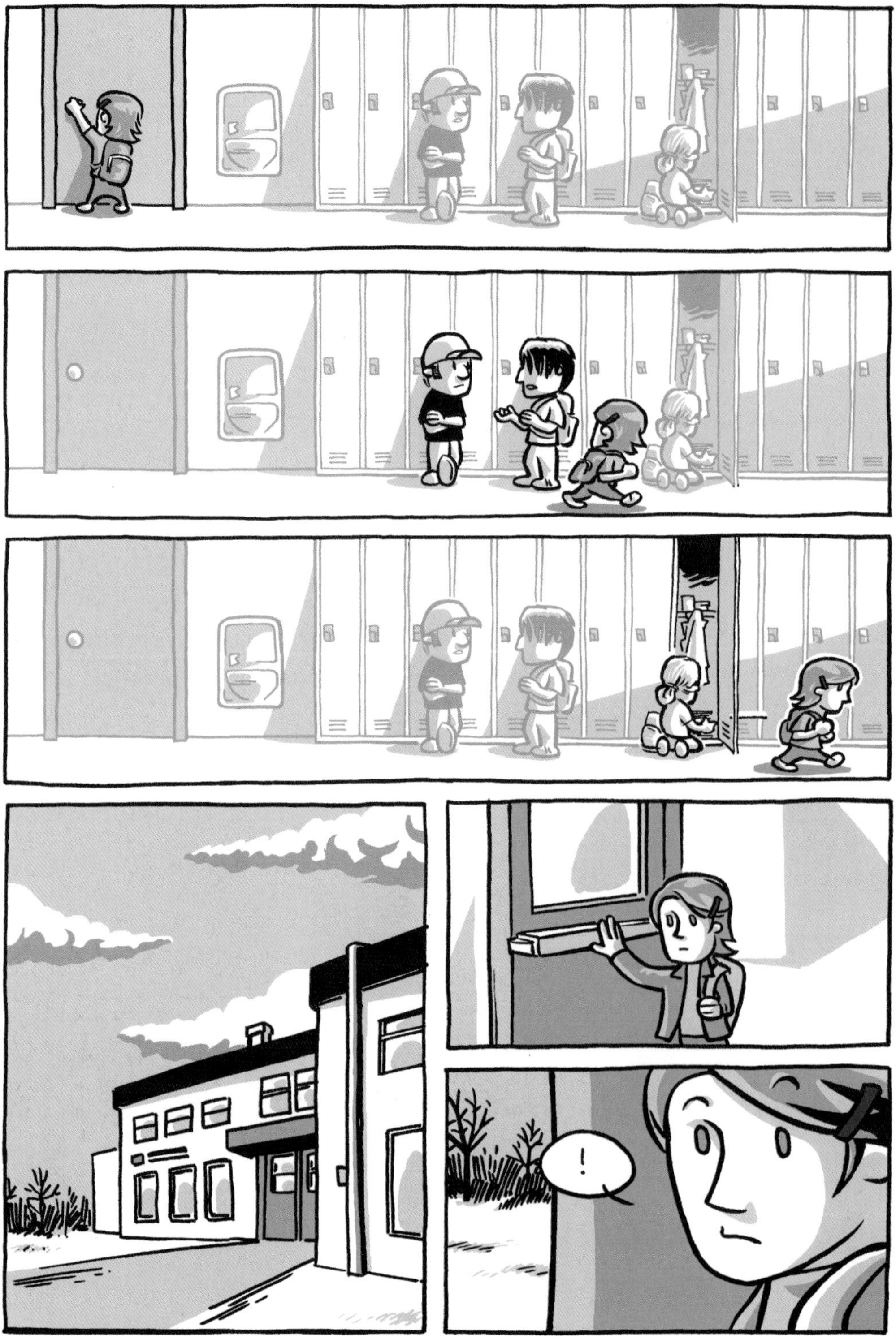
!

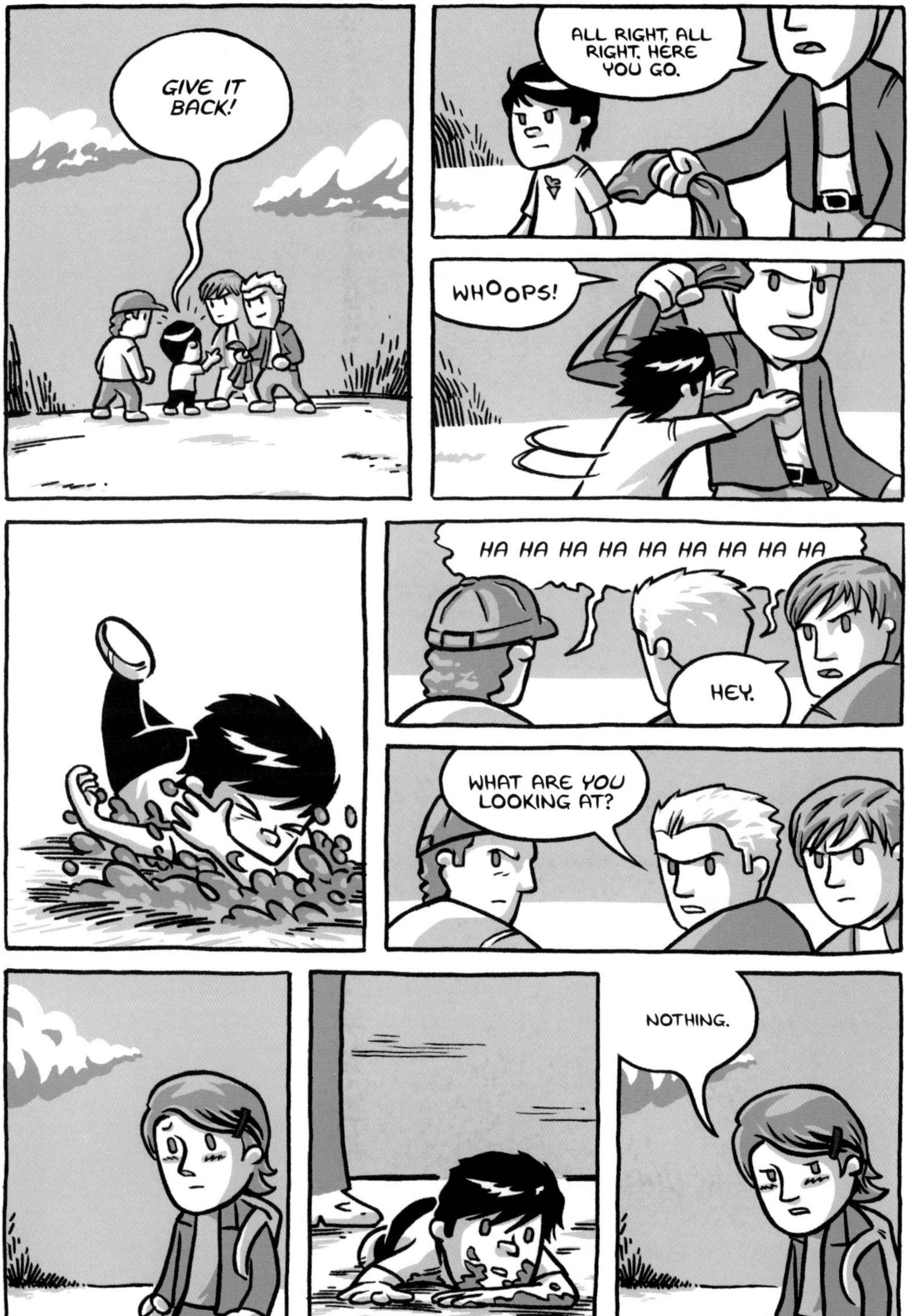
GIVE IT BACK!
ALL RIGHT, ALL RIGHT. HERE YOU GO.
WHOOPS!
HA HA HA HA HA HA HA HA HA
HEY.
WHAT ARE YOU LOOKING AT?
NOTHING.

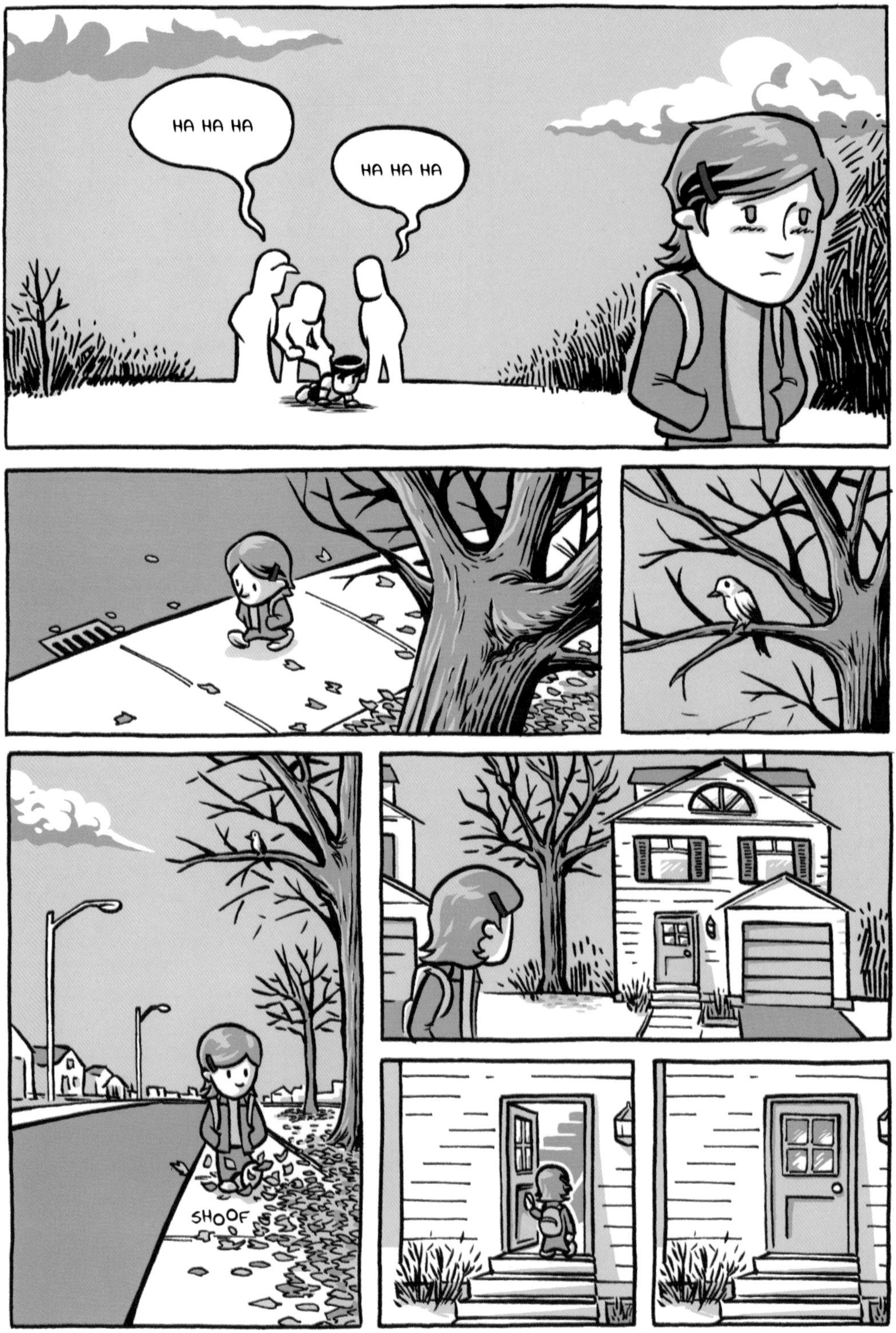
HA HA HA
HA HA HA
SHOOF

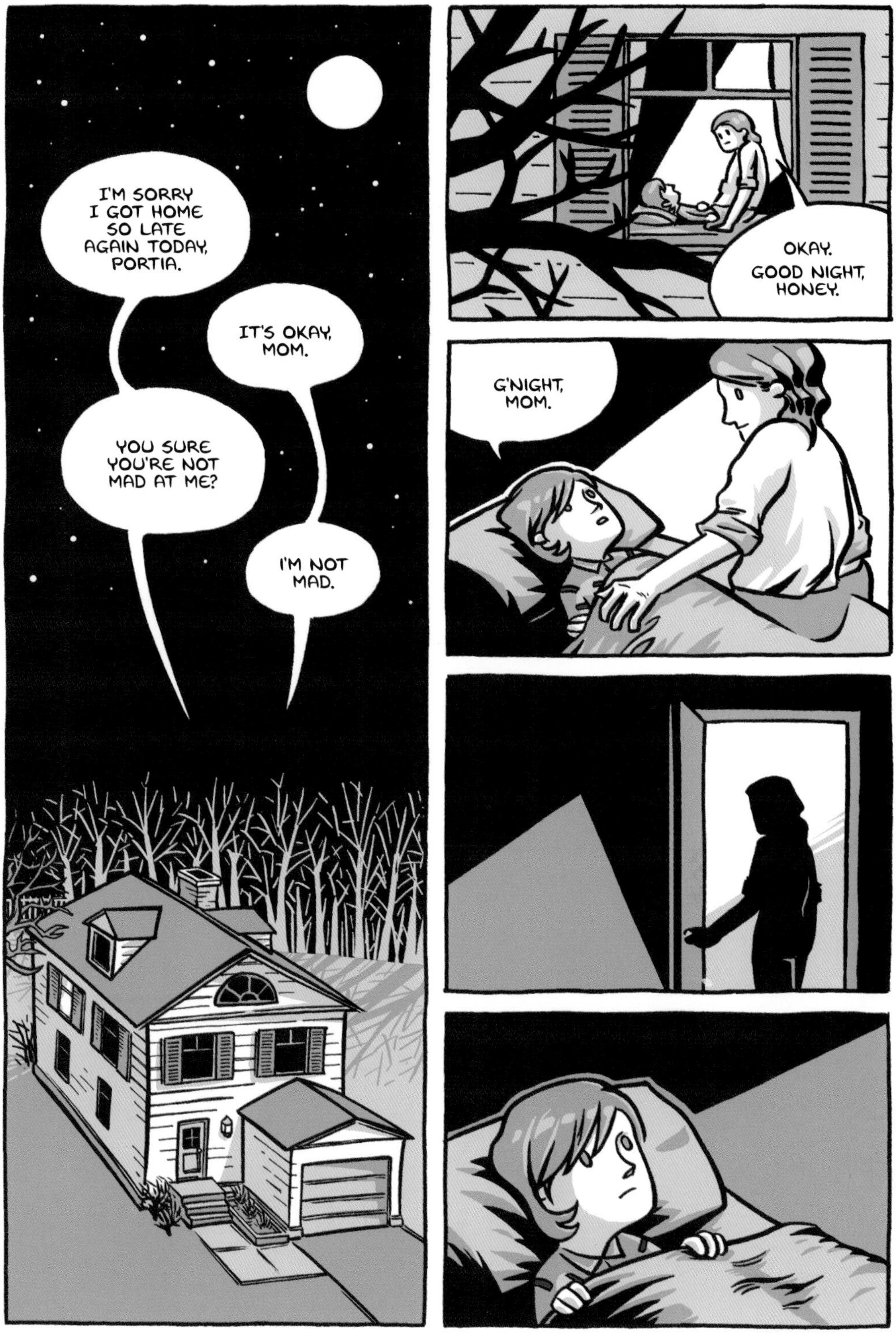
I'M SORRY I GOT HOME SO LATE AGAIN TODAY, PORTIA.
IT'S OKAY, MOM.
YOU SURE YOU'RE NOT MAD AT ME?
I'M NOT MAD.
OKAY. GOOD NIGHT, HONEY.
G'NIGHT, MOM.

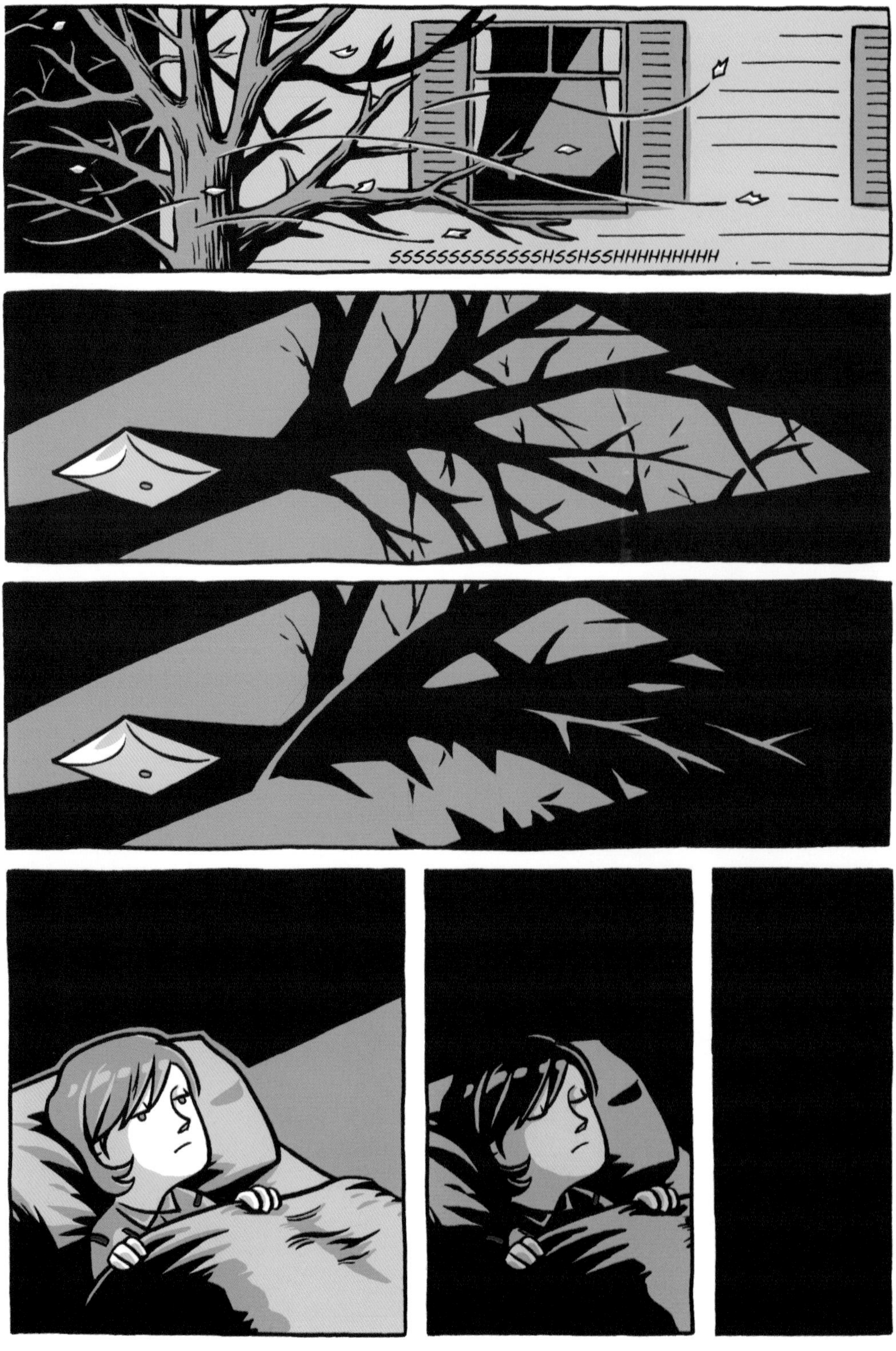
SSSSSSSSSSSSSSHSSHSSHHHHHHHHHH

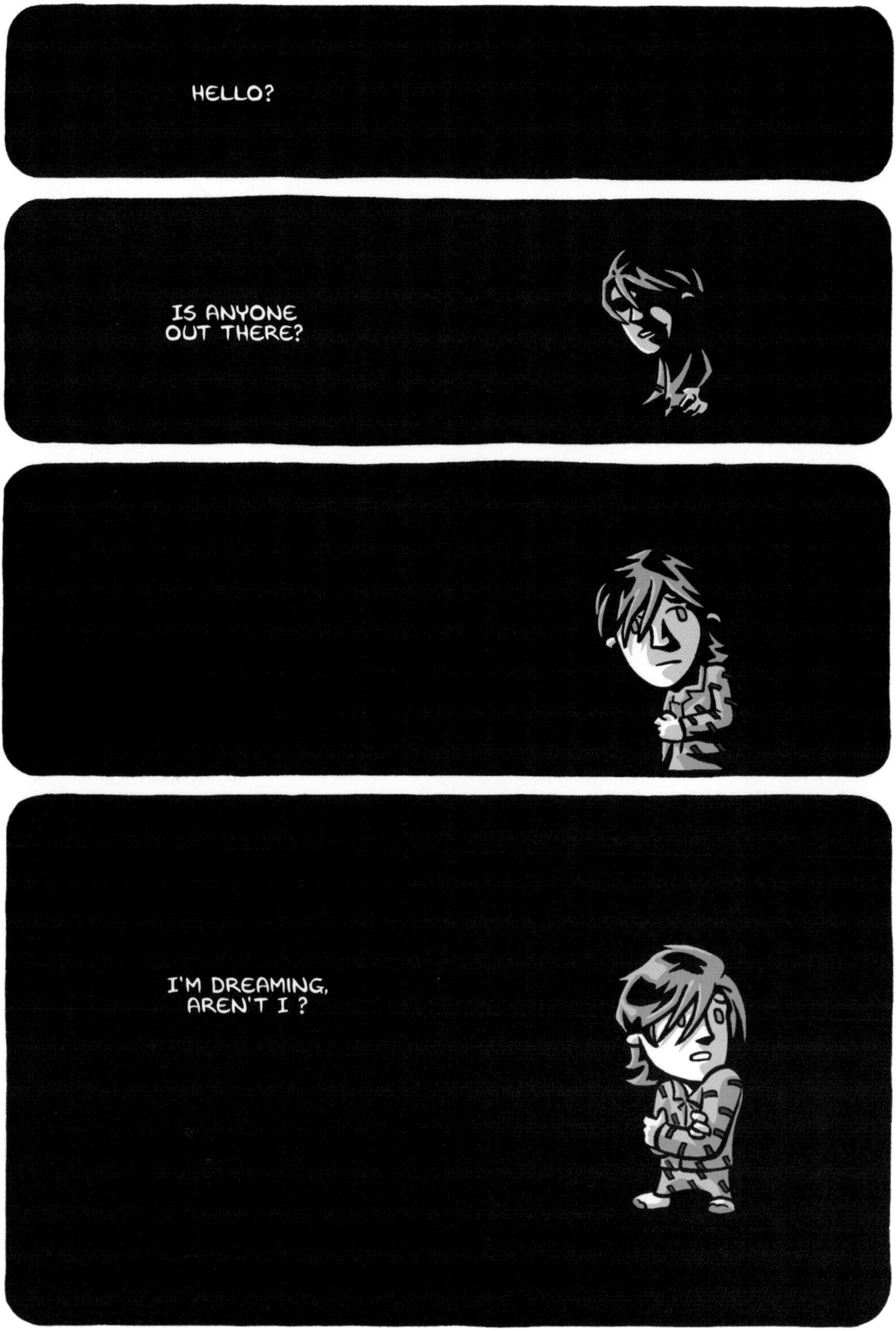
HELLO?
IS ANYONE OUT THERE?
I'M DREAMING, AREN'T I ?

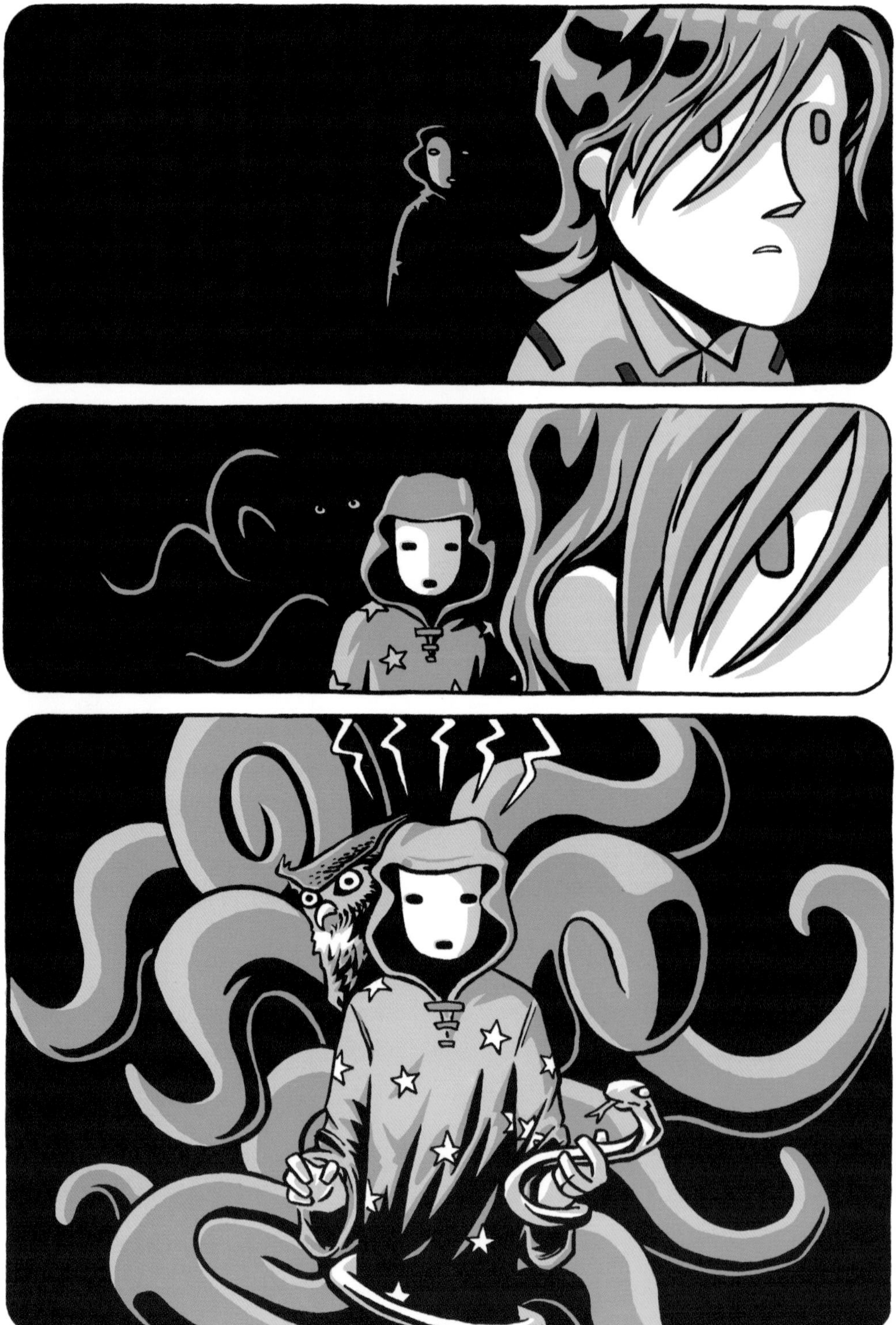

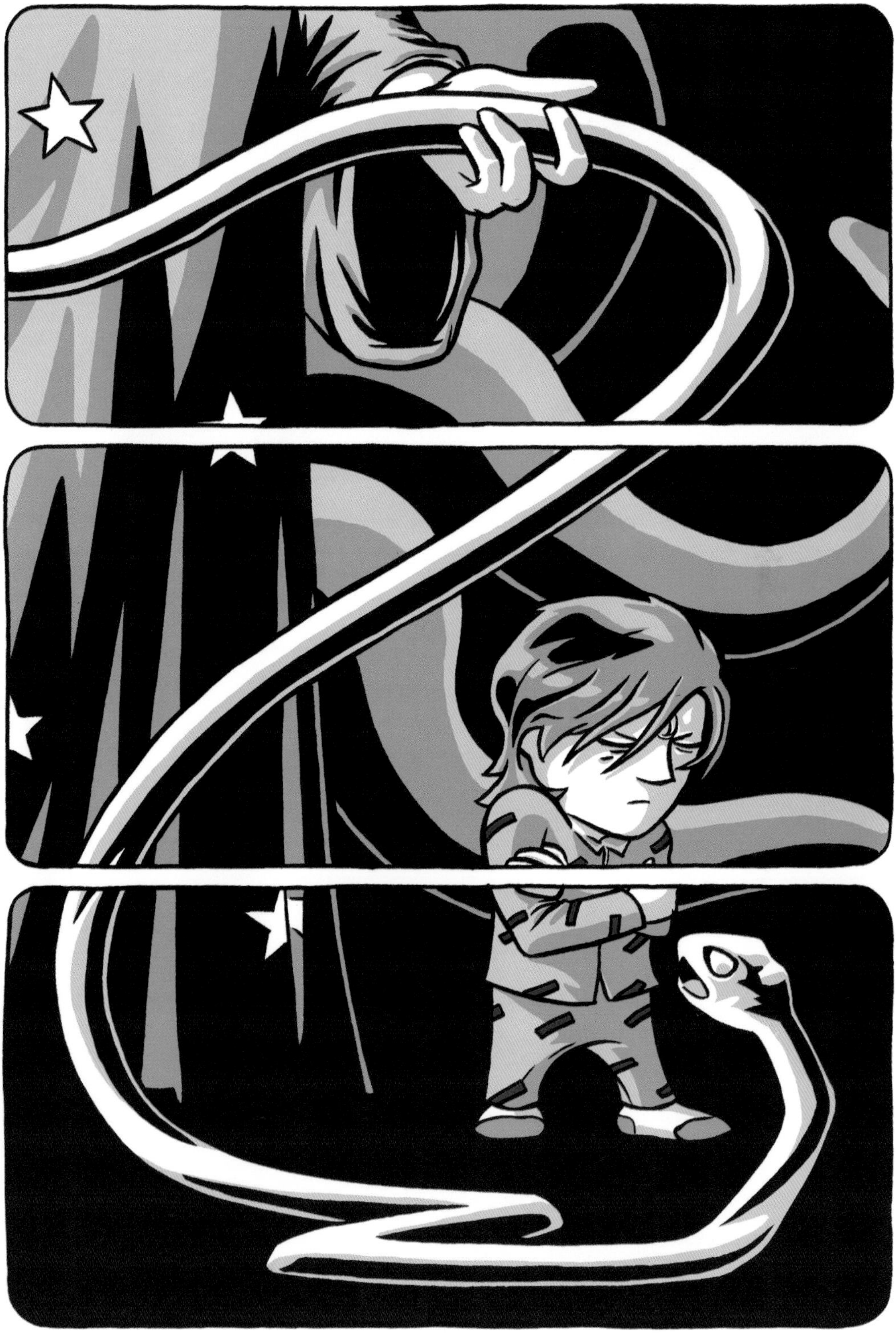

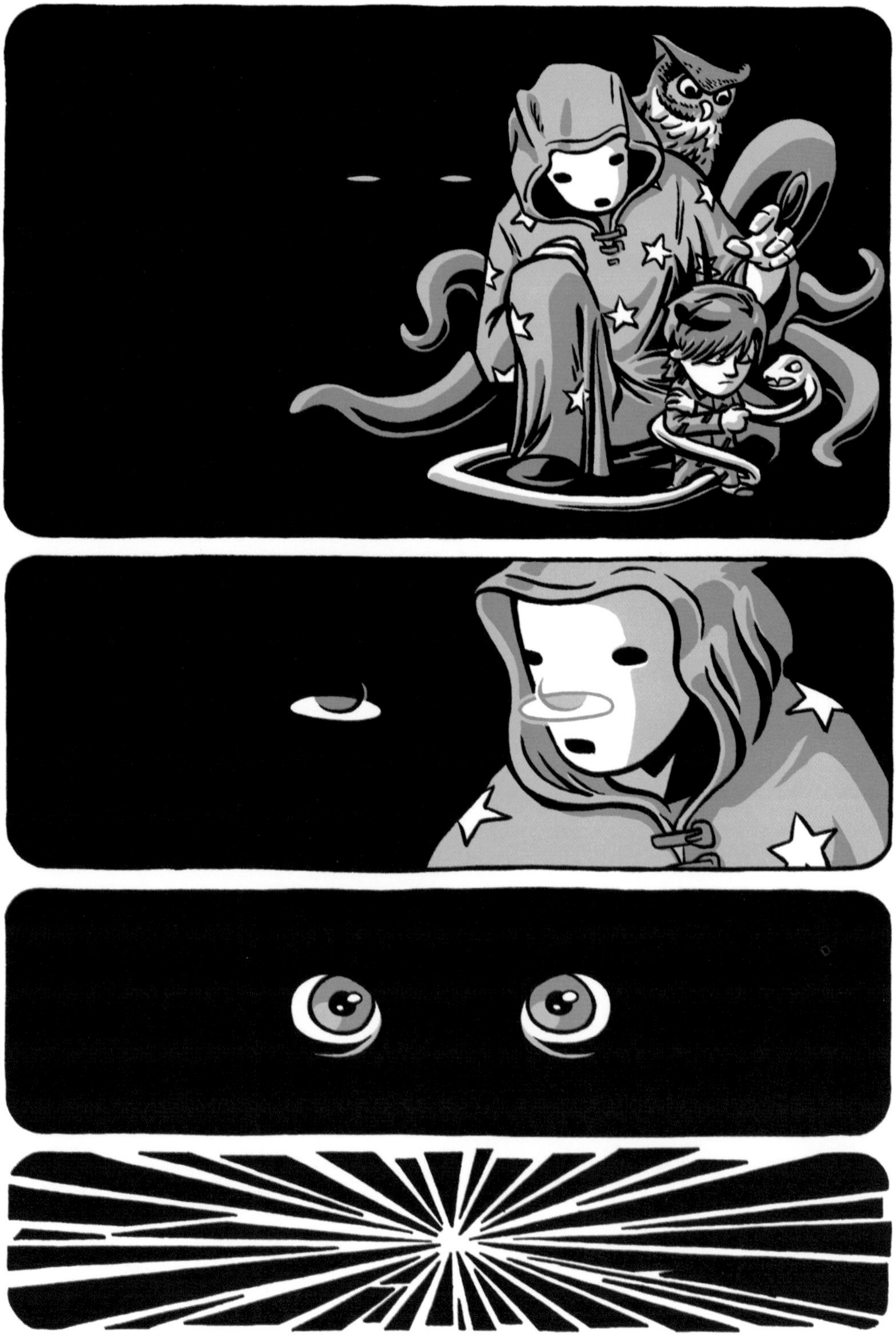

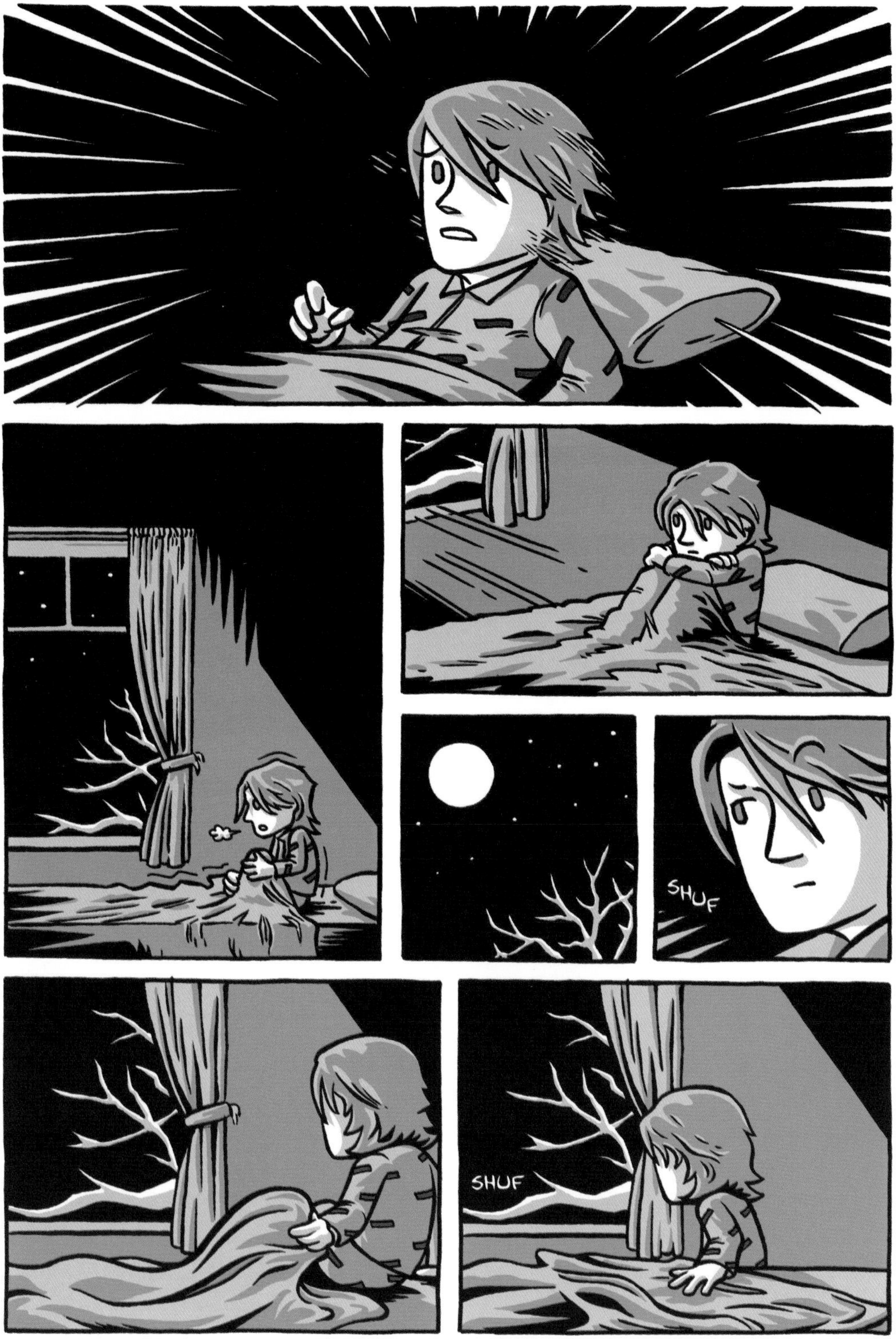
SHUF
SHUF

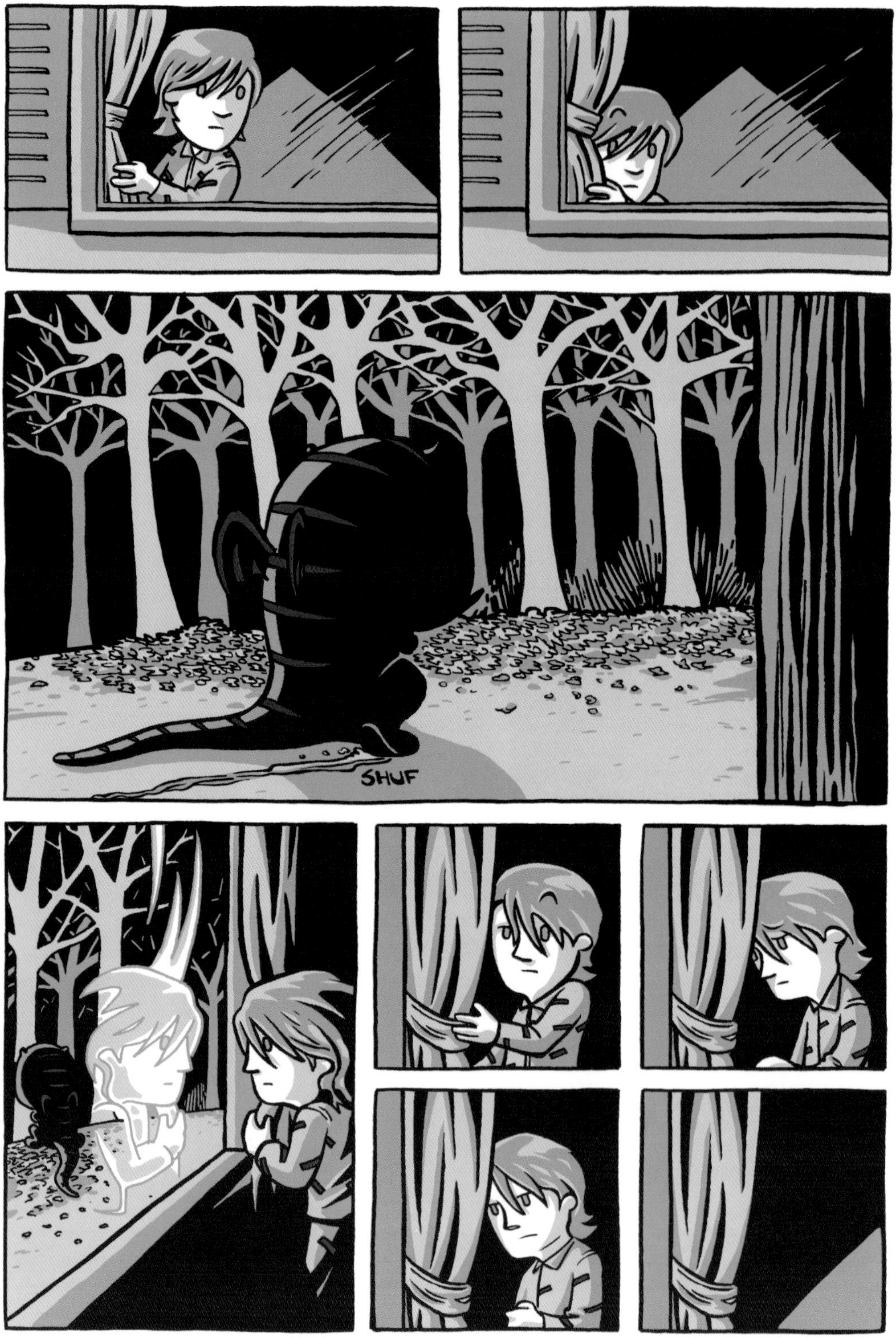
SHUF

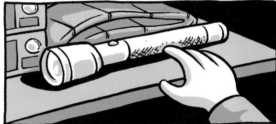

CREEEEEE...

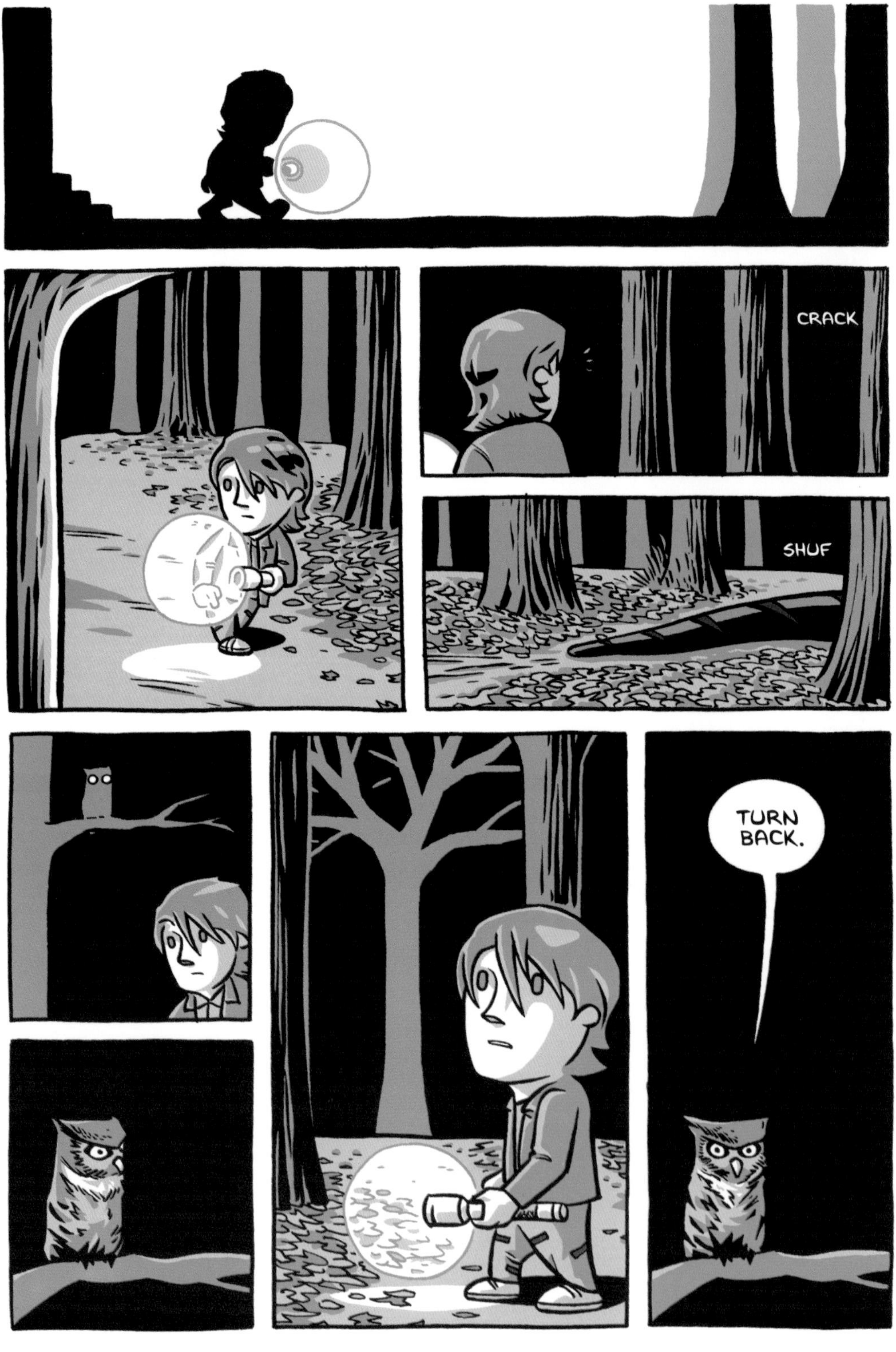
CRACK
SHUF
TURN BACK.

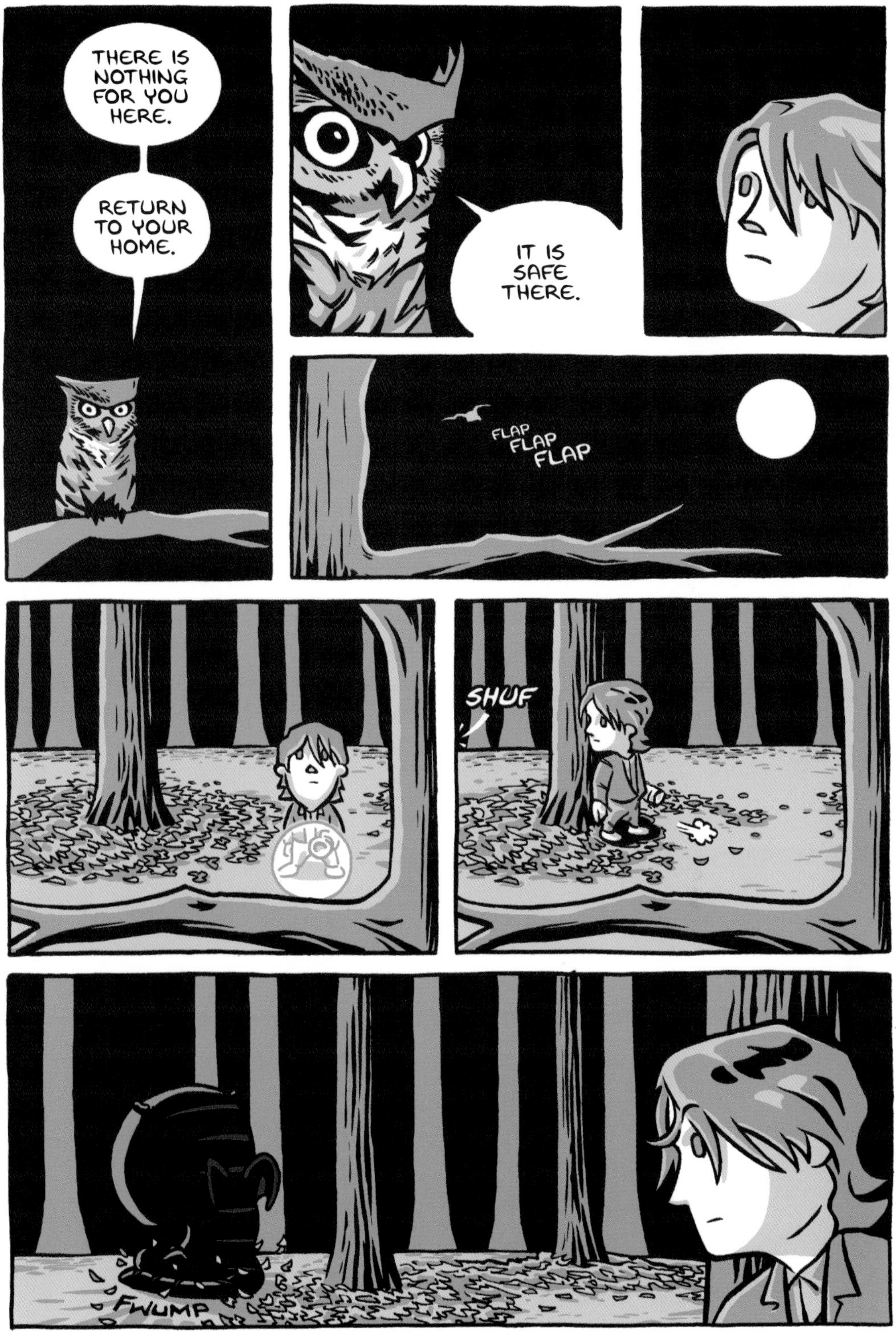
THERE IS NOTHING FOR YOU HERE.
RETURN TO YOUR HOME.
IT IS SAFE THERE.
FLAP FLAP FLAP
SHUF
FWUMP

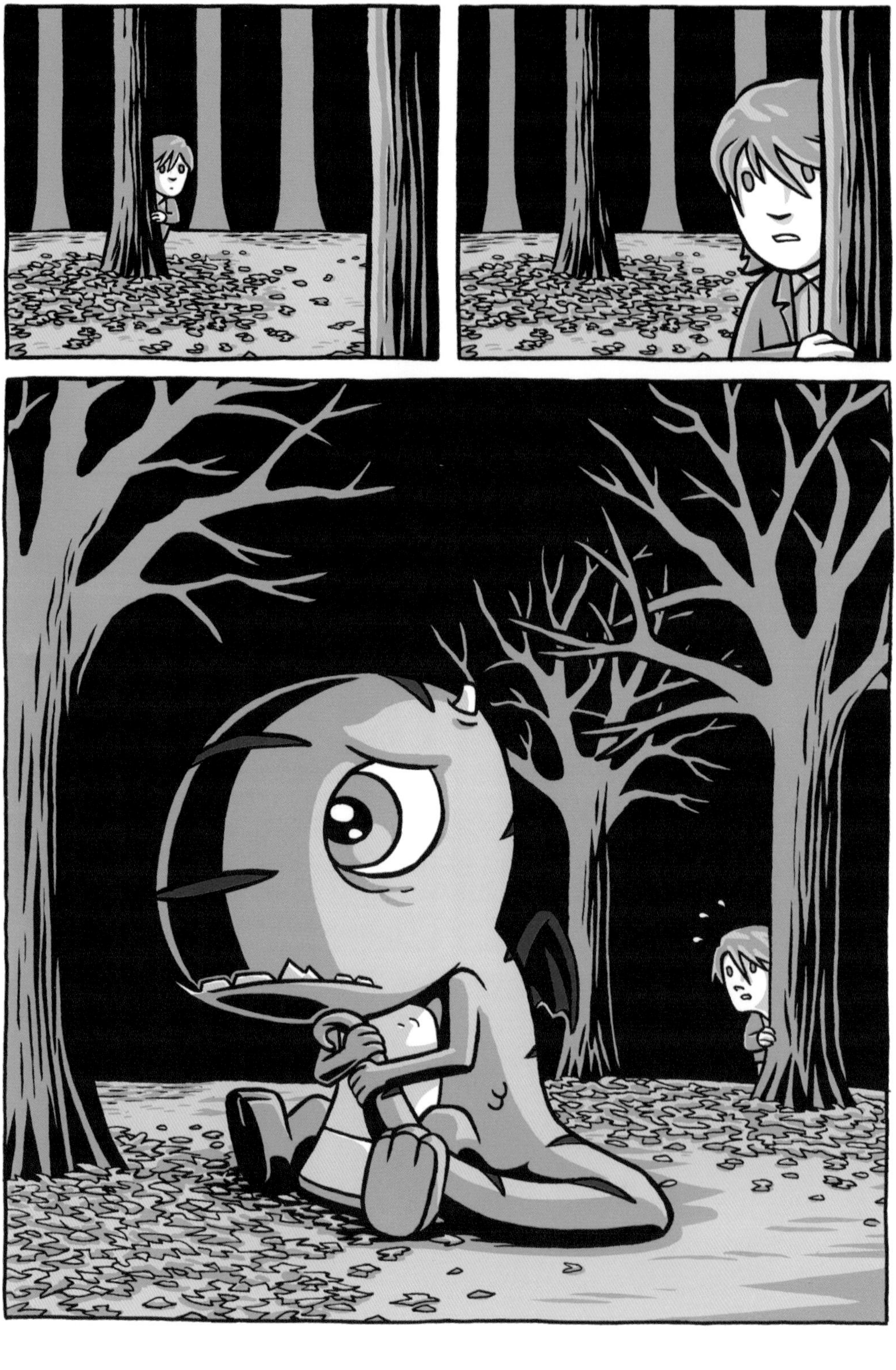

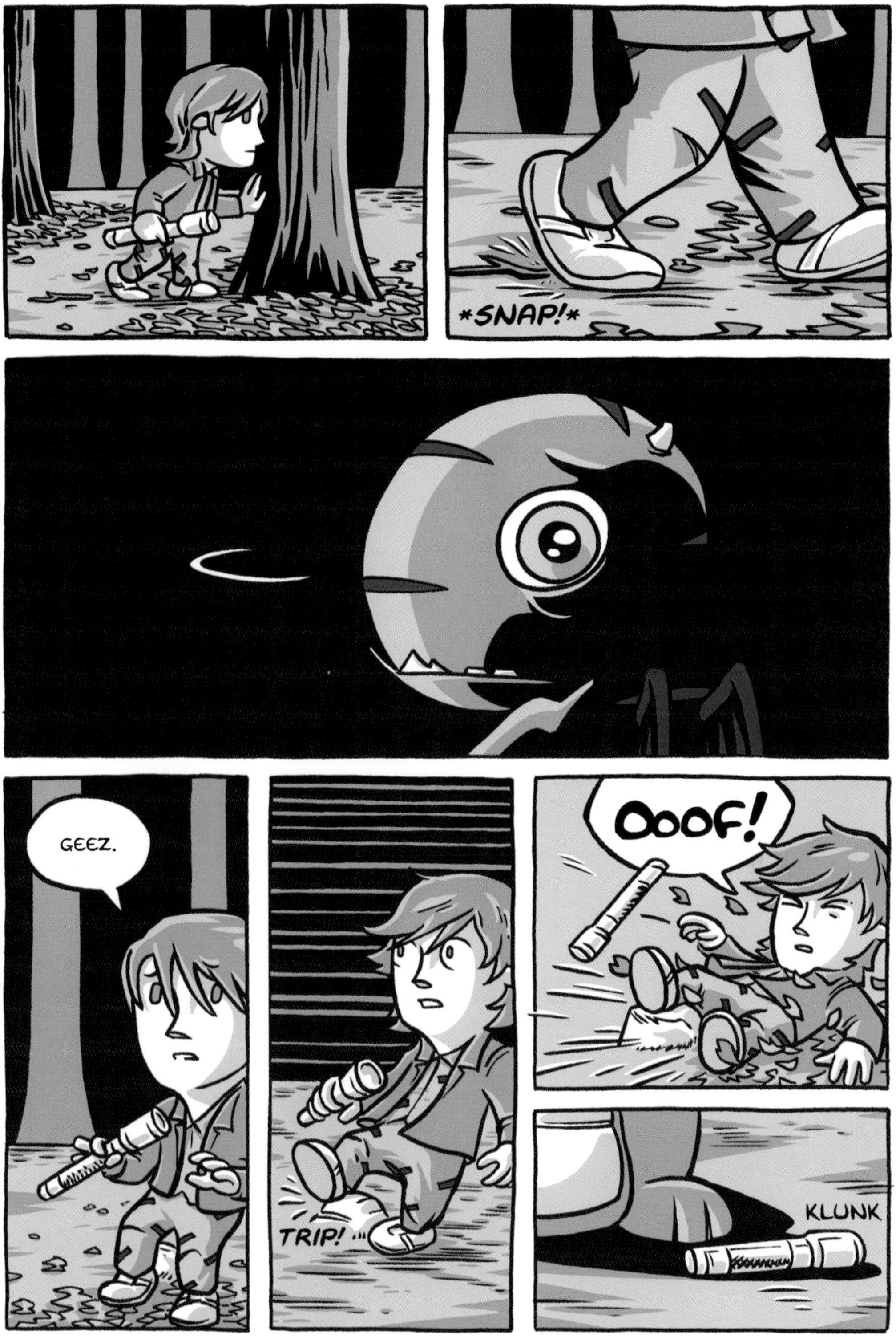
SNAP!
GEEZ.
TRIP!
OOOF!
KLUNK

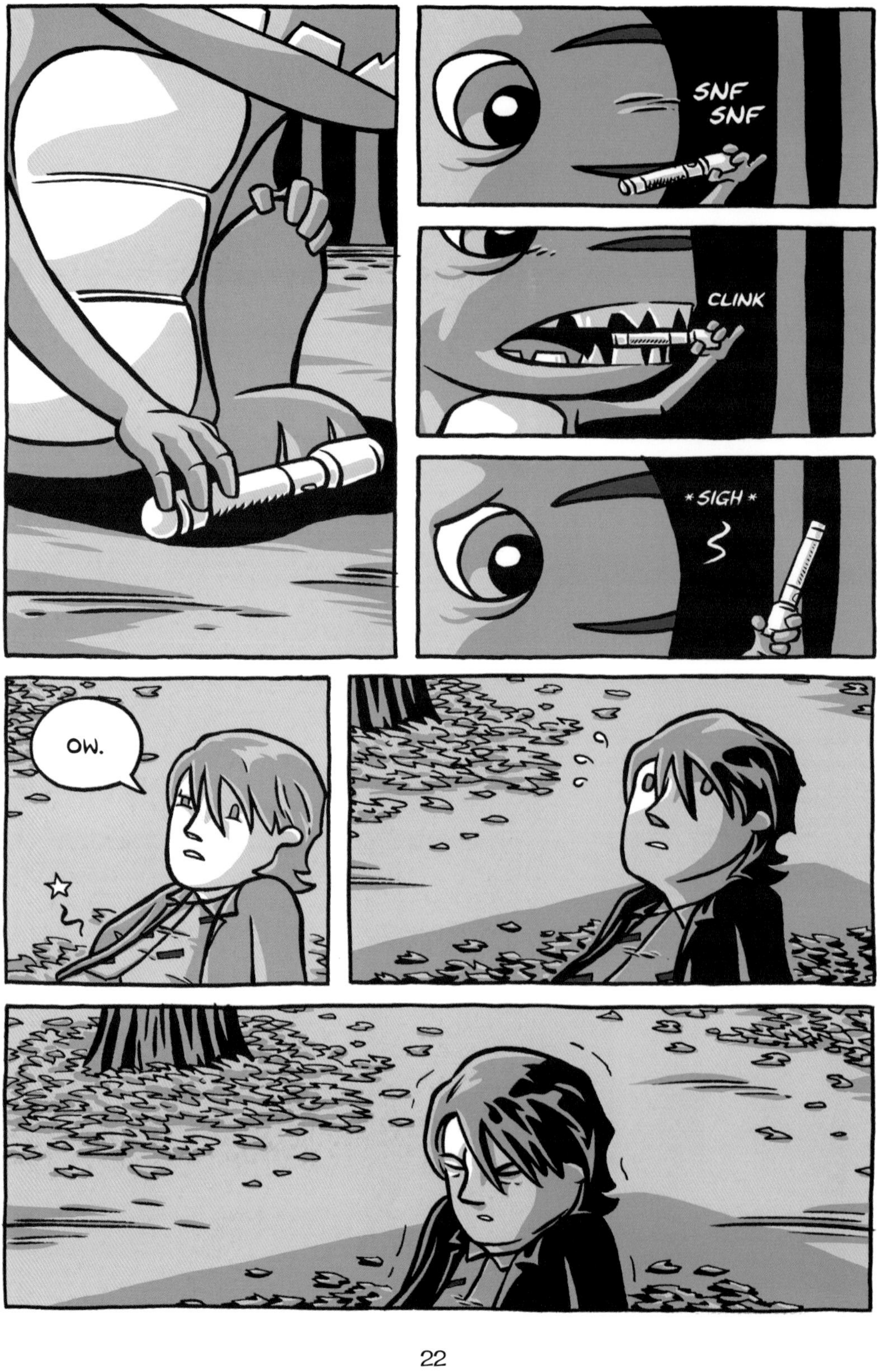
SNF
SNF
CLINK
SIGH
OW.

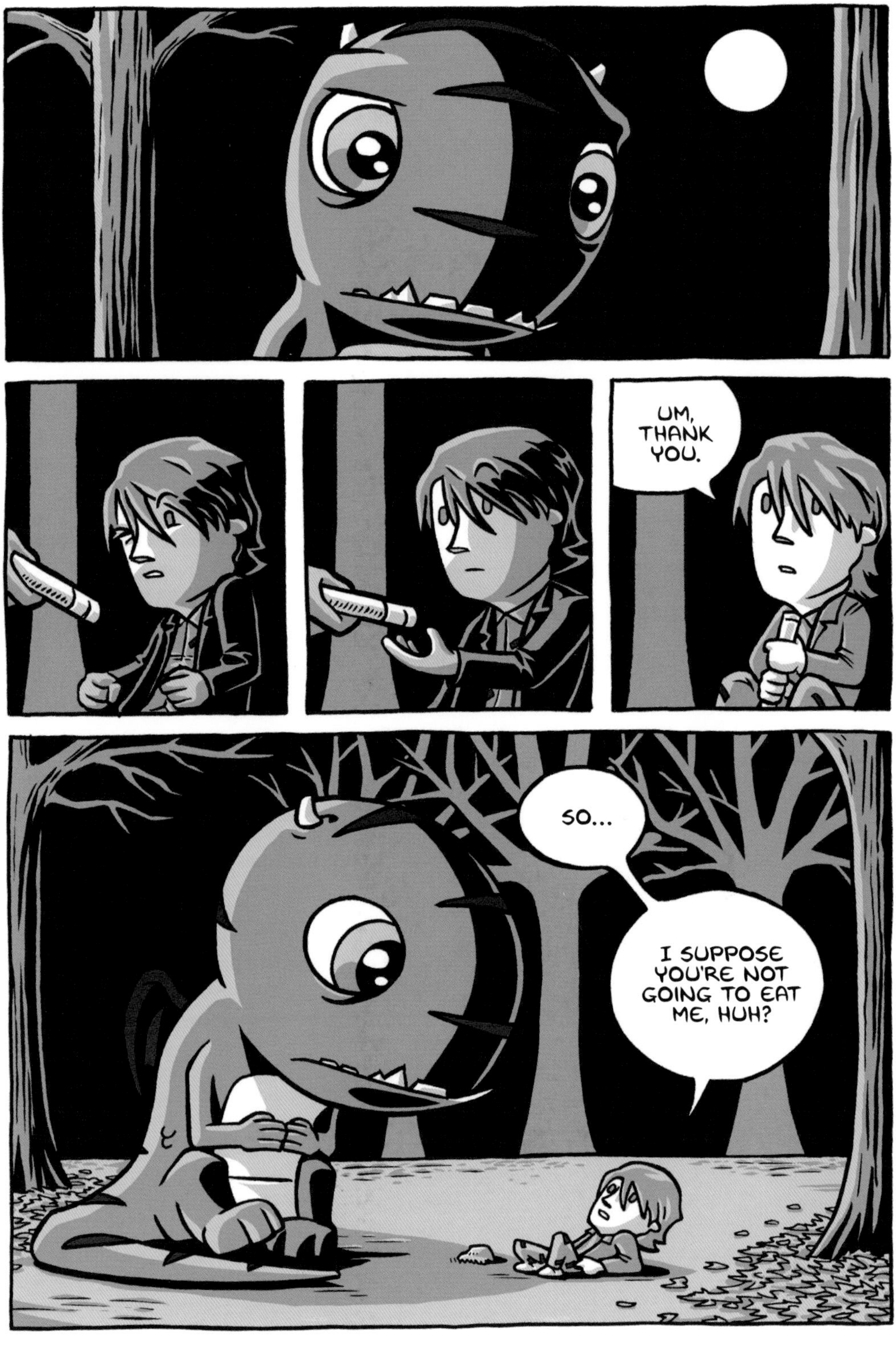
UM, THANK YOU.
SO...
I SUPPOSE YOU'RE NOT GOING TO EAT ME, HUH?

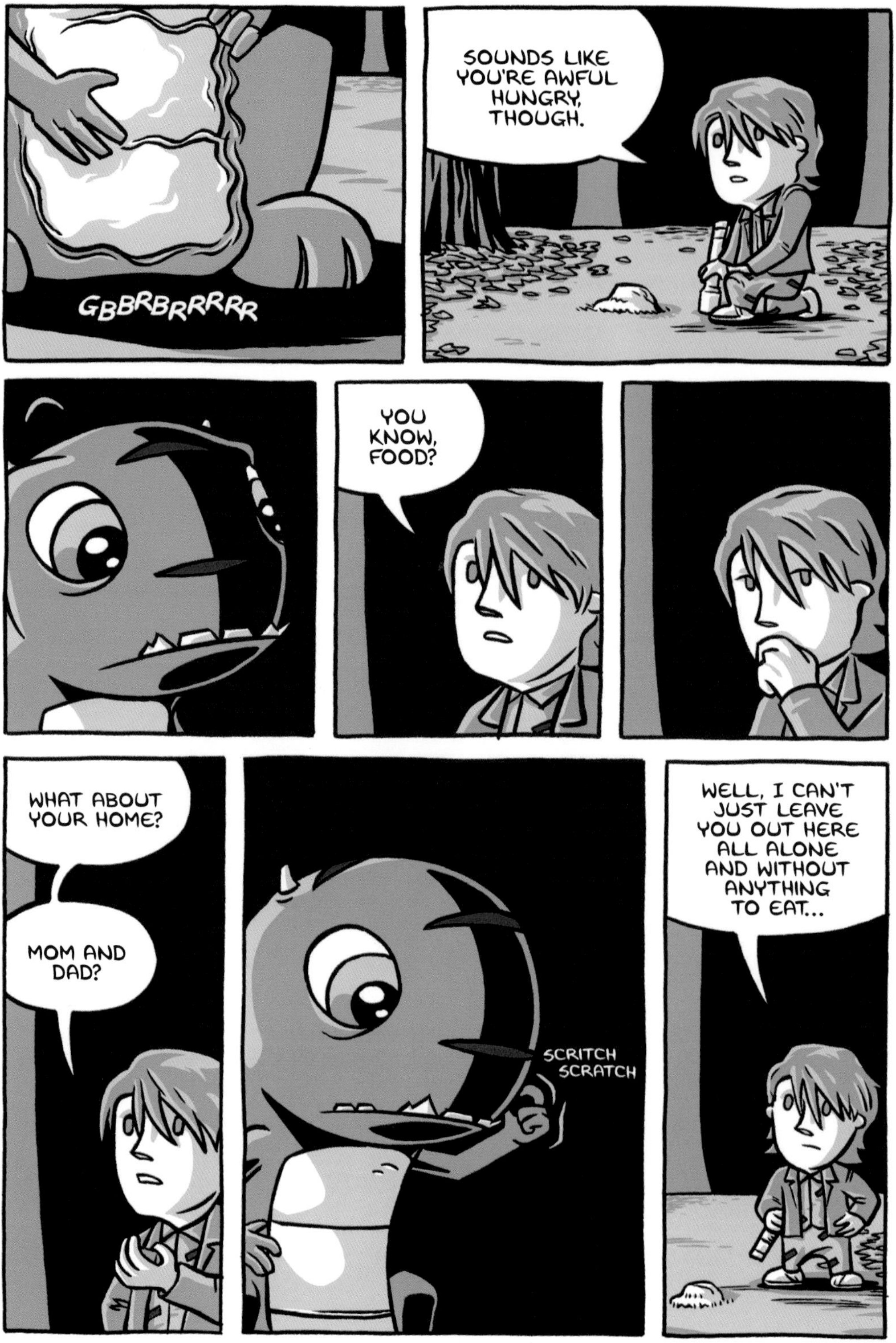
GBBRBRRRRR
SOUNDS LIKE YOU'RE AWFUL HUNGRY, THOUGH.
YOU KNOW, FOOD?
WHAT ABOUT YOUR HOME?
MOM AND DAD?
SCRITCH SCRATCH
WELL, I CAN'T JUST LEAVE YOU OUT HERE ALL ALONE AND WITHOUT ANYTHING TO EAT...

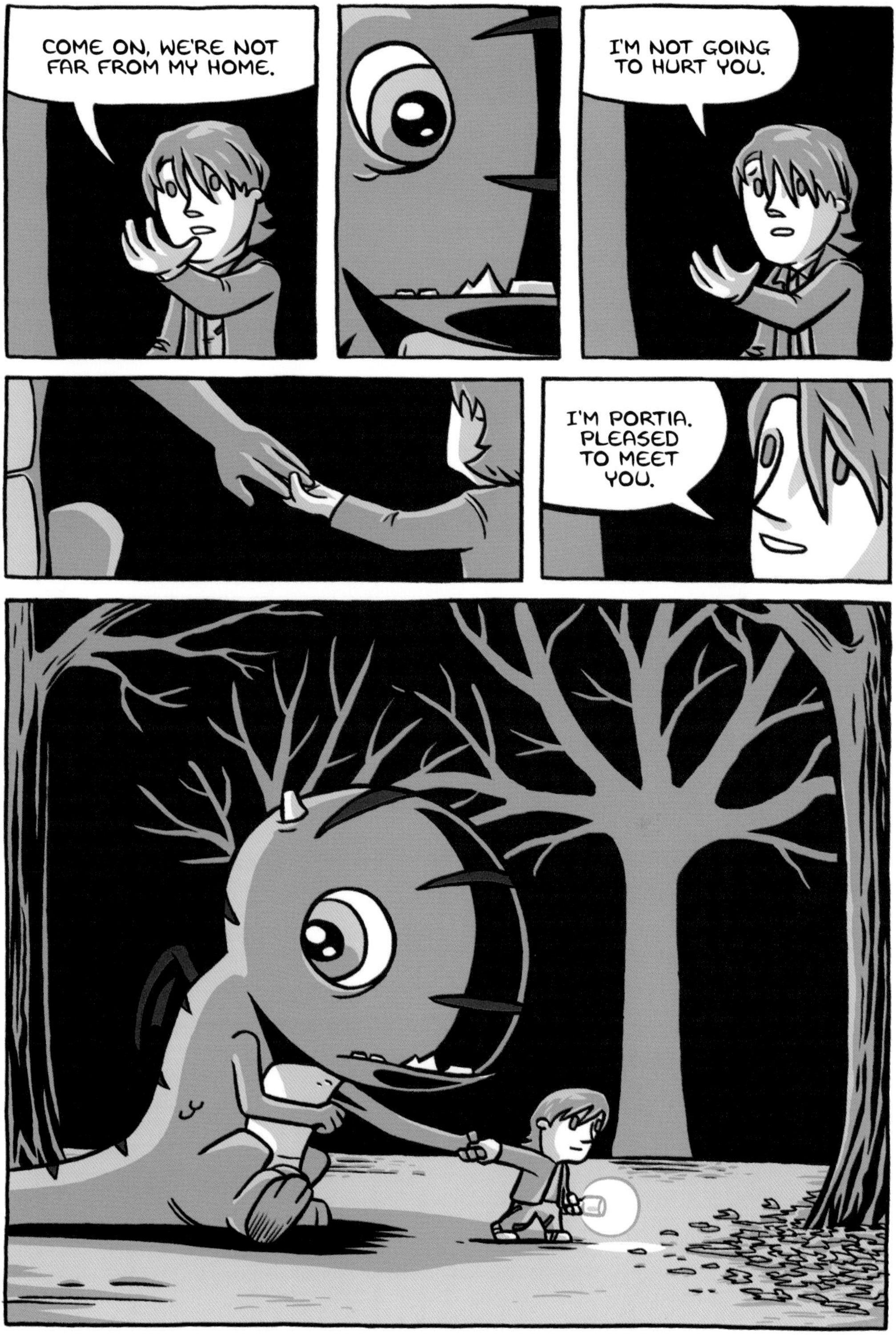
COME ON, WE'RE NOT FAR FROM MY HOME.
I'M NOT GOING TO HURT YOU.
I'M PORTIA. PLEASED TO MEET YOU.

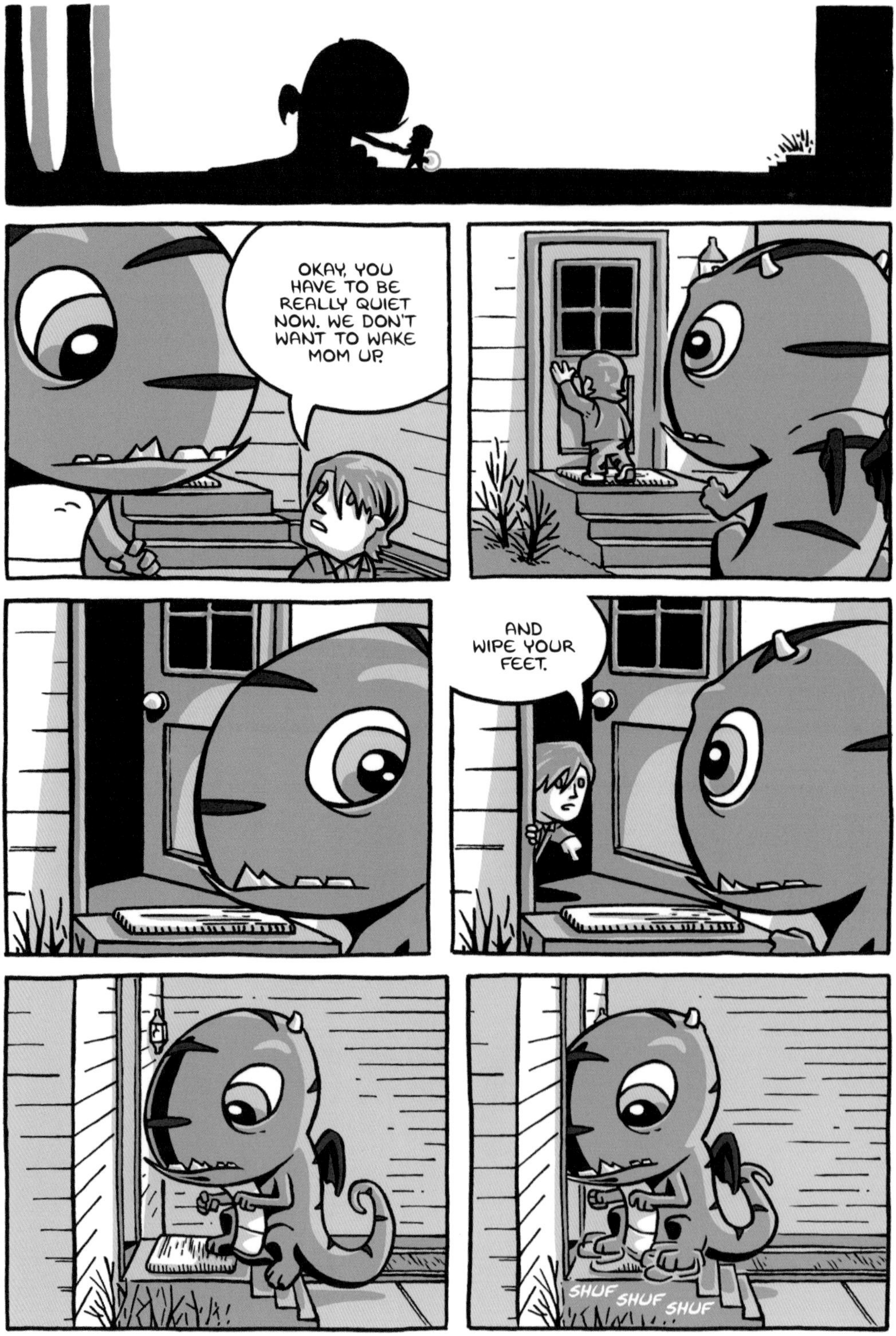
OKAY, YOU HAVE TO BE REALLY QUIET NOW. WE DON'T WANT TO WAKE MOM UP.
AND WIPE YOUR FEET.
SHUF SHUF SHUF

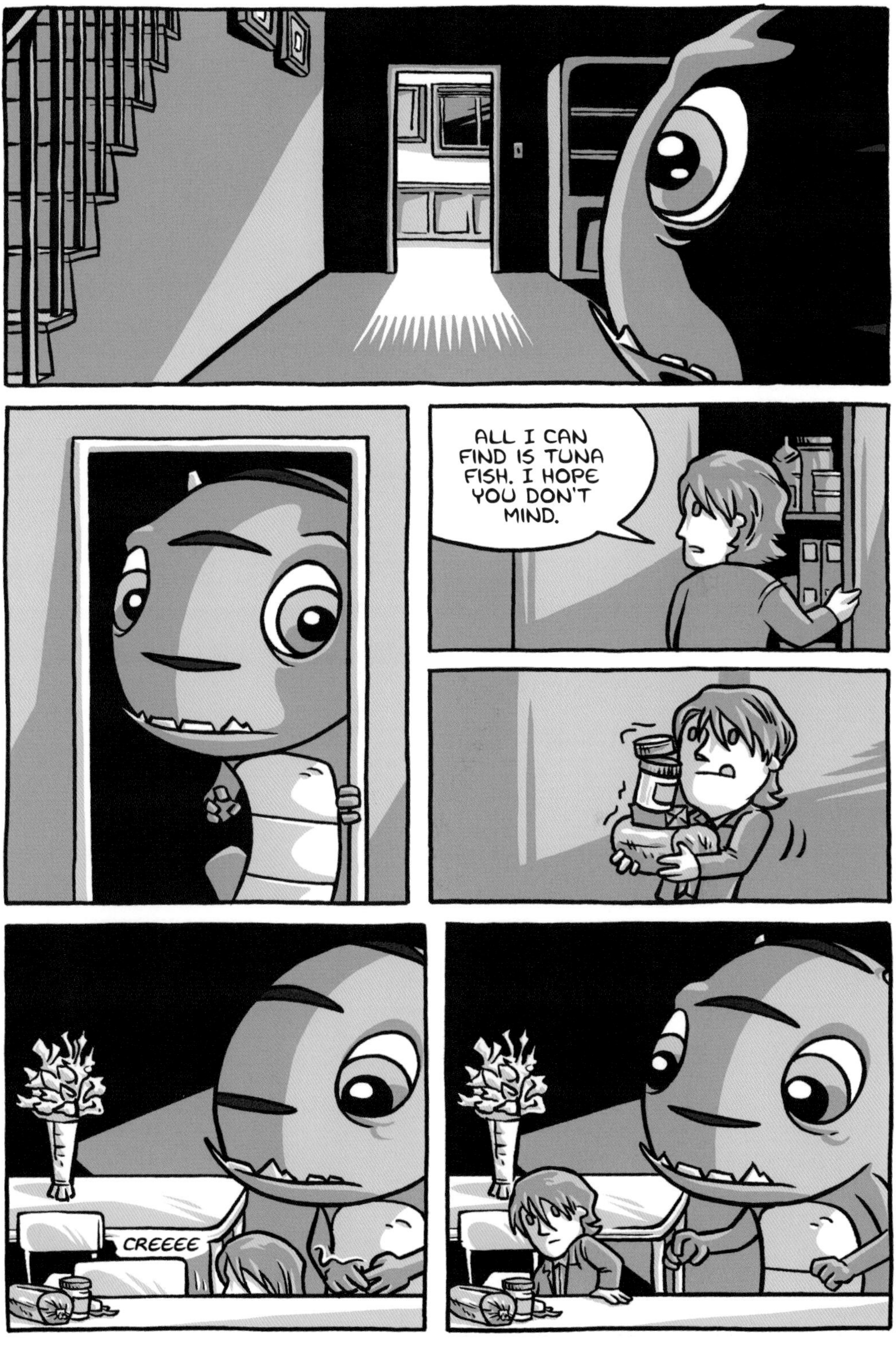
ALL I CAN FIND IS TUNA FISH. I HOPE YOU DON'T MIND.
CREEEE

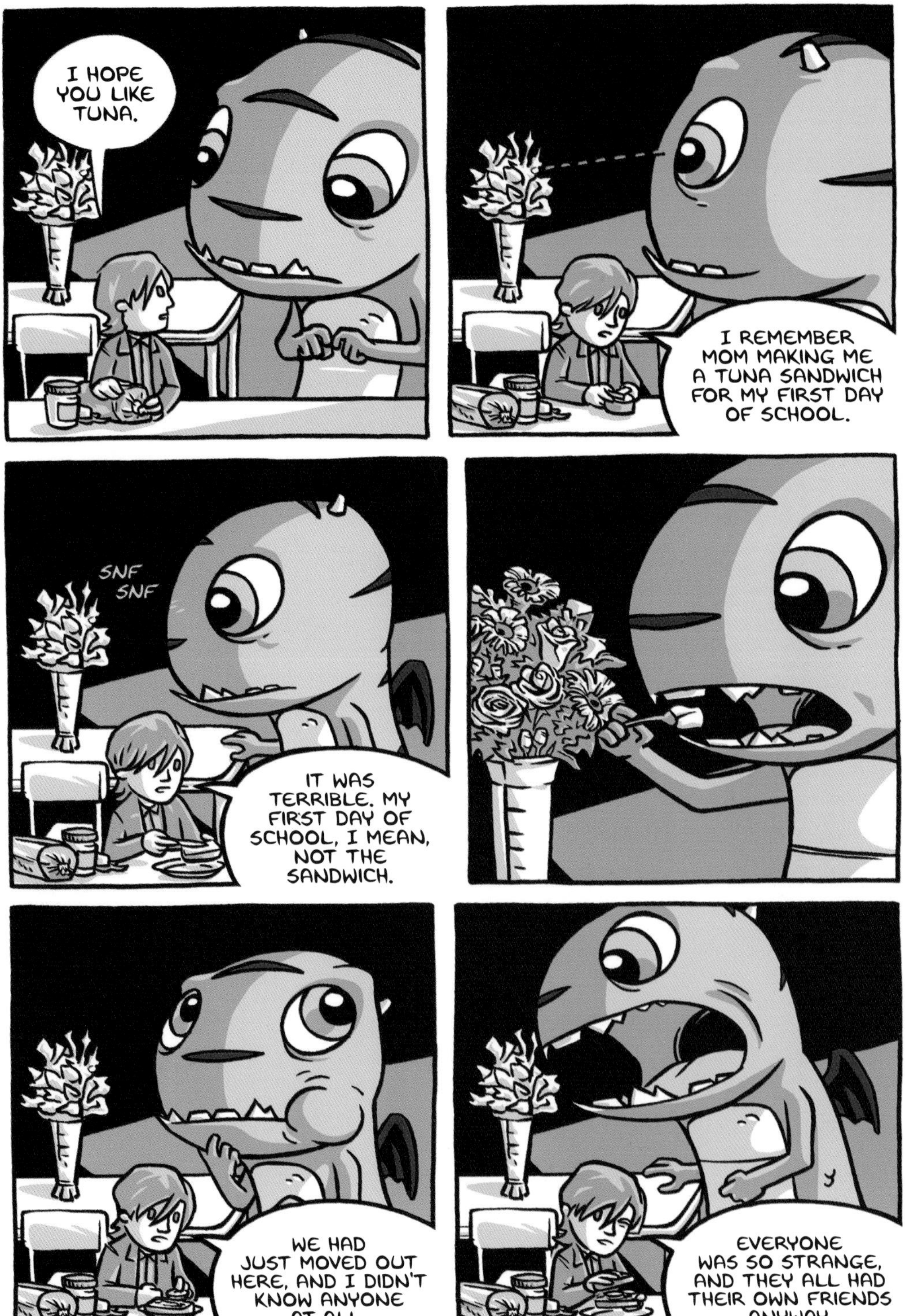
I HOPE YOU LIKE TUNA.
I REMEMBER MOM MAKING ME A TUNA SANDWICH FOR MY FIRST DAY OF SCHOOL.
SNF SNF
IT WAS TERRIBLE. MY FIRST DAY OF SCHOOL, I MEAN, NOT THE SANDWICH.
WE HAD JUST MOVED OUT HERE, AND I DIDN'T KNOW ANYONE AT ALL.
EVERYONE WAS SO STRANGE, AND THEY ALL HAD THEIR OWN FRIENDS ANYWAY.

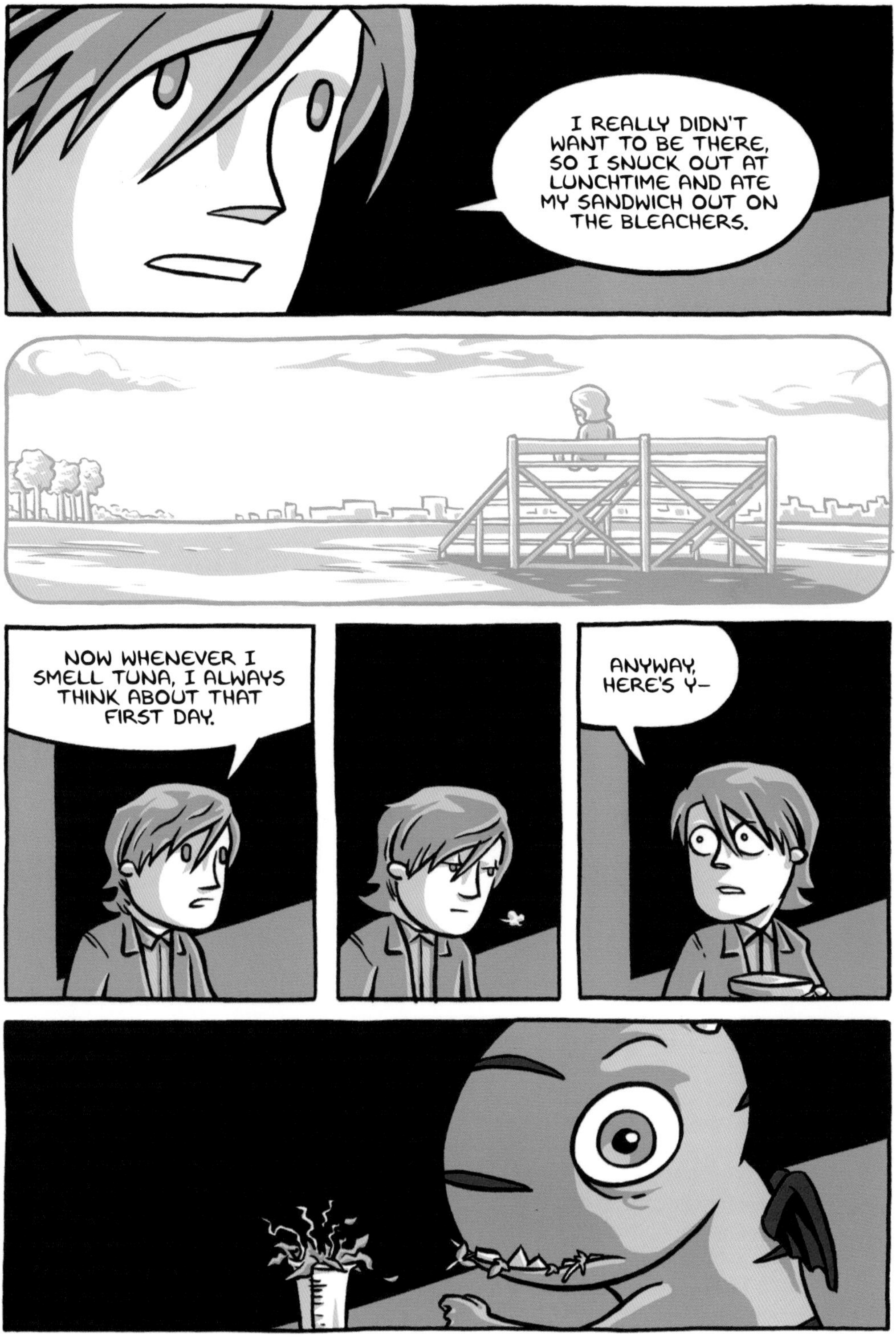
I REALLY DIDN'T WANT TO BE THERE, SO I SNUCK OUT AT LUNCHTIME AND ATE MY SANDWICH OUT ON THE BLEACHERS.
NOW WHENEVER I SMELL TUNA, I ALWAYS THINK ABOUT THAT FIRST DAY.
ANYWAY, HERE'S Y–

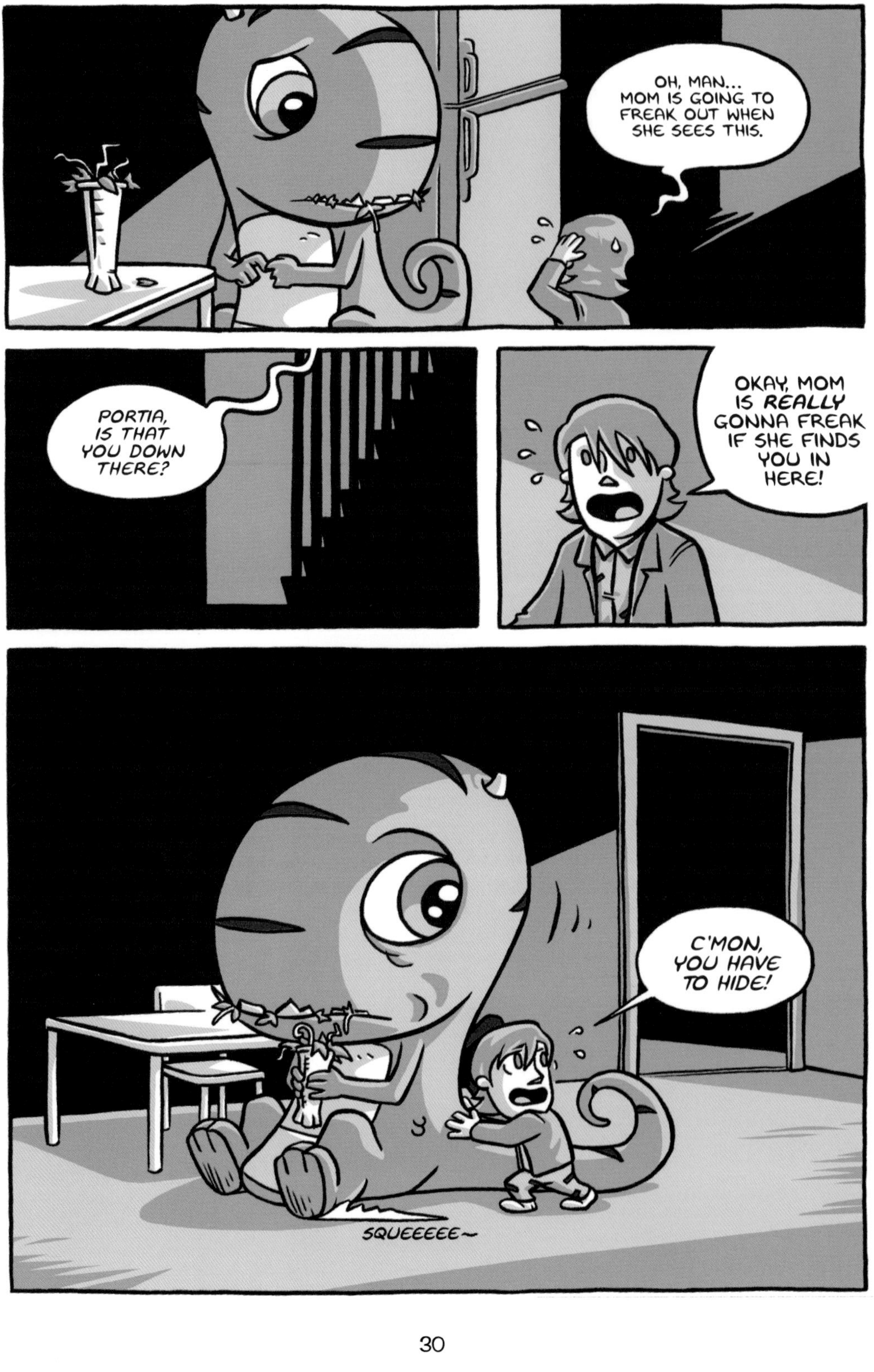
OH, MAN... MOM IS GOING TO FREAK OUT WHEN SHE SEES THIS.
PORTIA, IS THAT YOU DOWN THERE?
OKAY, MOM IS REALLY GONNA FREAK IF SHE FINDS YOU IN HERE!
C'MON, YOU HAVE TO HIDE!
SQUEEEEEE~

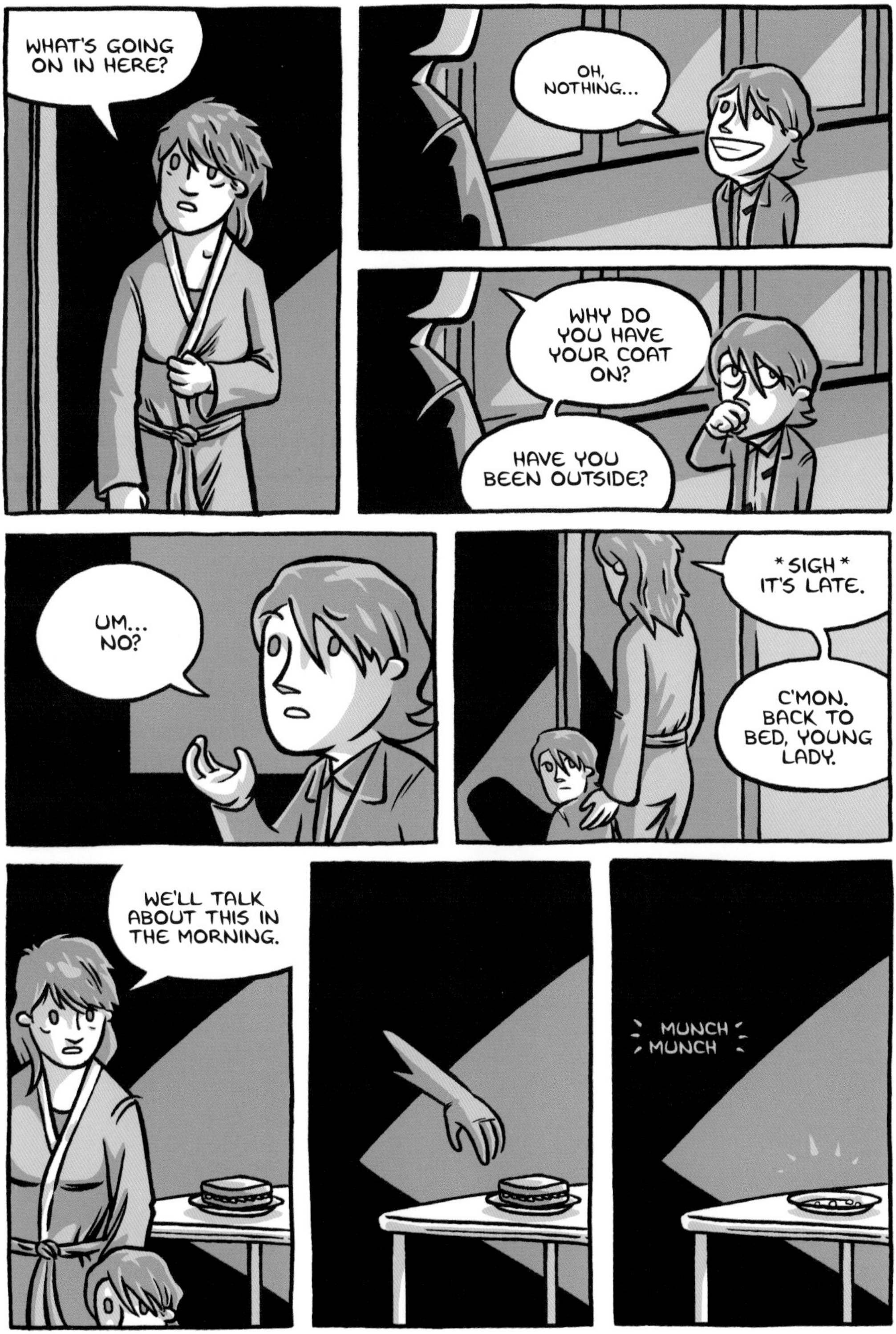
WHAT'S GOING ON IN HERE?
OH, NOTHING...
WHY DO YOU HAVE YOUR COAT ON?
HAVE YOU BEEN OUTSIDE?
UM... NO?
SIGH IT'S LATE.
C'MON. BACK TO BED, YOUNG LADY.
WE'LL TALK ABOUT THIS IN THE MORNING.
MUNCH MUNCH

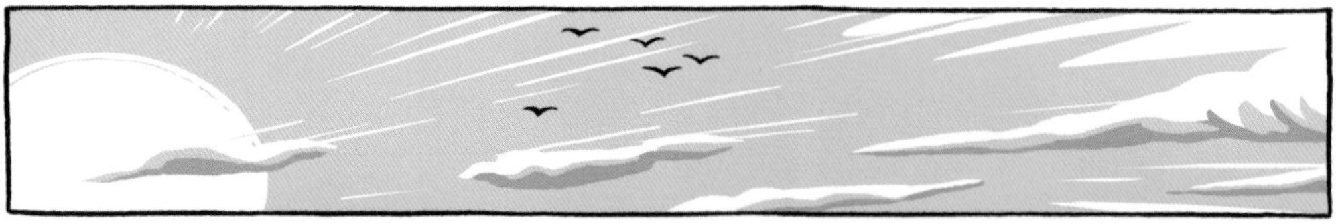

CHAPTER TWO

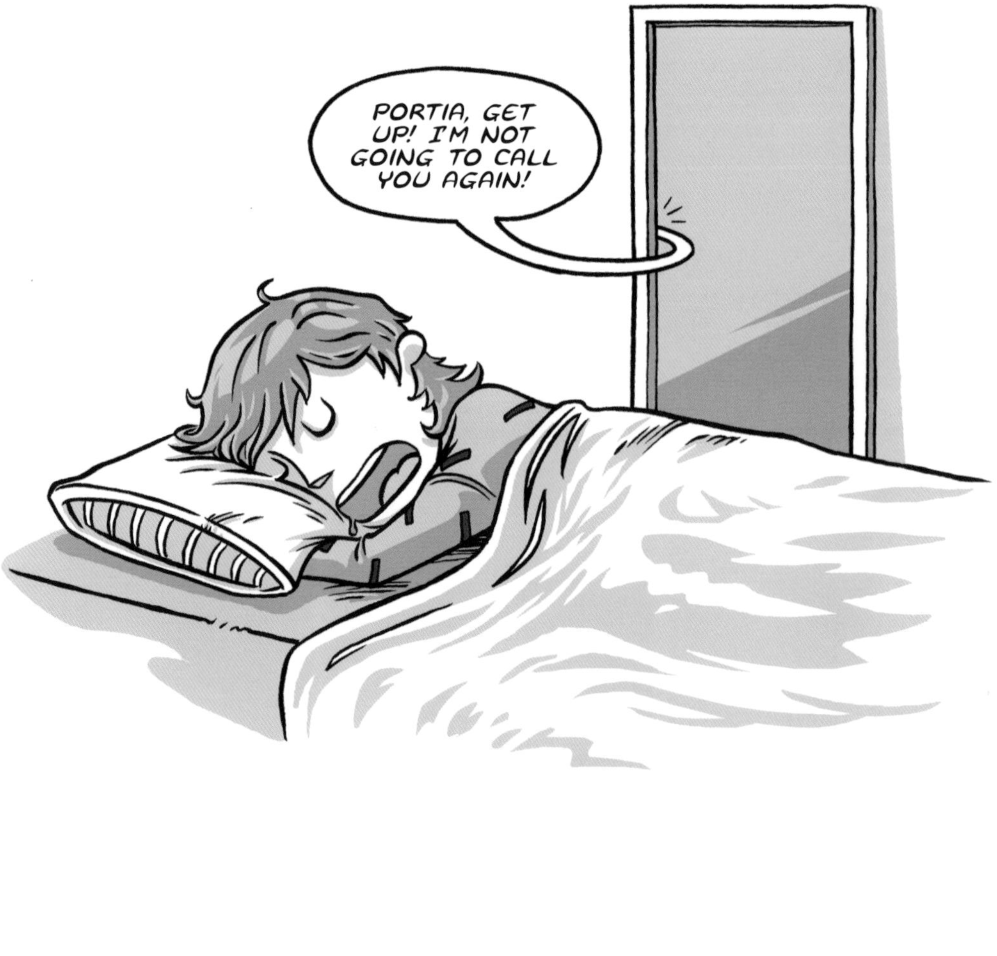
PORTIA, GET UP! I'M NOT GOING TO CALL YOU AGAIN!

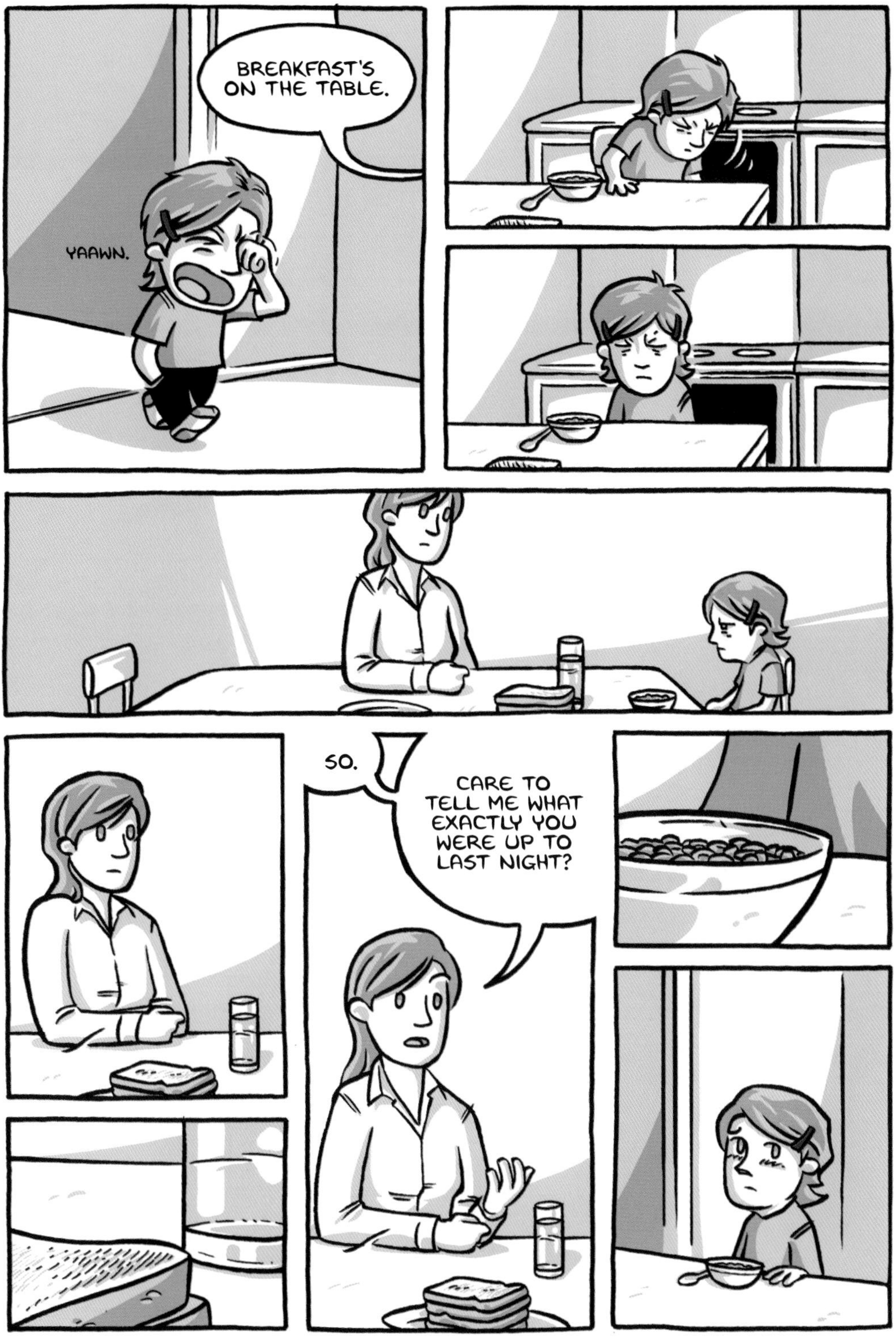
BREAKFAST'S ON THE TABLE.
YAAWN.
SO.
CARE TO TELL ME WHAT EXACTLY YOU WERE UP TO LAST NIGHT?

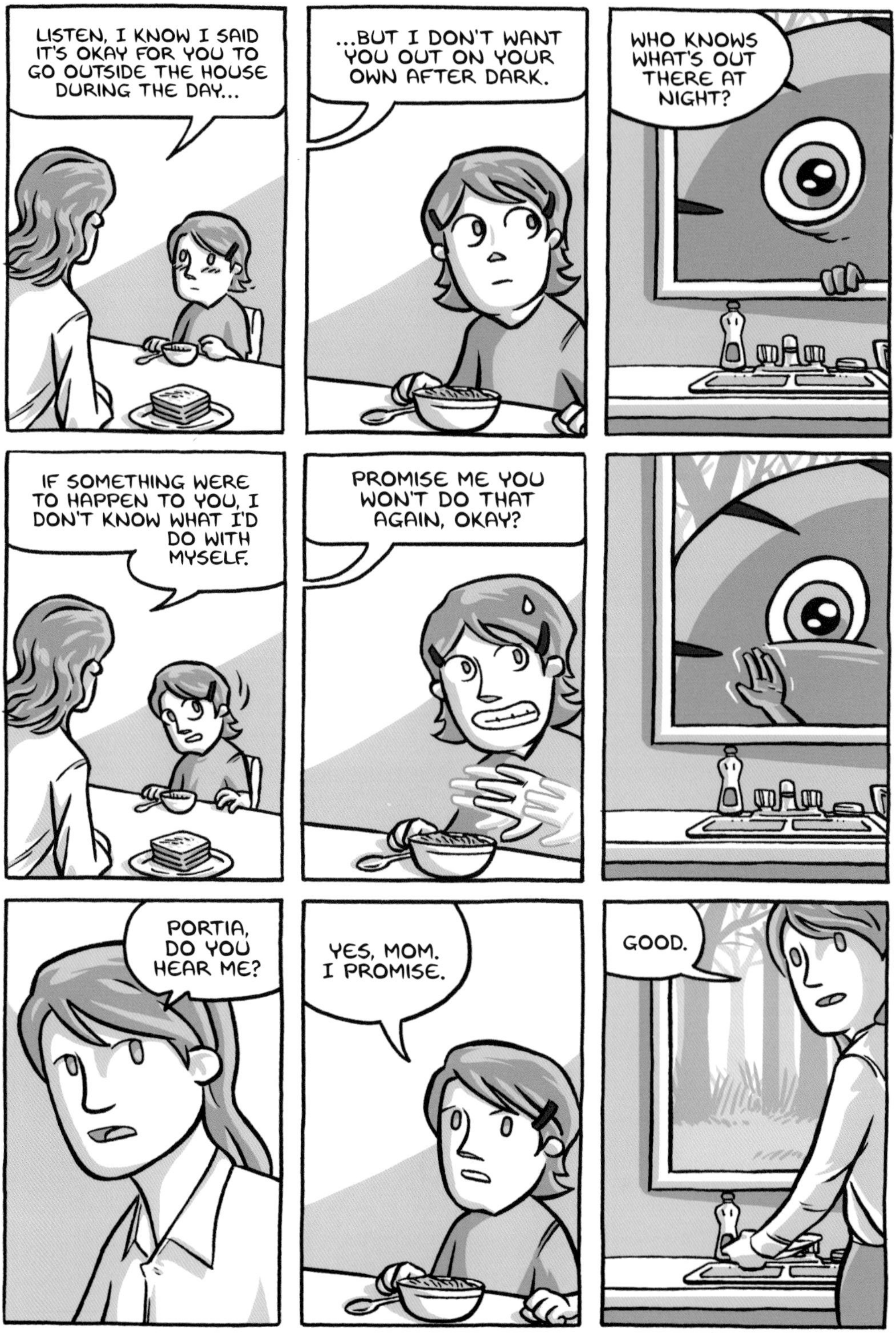
LISTEN, I KNOW I SAID IT'S OKAY FOR YOU TO GO OUTSIDE THE HOUSE DURING THE DAY...
...BUT I DON'T WANT YOU OUT ON YOUR OWN AFTER DARK.
WHO KNOWS WHAT'S OUT THERE AT NIGHT?
IF SOMETHING WERE TO HAPPEN TO YOU, I DON'T KNOW WHAT I'D DO WITH MYSELF.
PROMISE ME YOU WON'T DO THAT AGAIN, OKAY?
PORTIA, DO YOU HEAR ME?
YES, MOM. I PROMISE.
GOOD.

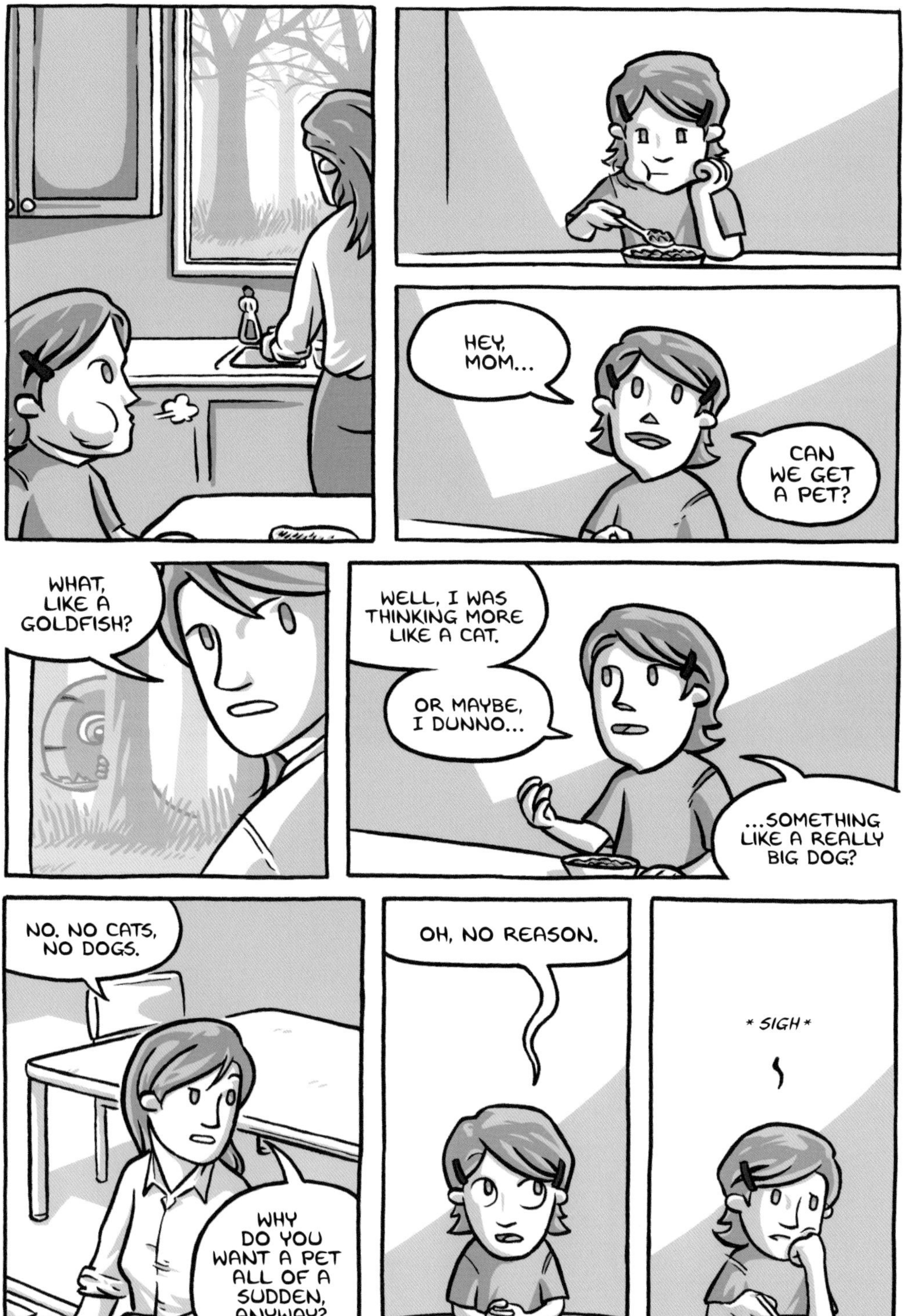
HEY, MOM...
CAN WE GET A PET?
WHAT, LIKE A GOLDFISH?
WELL, I WAS THINKING MORE LIKE A CAT.
OR MAYBE, I DUNNO...
...SOMETHING LIKE A REALLY BIG DOG?
NO. NO CATS, NO DOGS.
WHY DO YOU WANT A PET ALL OF A SUDDEN, ANYWAY?
OH, NO REASON.
* SIGH *

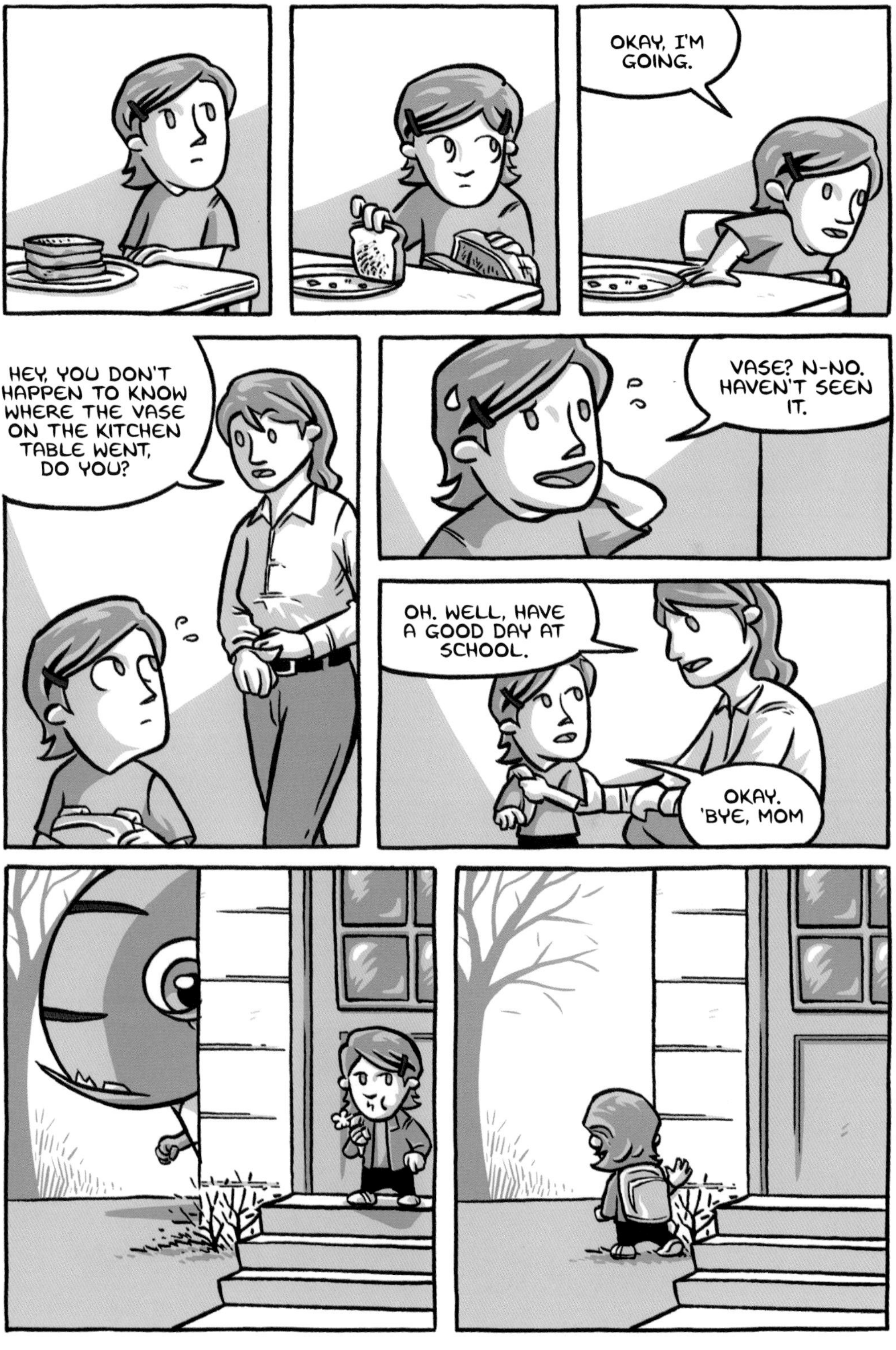
OKAY, I'M GOING.
HEY, YOU DON'T HAPPEN TO KNOW WHERE THE VASE ON THE KITCHEN TABLE WENT, DO YOU?
VASE? N-NO. HAVEN'T SEEN IT.
OH. WELL, HAVE A GOOD DAY AT SCHOOL.
OKAY. 'BYE, MOM

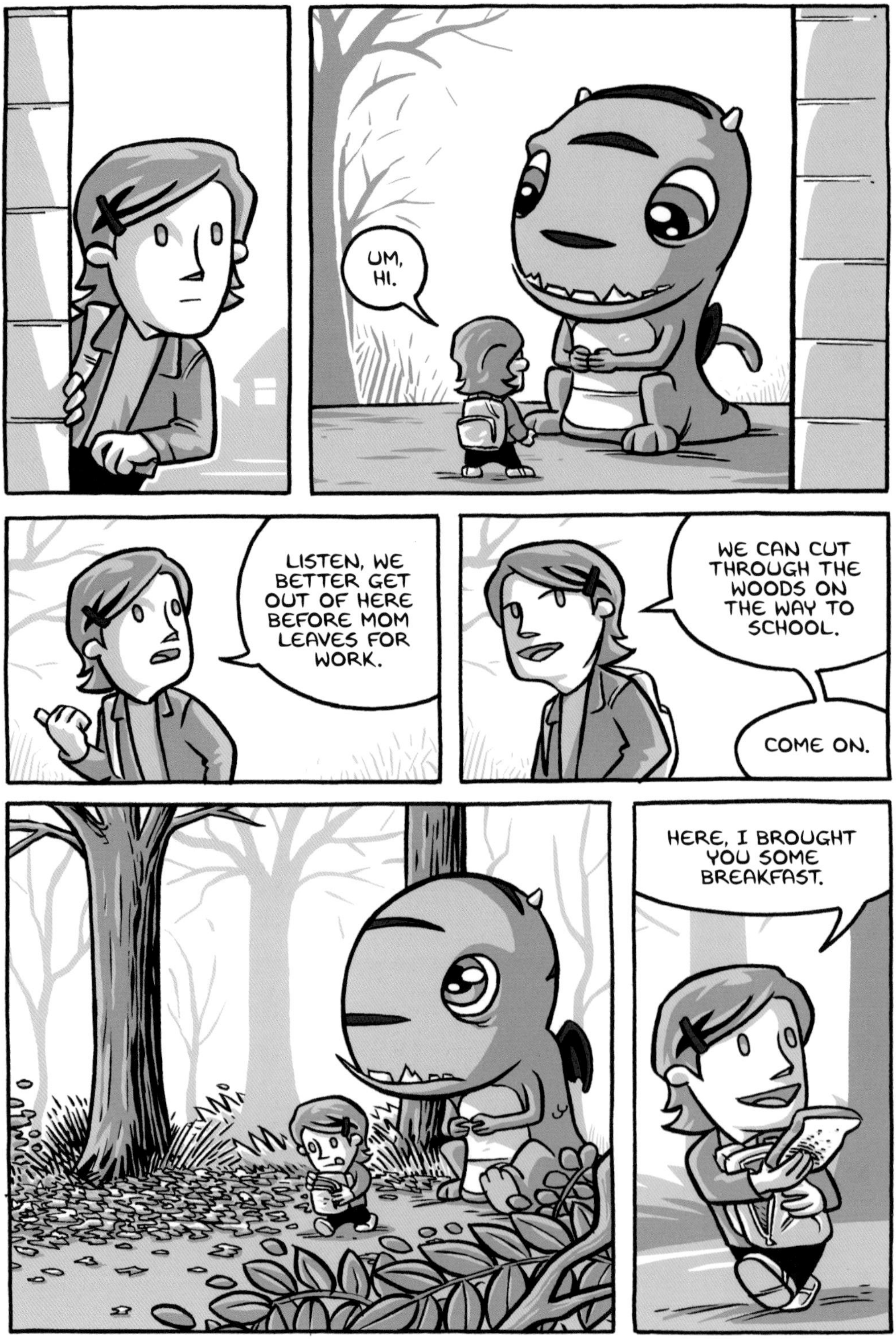
UM, HI.
LISTEN, WE BETTER GET OUT OF HERE BEFORE MOM LEAVES FOR WORK.
WE CAN CUT THROUGH THE WOODS ON THE WAY TO SCHOOL.
COME ON.
HERE, I BROUGHT YOU SOME BREAKFAST.

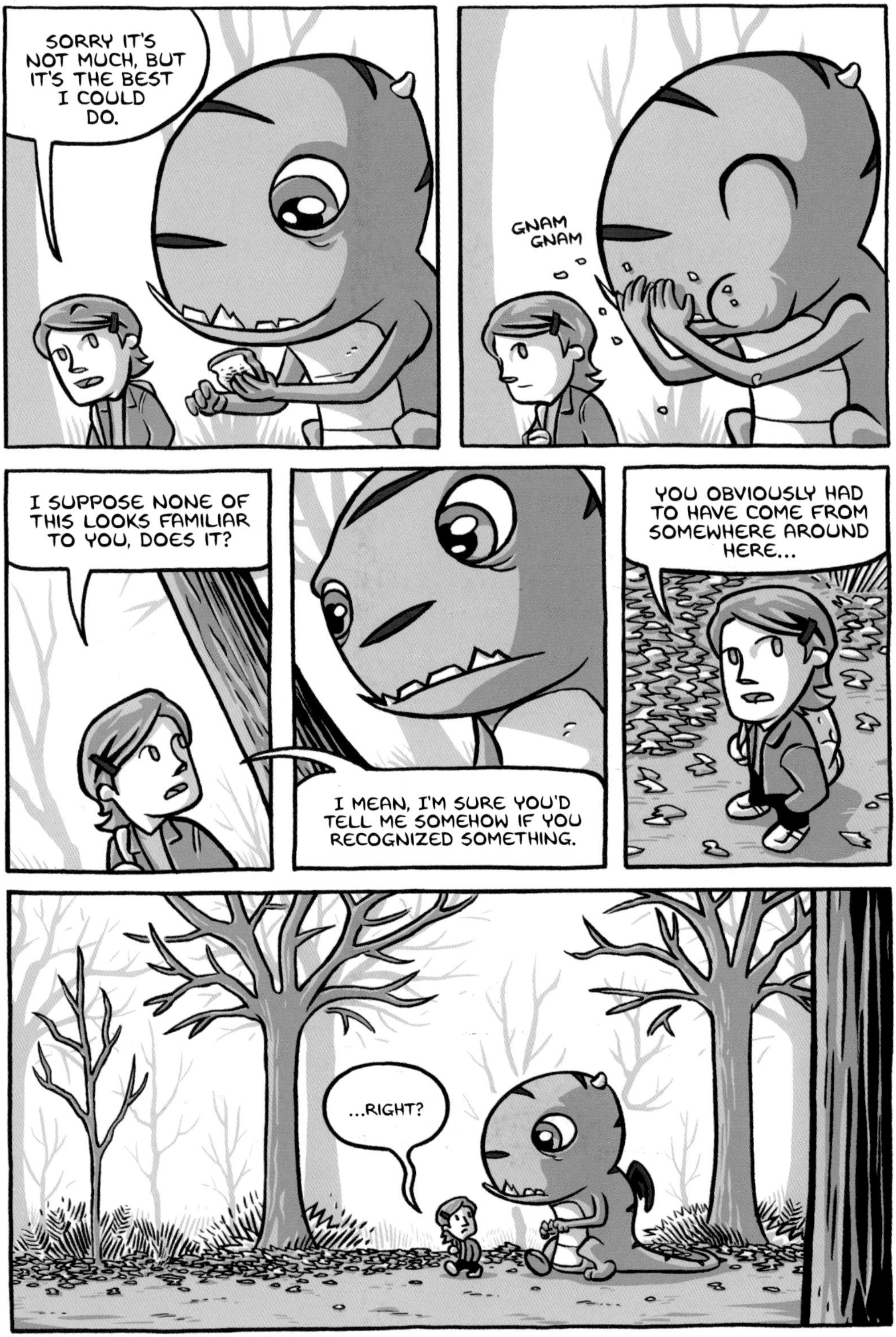

SORRY IT'S NOT MUCH, BUT IT'S THE BEST I COULD DO.
GNAM GNAM
I SUPPOSE NONE OF THIS LOOKS FAMILIAR TO YOU, DOES IT?
I MEAN, I'M SURE YOU'D TELL ME SOMEHOW IF YOU RECOGNIZED SOMETHING.
YOU OBVIOUSLY HAD TO HAVE COME FROM SOMEWHERE AROUND HERE...
...RIGHT?

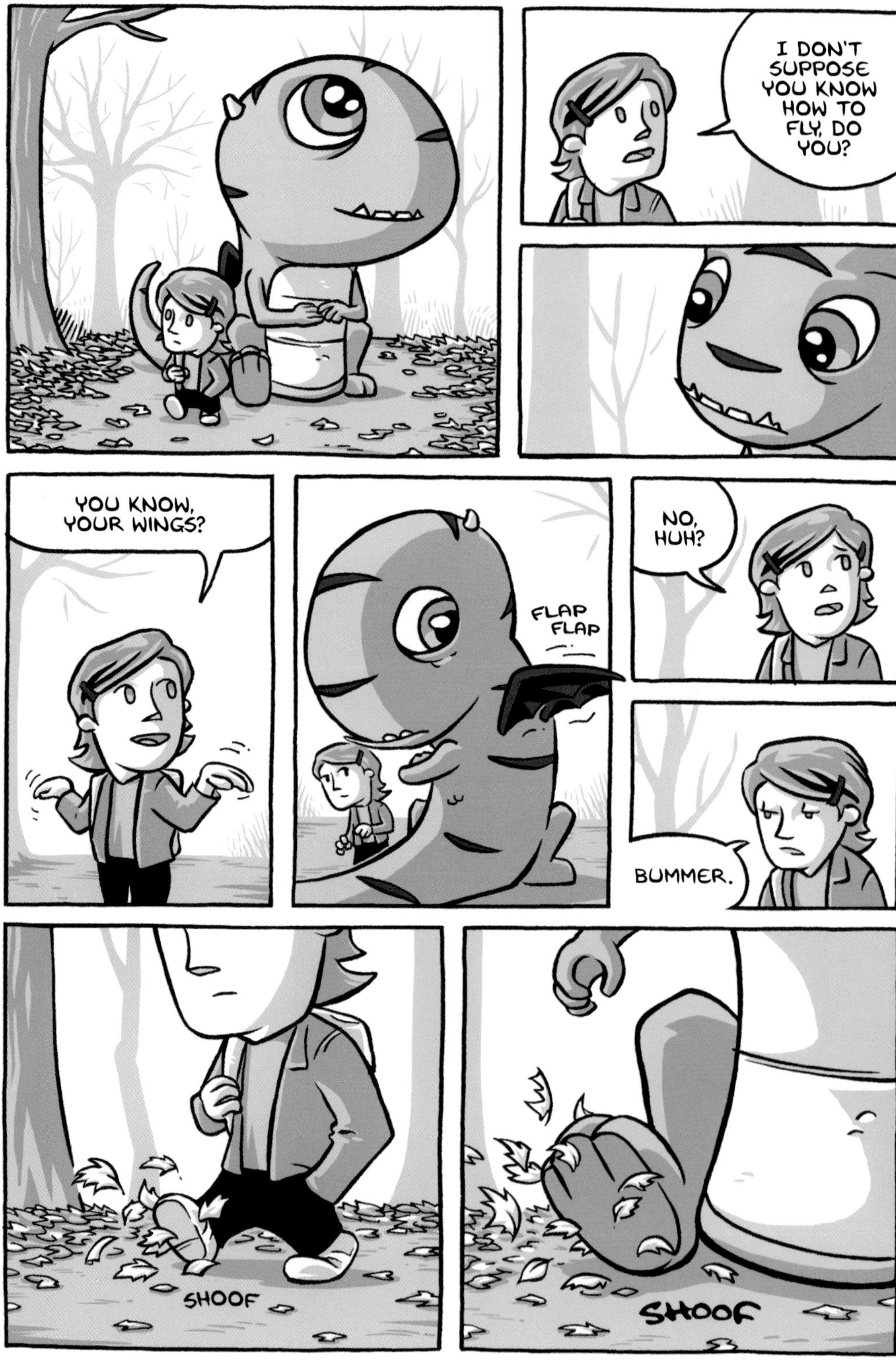
I DON'T SUPPOSE YOU KNOW HOW TO FLY, DO YOU?
YOU KNOW, YOUR WINGS?
FLAP FLAP
NO, HUH?
BUMMER.
SHOOF
SHOOF

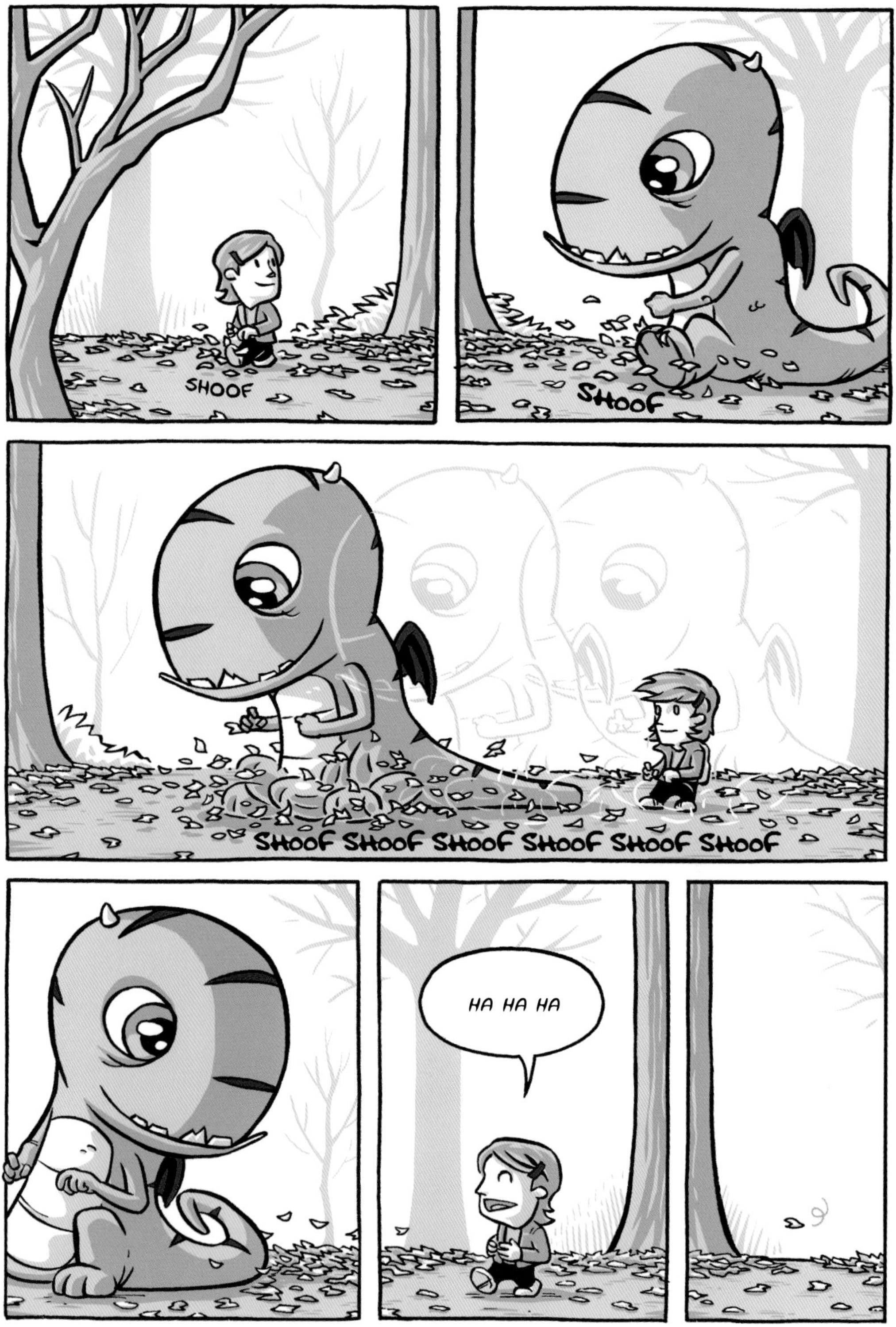
SHOOF
SHOOF
SHOOF SHOOF SHOOF SHOOF SHOOF SHOOF
HA HA HA

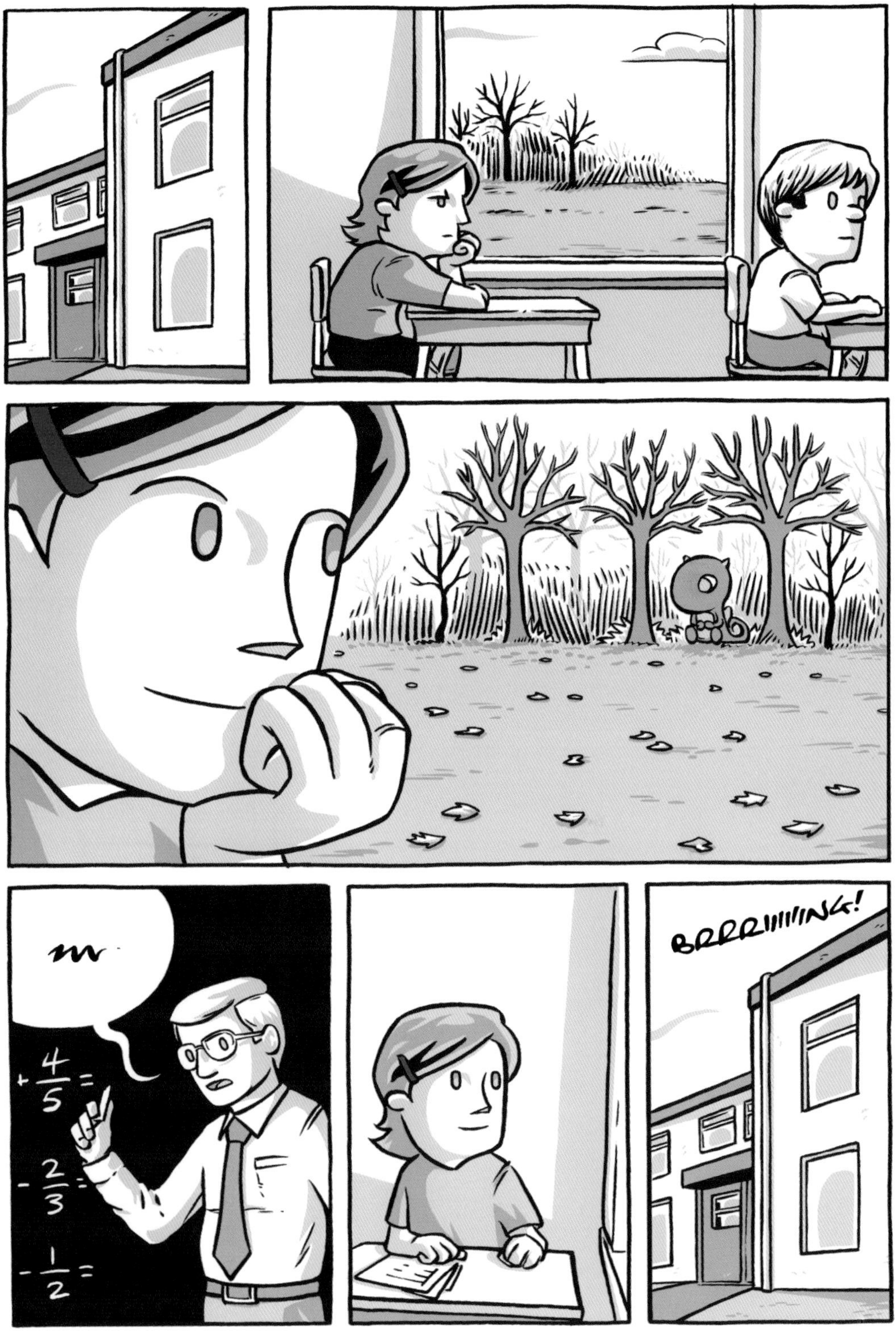
4/5 =
2/3 =
1/2 =
BRRRIIIIIIING!

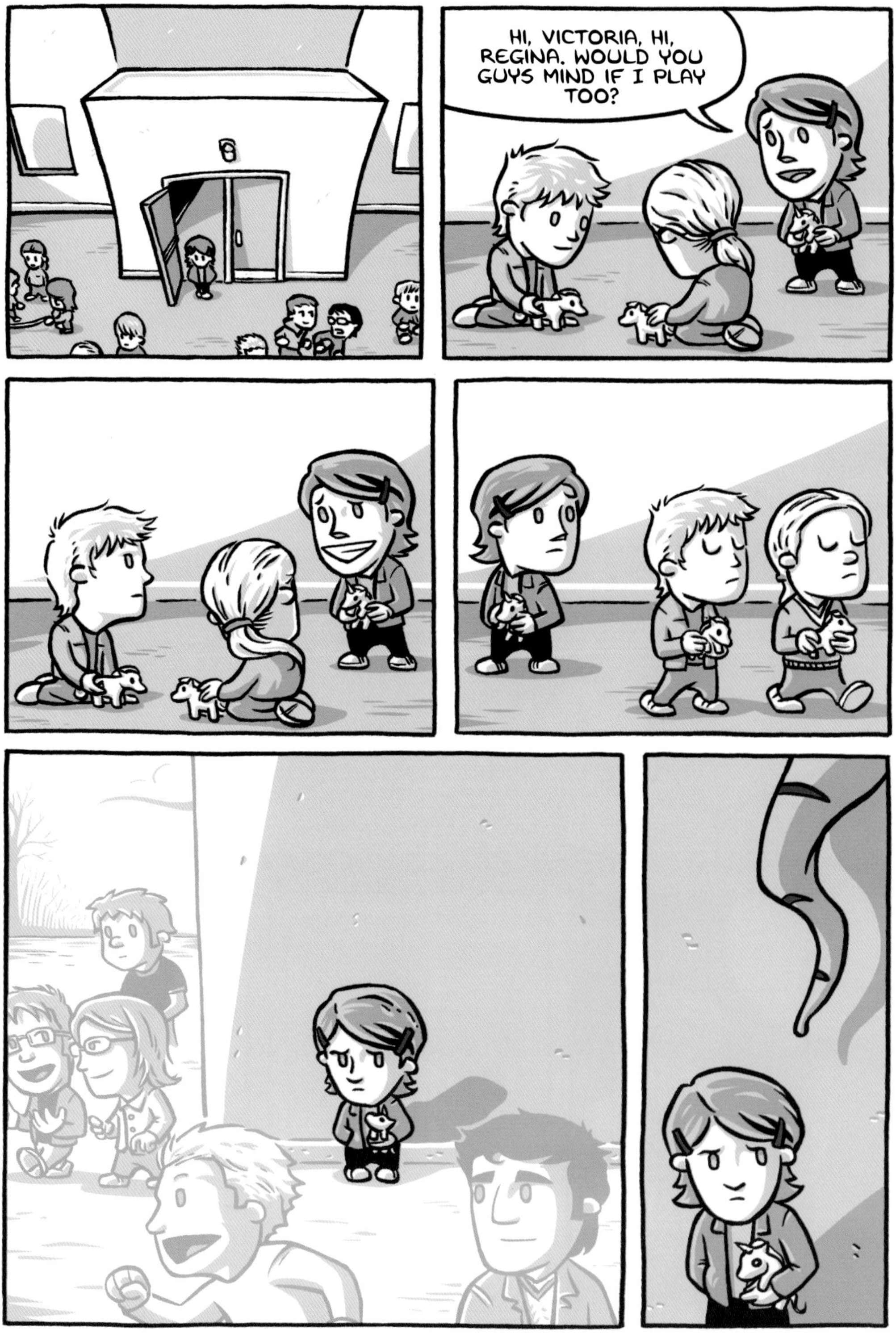
HI, VICTORIA, HI, REGINA. WOULD YOU GUYS MIND IF I PLAY TOO?

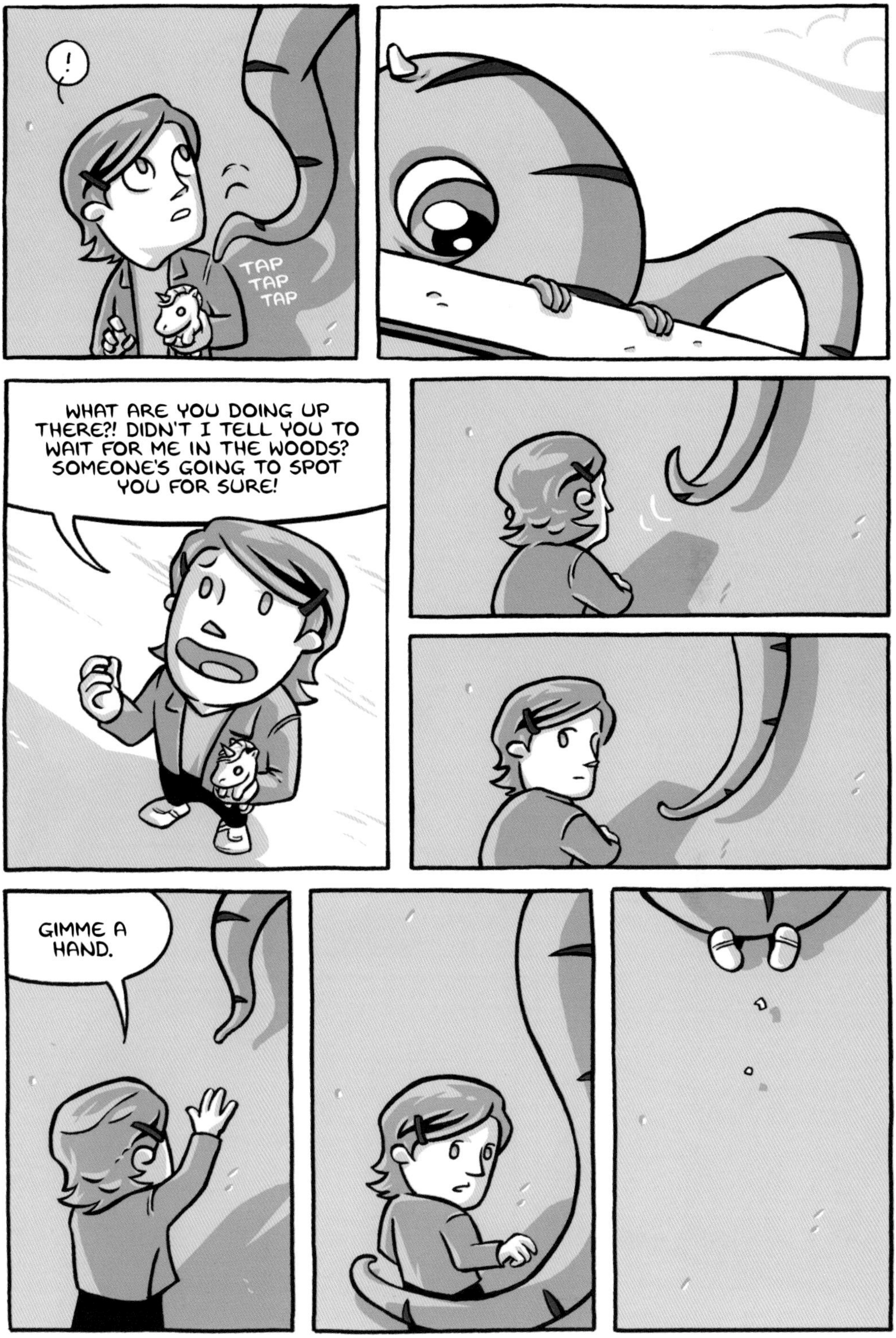
!
TAP
TAP
TAP
WHAT ARE YOU DOING UP THERE?! DIDN'T I TELL YOU TO WAIT FOR ME IN THE WOODS? SOMEONE'S GOING TO SPOT YOU FOR SURE!
GIMME A HAND.

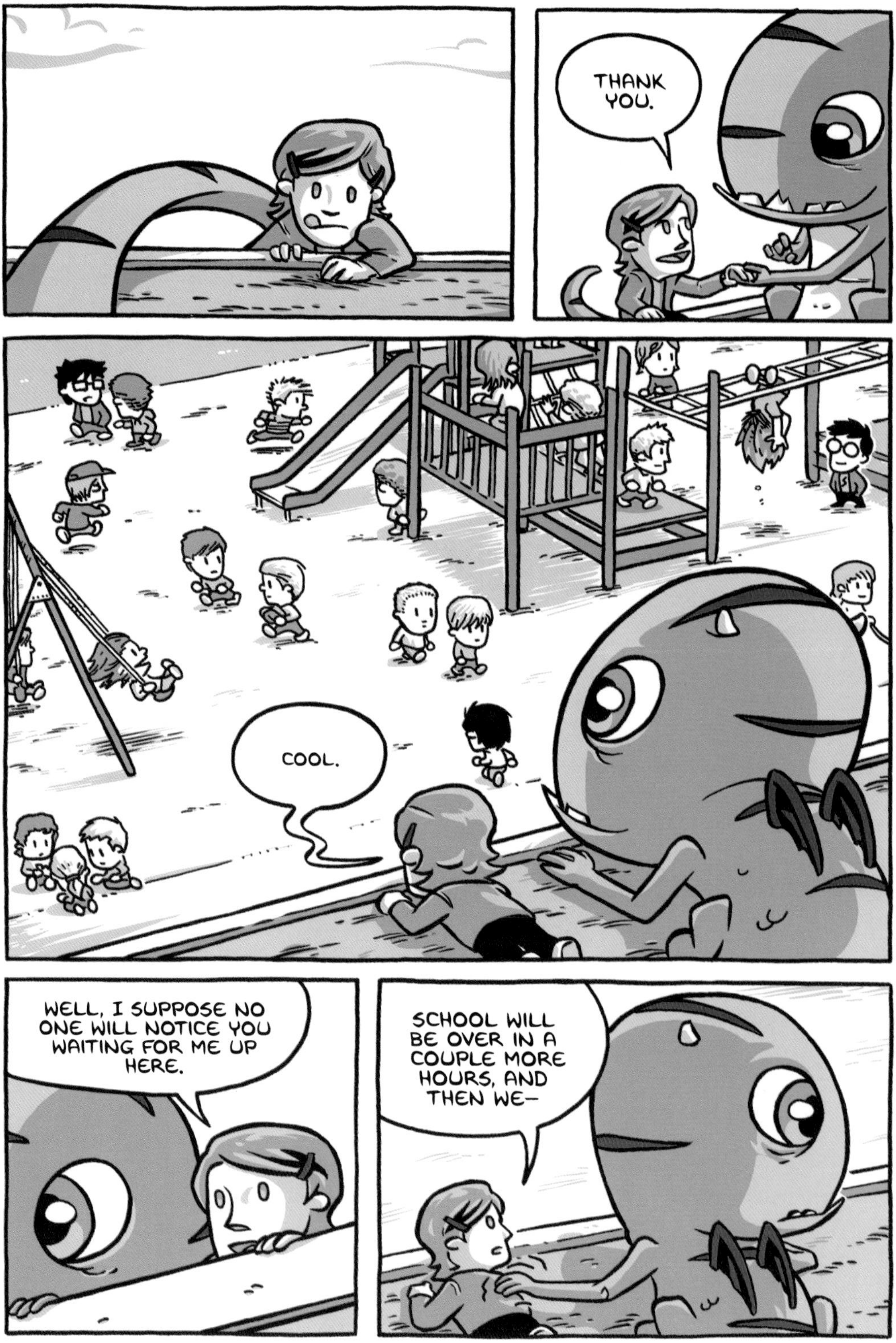
THANK YOU.
COOL.
WELL, I SUPPOSE NO ONE WILL NOTICE YOU WAITING FOR ME UP HERE.
SCHOOL WILL BE OVER IN A COUPLE MORE HOURS, AND THEN WE—

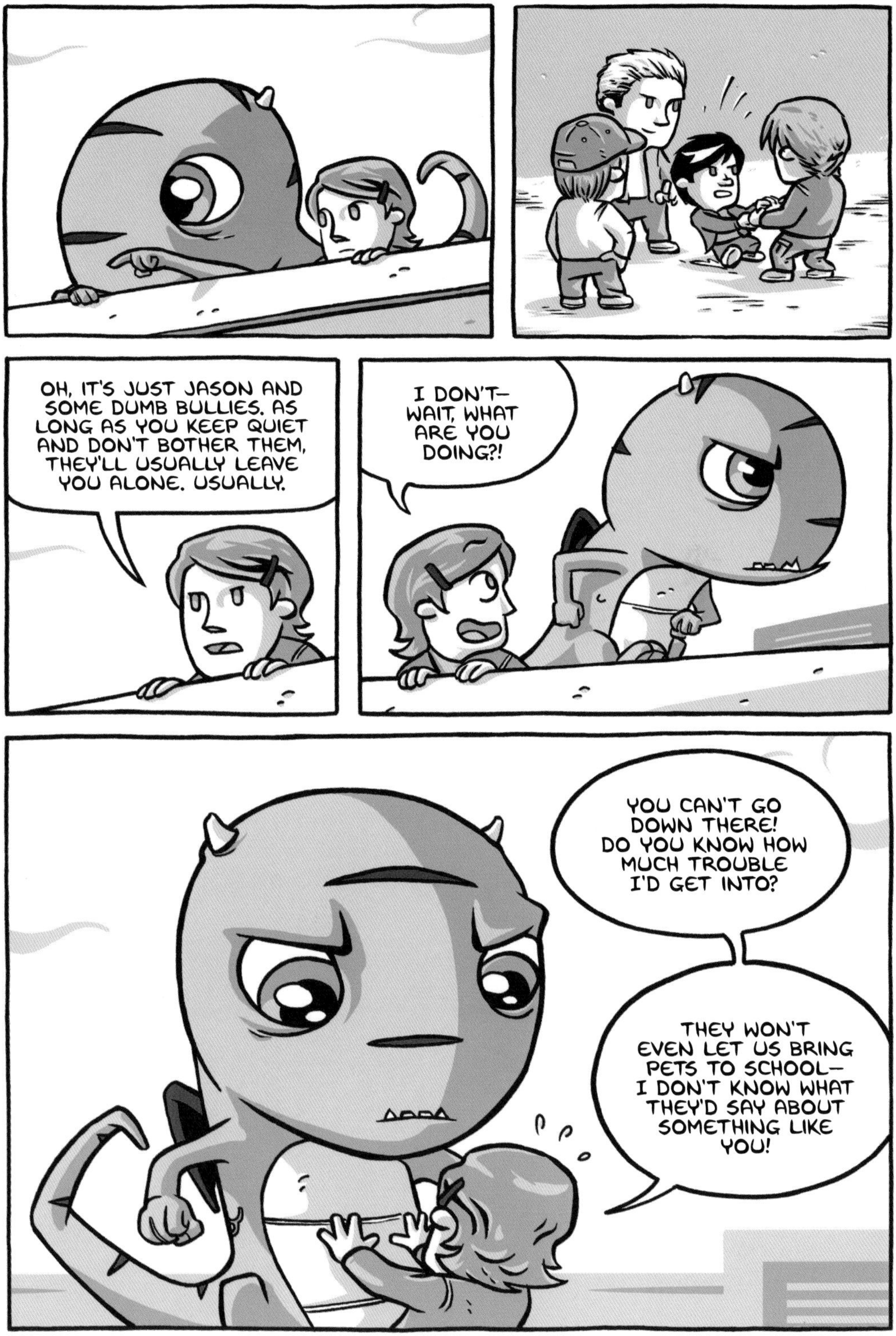
OH, IT'S JUST JASON AND SOME DUMB BULLIES. AS LONG AS YOU KEEP QUIET AND DON'T BOTHER THEM, THEY'LL USUALLY LEAVE YOU ALONE. USUALLY.
I DON'T— WAIT, WHAT ARE YOU DOING?!
YOU CAN'T GO DOWN THERE! DO YOU KNOW HOW MUCH TROUBLE I'D GET INTO?
THEY WON'T EVEN LET US BRING PETS TO SCHOOL— I DON'T KNOW WHAT THEY'D SAY ABOUT SOMETHING LIKE YOU!

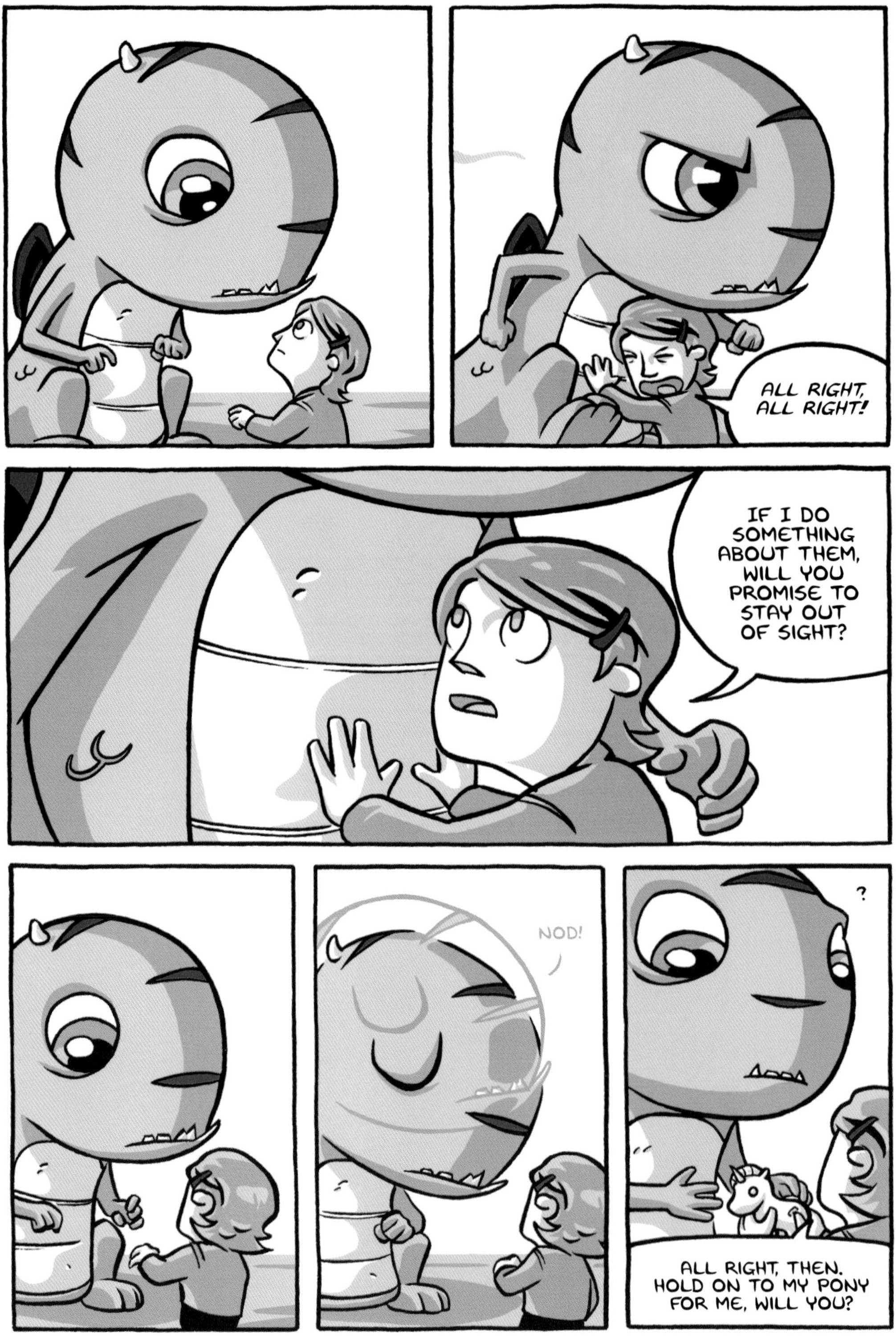
ALL RIGHT,
ALL RIGHT!
IF I DO SOMETHING ABOUT THEM, WILL YOU PROMISE TO STAY OUT OF SIGHT?
NOD!
?
ALL RIGHT, THEN. HOLD ON TO MY PONY FOR ME, WILL YOU?

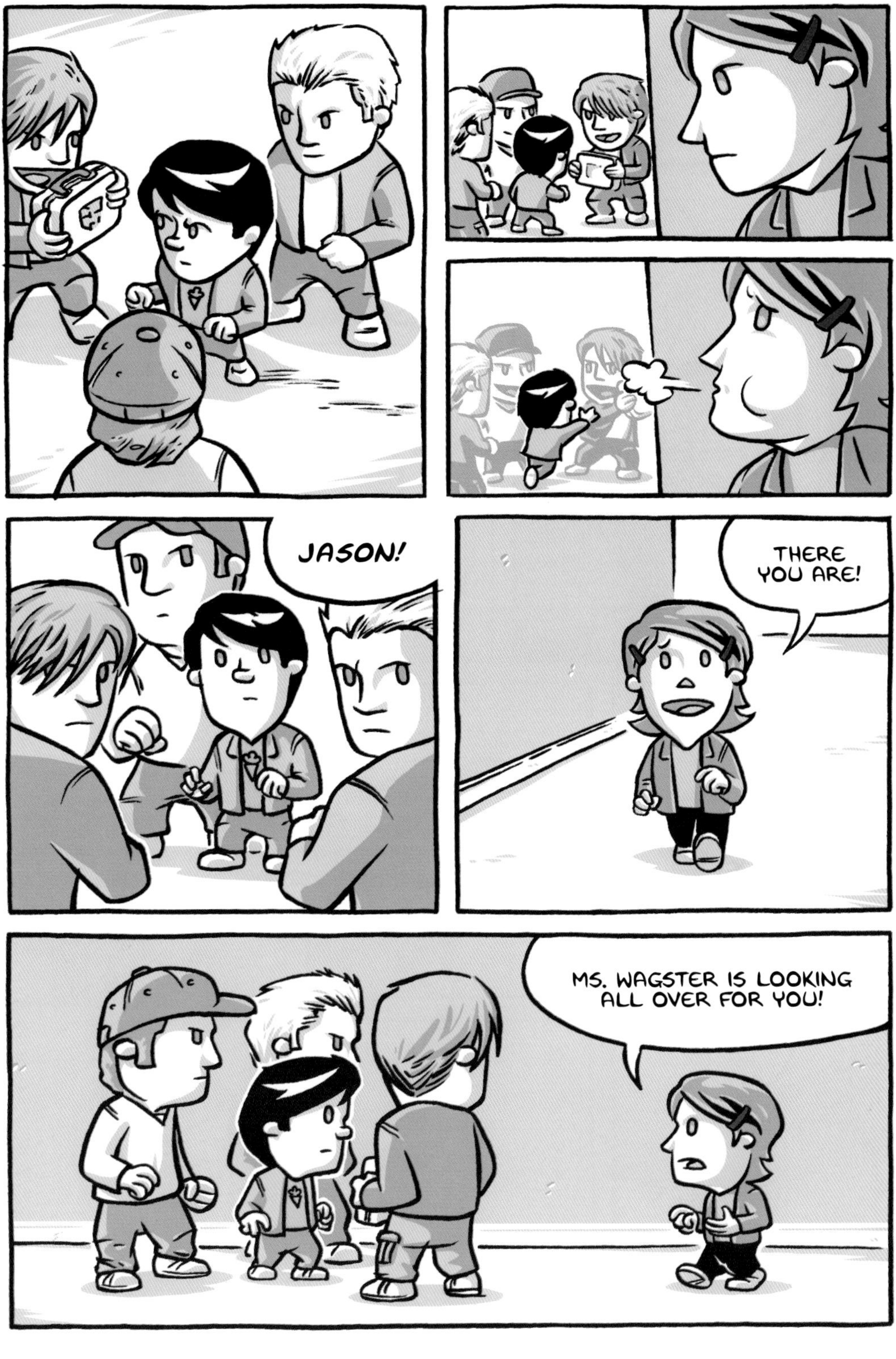
JASON!
THERE YOU ARE!
MS. WAGSTER IS LOOKING ALL OVER FOR YOU!

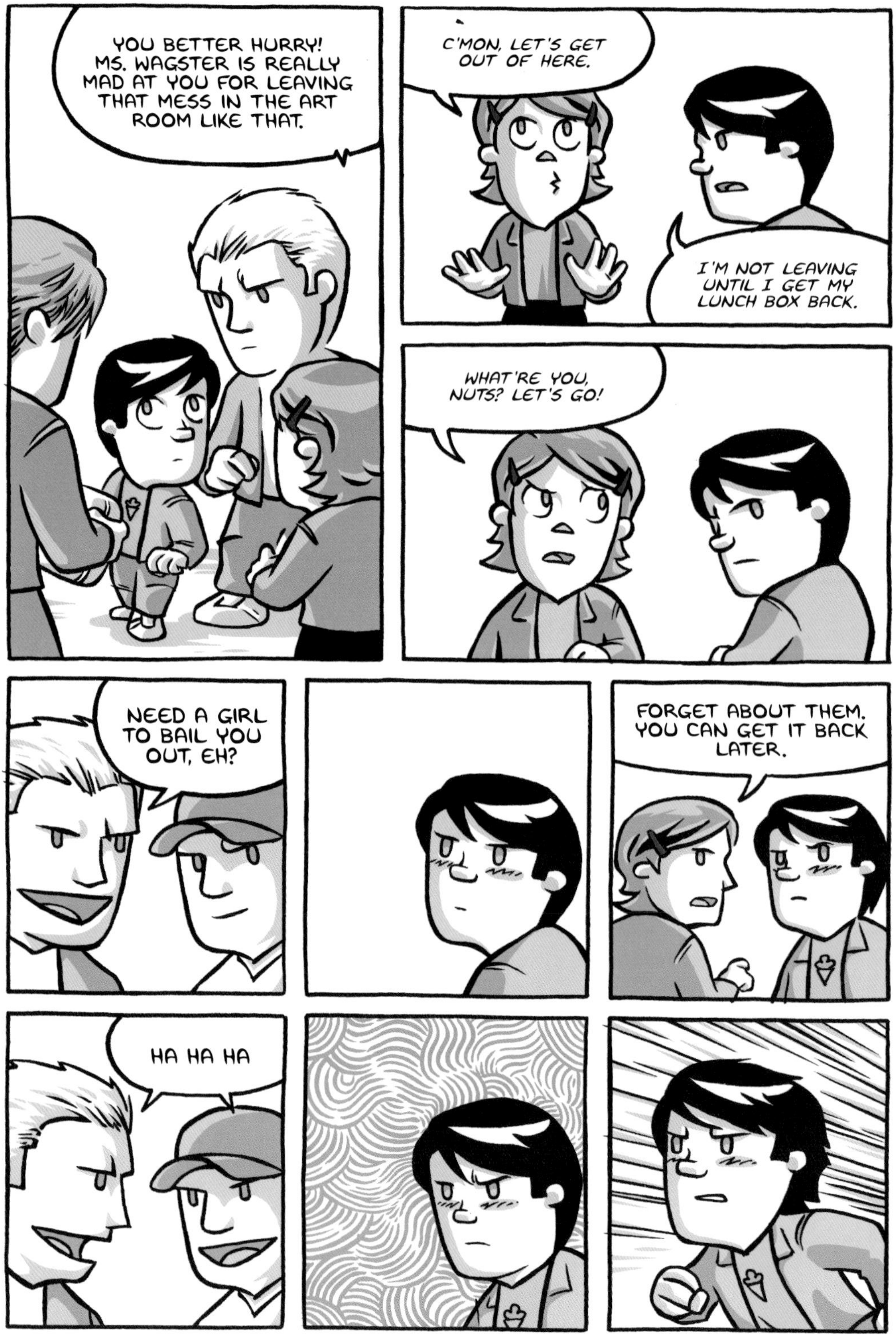
YOU BETTER HURRY! MS. WAGSTER IS REALLY MAD AT YOU FOR LEAVING THAT MESS IN THE ART ROOM LIKE THAT.
C'MON, LET'S GET OUT OF HERE.
I'M NOT LEAVING UNTIL I GET MY LUNCH BOX BACK.
WHAT'RE YOU, NUTS? LET'S GO!
NEED A GIRL TO BAIL YOU OUT, EH?
FORGET ABOUT THEM. YOU CAN GET IT BACK LATER.
HA HA HA

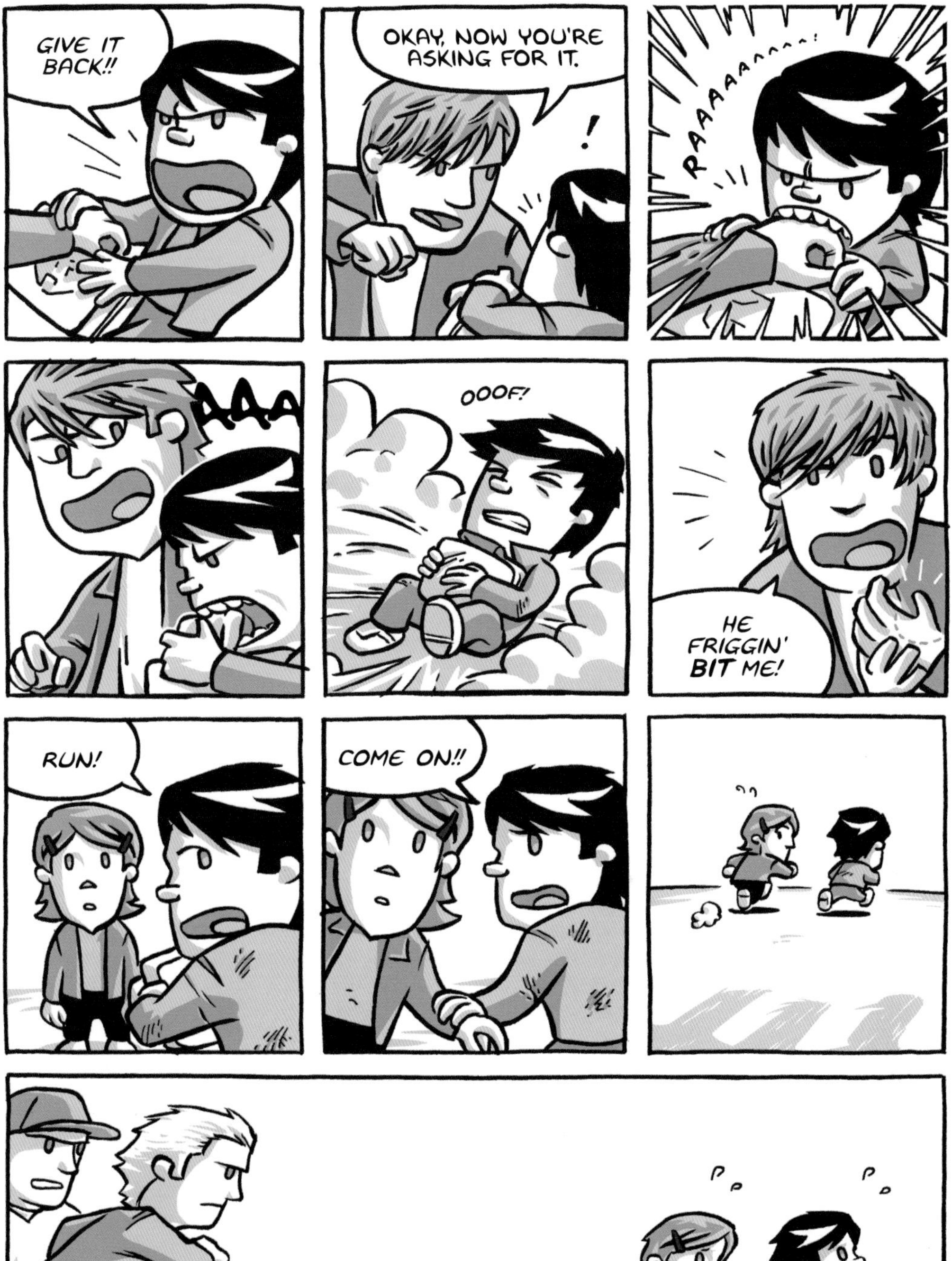
GIVE IT BACK!!
OKAY, NOW YOU'RE ASKING FOR IT.
!
RAAAAAAAAA!
AAA
OOOF!
HE FRIGGIN' BIT ME!
RUN!
COME ON!!

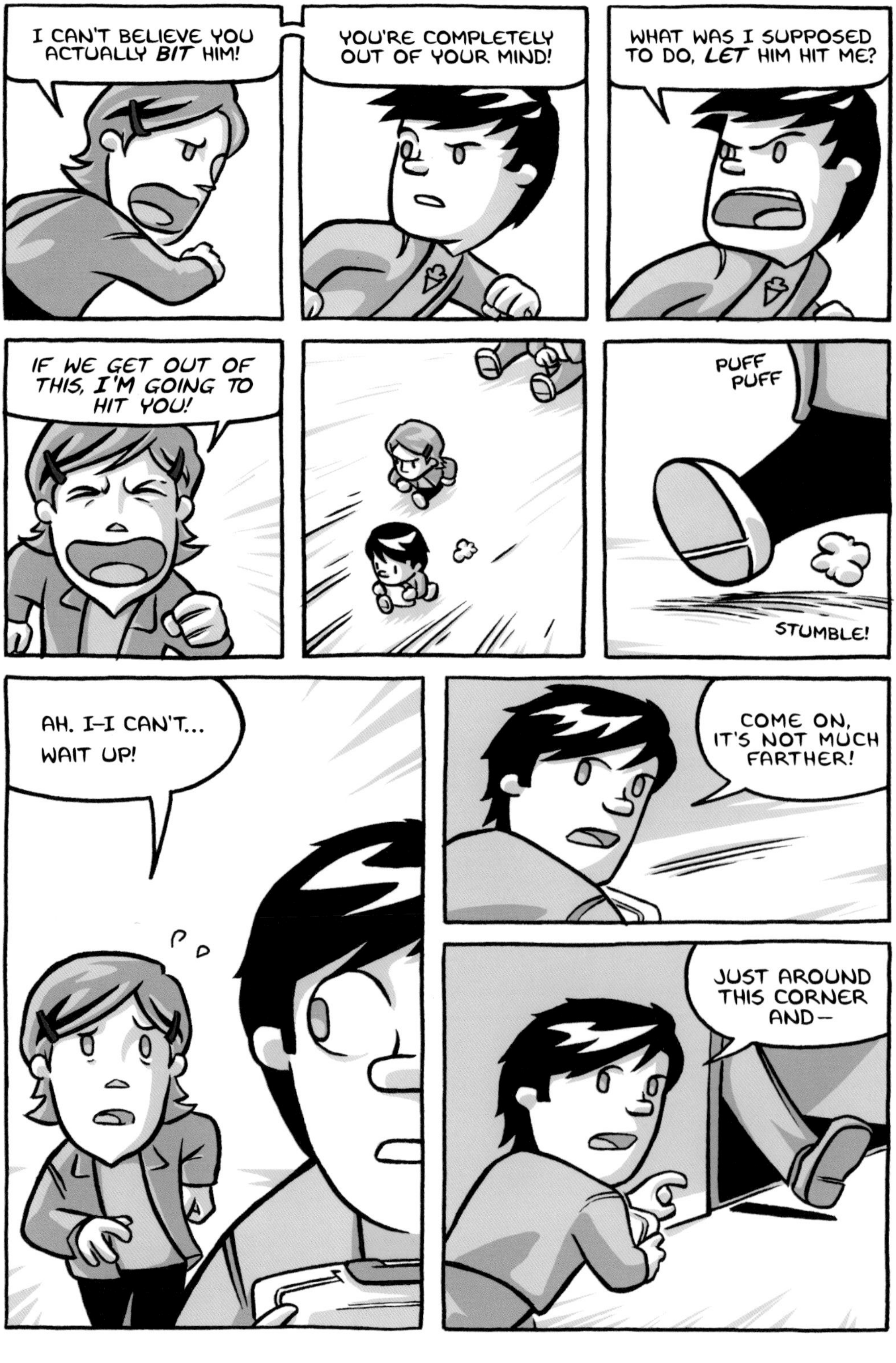

I CAN'T BELIEVE YOU ACTUALLY *BIT* HIM!
YOU'RE COMPLETELY OUT OF YOUR MIND!
WHAT WAS I SUPPOSED TO DO, *LET* HIM HIT ME?
IF WE GET OUT OF THIS, I'M GOING TO HIT YOU!
PUFF PUFF
STUMBLE!
AH. I-I CAN'T...
WAIT UP!
COME ON, IT'S NOT MUCH FARTHER!
JUST AROUND THIS CORNER AND—

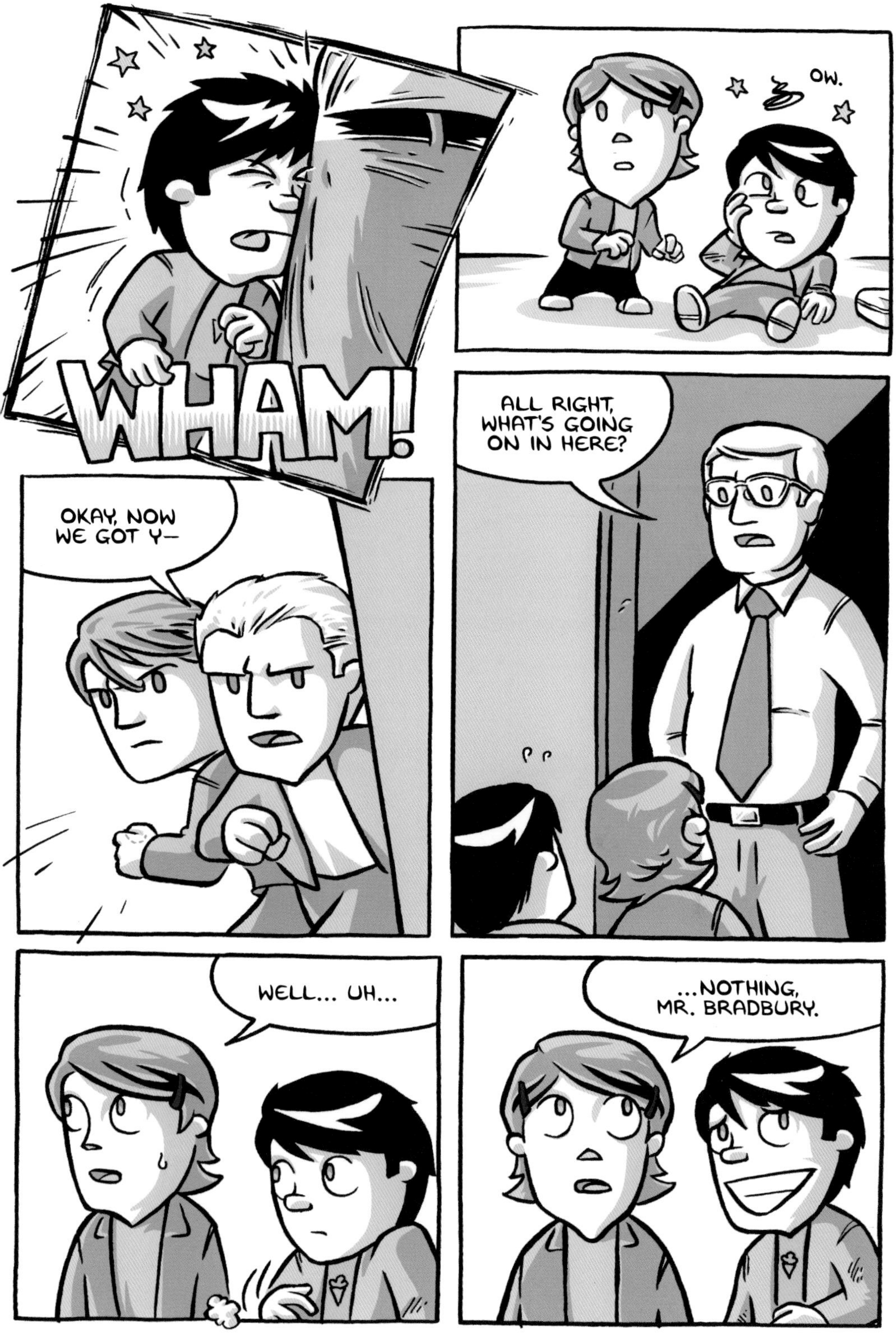
WHAM!
OW.
OKAY, NOW WE GOT Y—
ALL RIGHT, WHAT'S GOING ON IN HERE?
WELL... UH...
...NOTHING, MR. BRADBURY.

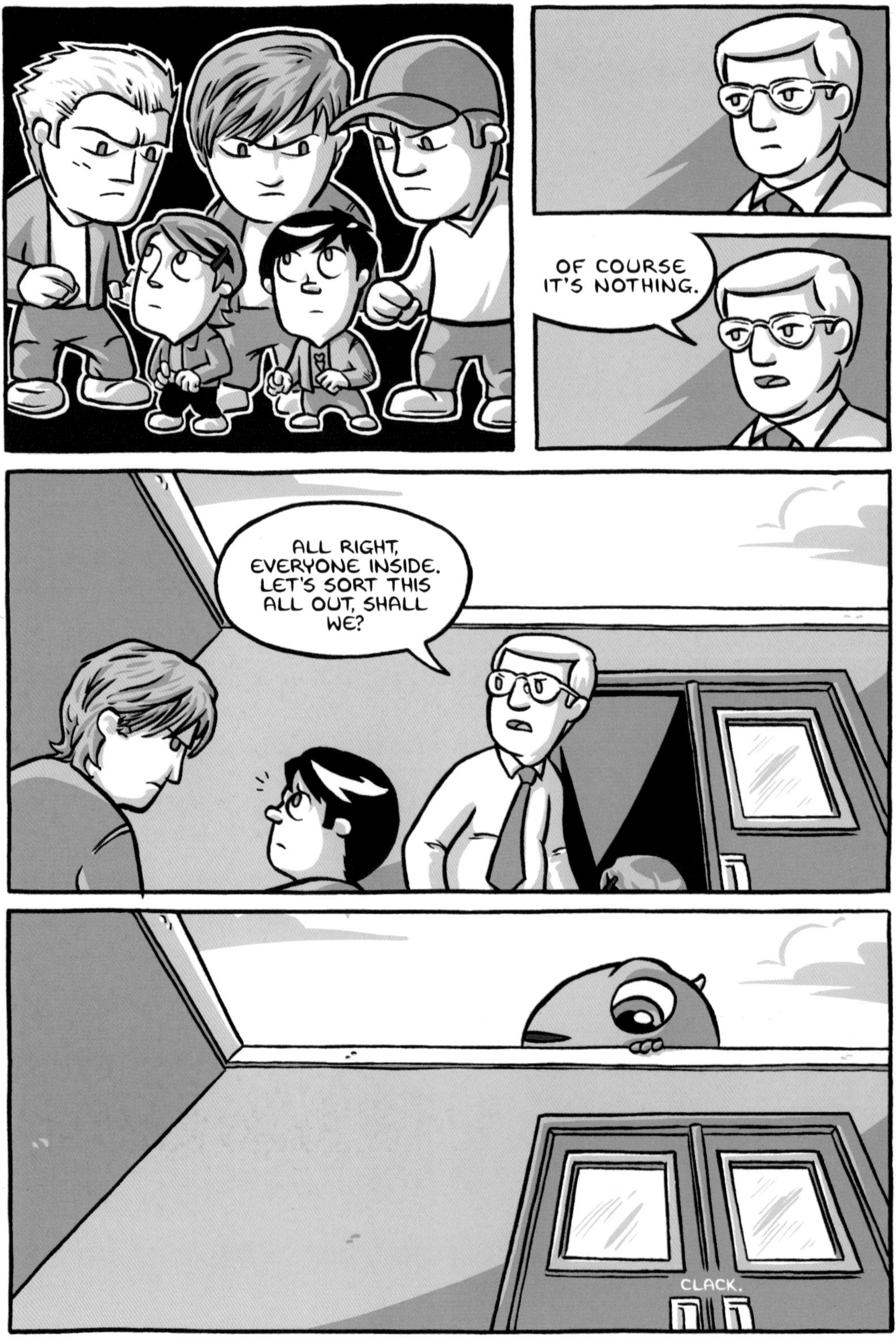
OF COURSE IT'S NOTHING.
ALL RIGHT, EVERYONE INSIDE. LET'S SORT THIS ALL OUT, SHALL WE?
CLACK.

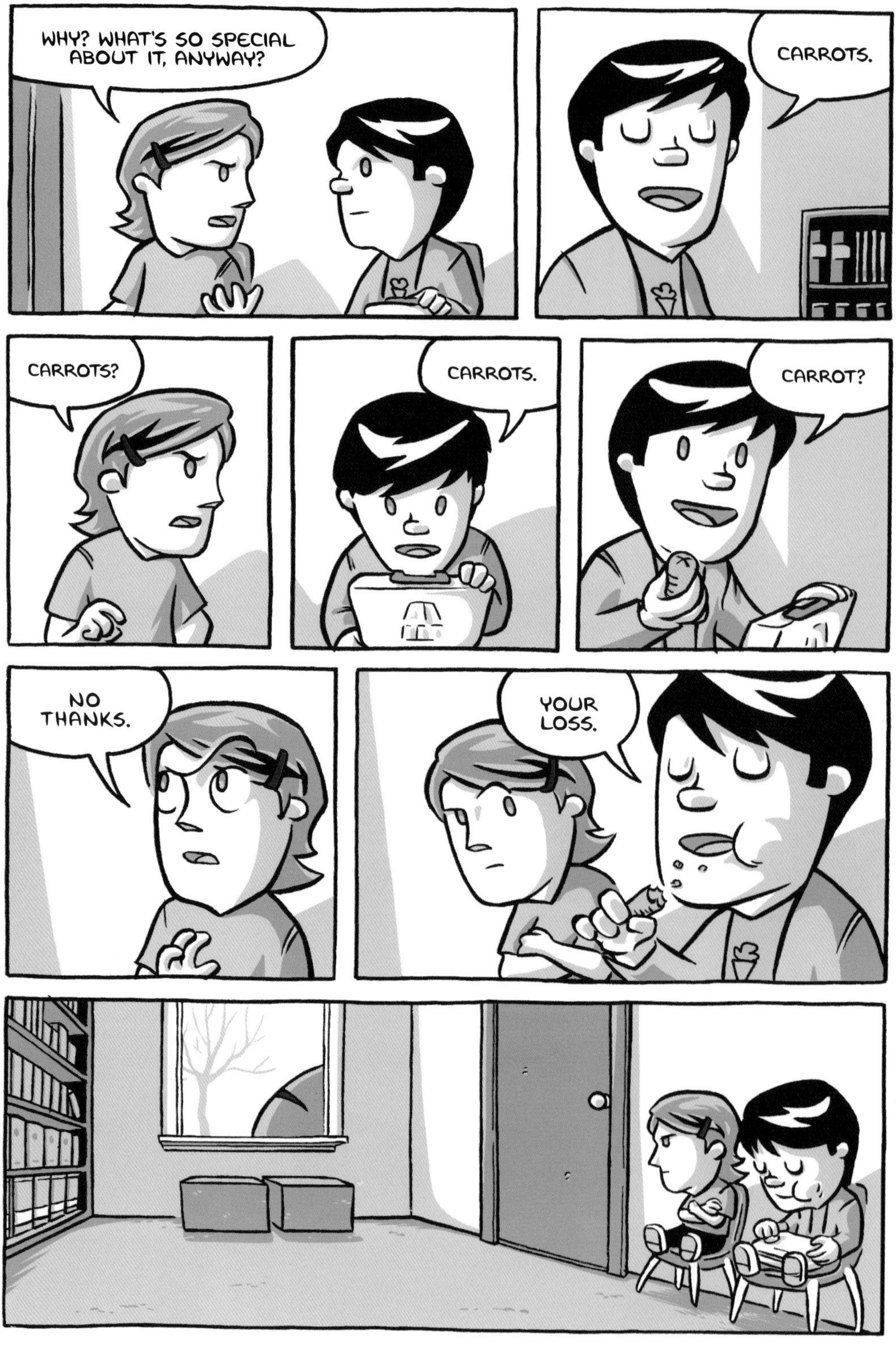
WHY? WHAT'S SO SPECIAL ABOUT IT, ANYWAY?
CARROTS.
CARROTS?
CARROTS.
CARROT?
NO THANKS.
YOUR LOSS.

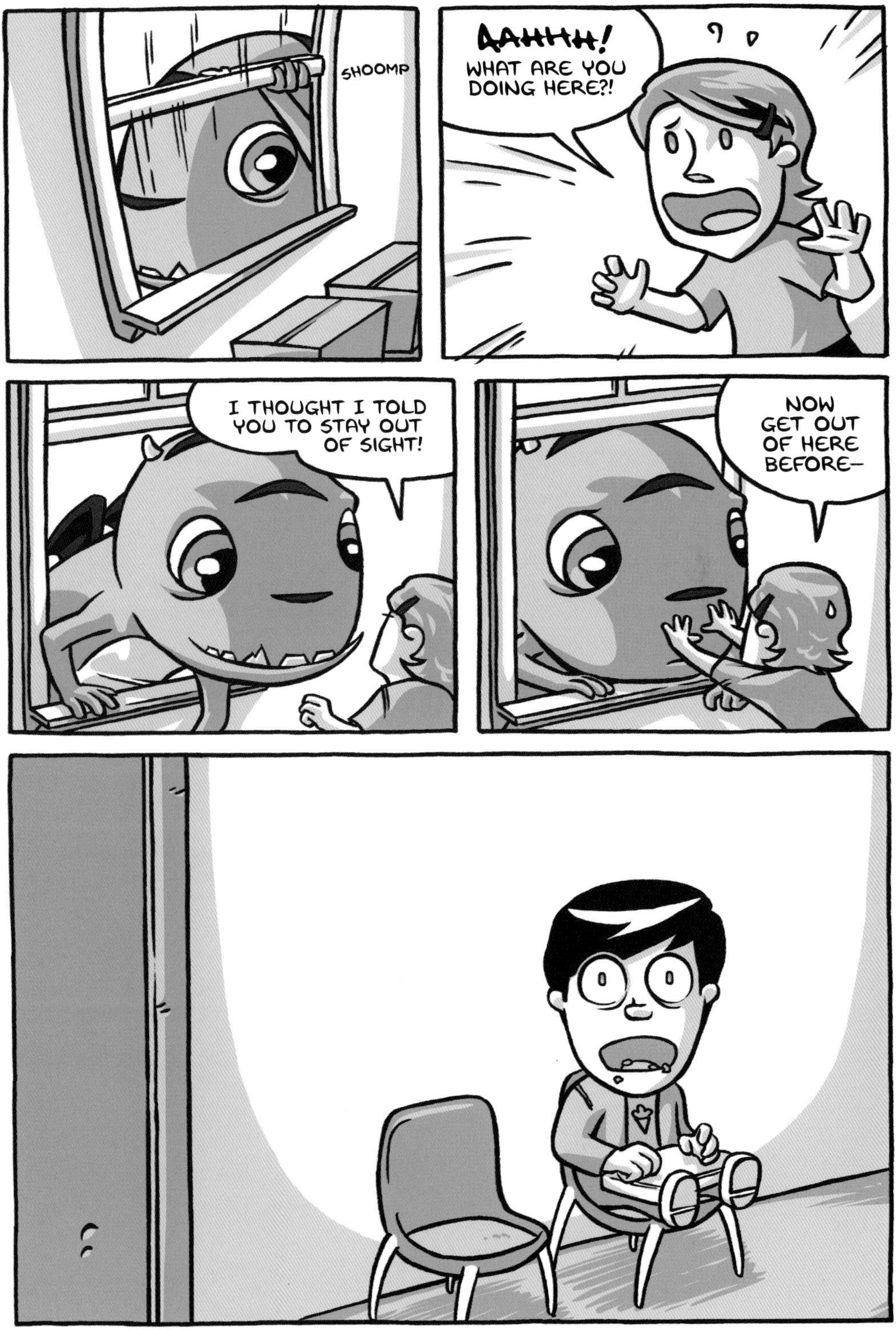
SHOOMP
AAHHH! WHAT ARE YOU DOING HERE?!
I THOUGHT I TOLD YOU TO STAY OUT OF SIGHT!
NOW GET OUT OF HERE BEFORE—

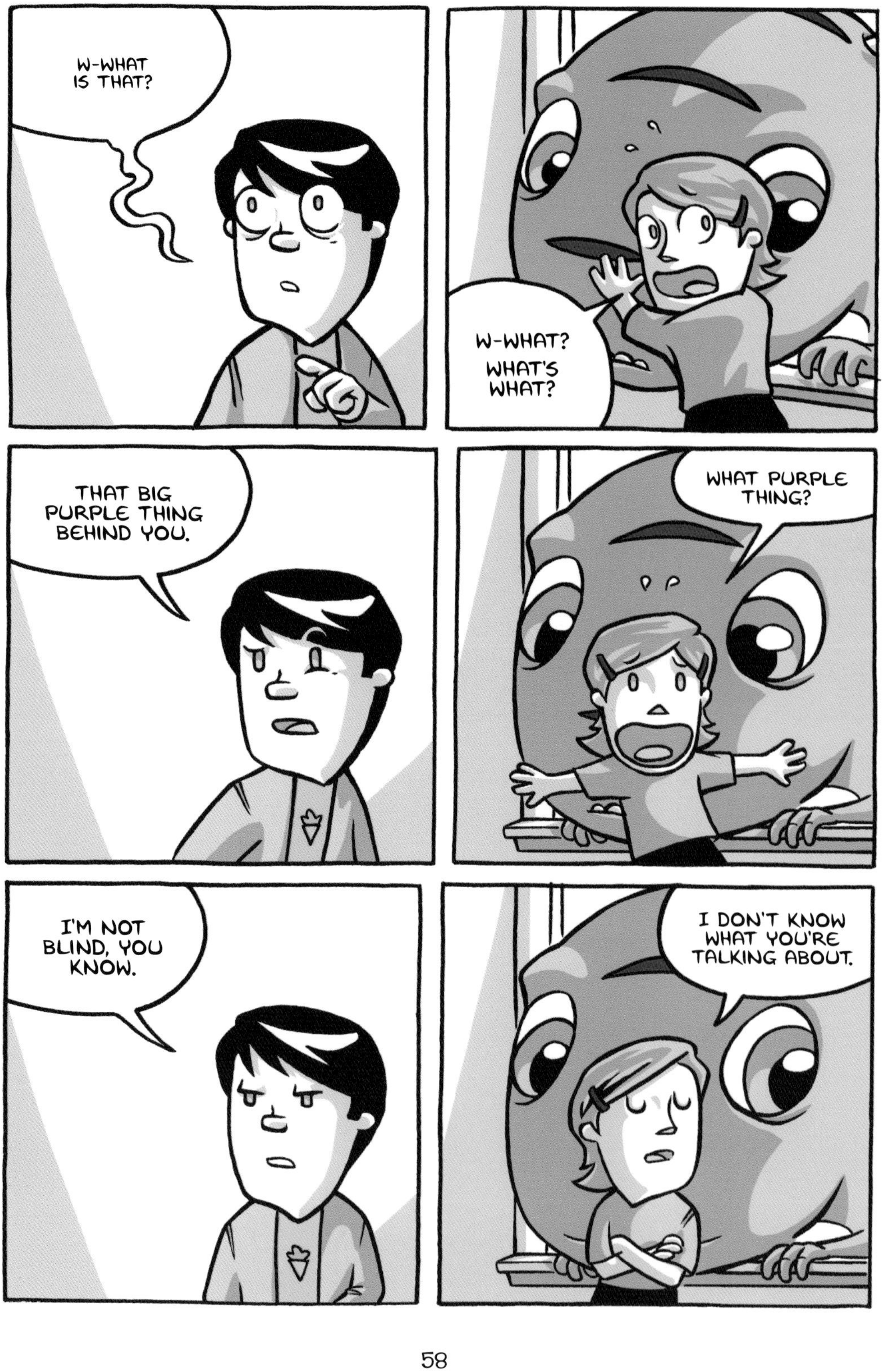
W-WHAT IS THAT?
W-WHAT? WHAT'S WHAT?
THAT BIG PURPLE THING BEHIND YOU.
WHAT PURPLE THING?
I'M NOT BLIND, YOU KNOW.
I DON'T KNOW WHAT YOU'RE TALKING ABOUT.

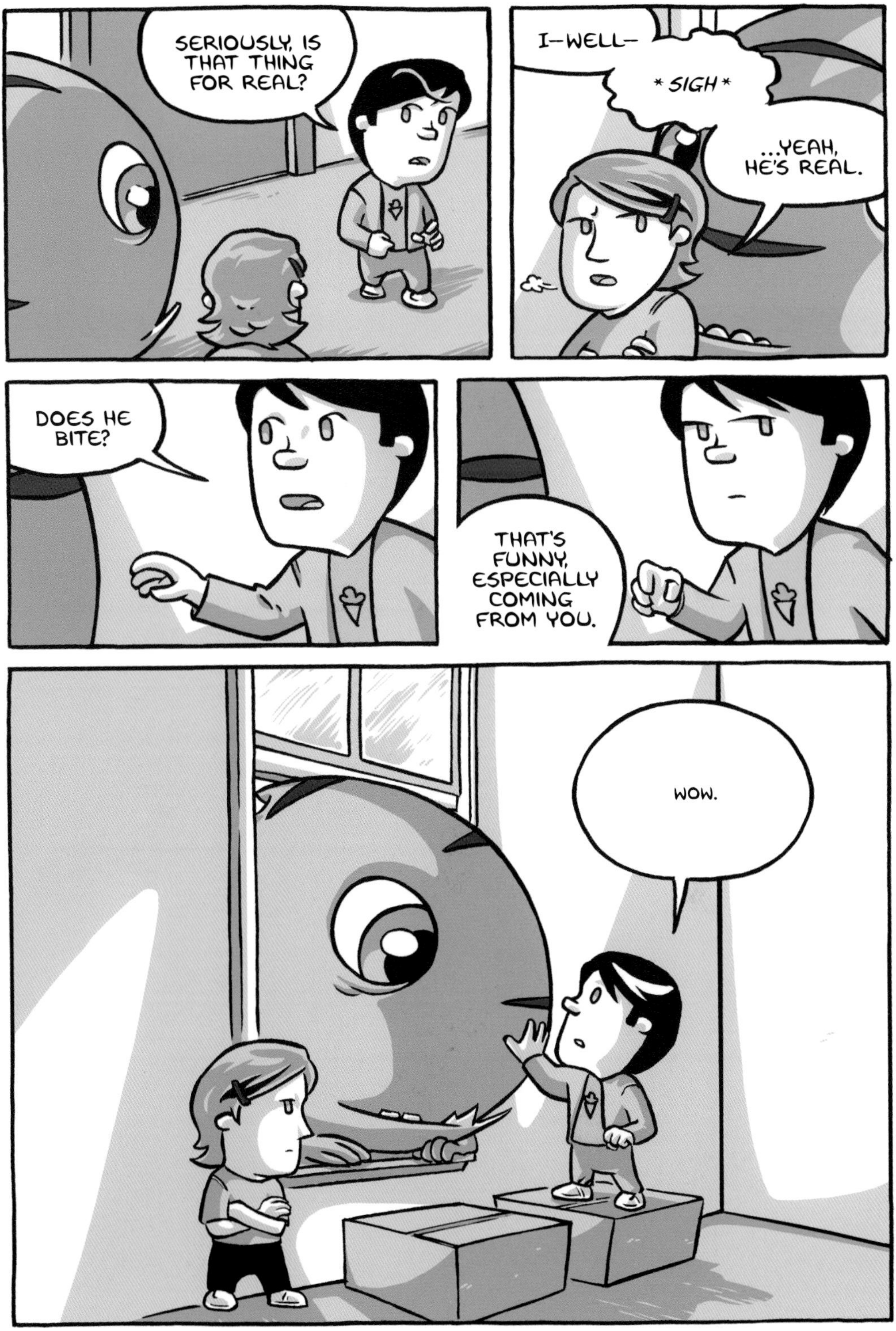
SERIOUSLY, IS THAT THING FOR REAL?
I—WELL—
* SIGH *
...YEAH, HE'S REAL.
DOES HE BITE?
THAT'S FUNNY, ESPECIALLY COMING FROM YOU.
WOW.

61

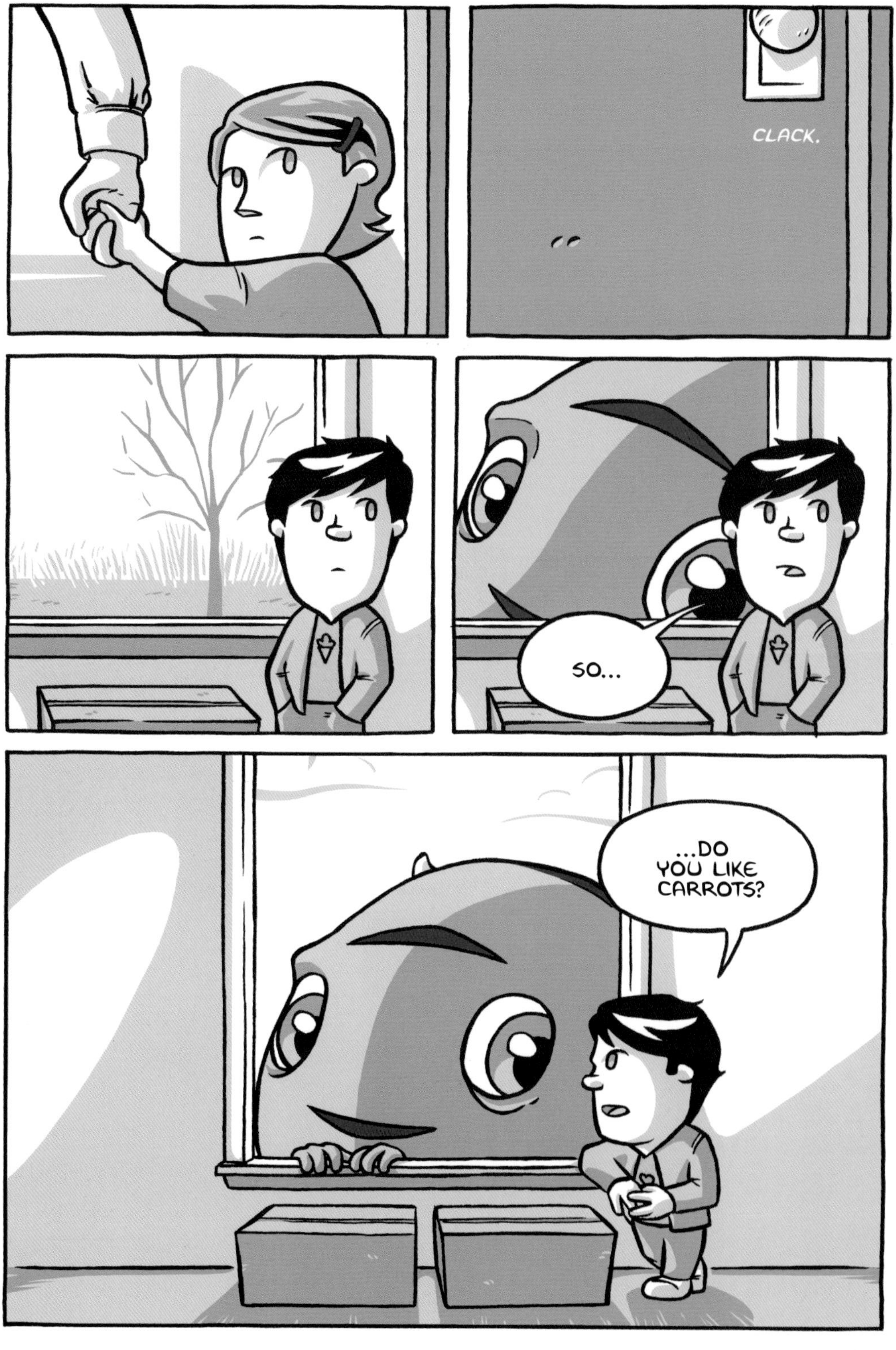
CLACK.
SO...
...DO YOU LIKE CARROTS?

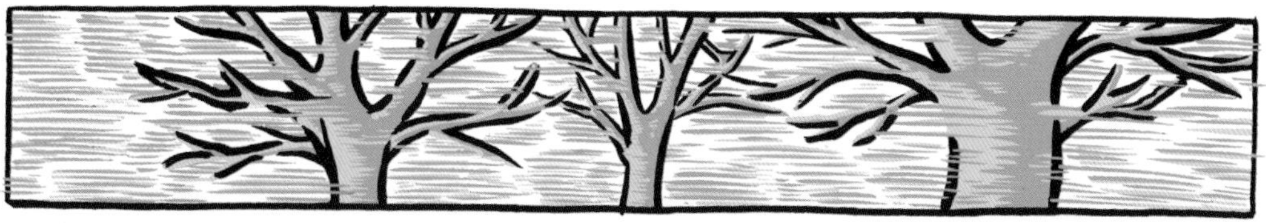

CHAPTER THREE

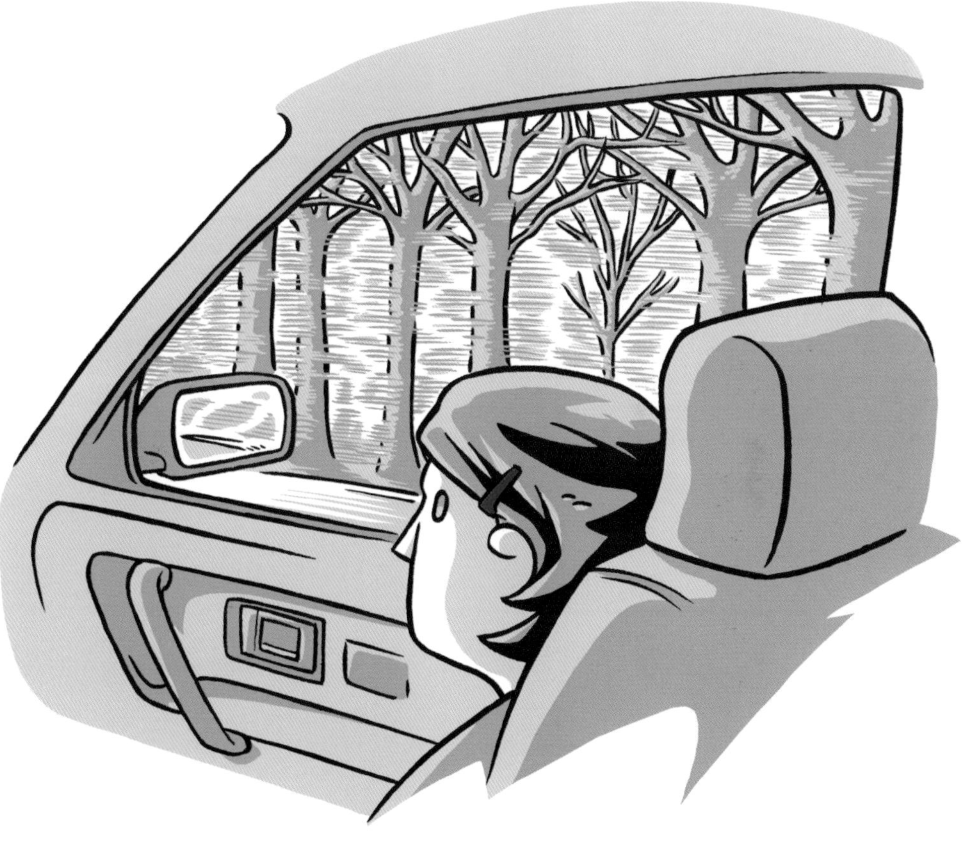

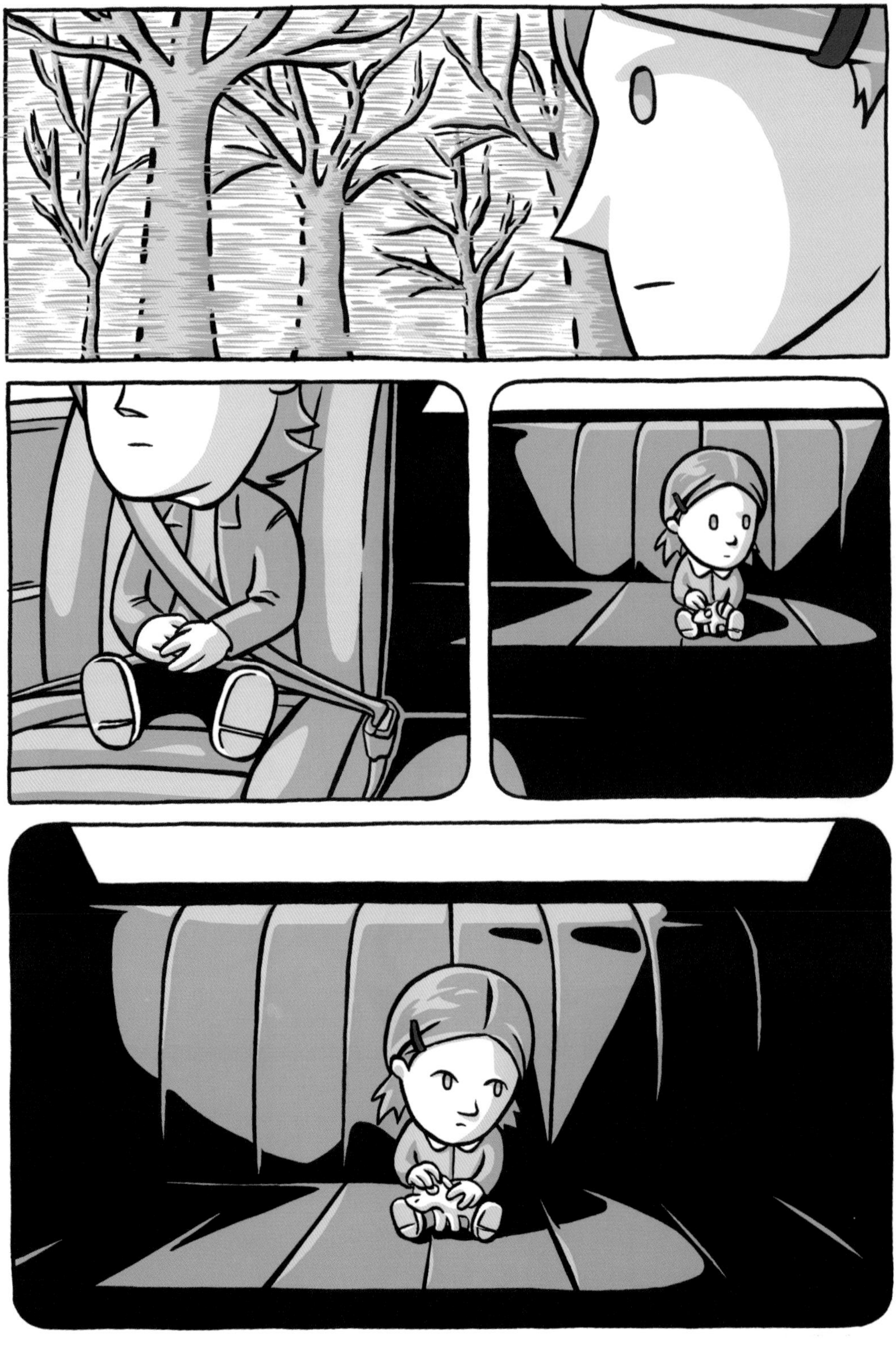

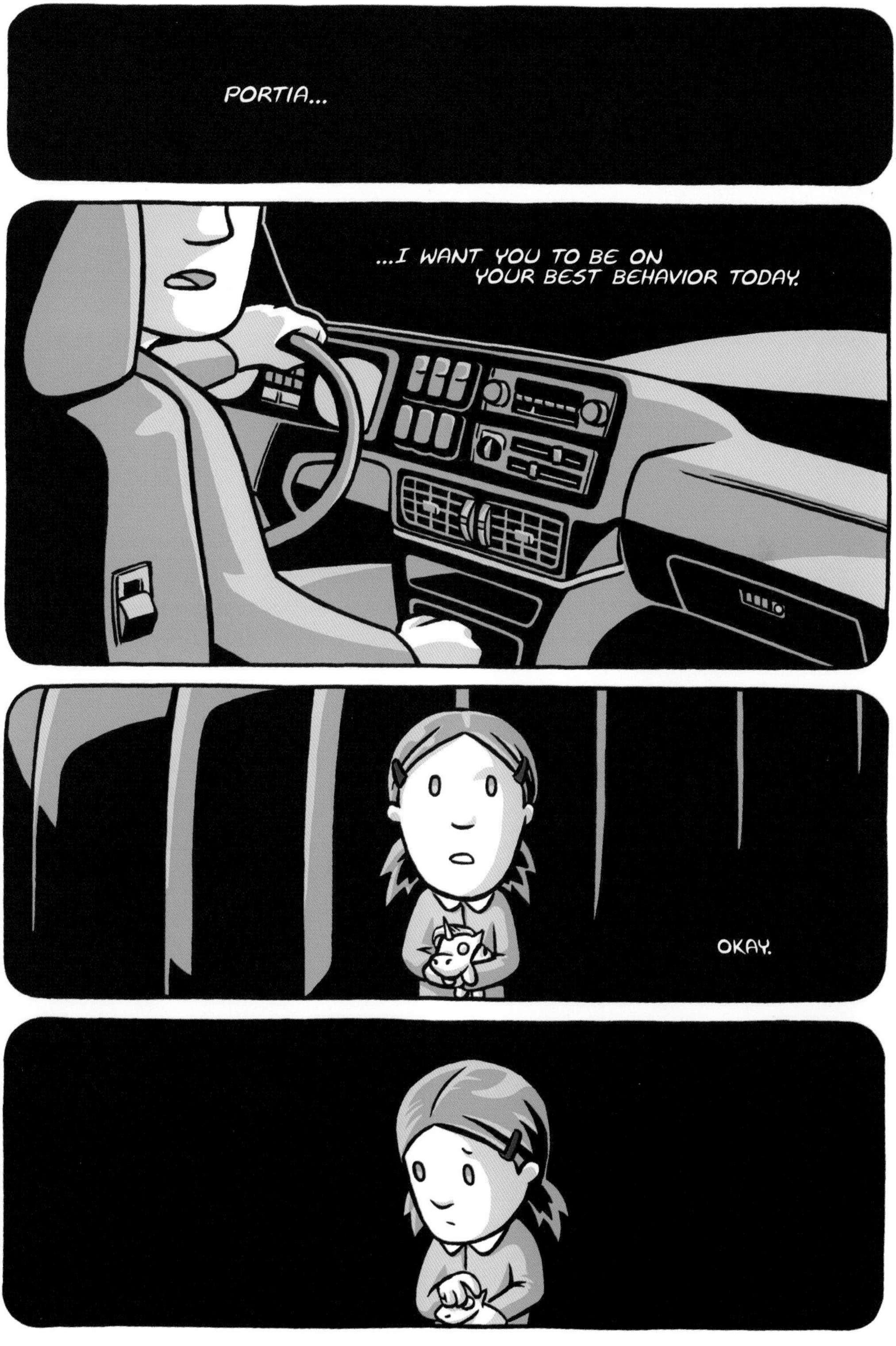
PORTIA...
...I WANT YOU TO BE ON YOUR BEST BEHAVIOR TODAY.
OKAY.

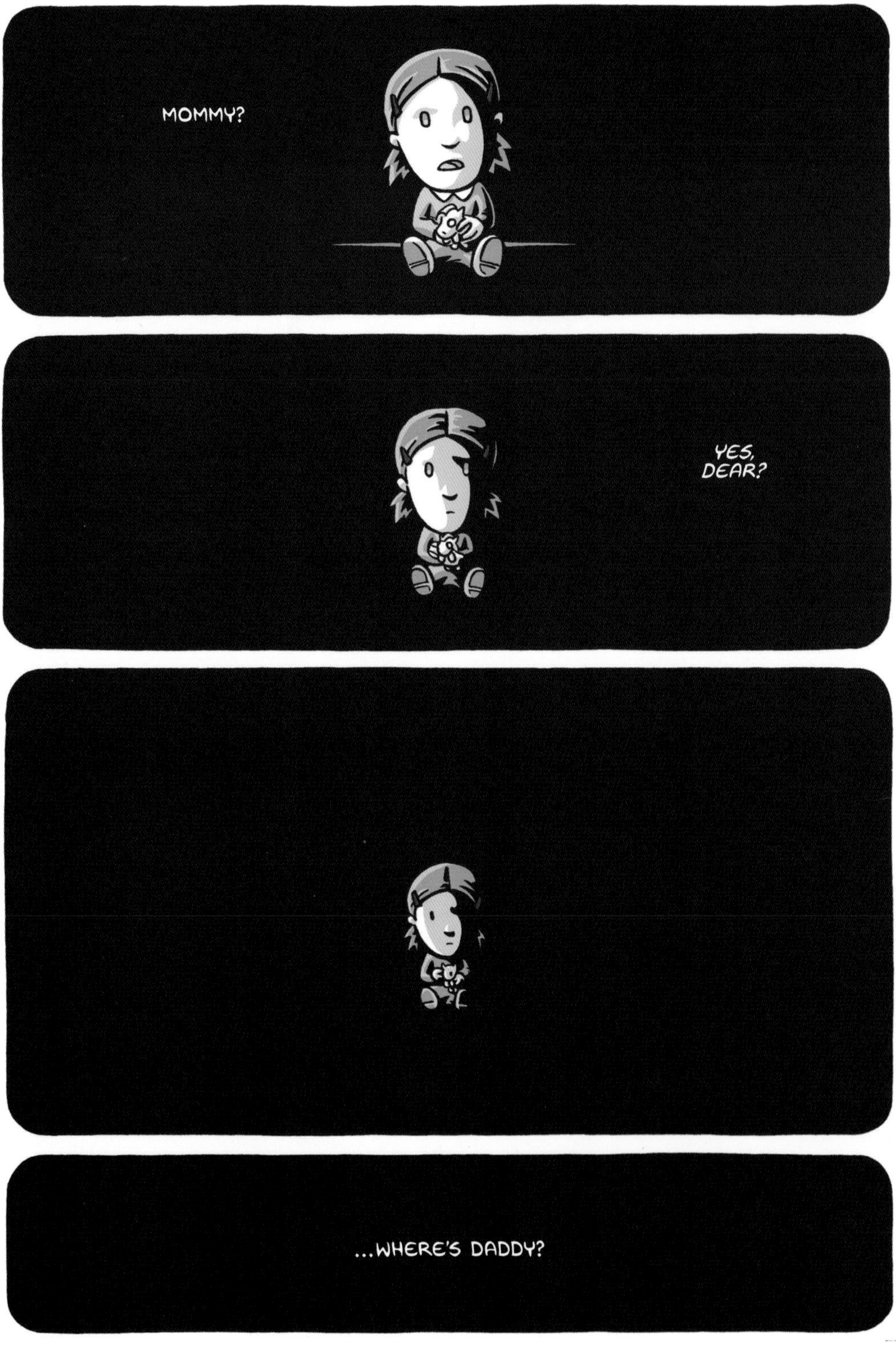
MOMMY?
YES, DEAR?
...WHERE'S DADDY?

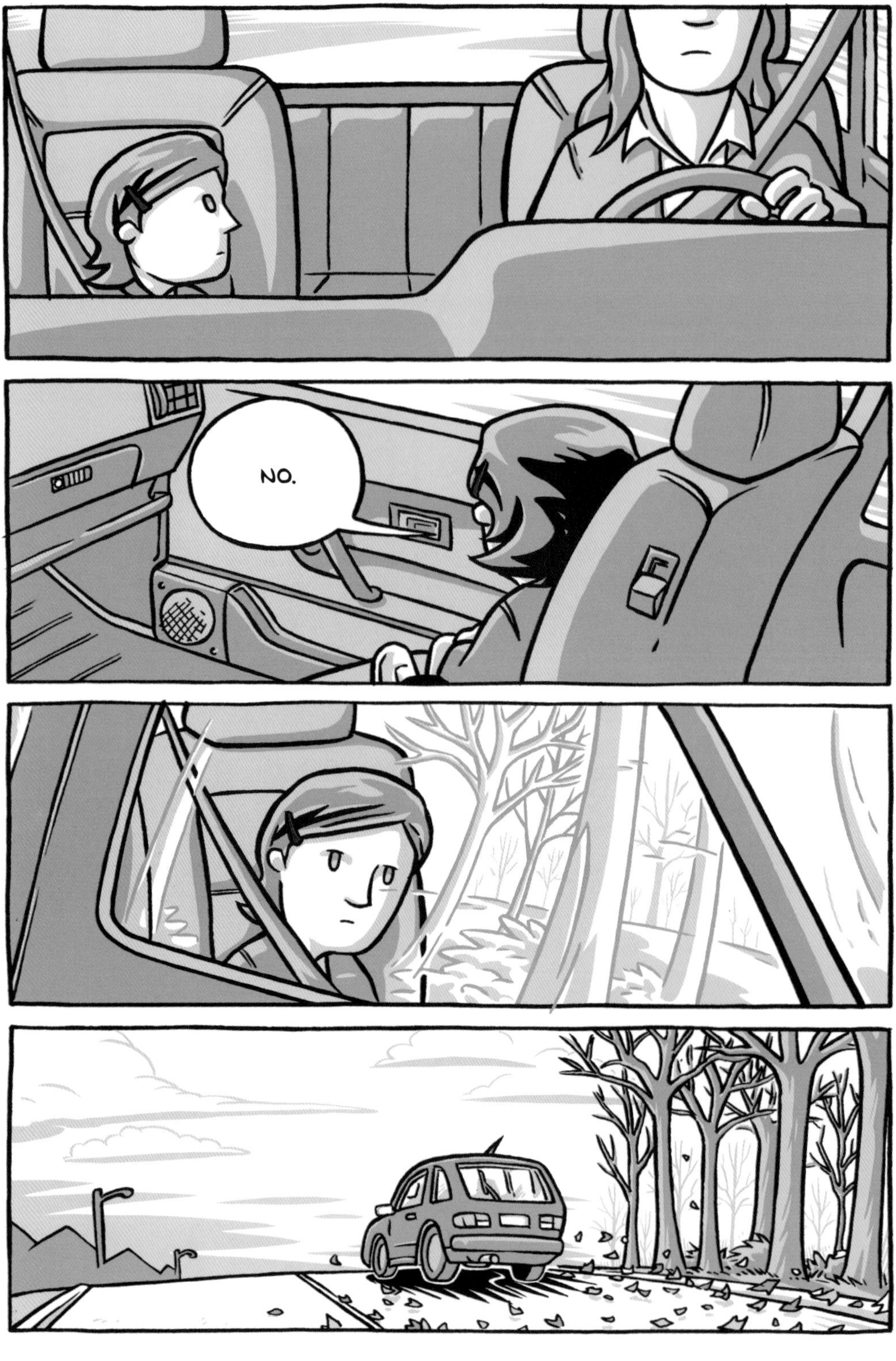
NO.

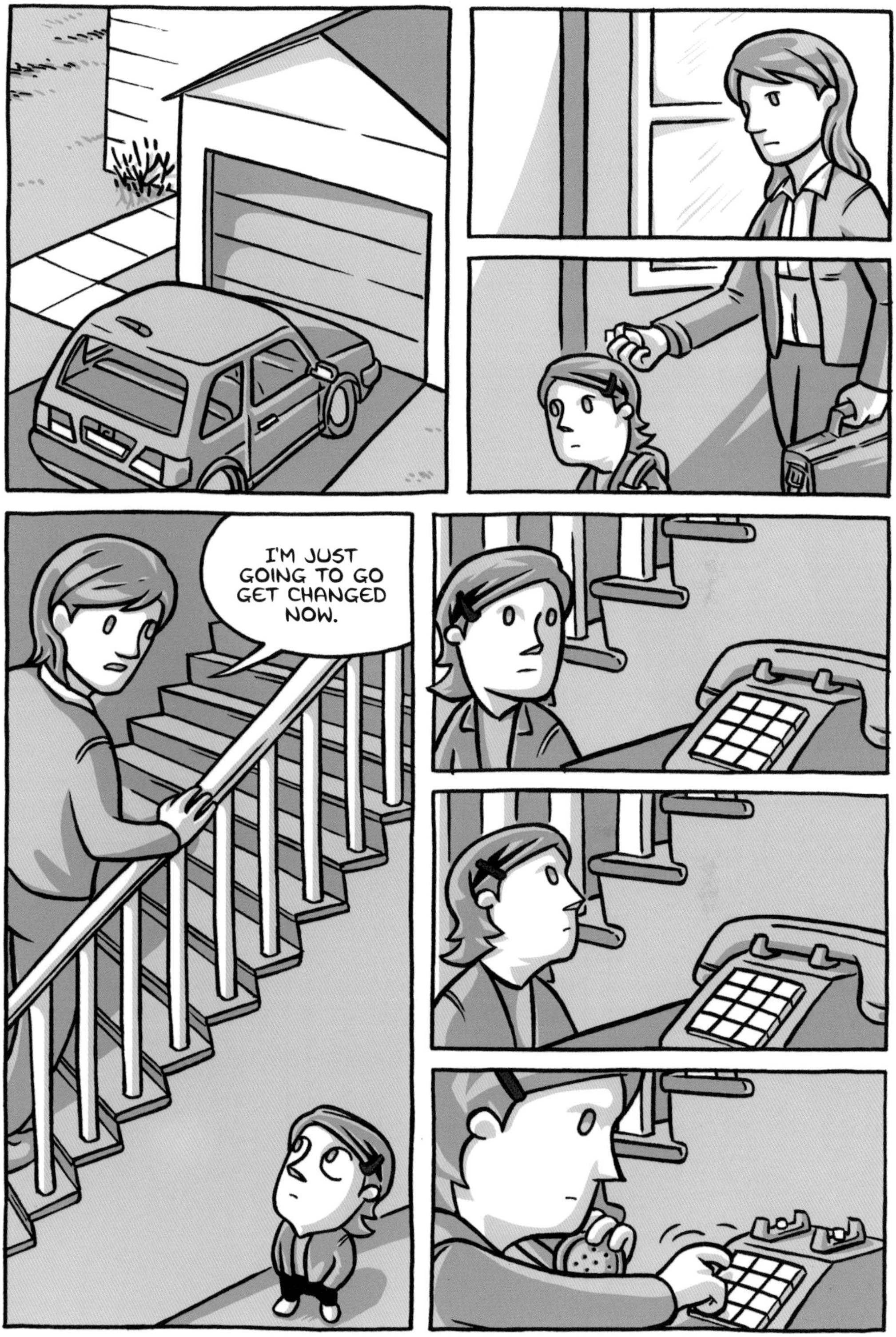
I'M JUST GOING TO GO GET CHANGED NOW.

71

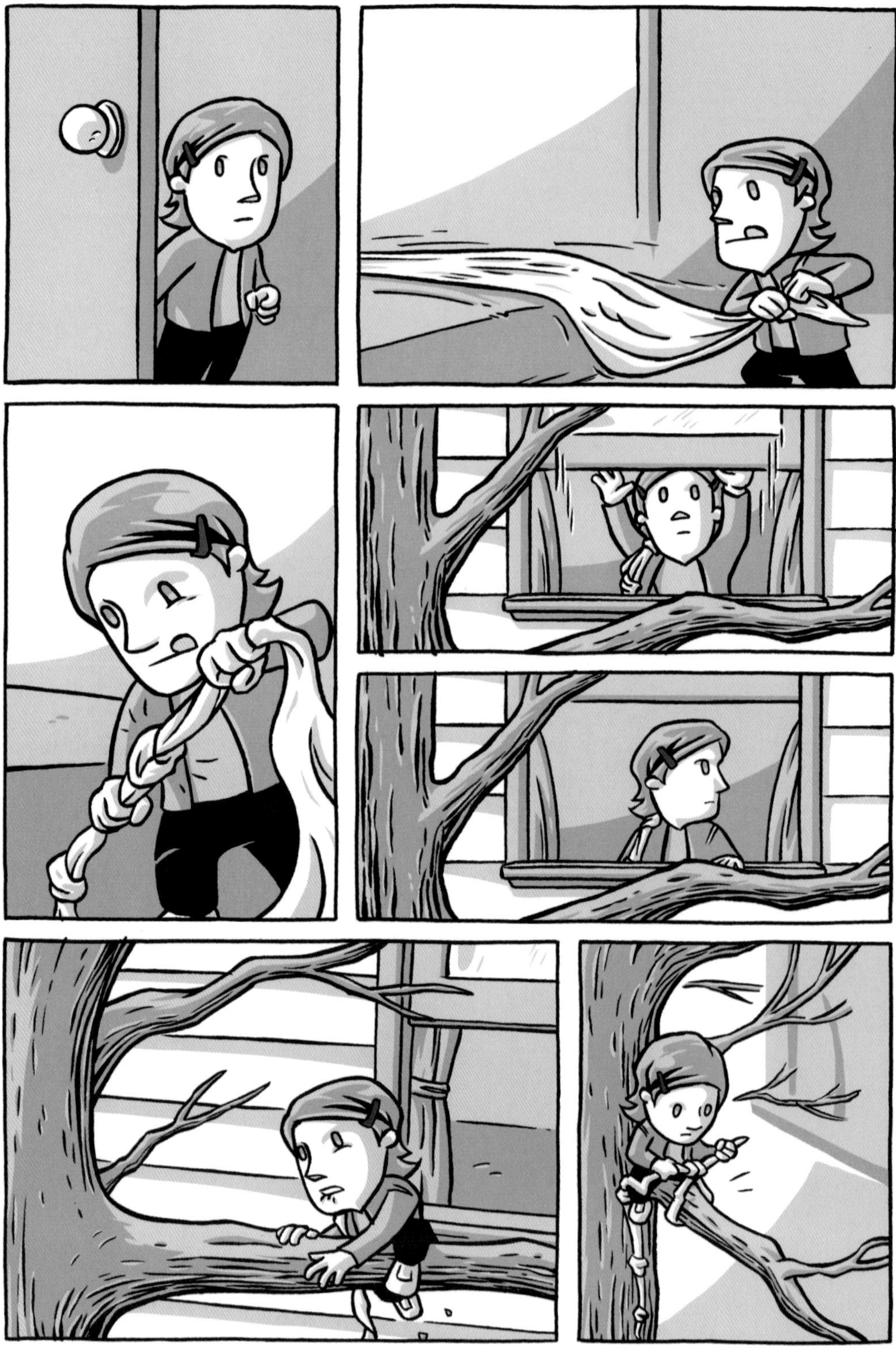

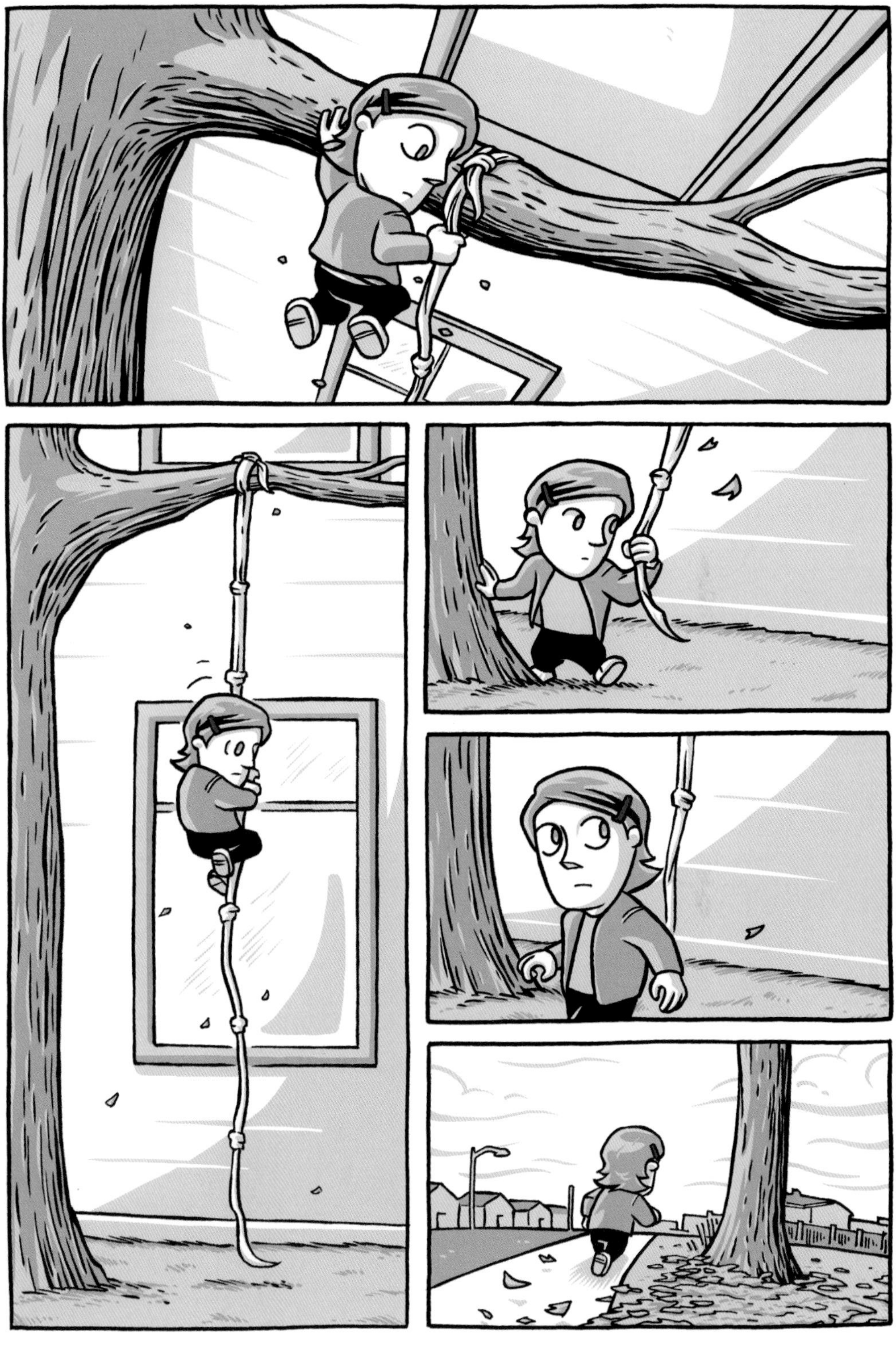

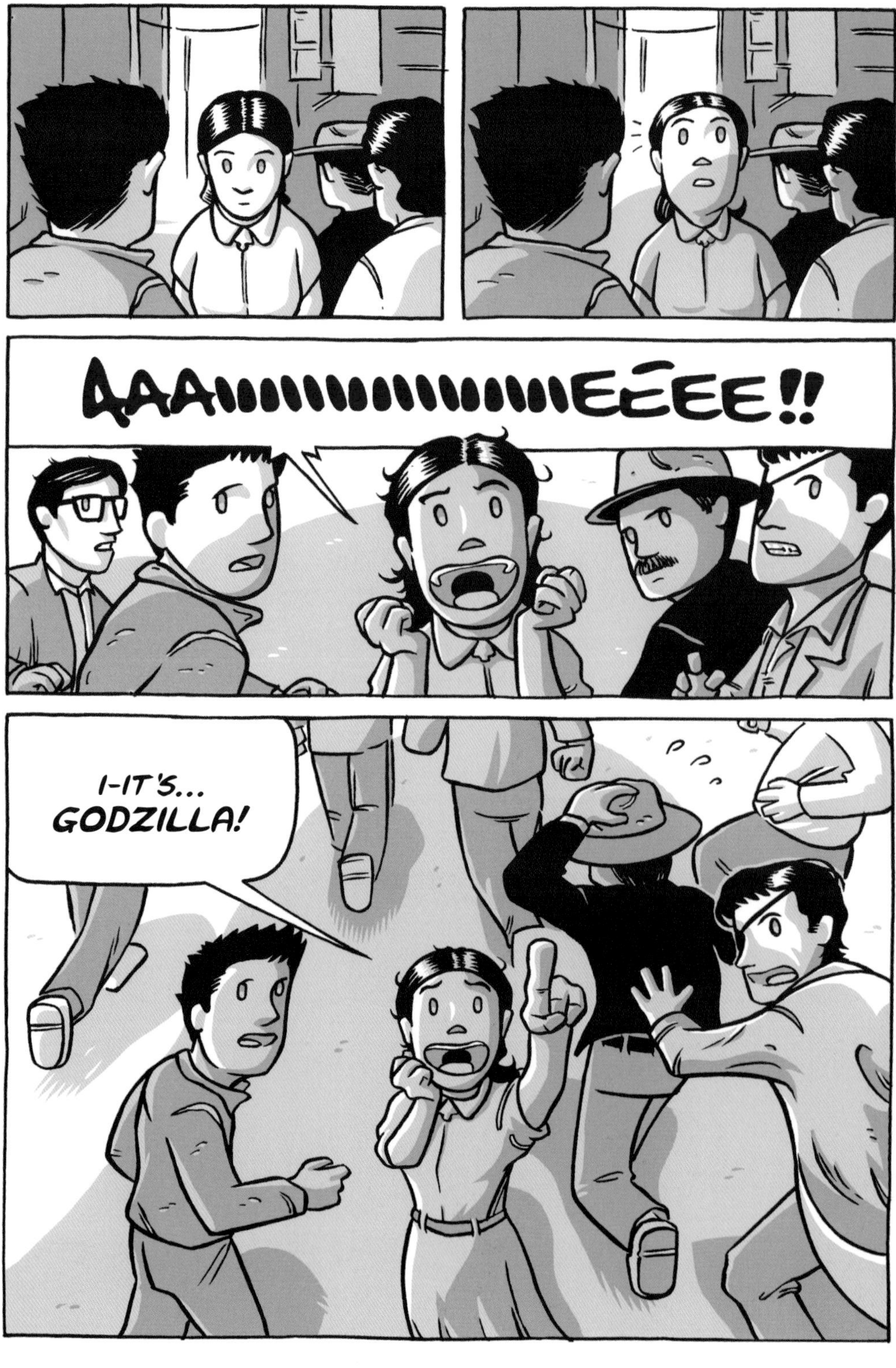
AAAIIIIIIIIIIIIIIIIIEEEEE!!
I-IT'S... GODZILLA!

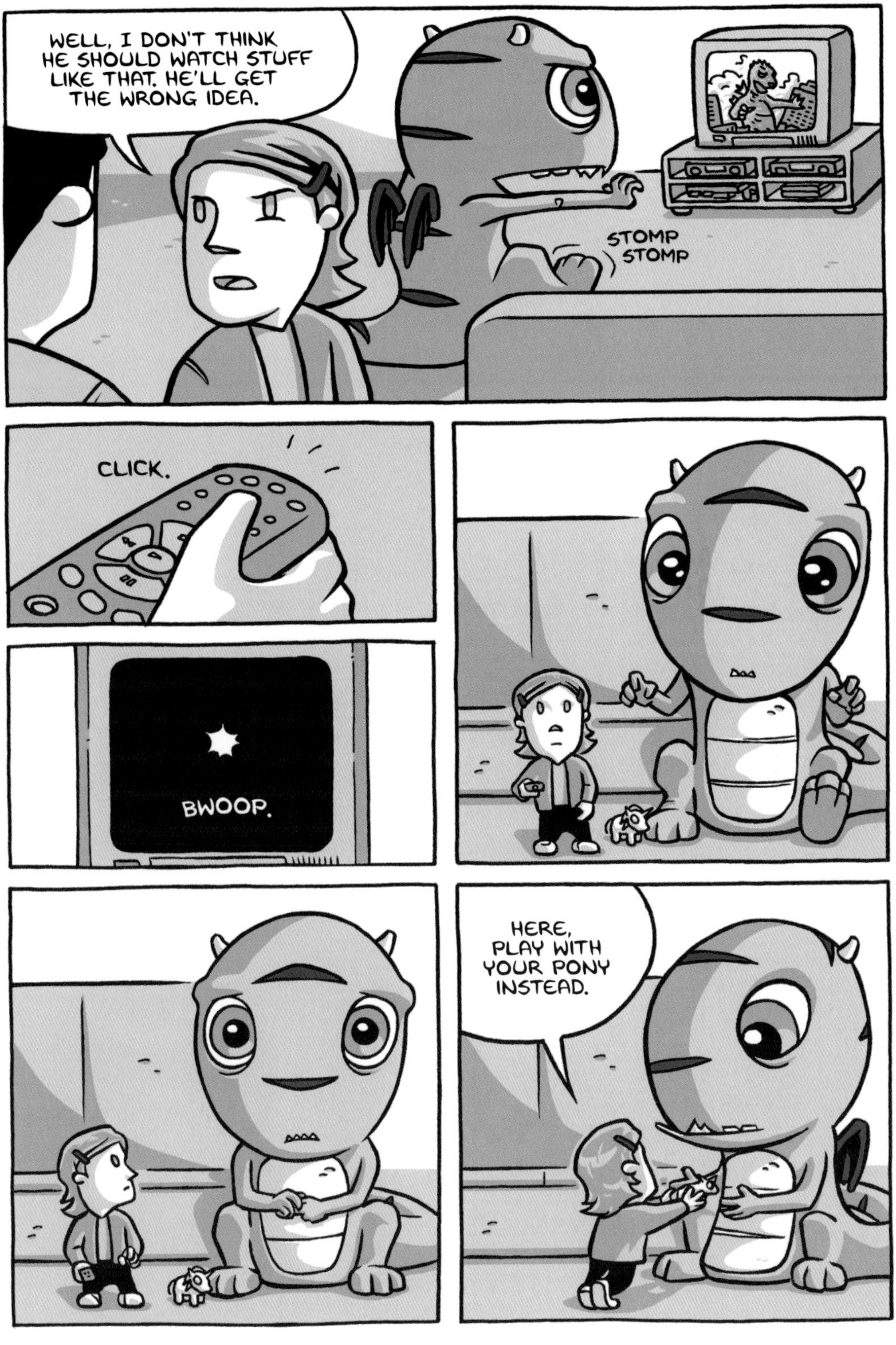

WELL, I DON'T THINK HE SHOULD WATCH STUFF LIKE THAT. HE'LL GET THE WRONG IDEA.
STOMP STOMP
CLICK.
BWOOP.
HERE, PLAY WITH YOUR PONY INSTEAD.

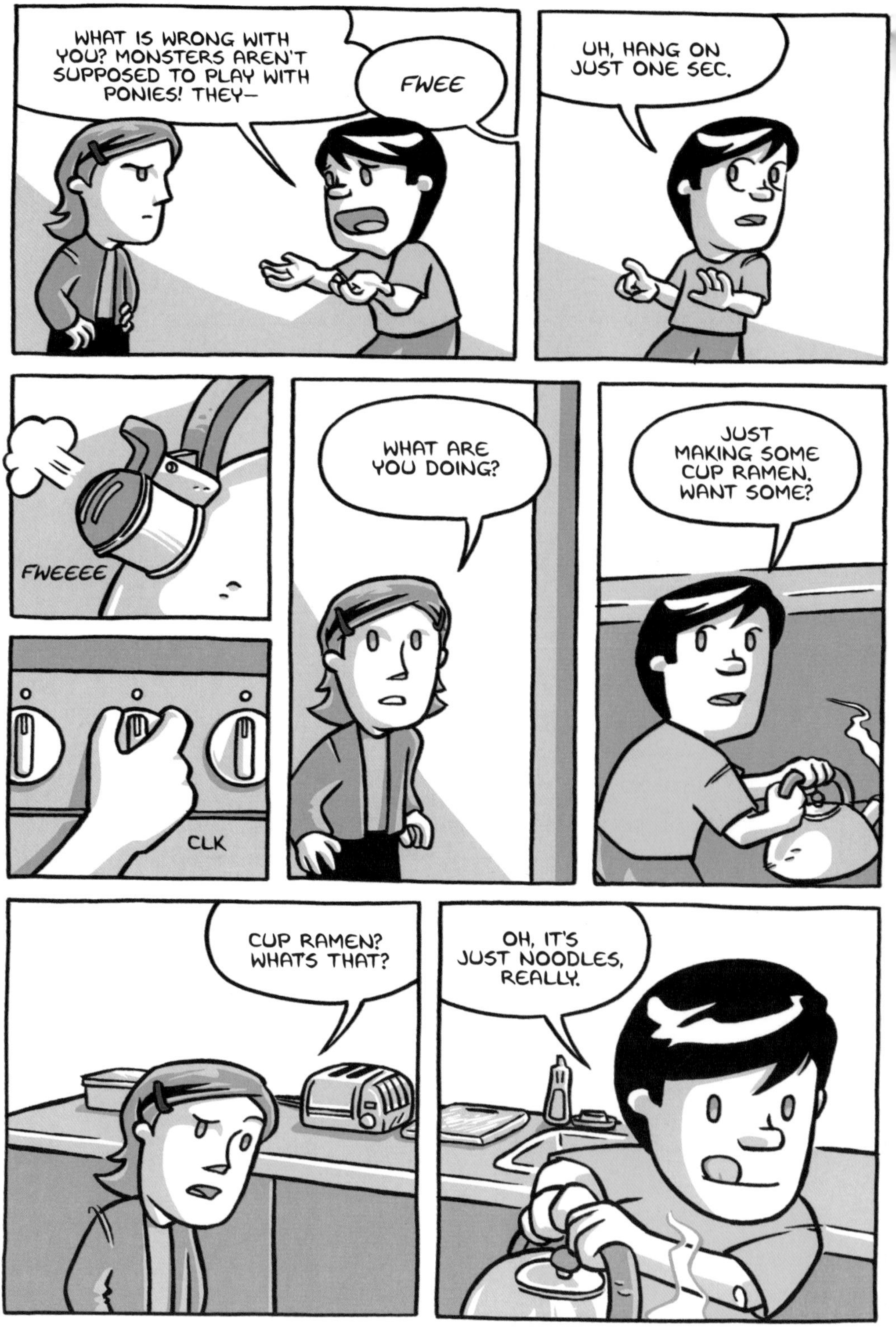
WHAT IS WRONG WITH YOU? MONSTERS AREN'T SUPPOSED TO PLAY WITH PONIES! THEY—
FWEE
UH, HANG ON JUST ONE SEC.
FWEEEE
CLK
WHAT ARE YOU DOING?
JUST MAKING SOME CUP RAMEN. WANT SOME?
CUP RAMEN? WHAT'S THAT?
OH, IT'S JUST NOODLES, REALLY.

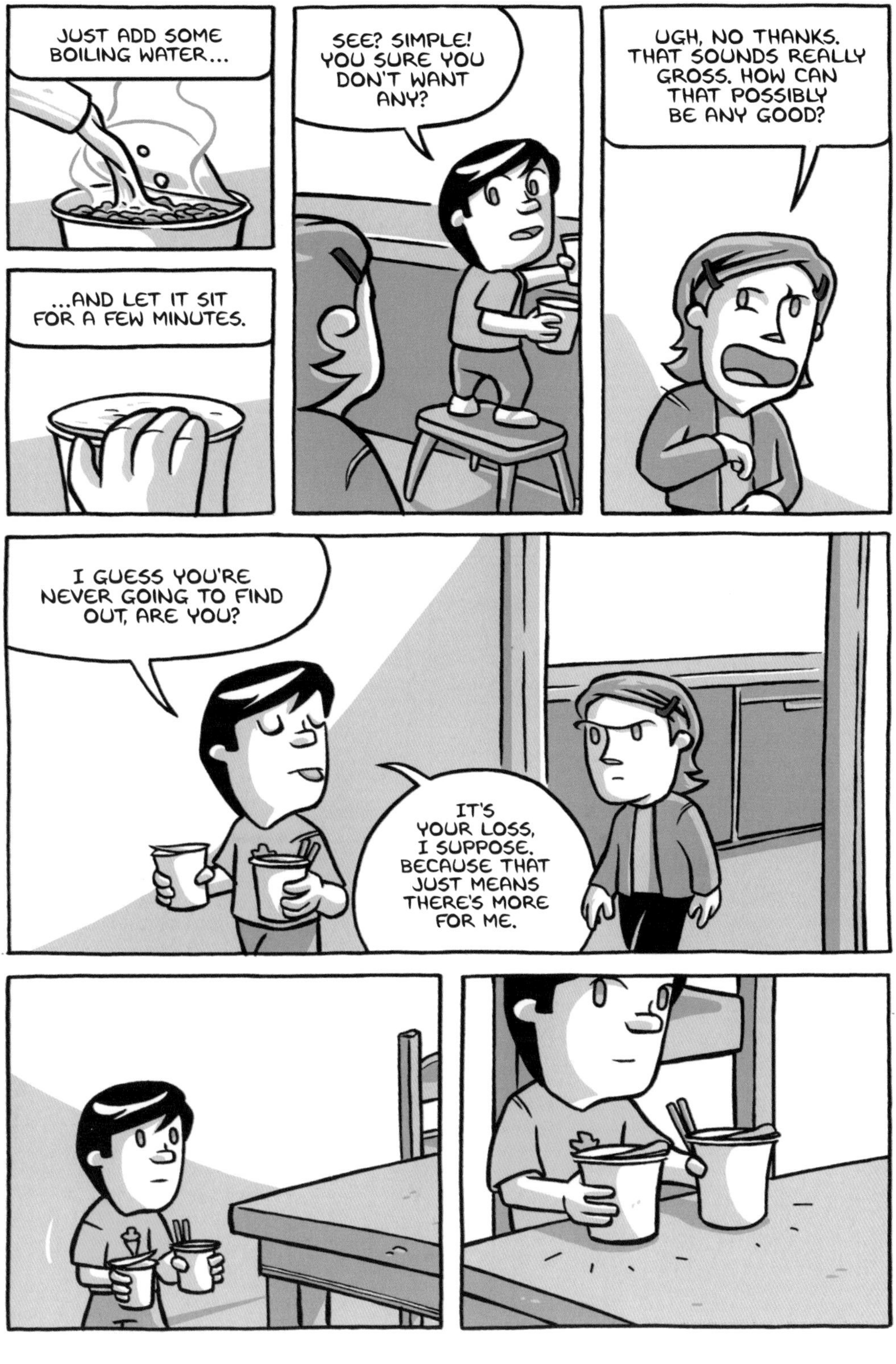
JUST ADD SOME BOILING WATER...
SEE? SIMPLE! YOU SURE YOU DON'T WANT ANY?
UGH, NO THANKS. THAT SOUNDS REALLY GROSS. HOW CAN THAT POSSIBLY BE ANY GOOD?
...AND LET IT SIT FOR A FEW MINUTES.
I GUESS YOU'RE NEVER GOING TO FIND OUT, ARE YOU?
IT'S YOUR LOSS, I SUPPOSE. BECAUSE THAT JUST MEANS THERE'S MORE FOR ME.

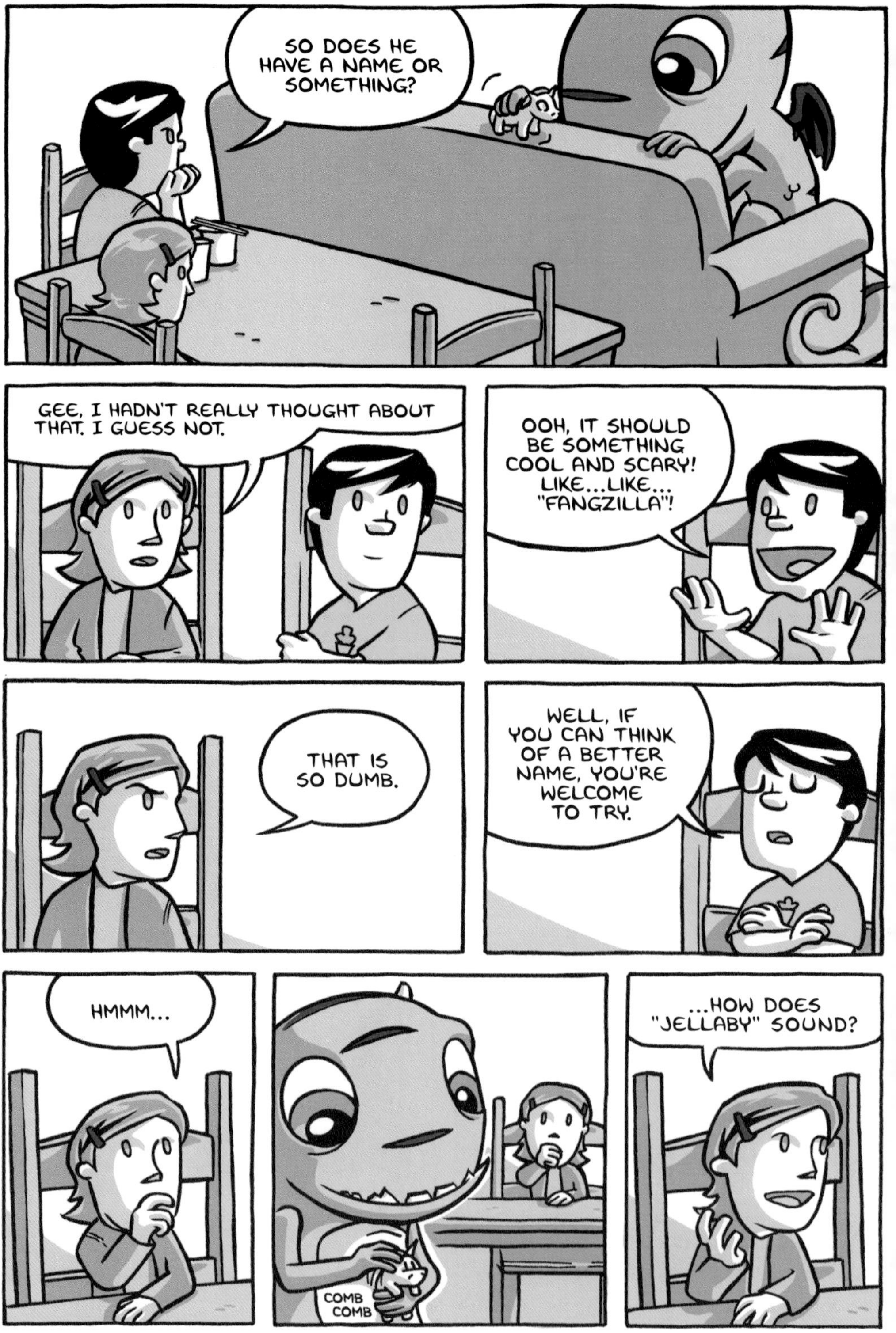
SO DOES HE HAVE A NAME OR SOMETHING?
GEE, I HADN'T REALLY THOUGHT ABOUT THAT. I GUESS NOT.
OOH, IT SHOULD BE SOMETHING COOL AND SCARY! LIKE...LIKE... "FANGZILLA"!
THAT IS SO DUMB.
WELL, IF YOU CAN THINK OF A BETTER NAME, YOU'RE WELCOME TO TRY.
HMMM...
COMB COMB
...HOW DOES "JELLABY" SOUND?

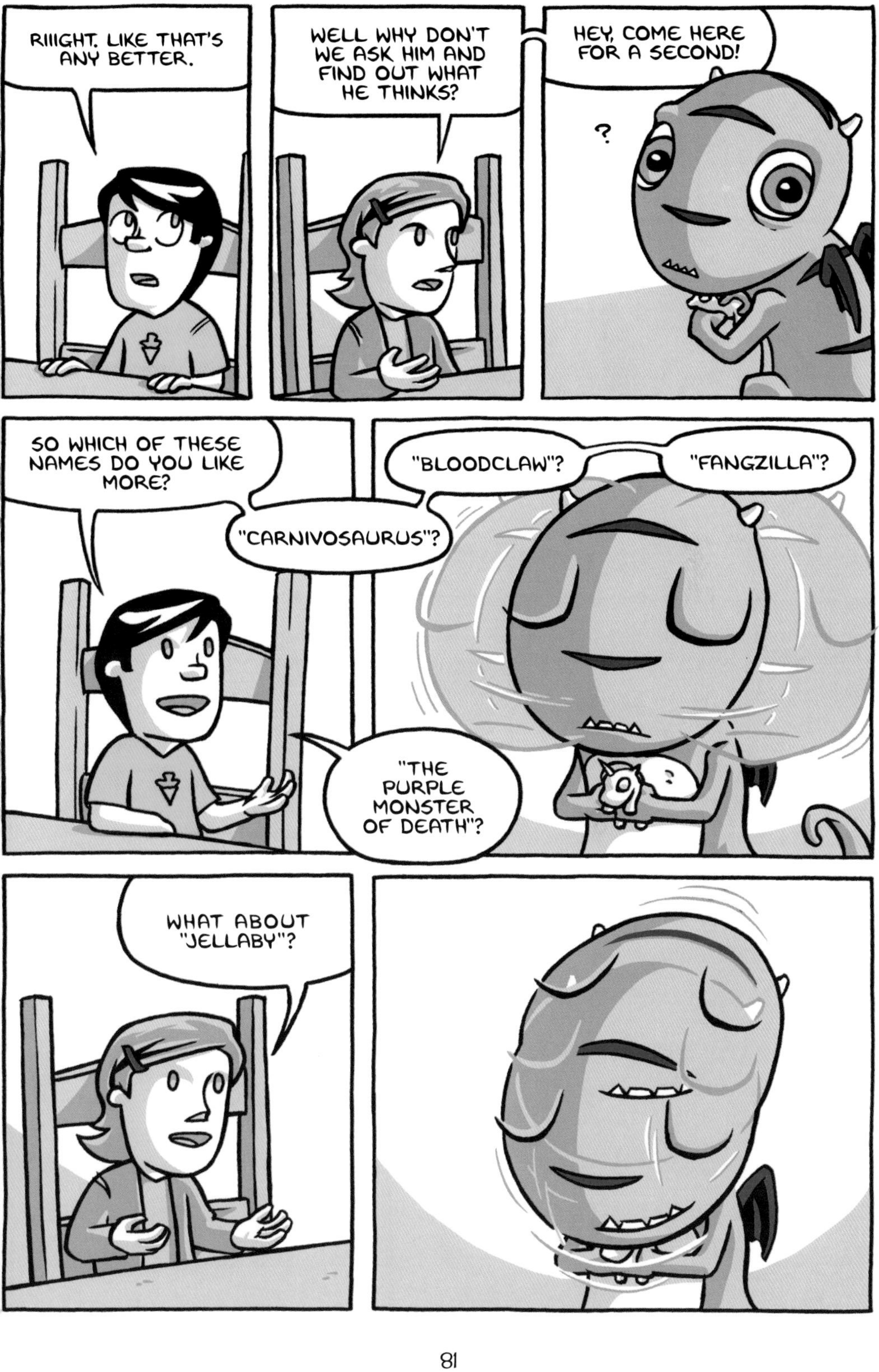
RIIIGHT. LIKE THAT'S ANY BETTER.
WELL WHY DON'T WE ASK HIM AND FIND OUT WHAT HE THINKS?
HEY, COME HERE FOR A SECOND!
?
SO WHICH OF THESE NAMES DO YOU LIKE MORE?
"CARNIVOSAURUS"?
"BLOODCLAW"?
"FANGZILLA"?
"THE PURPLE MONSTER OF DEATH"?
WHAT ABOUT "JELLABY"?

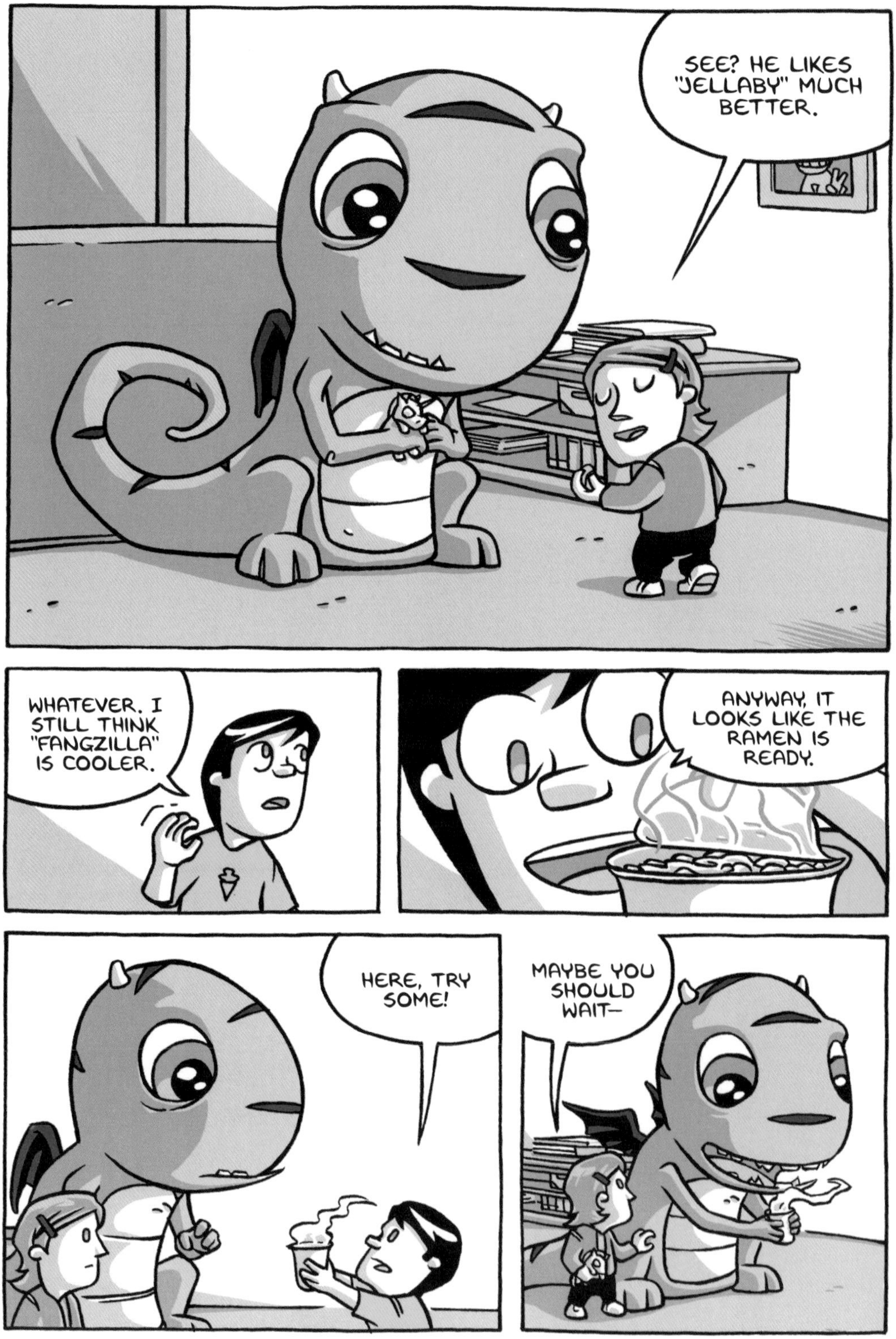
SEE? HE LIKES "JELLABY" MUCH BETTER.
WHATEVER. I STILL THINK "FANGZILLA" IS COOLER.
ANYWAY, IT LOOKS LIKE THE RAMEN IS READY.
HERE, TRY SOME!
MAYBE YOU SHOULD WAIT—

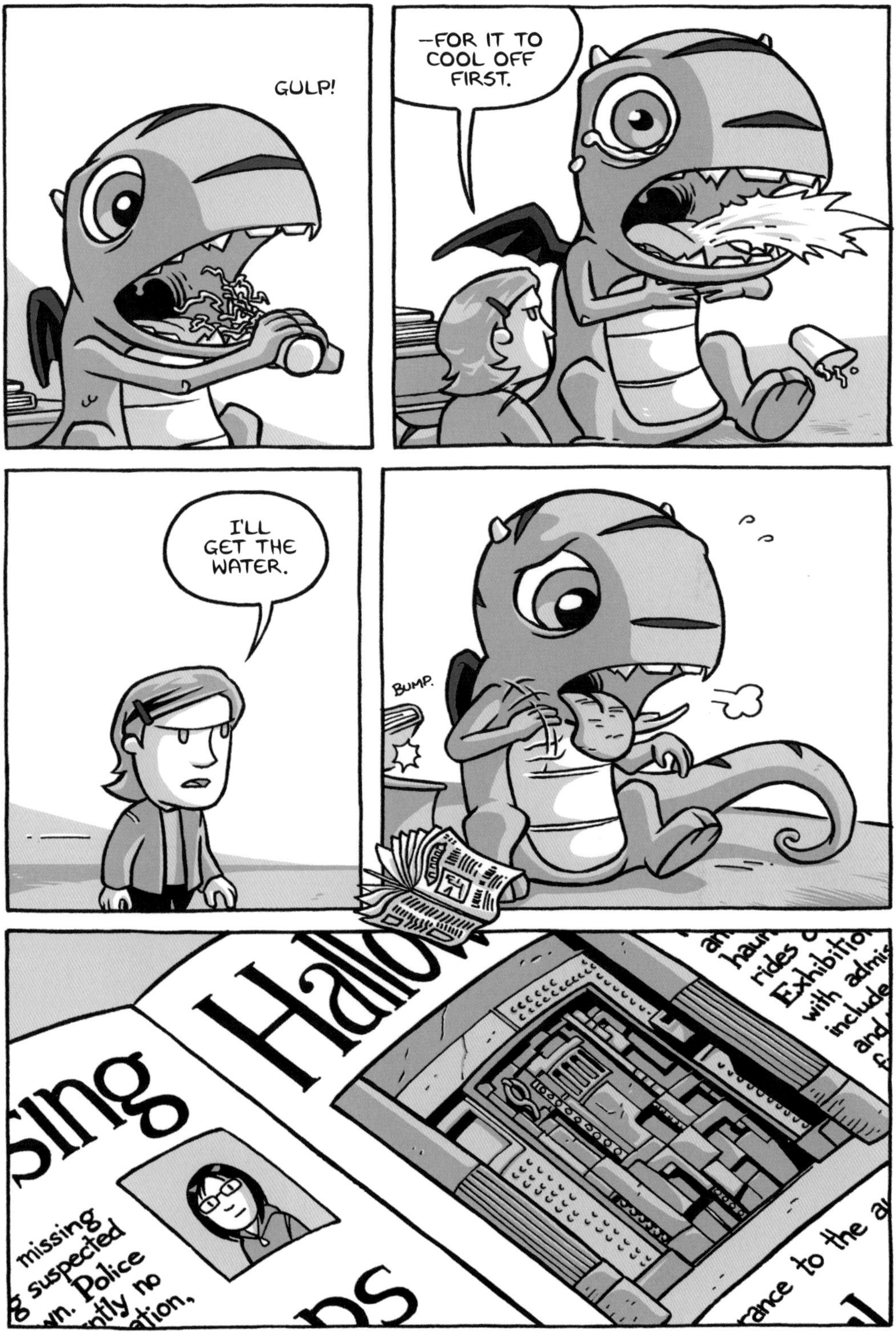
GULP!
—FOR IT TO COOL OFF FIRST.
I'LL GET THE WATER.
BUMP.

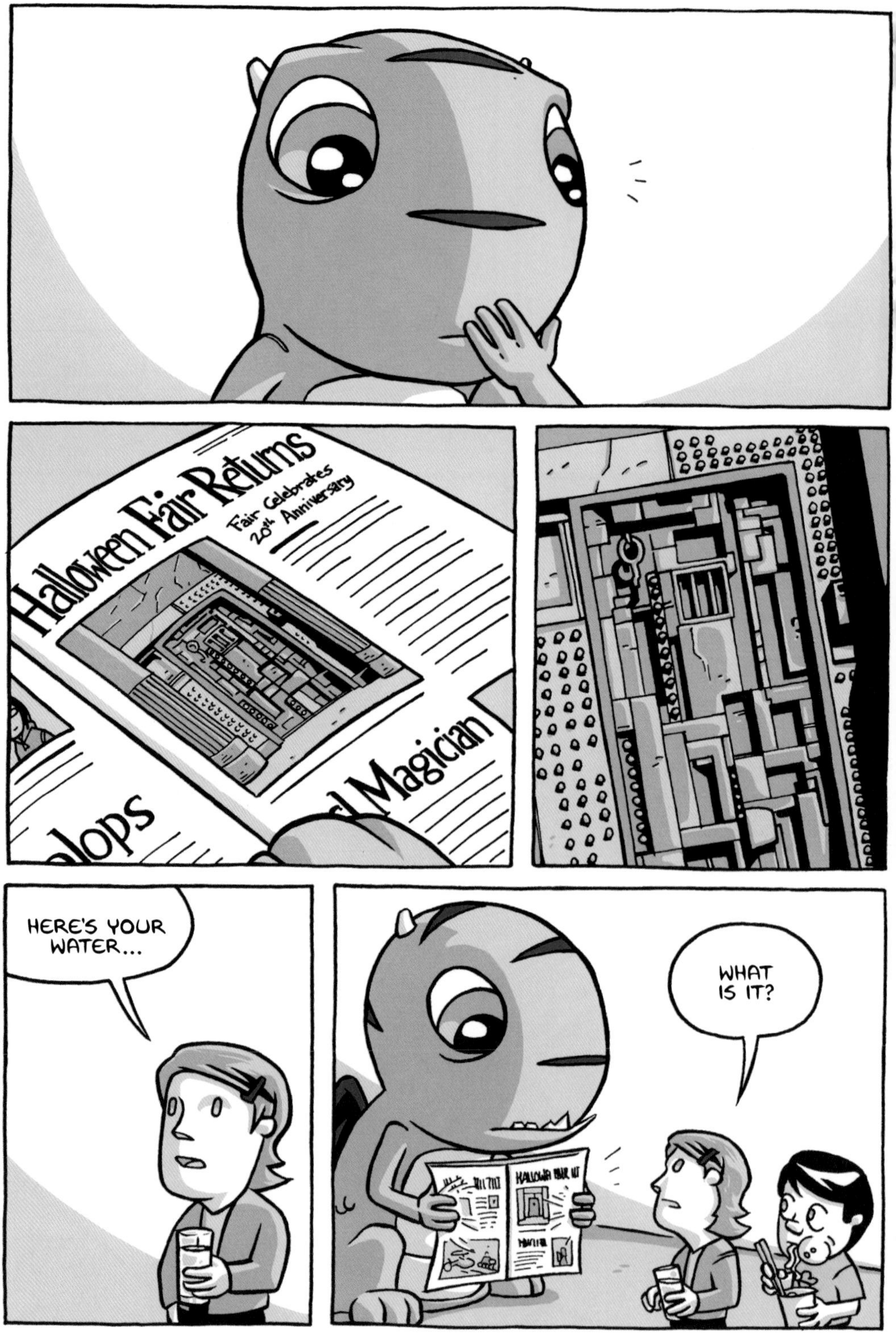
Halloween Fair Returns
Fair Celebrates 20th Anniversary
Magician
lops
HERE'S YOUR WATER...
WHAT IS IT?

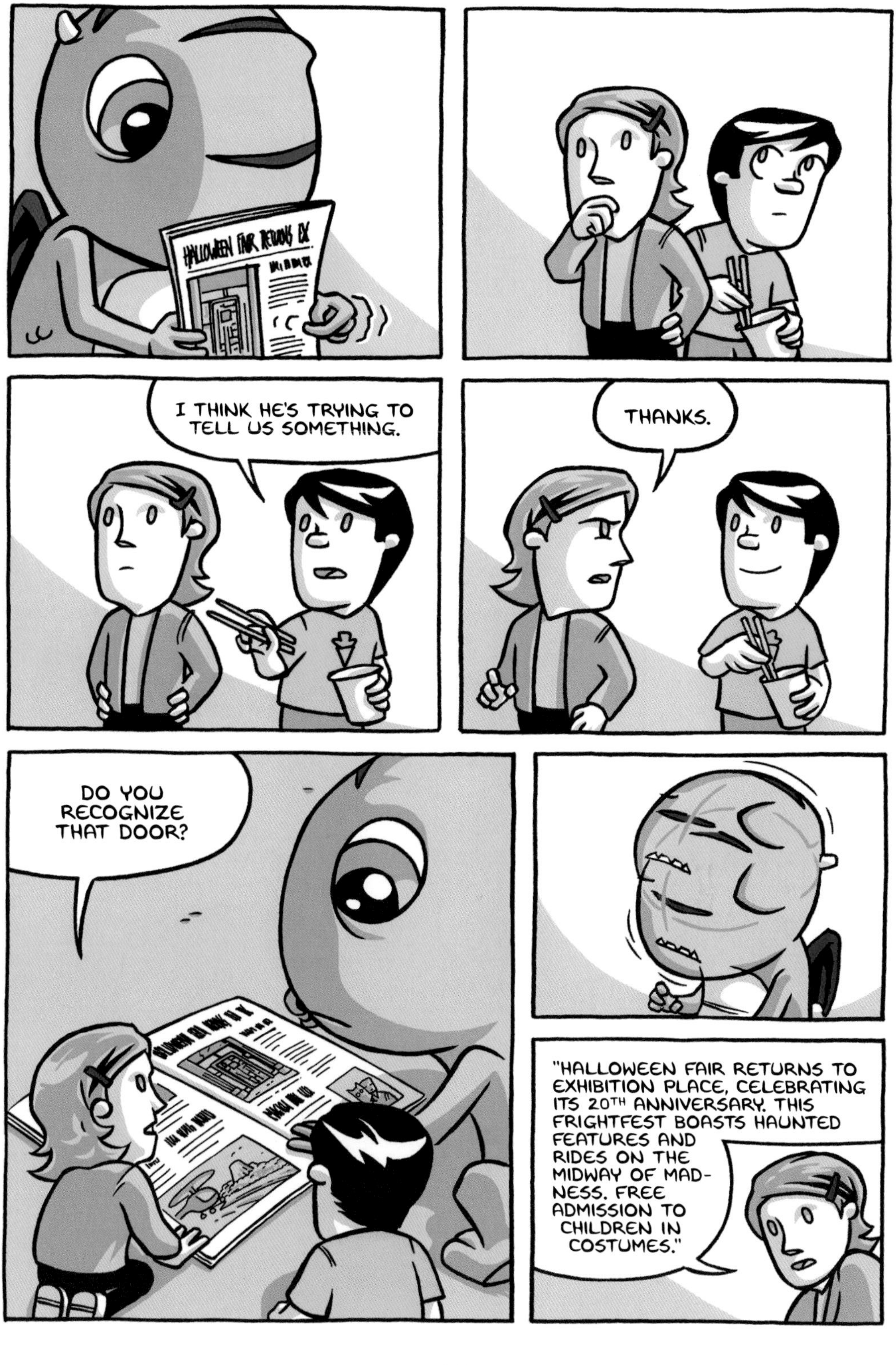
HALLOWEEN FAIR RETURNS EX
I THINK HE'S TRYING TO TELL US SOMETHING.
THANKS.
DO YOU RECOGNIZE THAT DOOR?
"HALLOWEEN FAIR RETURNS TO EXHIBITION PLACE, CELEBRATING ITS 20TH ANNIVERSARY. THIS FRIGHTFEST BOASTS HAUNTED FEATURES AND RIDES ON THE MIDWAY OF MADNESS. FREE ADMISSION TO CHILDREN IN COSTUMES."

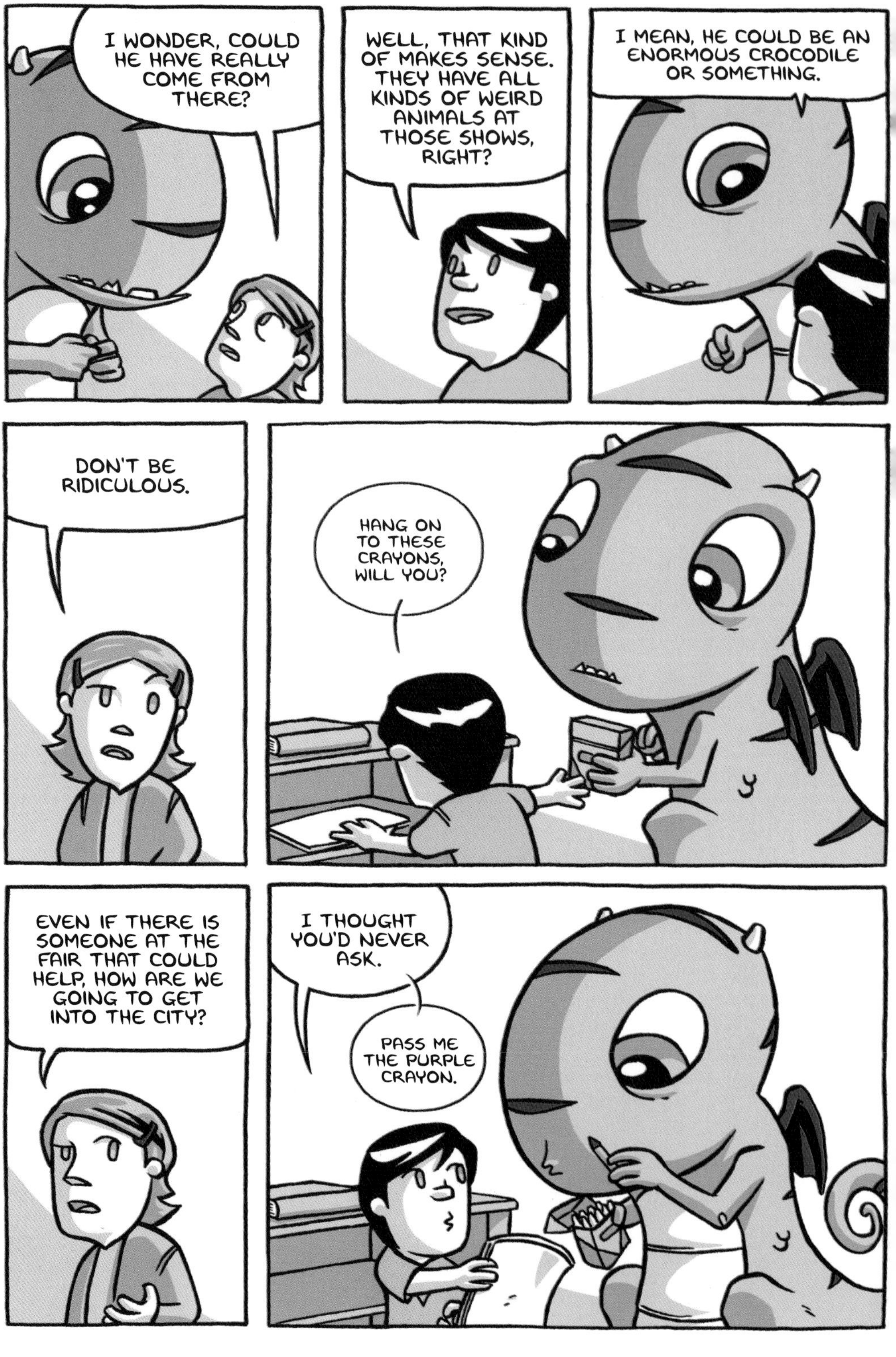
I WONDER, COULD HE HAVE REALLY COME FROM THERE?
WELL, THAT KIND OF MAKES SENSE. THEY HAVE ALL KINDS OF WEIRD ANIMALS AT THOSE SHOWS, RIGHT?
I MEAN, HE COULD BE AN ENORMOUS CROCODILE OR SOMETHING.
DON'T BE RIDICULOUS.
HANG ON TO THESE CRAYONS, WILL YOU?
EVEN IF THERE IS SOMEONE AT THE FAIR THAT COULD HELP, HOW ARE WE GOING TO GET INTO THE CITY?
I THOUGHT YOU'D NEVER ASK.
PASS ME THE PURPLE CRAYON.

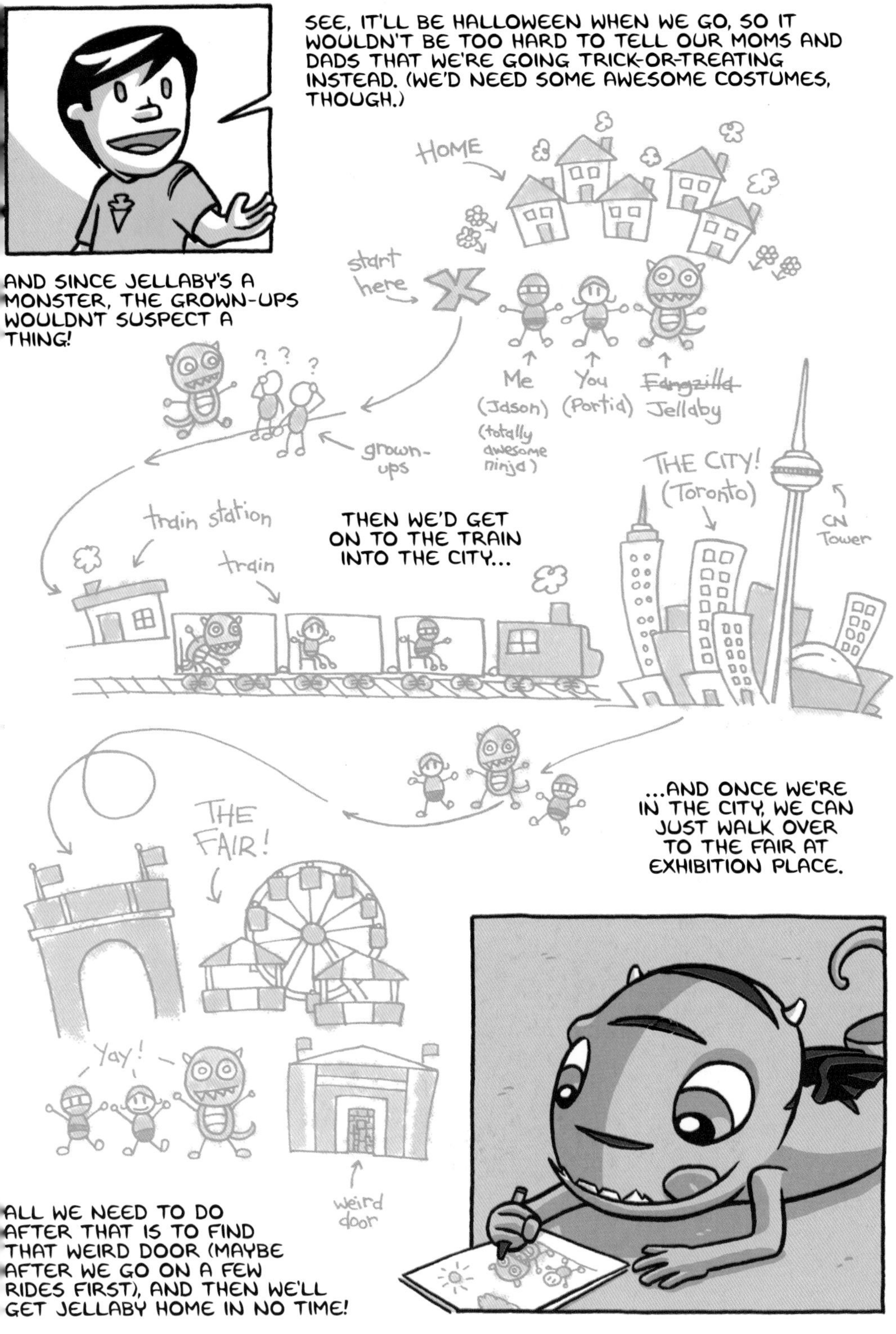
SEE, IT'LL BE HALLOWEEN WHEN WE GO, SO IT WOULDN'T BE TOO HARD TO TELL OUR MOMS AND DADS THAT WE'RE GOING TRICK-OR-TREATING INSTEAD. (WE'D NEED SOME AWESOME COSTUMES, THOUGH.)
HOME
start here
Me (Jason) (totally awesome ninja)
You (Portia)
Fangzilla Jellaby
AND SINCE JELLABY'S A MONSTER, THE GROWN-UPS WOULDN'T SUSPECT A THING!
? ? ?
grown-ups
THE CITY! (Toronto)
CN Tower
train station
train
THEN WE'D GET ON TO THE TRAIN INTO THE CITY...
...AND ONCE WE'RE IN THE CITY, WE CAN JUST WALK OVER TO THE FAIR AT EXHIBITION PLACE.
THE FAIR!
Yay!
weird door
ALL WE NEED TO DO AFTER THAT IS TO FIND THAT WEIRD DOOR (MAYBE AFTER WE GO ON A FEW RIDES FIRST), AND THEN WE'LL GET JELLABY HOME IN NO TIME!

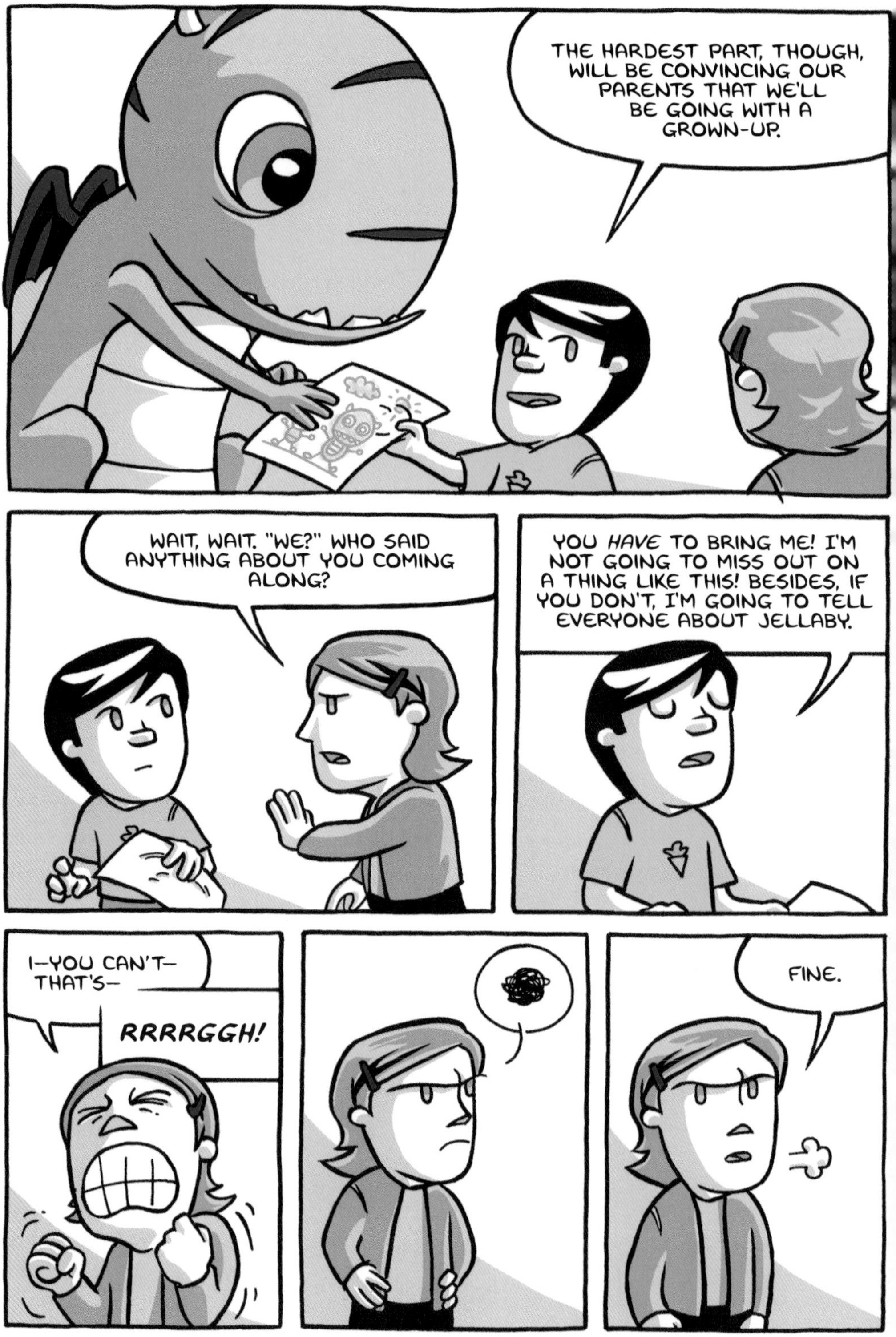
THE HARDEST PART, THOUGH, WILL BE CONVINCING OUR PARENTS THAT WE'LL BE GOING WITH A GROWN-UP.
WAIT, WAIT. "WE?" WHO SAID ANYTHING ABOUT YOU COMING ALONG?
YOU *HAVE* TO BRING ME! I'M NOT GOING TO MISS OUT ON A THING LIKE THIS! BESIDES, IF YOU DON'T, I'M GOING TO TELL EVERYONE ABOUT JELLABY.
I—YOU CAN'T— THAT'S—
RRRRGGH!
FINE.

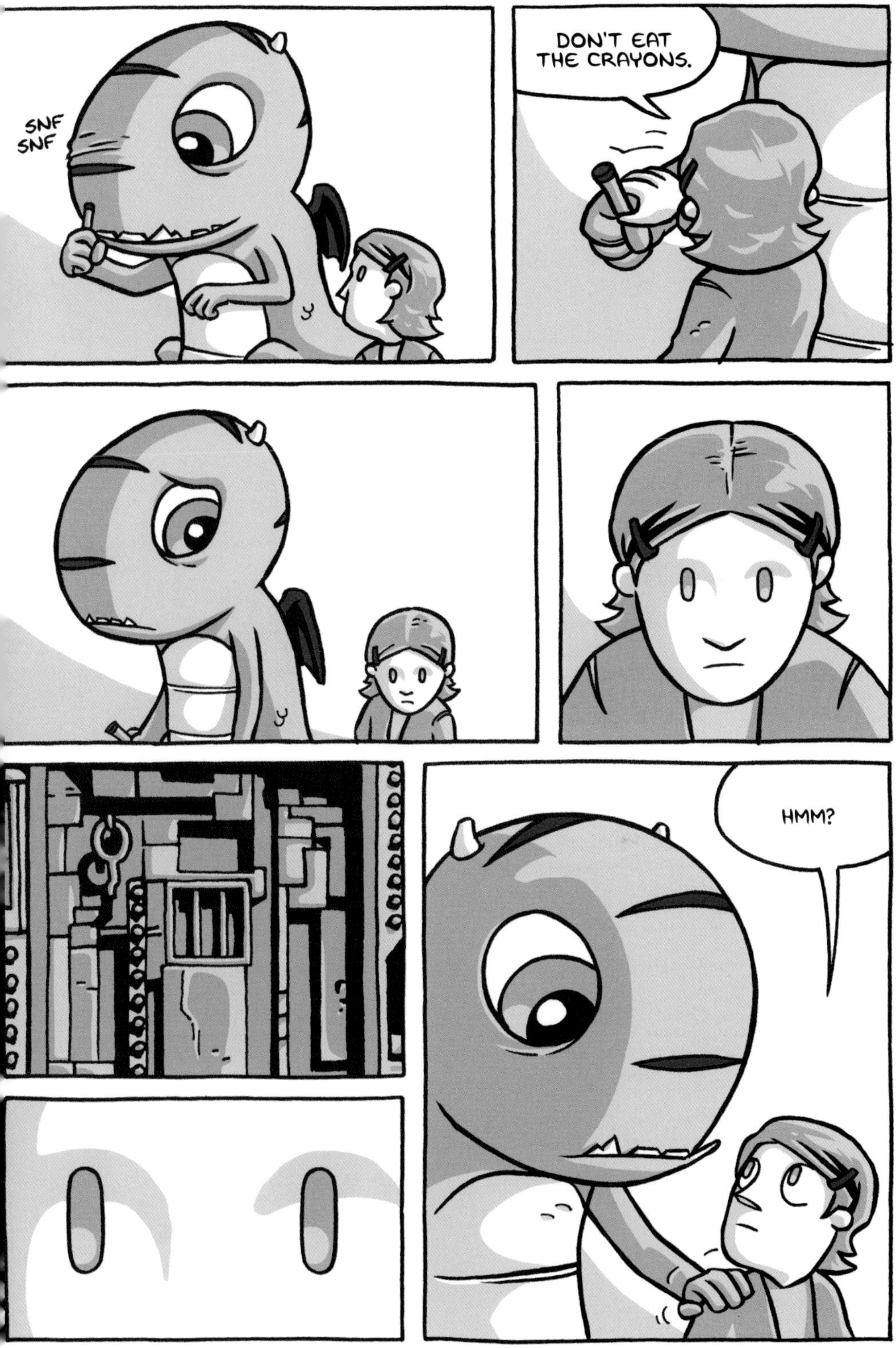
SNF
SNF
DON'T EAT THE CRAYONS.
HMM?

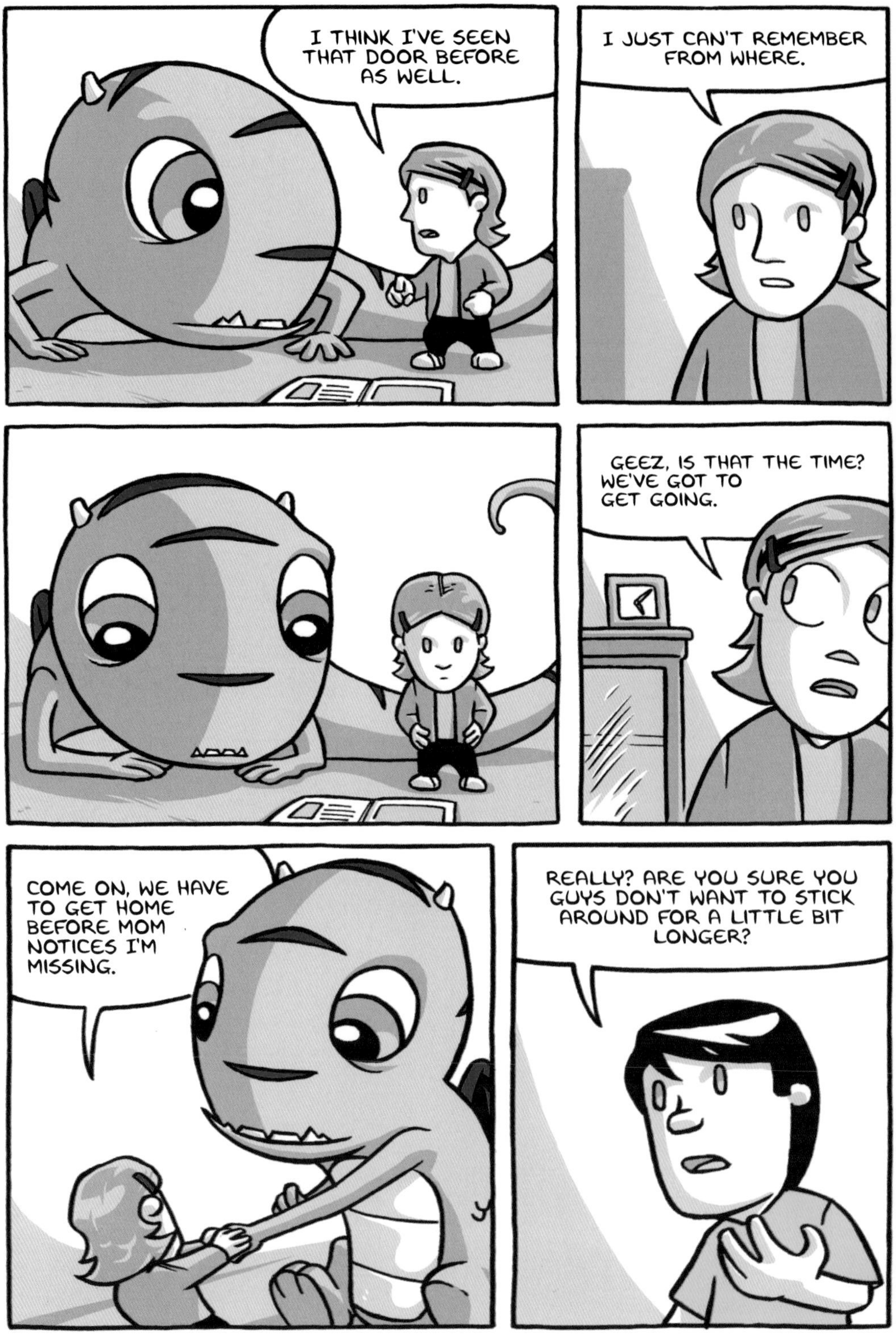
I THINK I'VE SEEN THAT DOOR BEFORE AS WELL.
I JUST CAN'T REMEMBER FROM WHERE.
GEEZ, IS THAT THE TIME? WE'VE GOT TO GET GOING.
COME ON, WE HAVE TO GET HOME BEFORE MOM NOTICES I'M MISSING.
REALLY? ARE YOU SURE YOU GUYS DON'T WANT TO STICK AROUND FOR A LITTLE BIT LONGER?

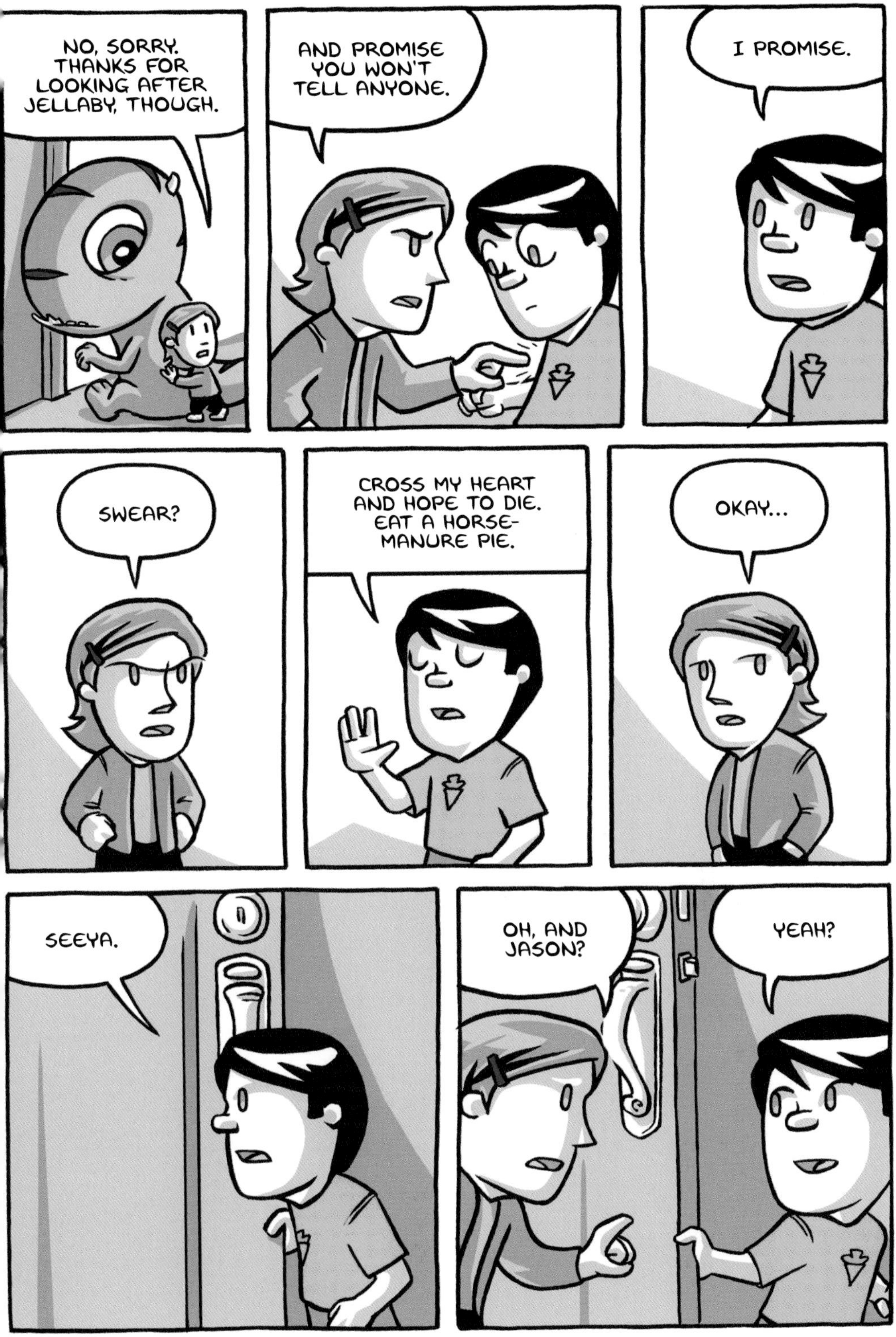
NO, SORRY. THANKS FOR LOOKING AFTER JELLABY, THOUGH.
AND PROMISE YOU WON'T TELL ANYONE.
I PROMISE.
SWEAR?
CROSS MY HEART AND HOPE TO DIE. EAT A HORSE-MANURE PIE.
OKAY...
SEEYA.
OH, AND JASON?
YEAH?

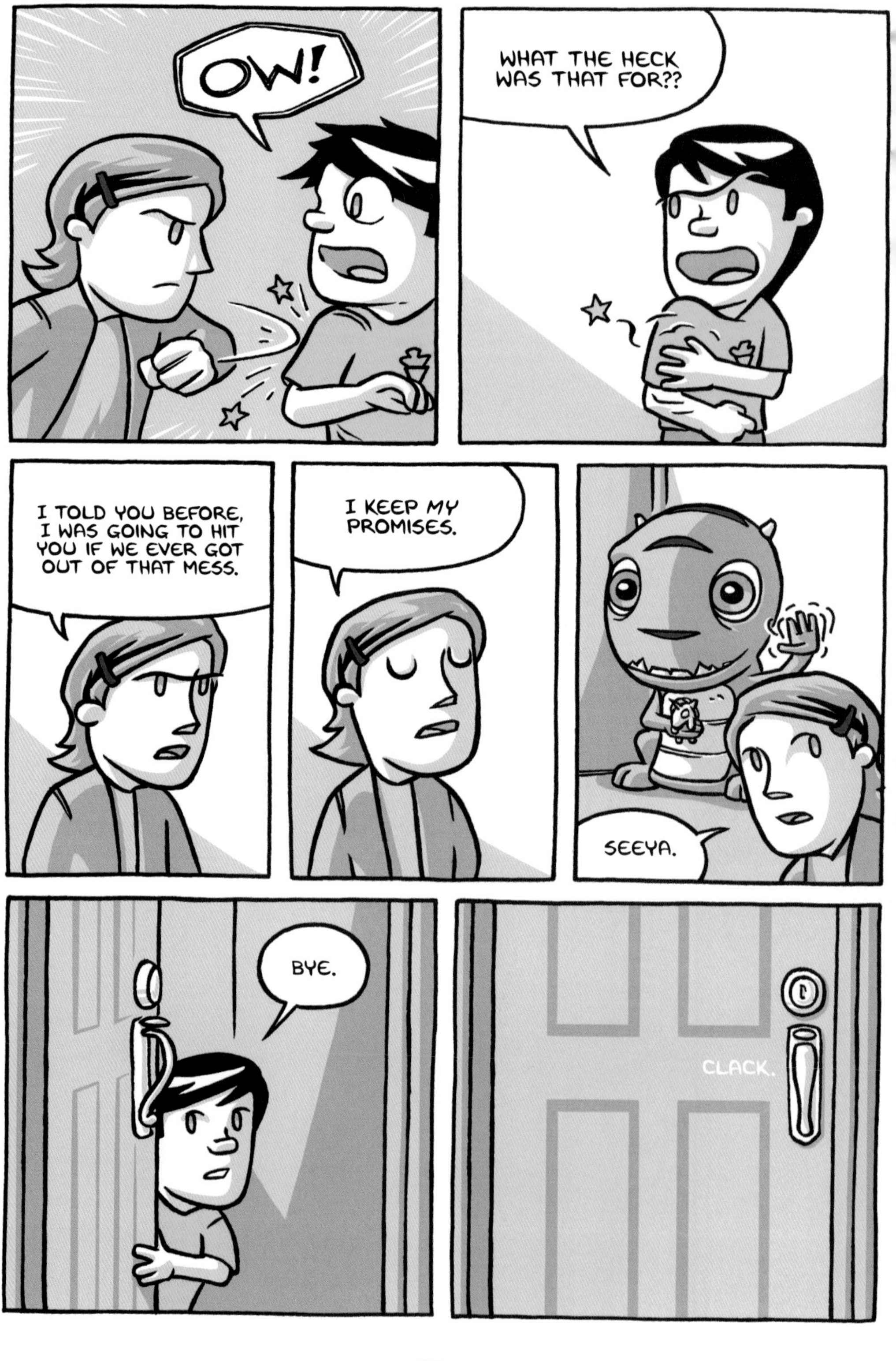
OW!
WHAT THE HECK WAS THAT FOR??
I TOLD YOU BEFORE, I WAS GOING TO HIT YOU IF WE EVER GOT OUT OF THAT MESS.
I KEEP MY PROMISES.
SEEYA.
BYE.
CLACK.

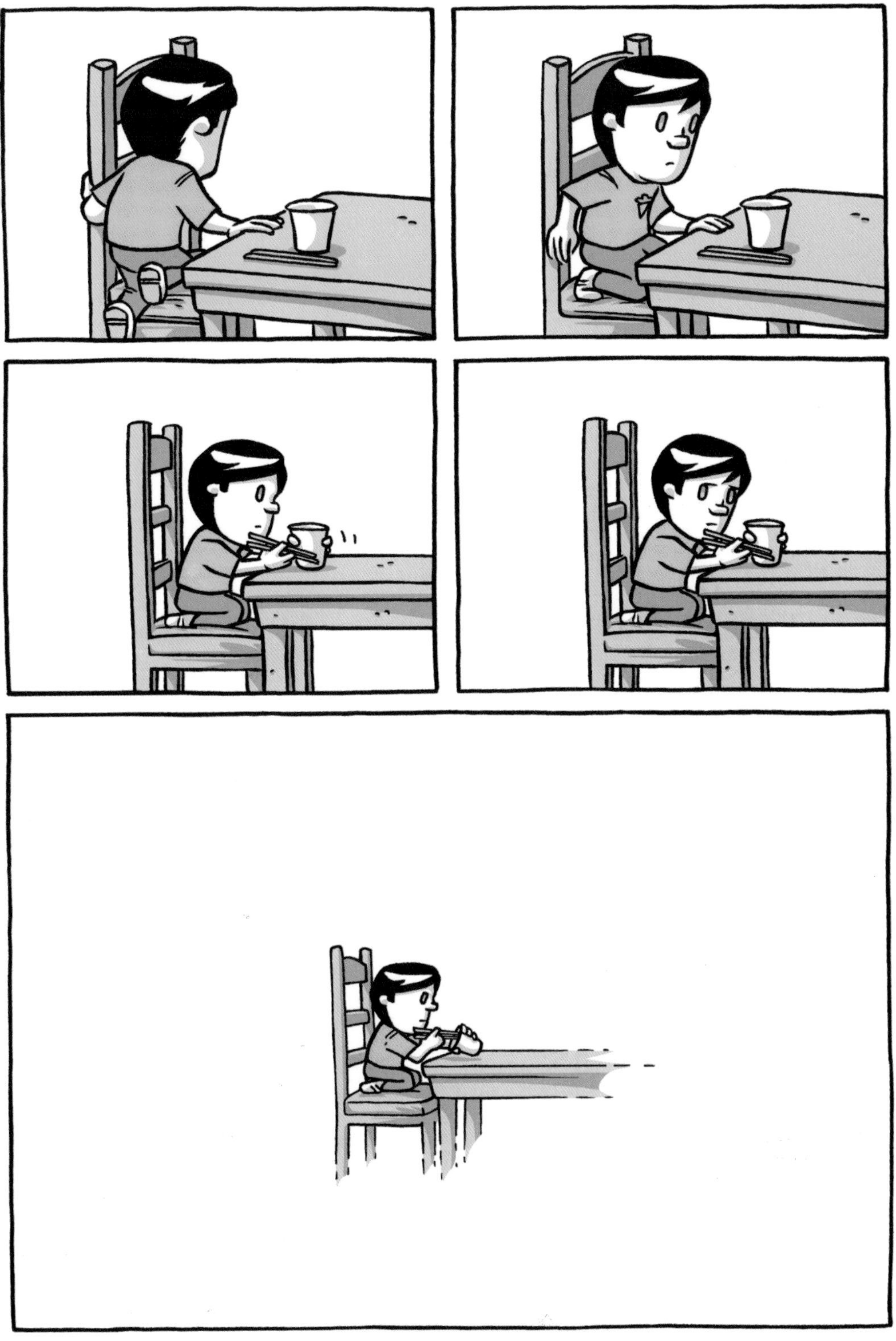

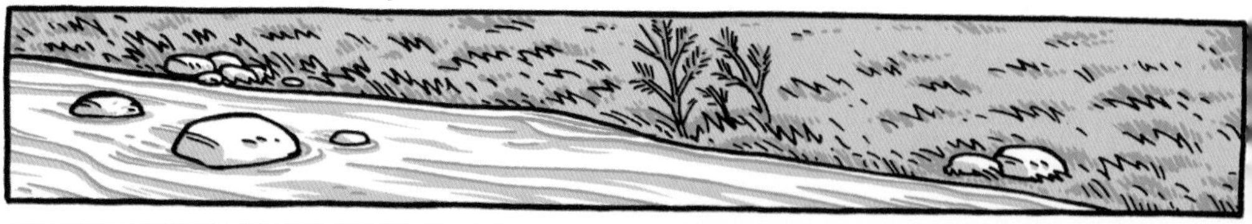

CHAPTER FOUR

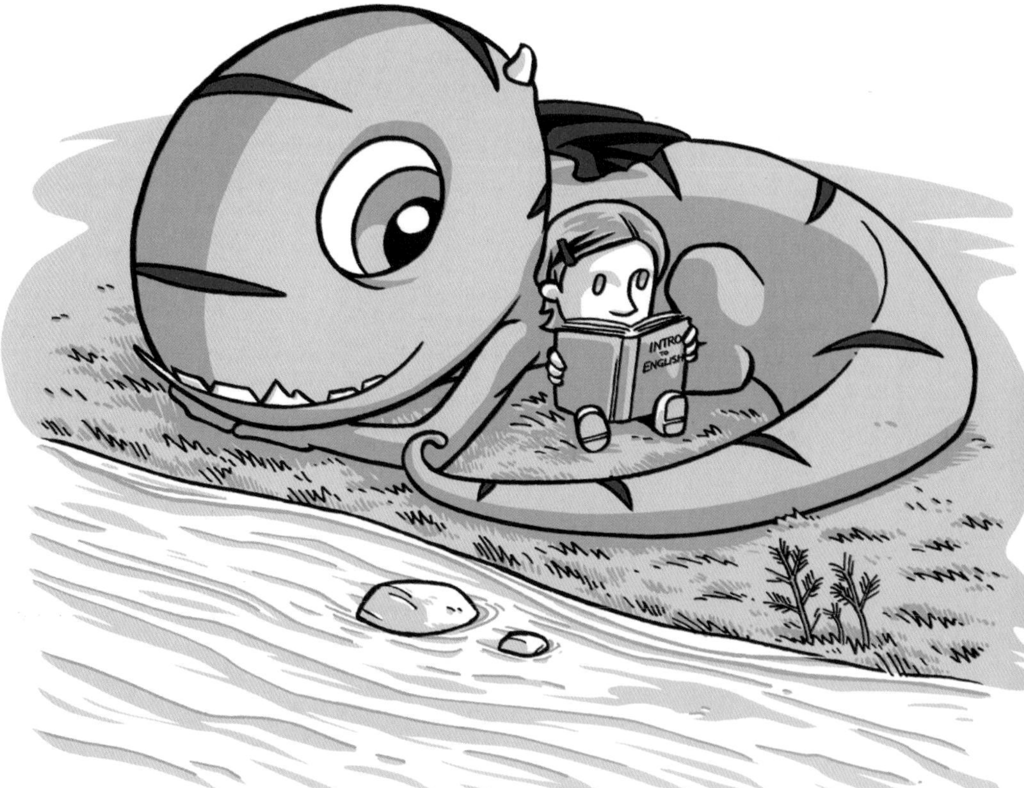
INTRO TO ENGLISH

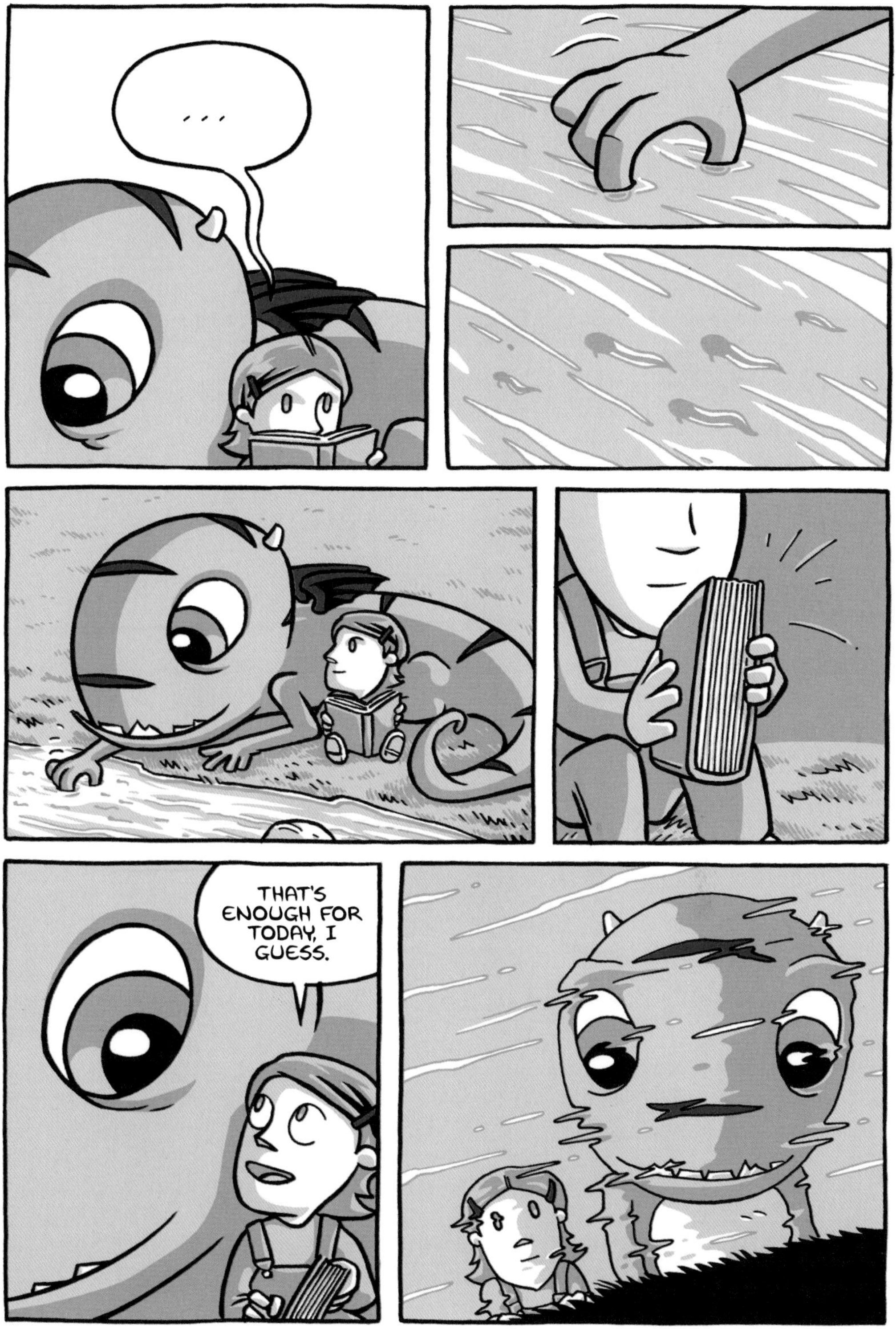
...
THAT'S ENOUGH FOR TODAY, I GUESS.

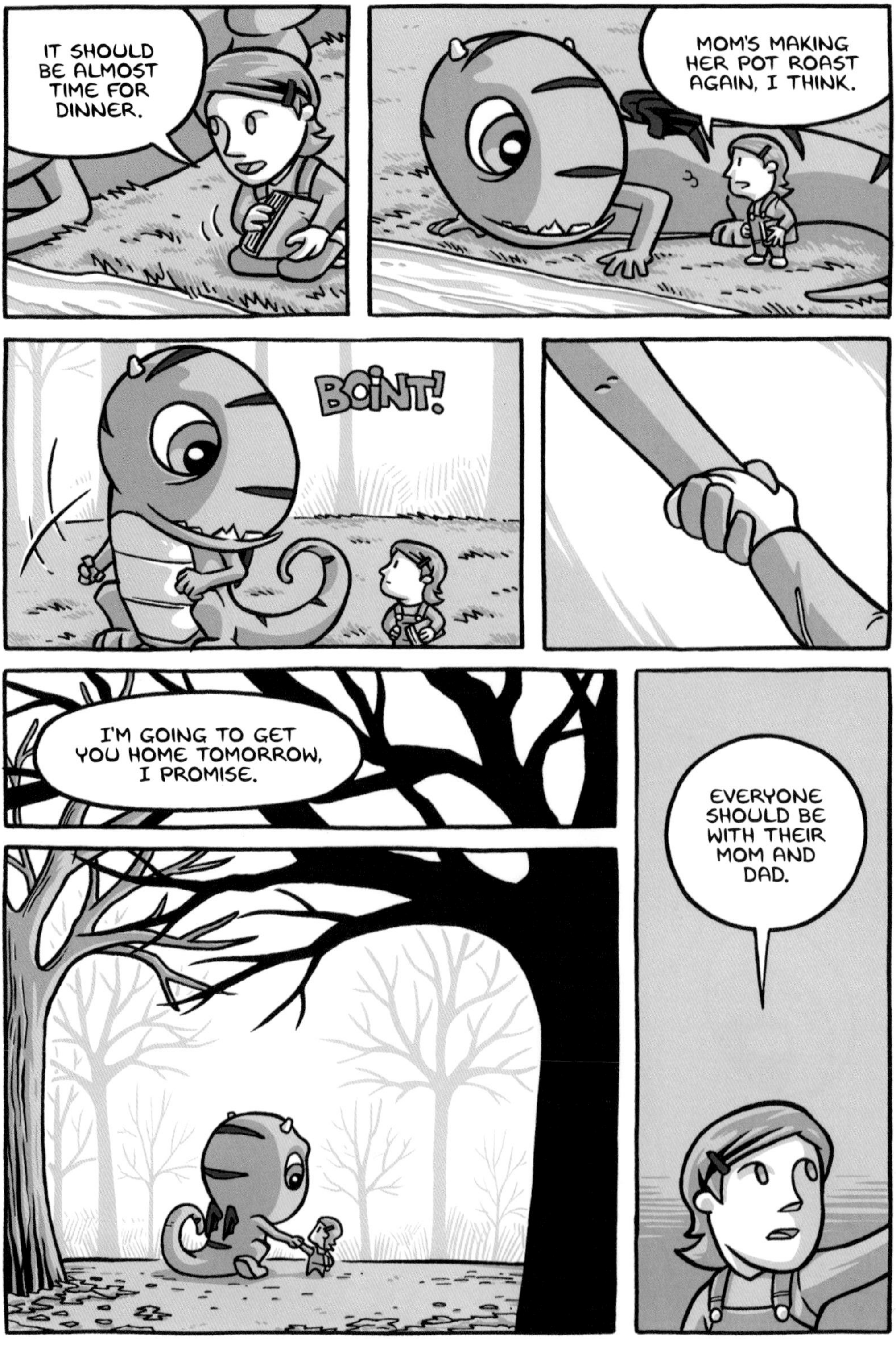
IT SHOULD BE ALMOST TIME FOR DINNER.
MOM'S MAKING HER POT ROAST AGAIN, I THINK.
BOINT!
I'M GOING TO GET YOU HOME TOMORROW, I PROMISE.
EVERYONE SHOULD BE WITH THEIR MOM AND DAD.

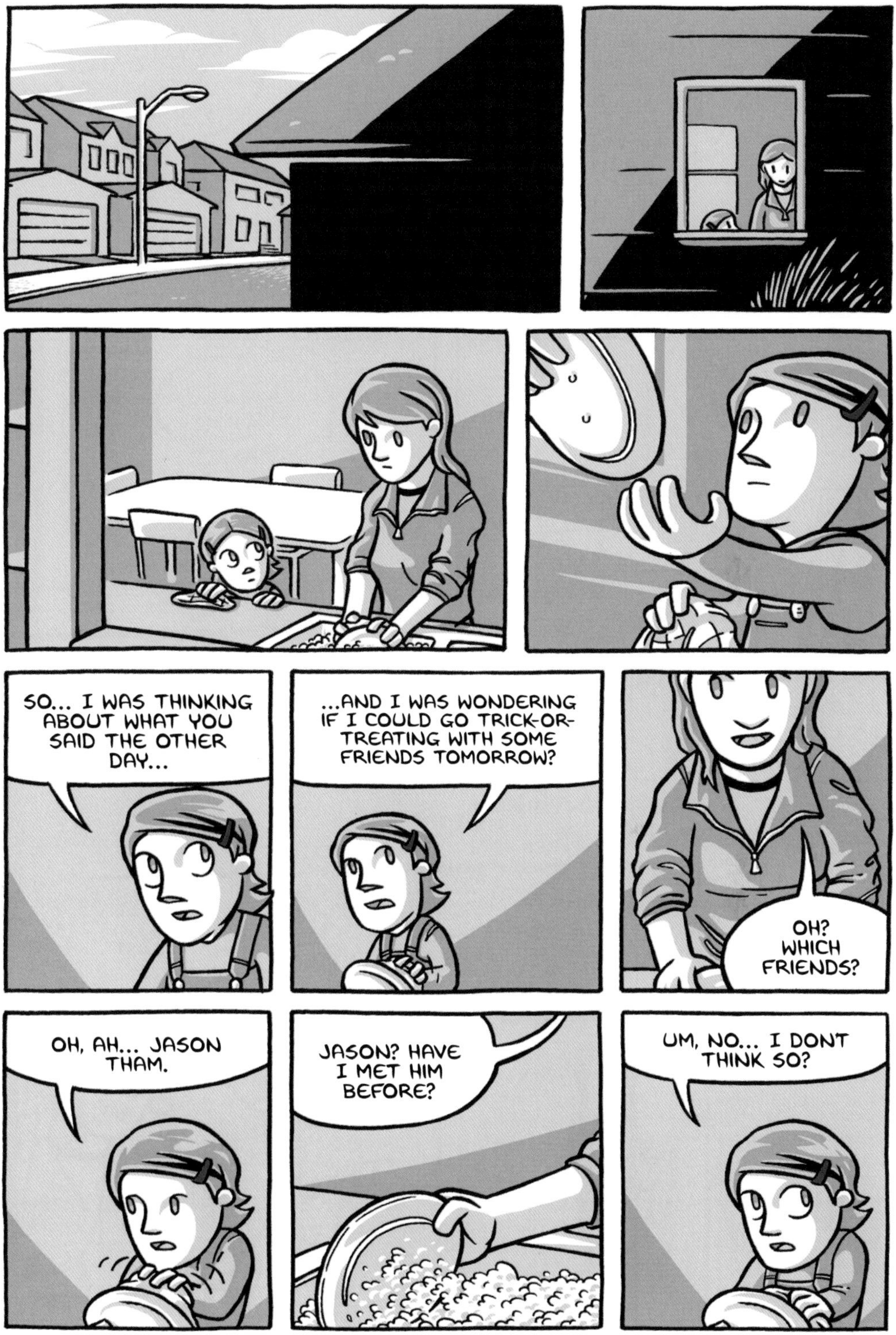
SO... I WAS THINKING ABOUT WHAT YOU SAID THE OTHER DAY...
...AND I WAS WONDERING IF I COULD GO TRICK-OR-TREATING WITH SOME FRIENDS TOMORROW?
OH? WHICH FRIENDS?
OH, AH... JASON THAM.
JASON? HAVE I MET HIM BEFORE?
UM, NO... I DON'T THINK SO?

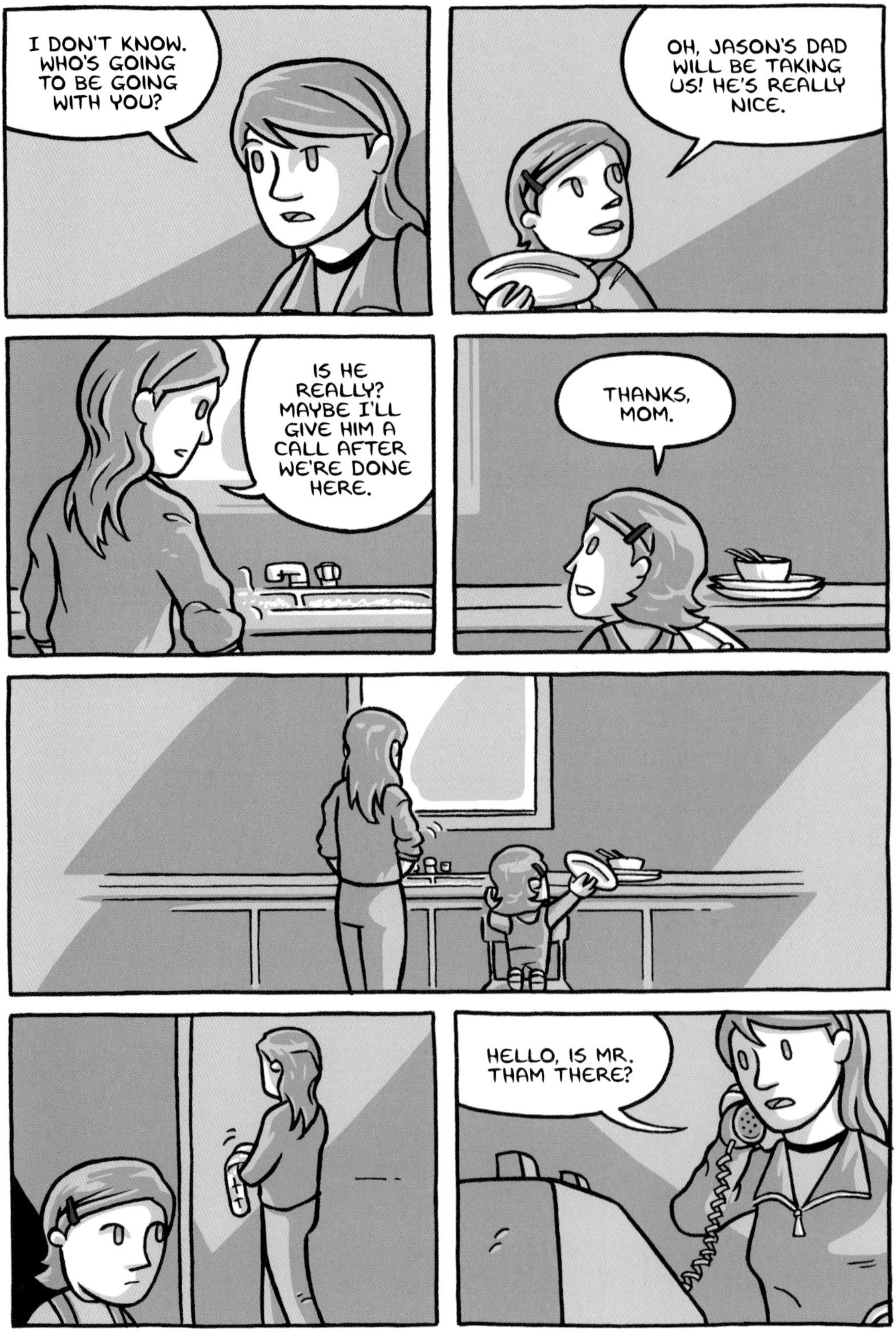
I DON'T KNOW. WHO'S GOING TO BE GOING WITH YOU?
OH, JASON'S DAD WILL BE TAKING US! HE'S REALLY NICE.
IS HE REALLY? MAYBE I'LL GIVE HIM A CALL AFTER WE'RE DONE HERE.
THANKS, MOM.
HELLO, IS MR. THAM THERE?

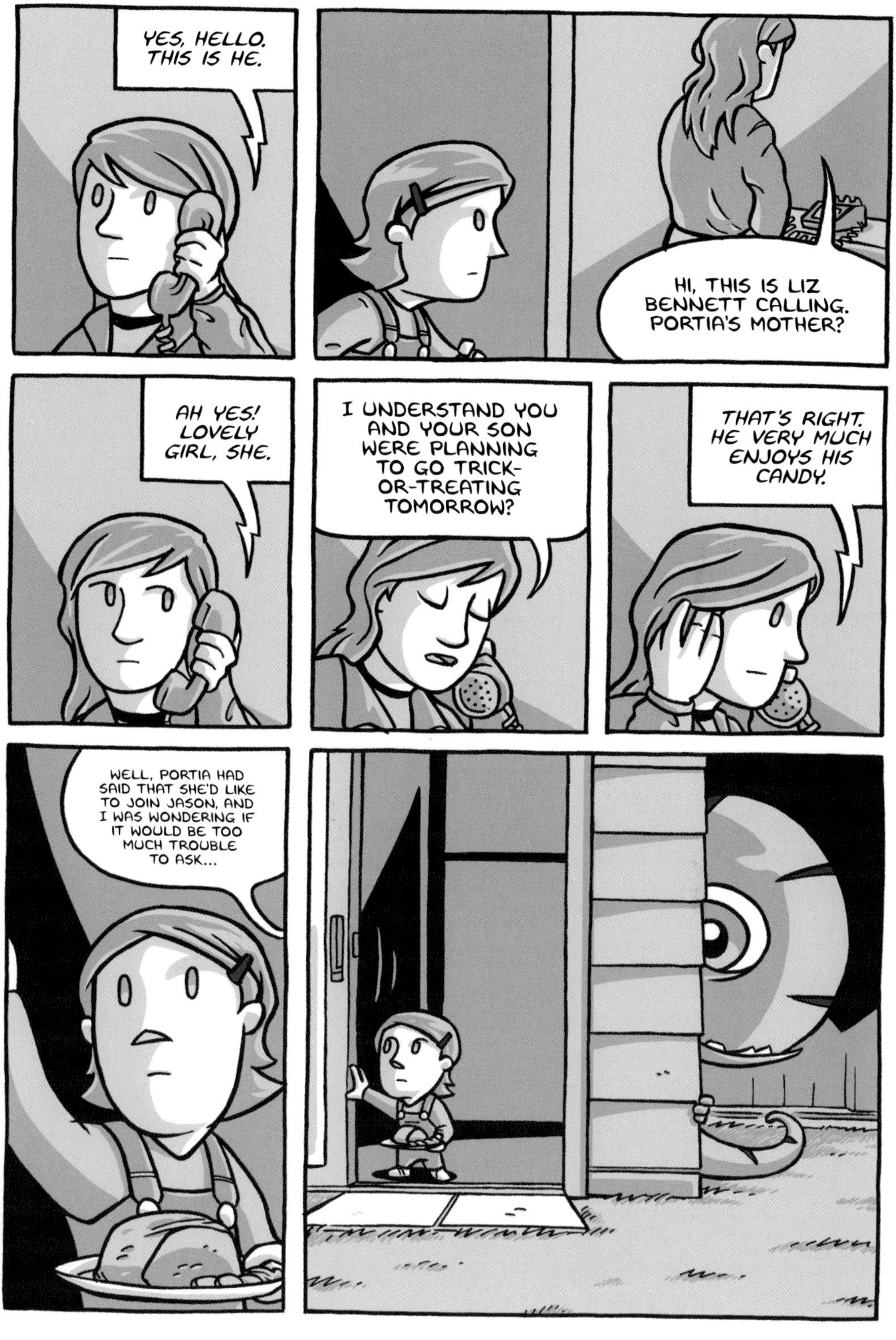
YES, HELLO. THIS IS HE.
HI, THIS IS LIZ BENNETT CALLING. PORTIA'S MOTHER?
AH YES! LOVELY GIRL, SHE.
I UNDERSTAND YOU AND YOUR SON WERE PLANNING TO GO TRICK-OR-TREATING TOMORROW?
THAT'S RIGHT. HE VERY MUCH ENJOYS HIS CANDY.
WELL, PORTIA HAD SAID THAT SHE'D LIKE TO JOIN JASON, AND I WAS WONDERING IF IT WOULD BE TOO MUCH TROUBLE TO ASK...

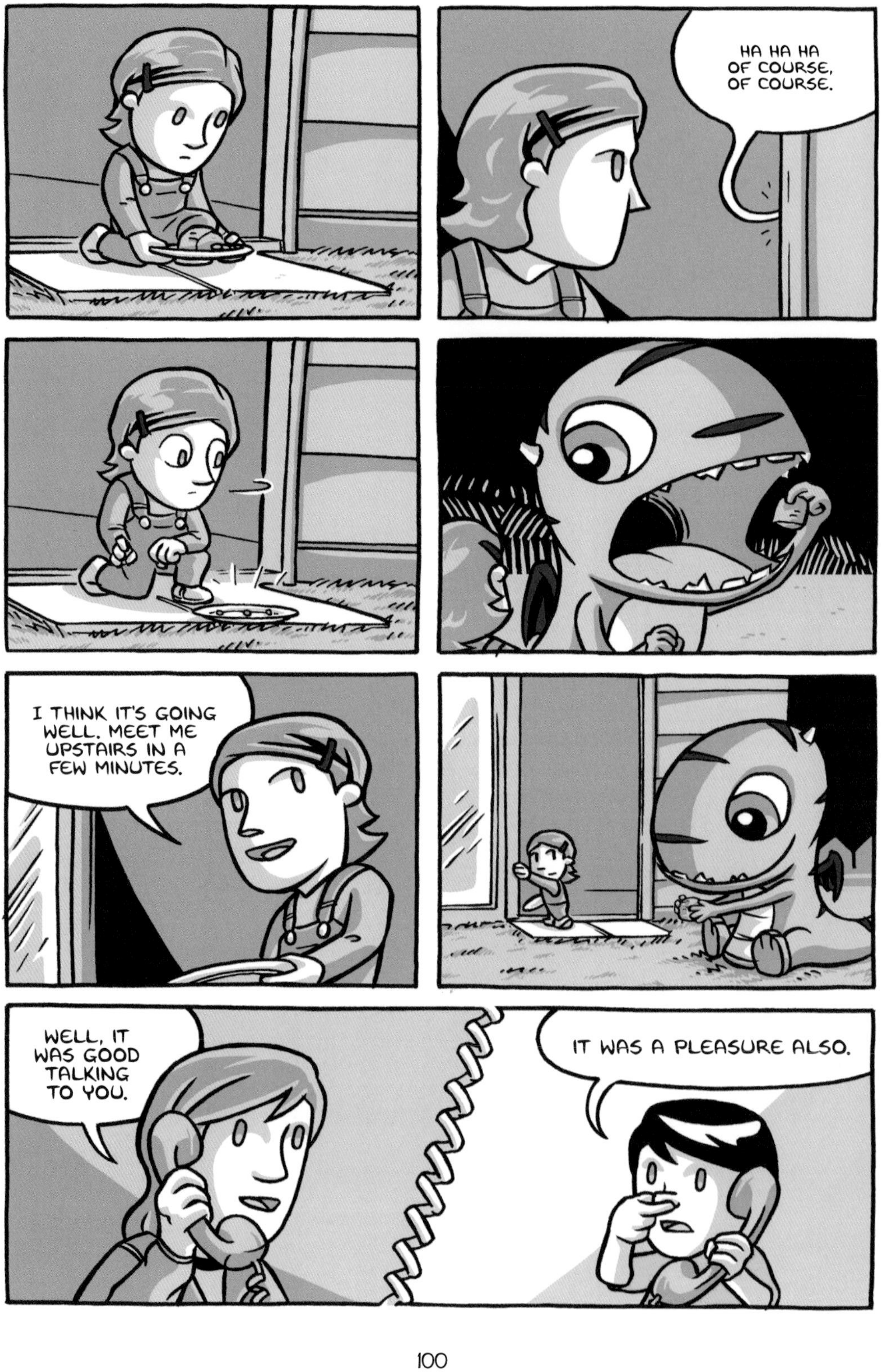
HA HA HA
OF COURSE,
OF COURSE.
I THINK IT'S GOING WELL. MEET ME UPSTAIRS IN A FEW MINUTES.
WELL, IT WAS GOOD TALKING TO YOU.
IT WAS A PLEASURE ALSO.

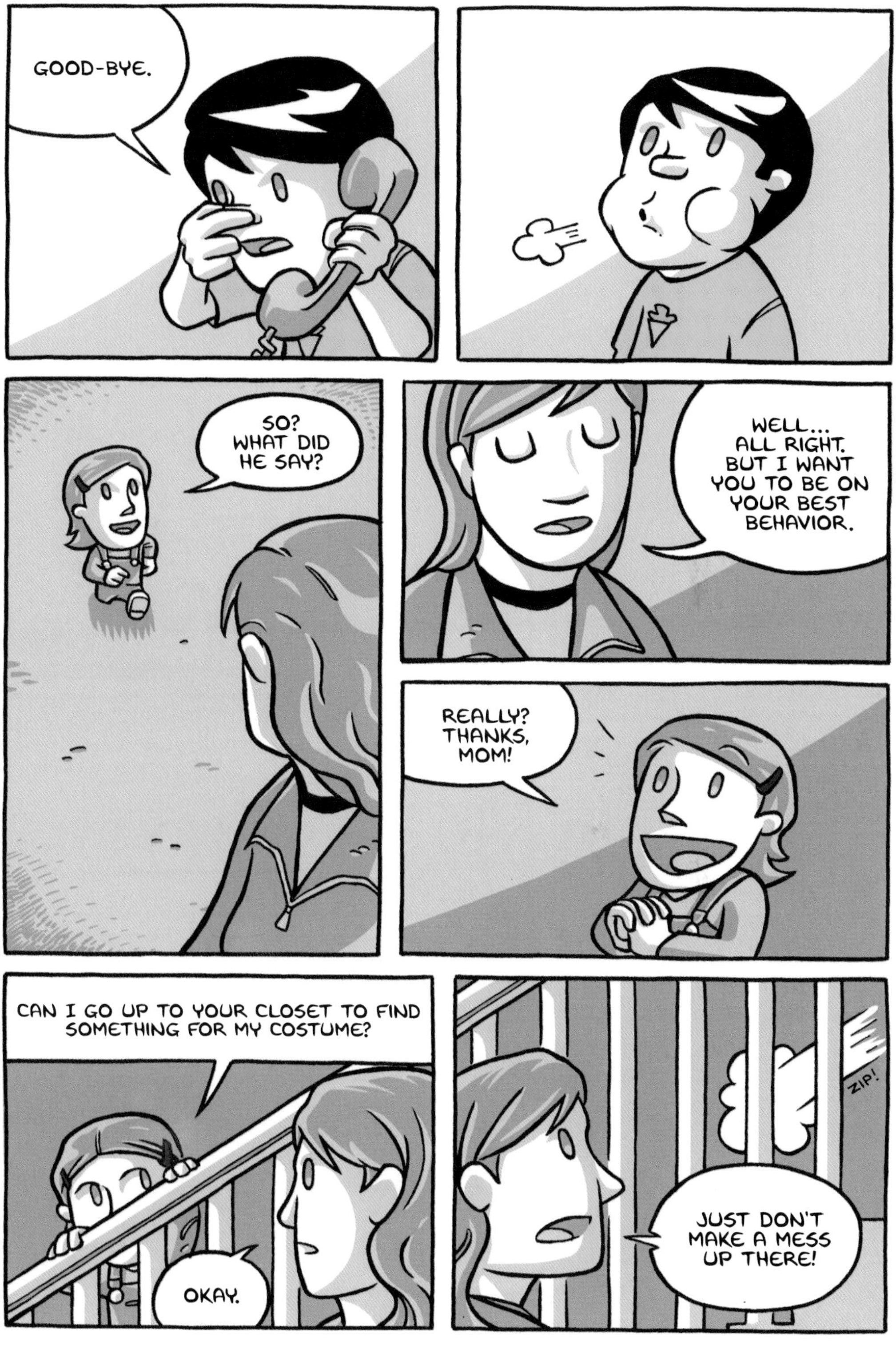
GOOD-BYE.
SO? WHAT DID HE SAY?
WELL... ALL RIGHT. BUT I WANT YOU TO BE ON YOUR BEST BEHAVIOR.
REALLY? THANKS, MOM!
CAN I GO UP TO YOUR CLOSET TO FIND SOMETHING FOR MY COSTUME?
OKAY.
ZIP!
JUST DON'T MAKE A MESS UP THERE!

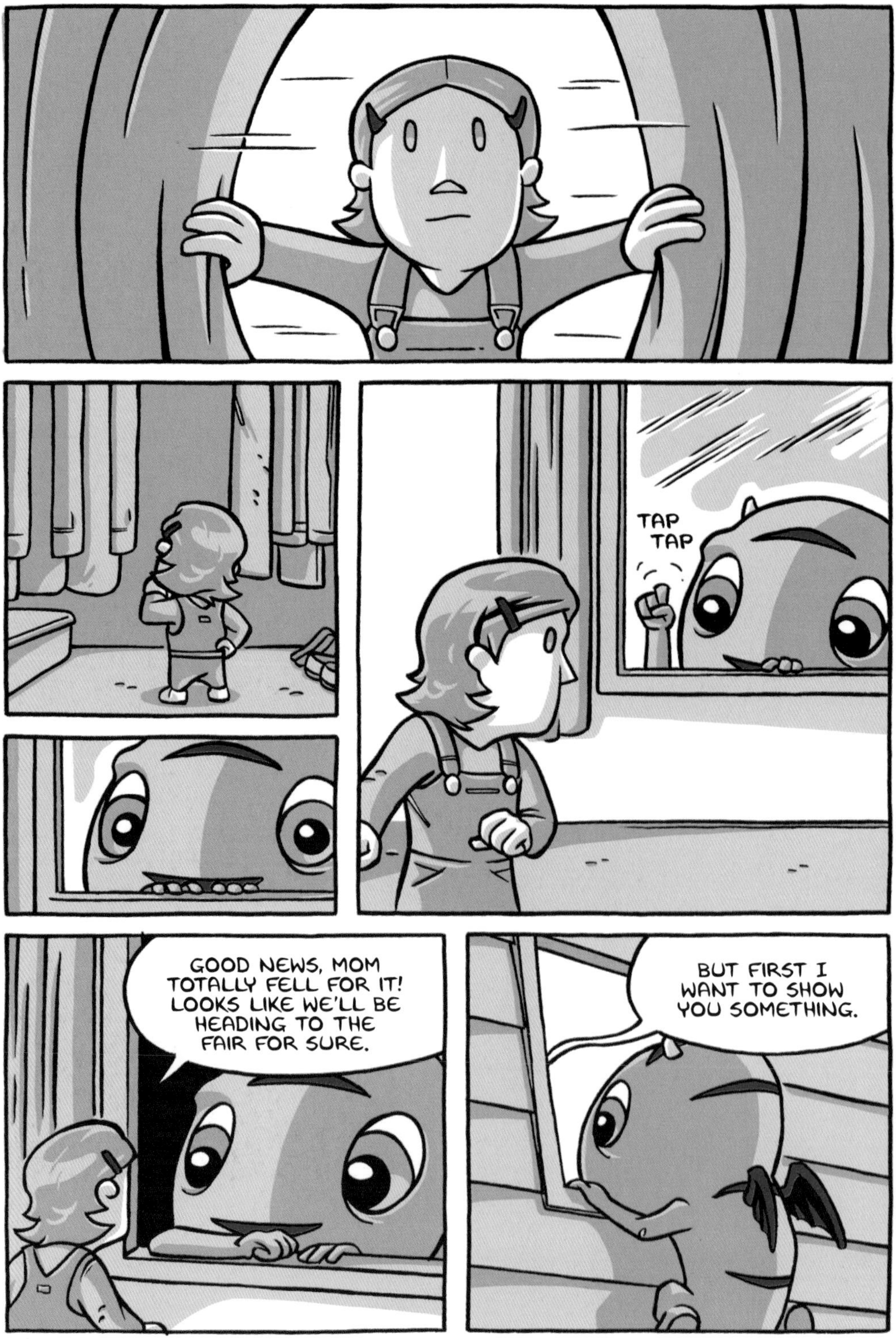
TAP TAP
GOOD NEWS, MOM TOTALLY FELL FOR IT! LOOKS LIKE WE'LL BE HEADING TO THE FAIR FOR SURE.
BUT FIRST I WANT TO SHOW YOU SOMETHING.

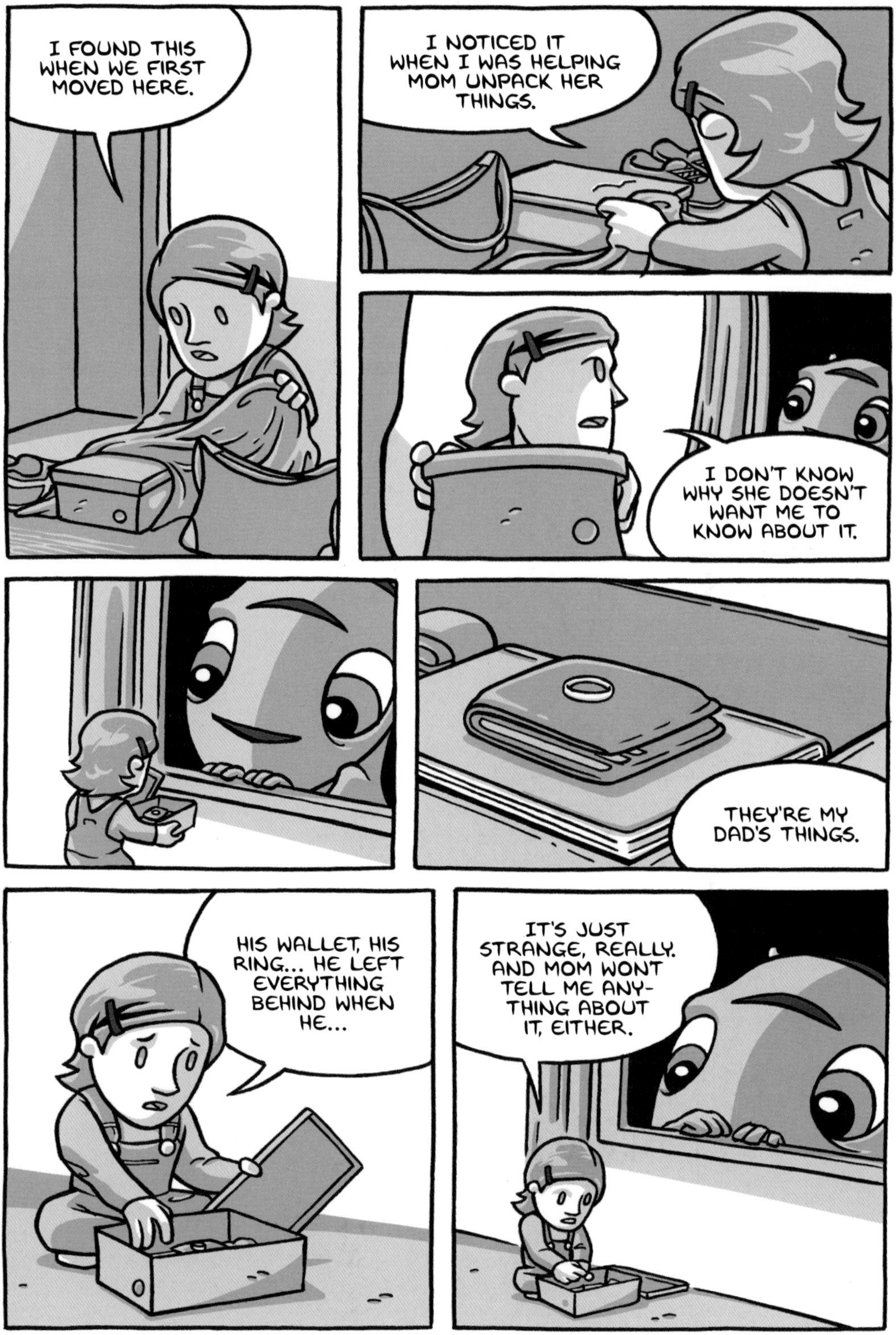
I FOUND THIS WHEN WE FIRST MOVED HERE.
I NOTICED IT WHEN I WAS HELPING MOM UNPACK HER THINGS.
I DON'T KNOW WHY SHE DOESN'T WANT ME TO KNOW ABOUT IT.
THEY'RE MY DAD'S THINGS.
HIS WALLET, HIS RING... HE LEFT EVERYTHING BEHIND WHEN HE...
IT'S JUST STRANGE, REALLY. AND MOM WON'T TELL ME ANY-THING ABOUT IT, EITHER.

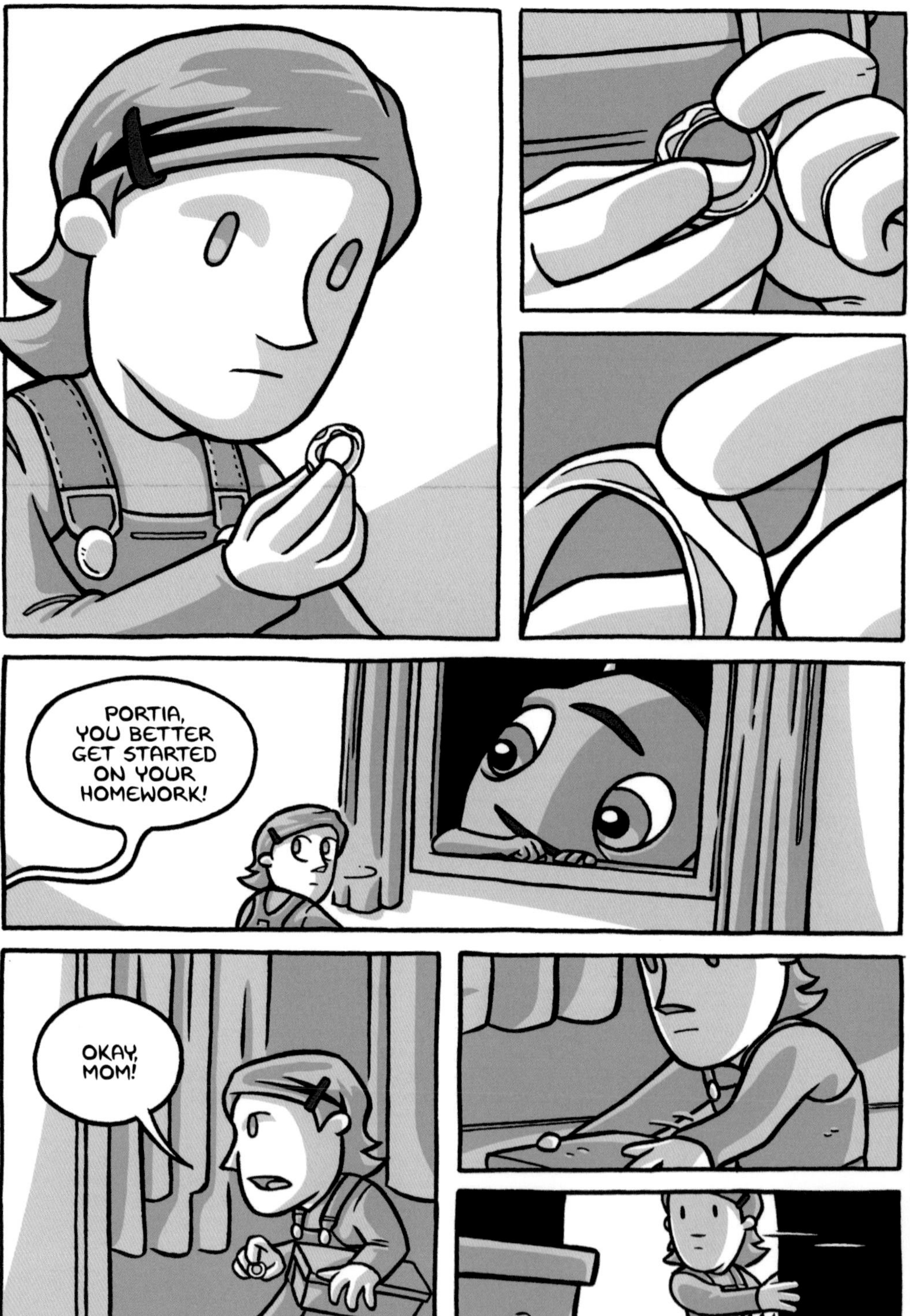
PORTIA, YOU BETTER GET STARTED ON YOUR HOMEWORK!
OKAY, MOM!

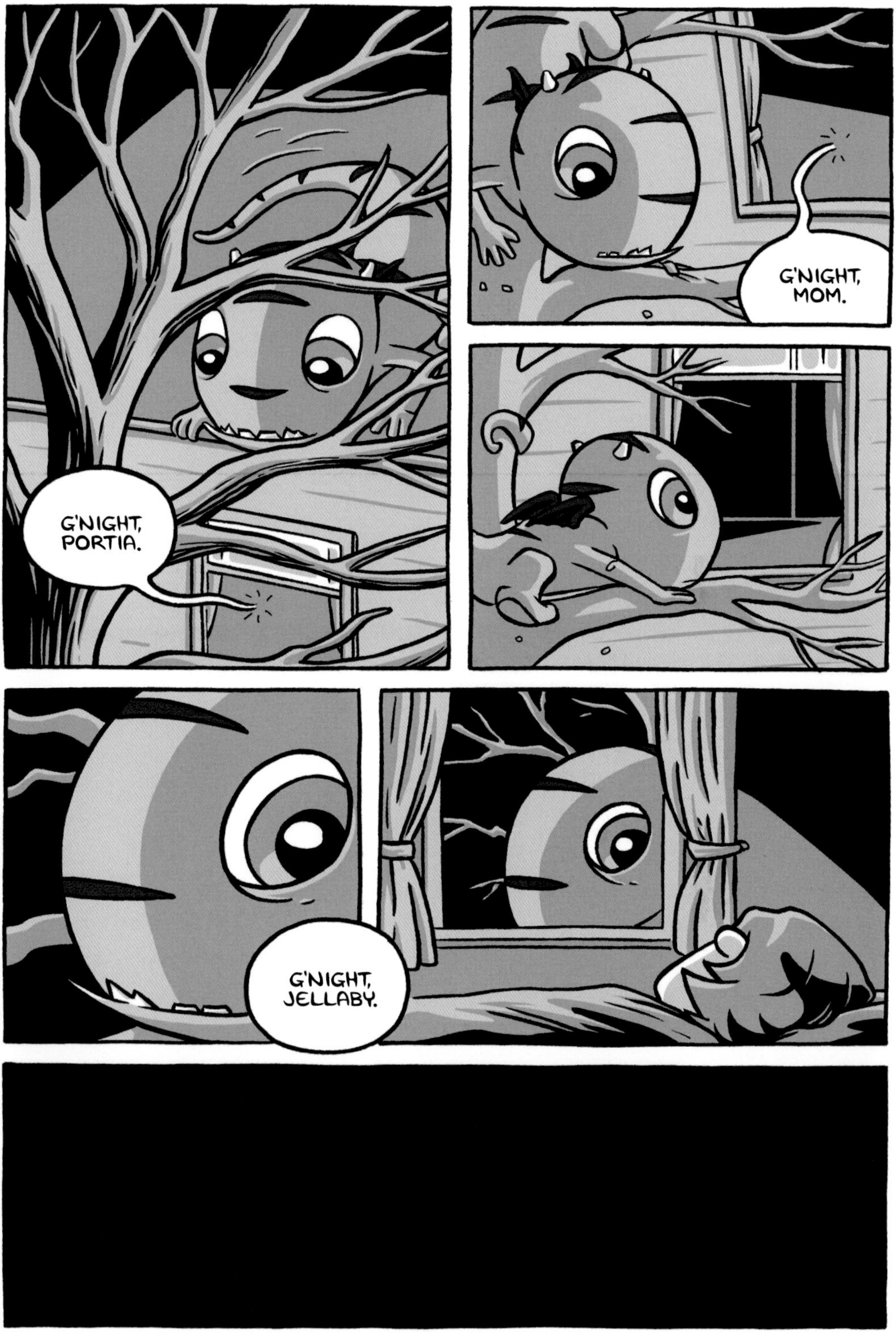
G'NIGHT, PORTIA.
G'NIGHT, MOM.
G'NIGHT, JELLABY.

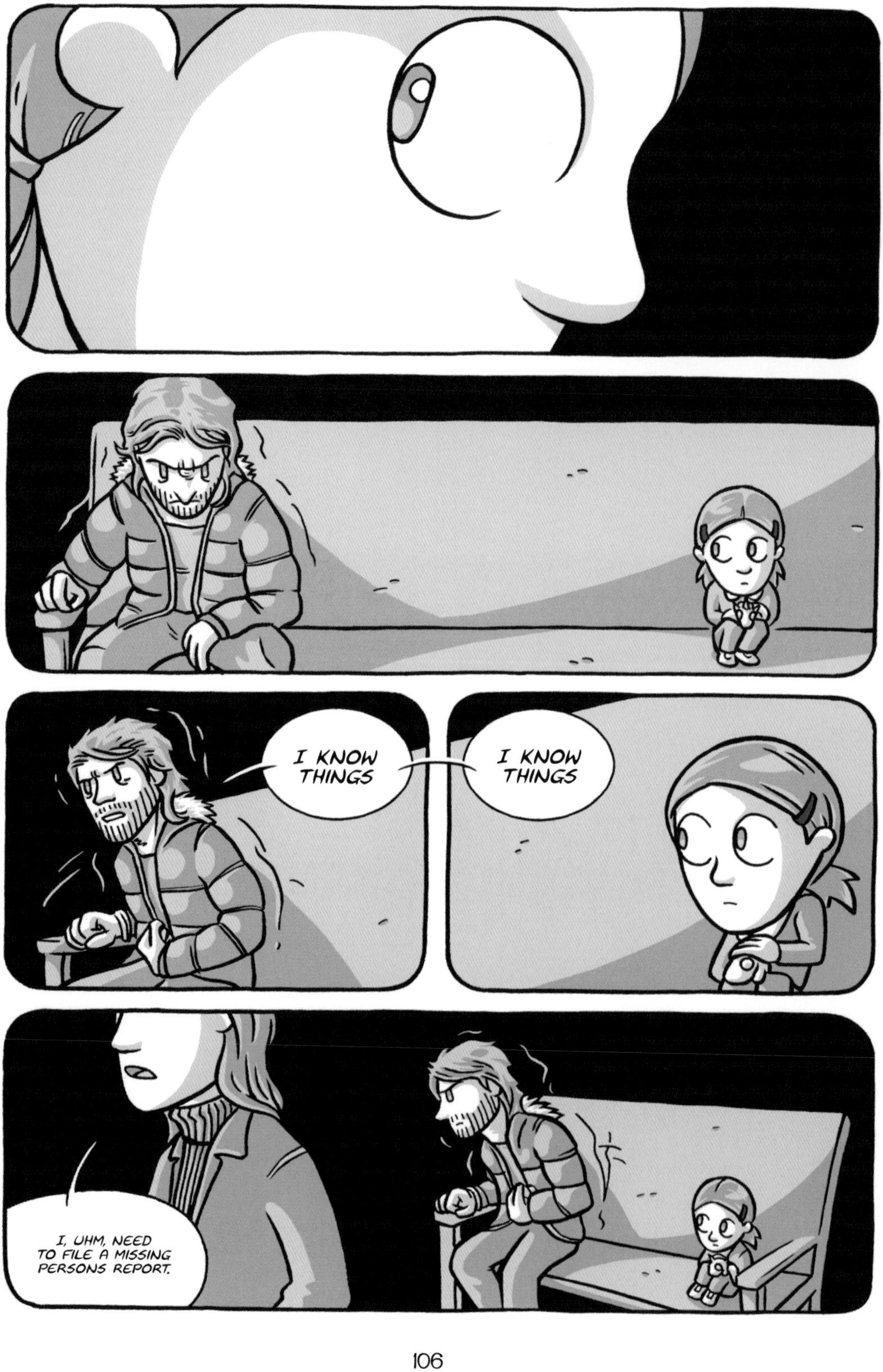
I KNOW THINGS
I KNOW THINGS
I, UHM, NEED TO FILE A MISSING PERSONS REPORT.

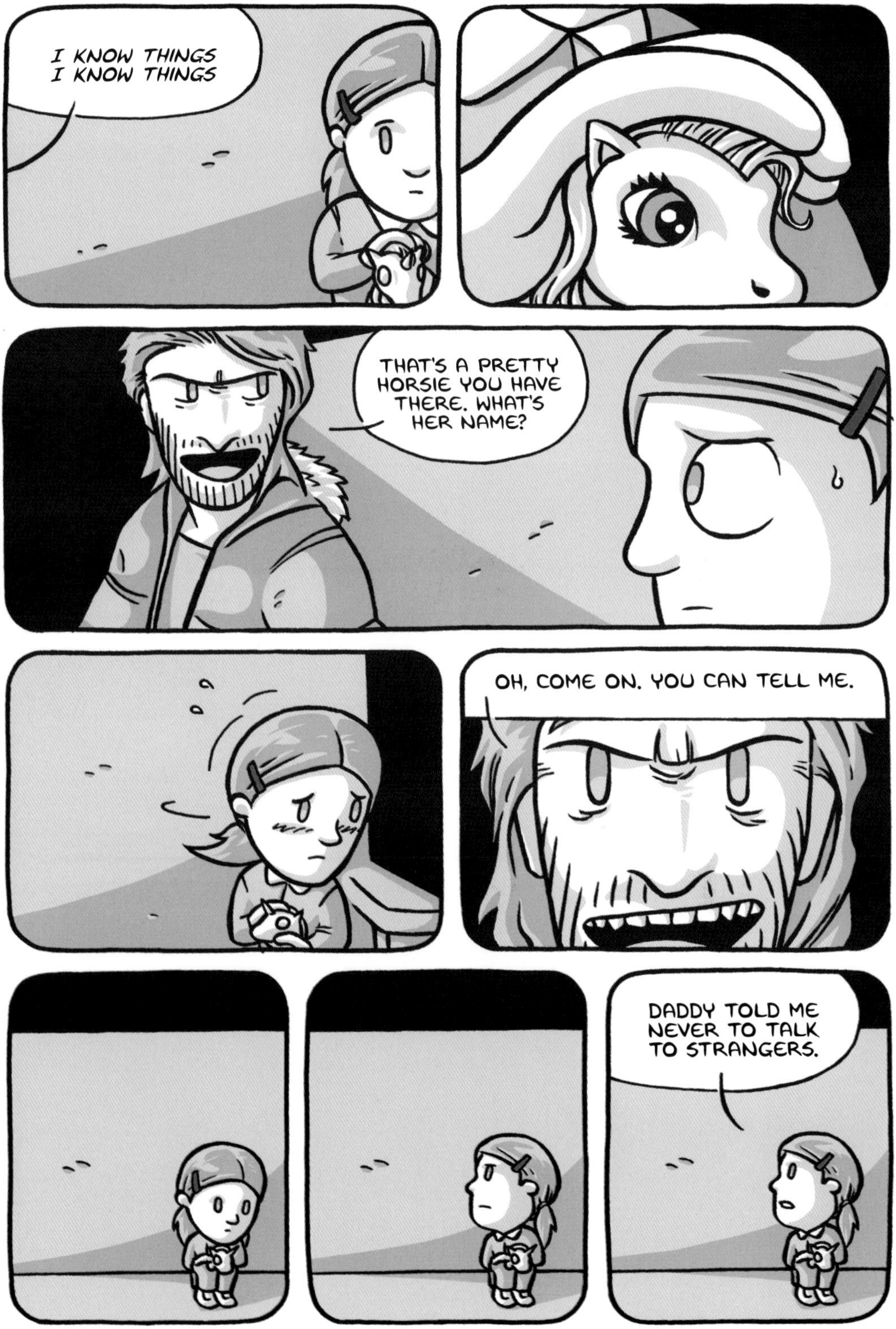
I KNOW THINGS I KNOW THINGS
THAT'S A PRETTY HORSIE YOU HAVE THERE. WHAT'S HER NAME?
OH, COME ON. YOU CAN TELL ME.
DADDY TOLD ME NEVER TO TALK TO STRANGERS.

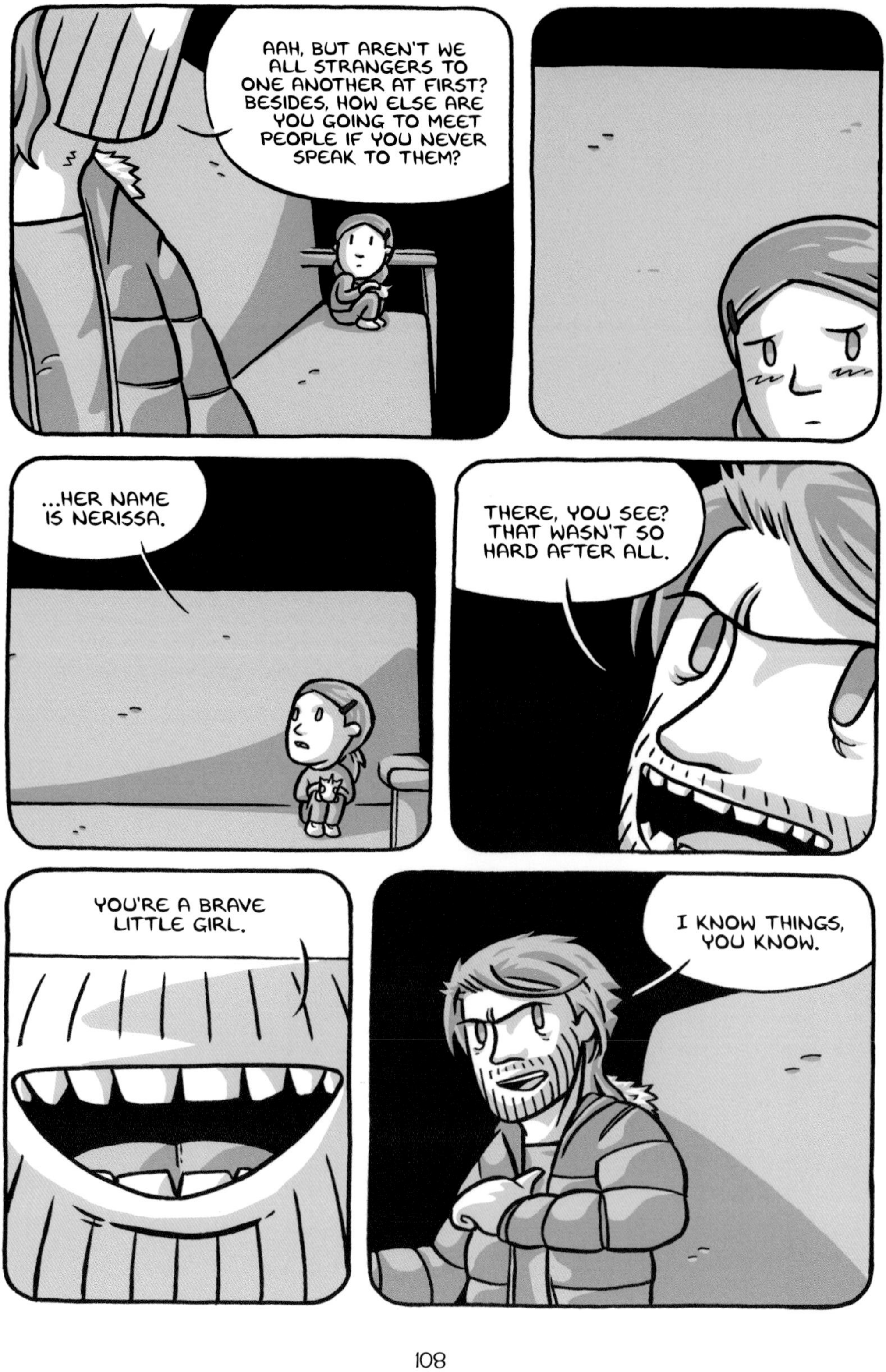
AAH, BUT AREN'T WE ALL STRANGERS TO ONE ANOTHER AT FIRST? BESIDES, HOW ELSE ARE YOU GOING TO MEET PEOPLE IF YOU NEVER SPEAK TO THEM?
...HER NAME IS NERISSA.
THERE, YOU SEE? THAT WASN'T SO HARD AFTER ALL.
YOU'RE A BRAVE LITTLE GIRL.
I KNOW THINGS, YOU KNOW.

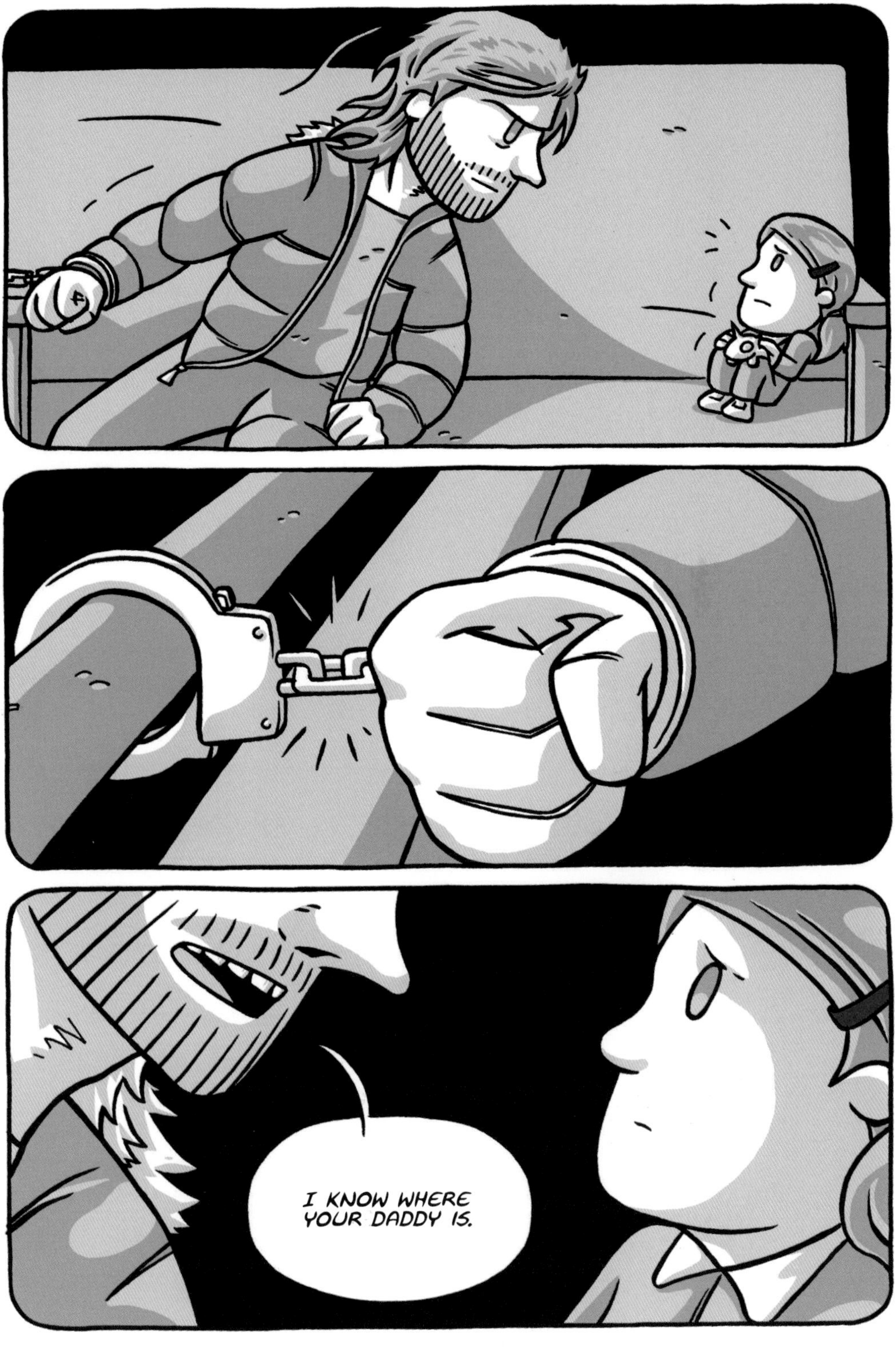
I KNOW WHERE YOUR DADDY IS.

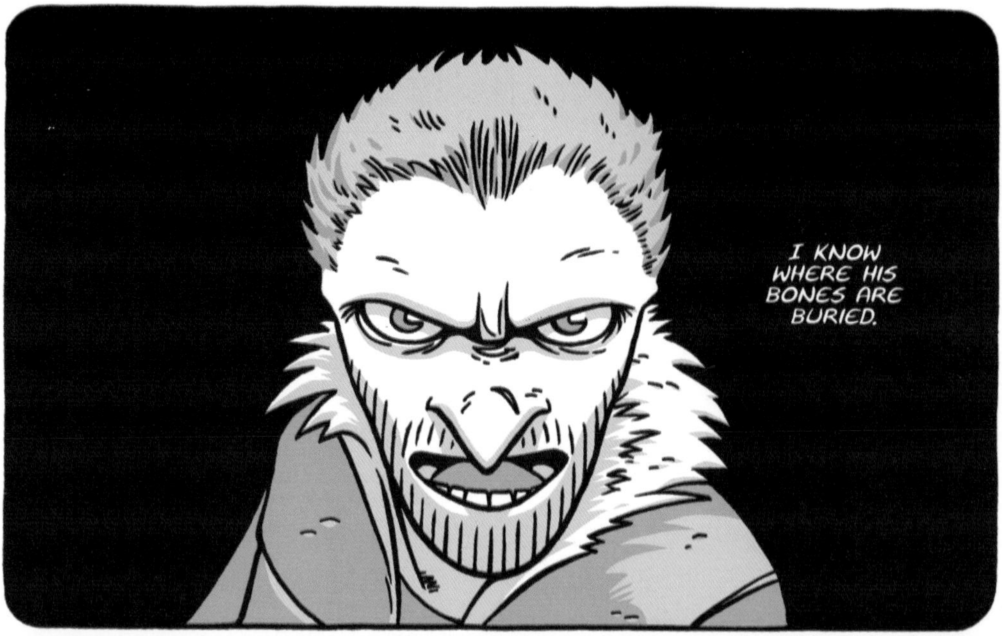
I KNOW WHERE HIS BONES ARE BURIED.

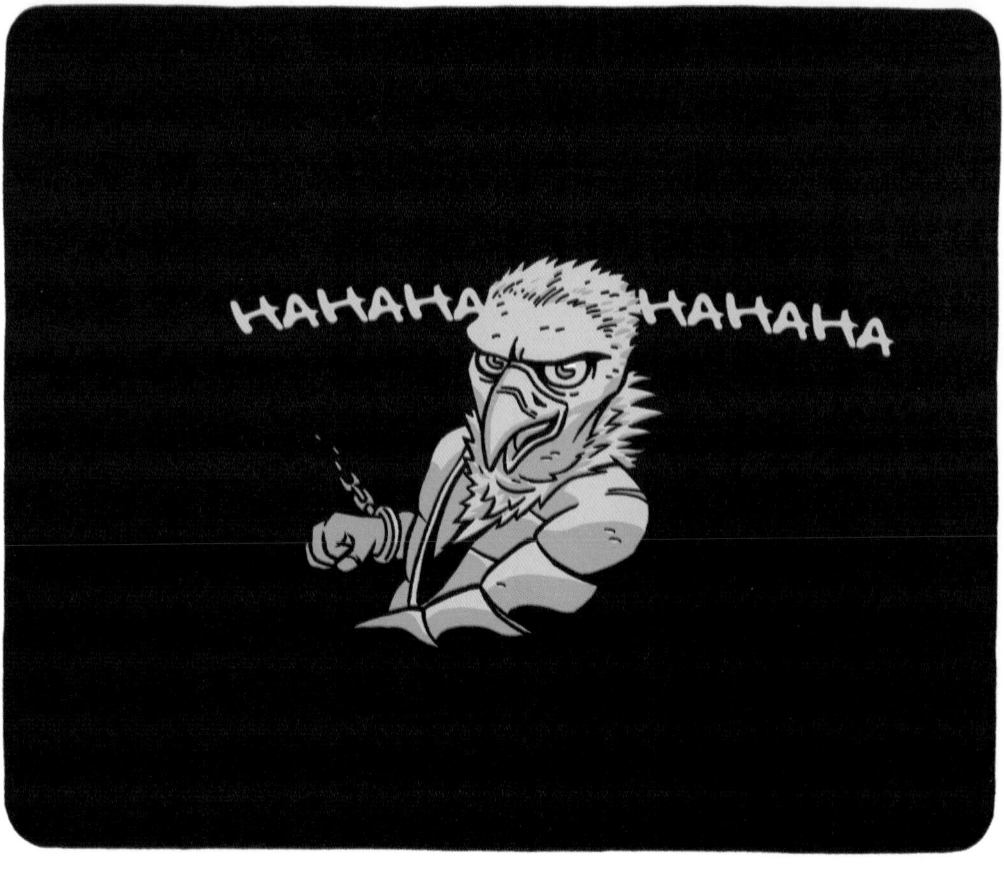
HAHAHAHAHAHAHA

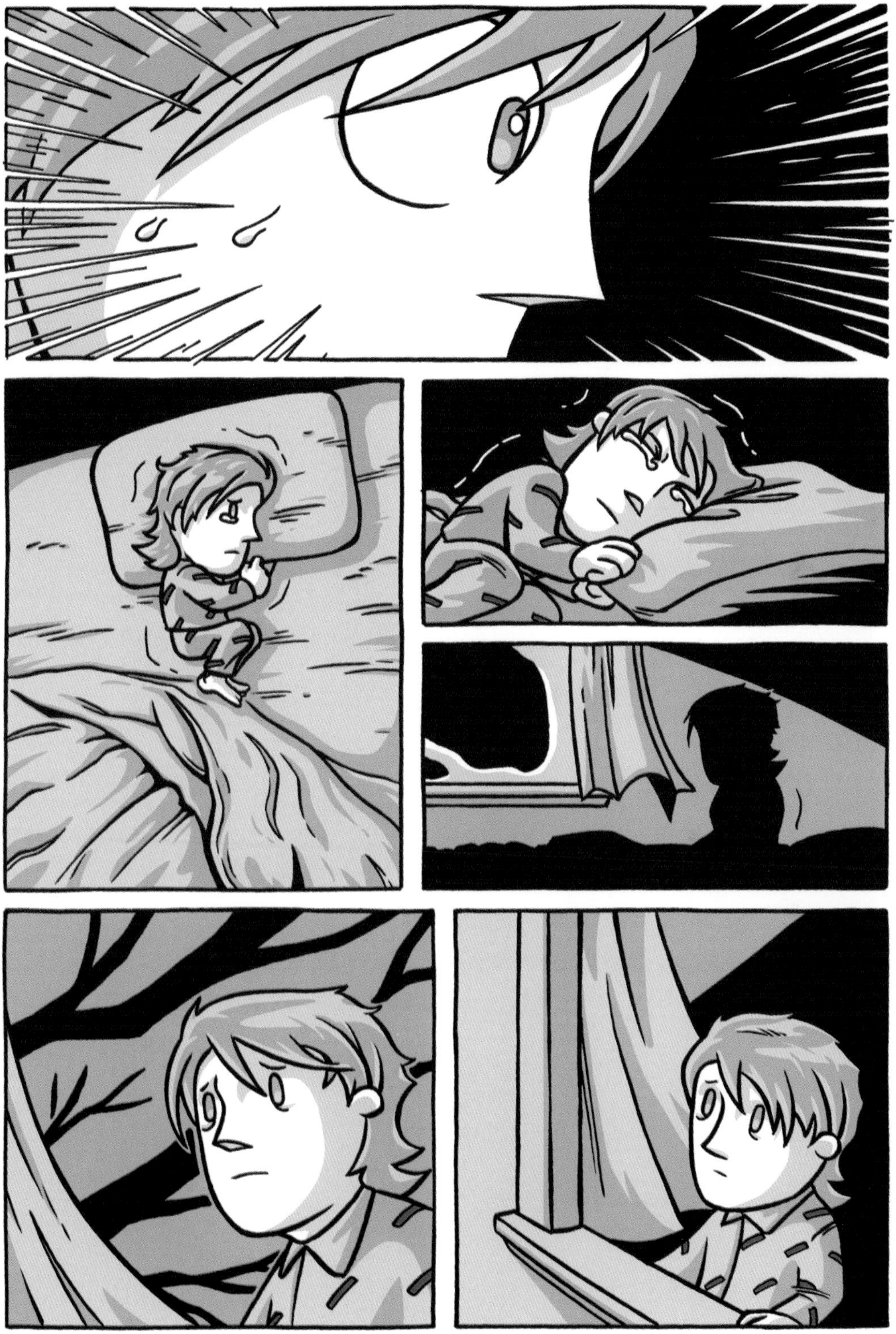

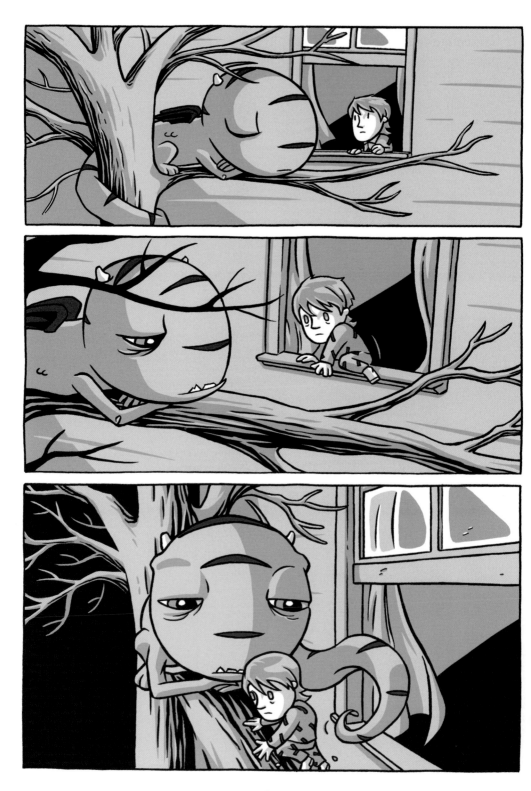

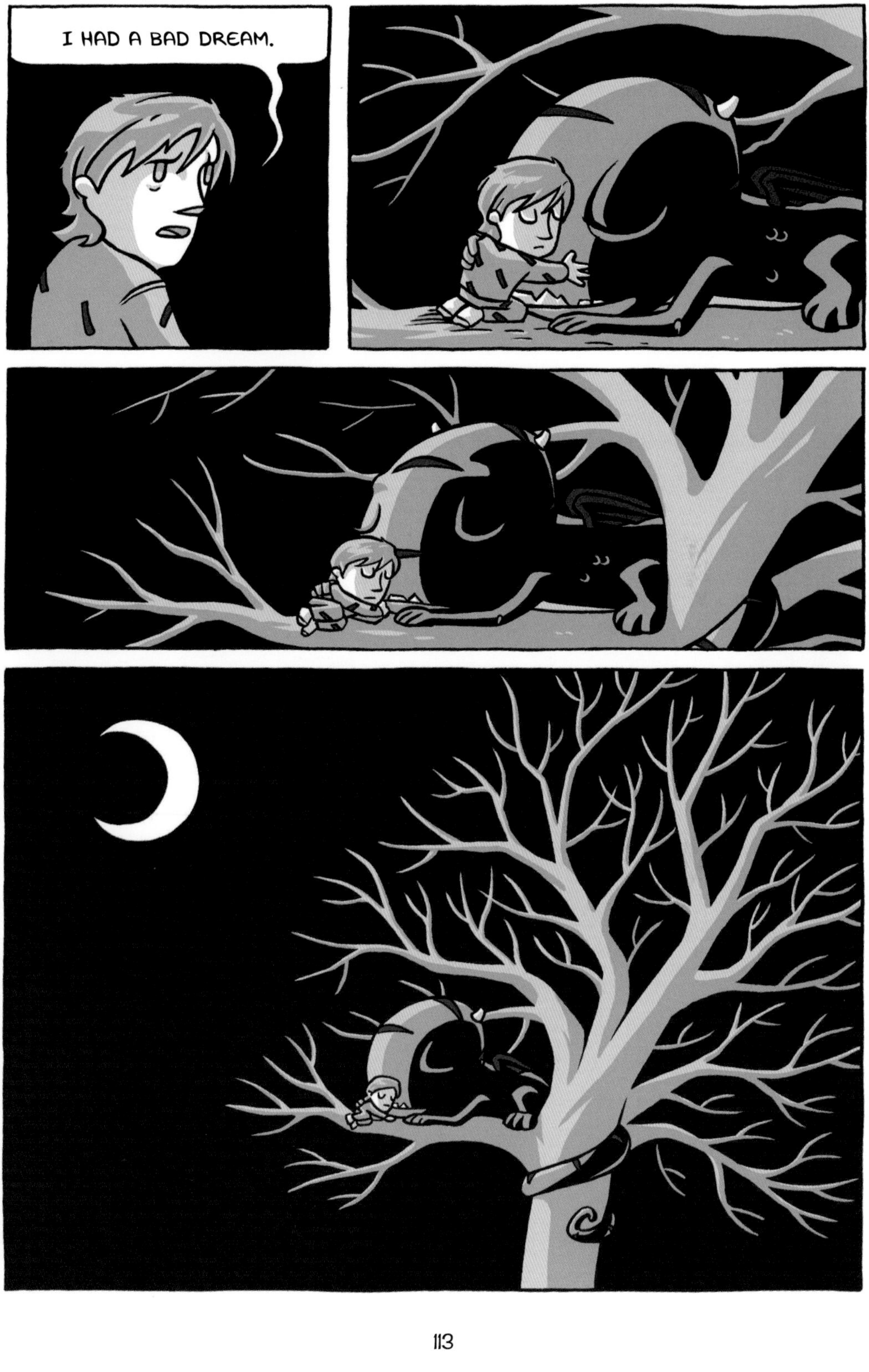
I HAD A BAD DREAM.

CHAPTER FIVE

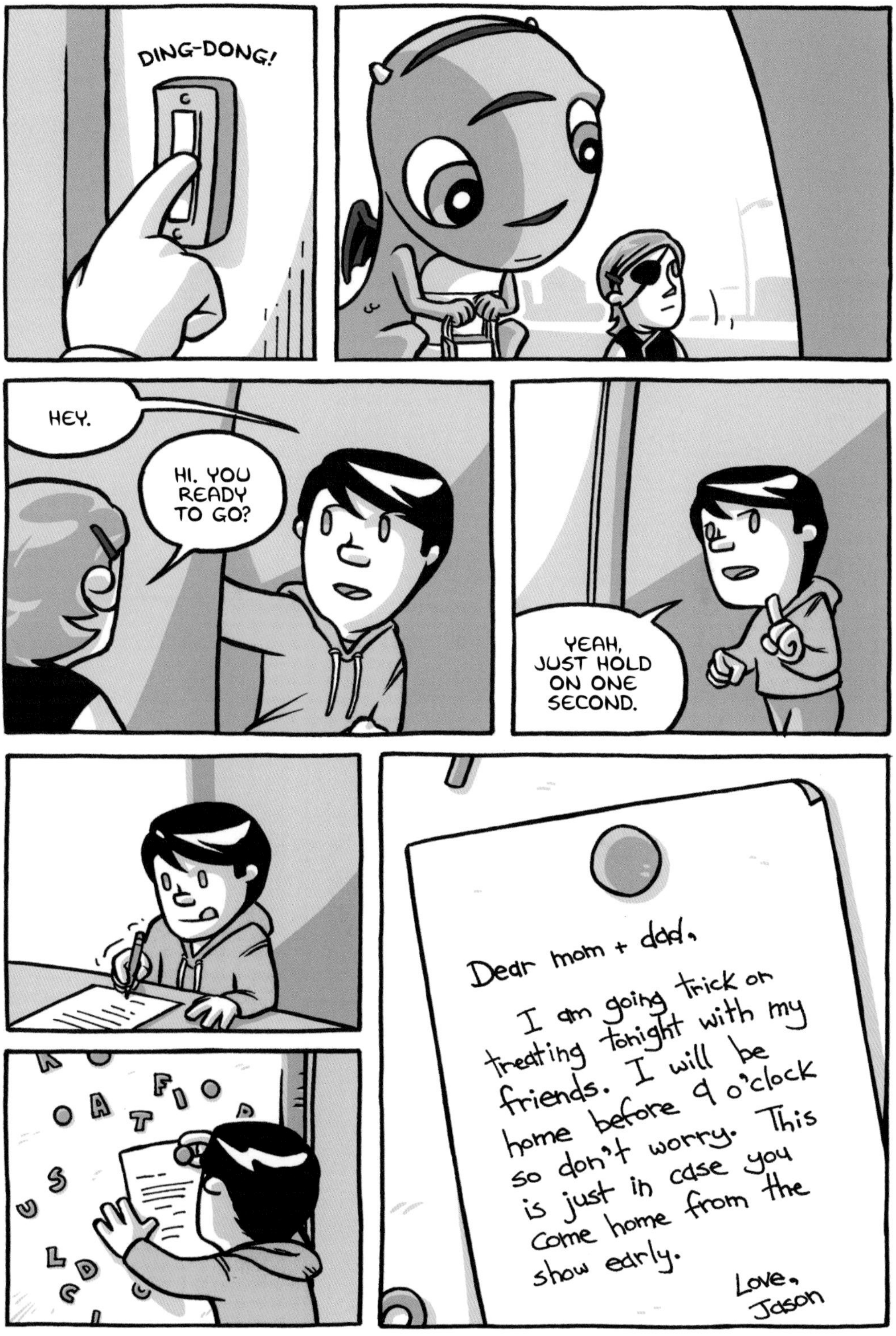
DING-DONG!
HEY.
HI. YOU READY TO GO?
YEAH, JUST HOLD ON ONE SECOND.
Dear mom + dad,
I am going trick or treating tonight with my friends. I will be home before 9 o'clock so don't worry. This is just in case you come home from the show early.
Love,
Jason

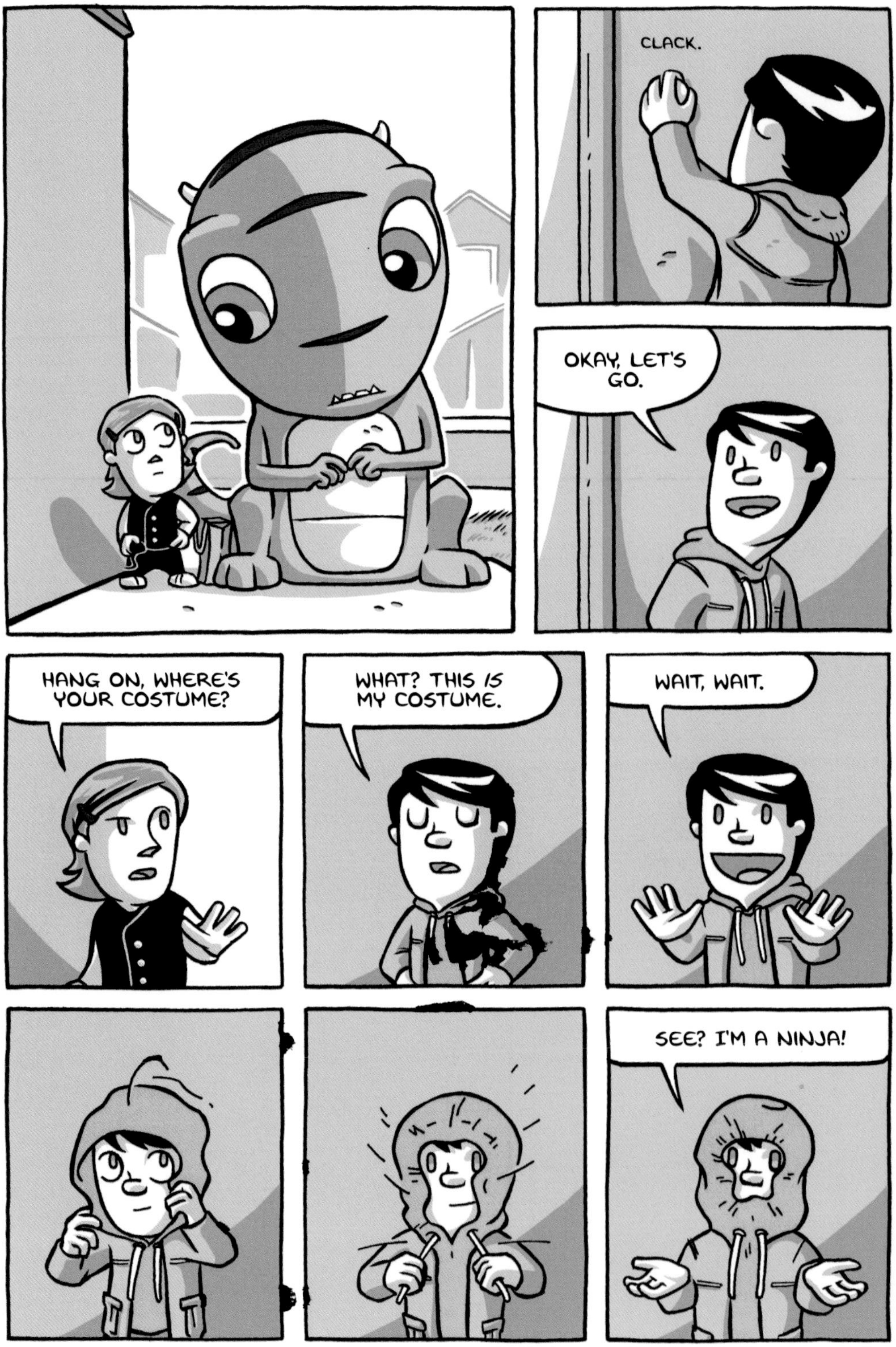
CLACK.
OKAY, LET'S GO.
HANG ON, WHERE'S YOUR COSTUME?
WHAT? THIS *IS* MY COSTUME.
WAIT, WAIT.
SEE? I'M A NINJA!

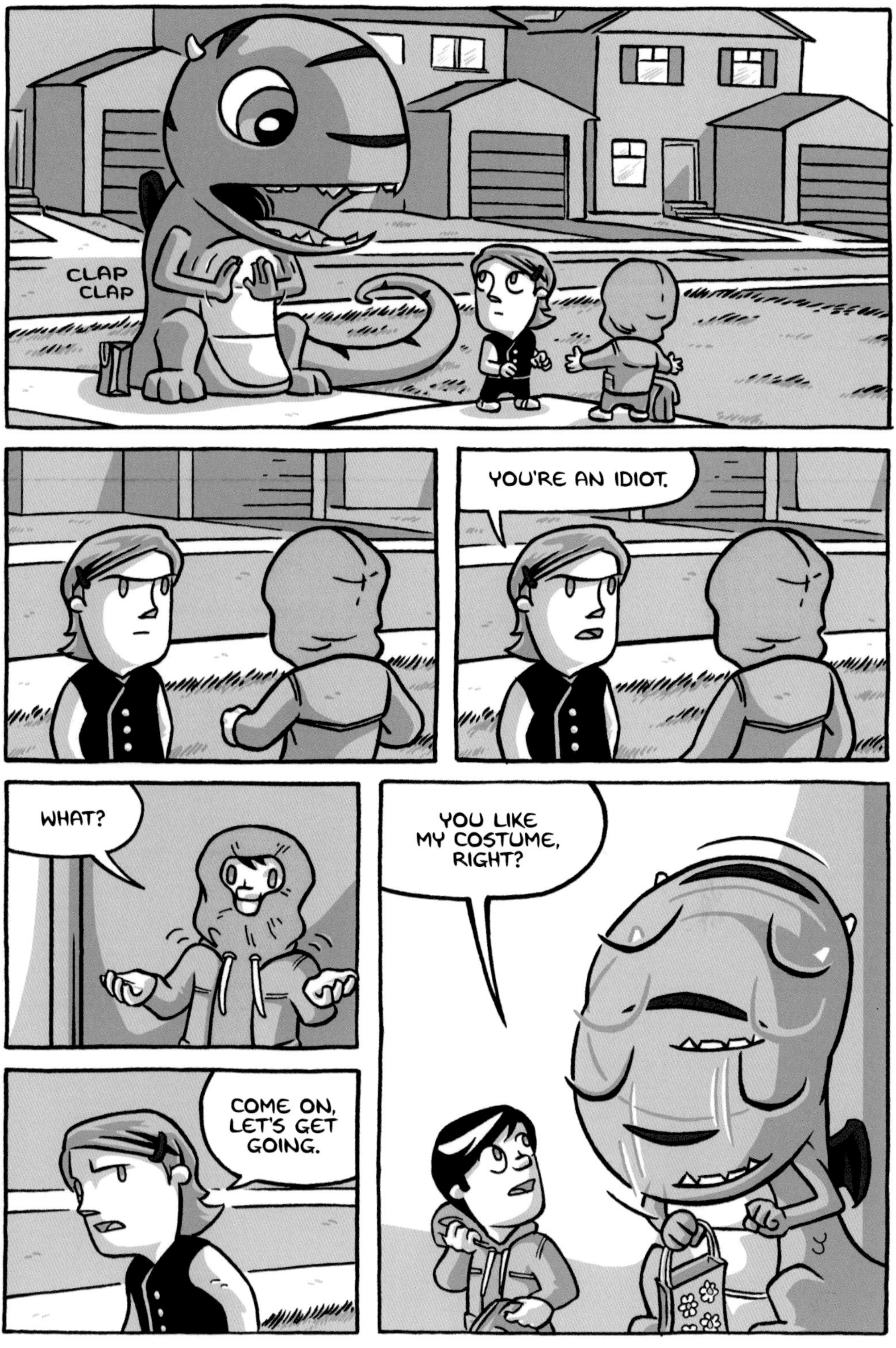
CLAP
CLAP
YOU'RE AN IDIOT.
WHAT?
YOU LIKE MY COSTUME, RIGHT?
COME ON, LET'S GET GOING.

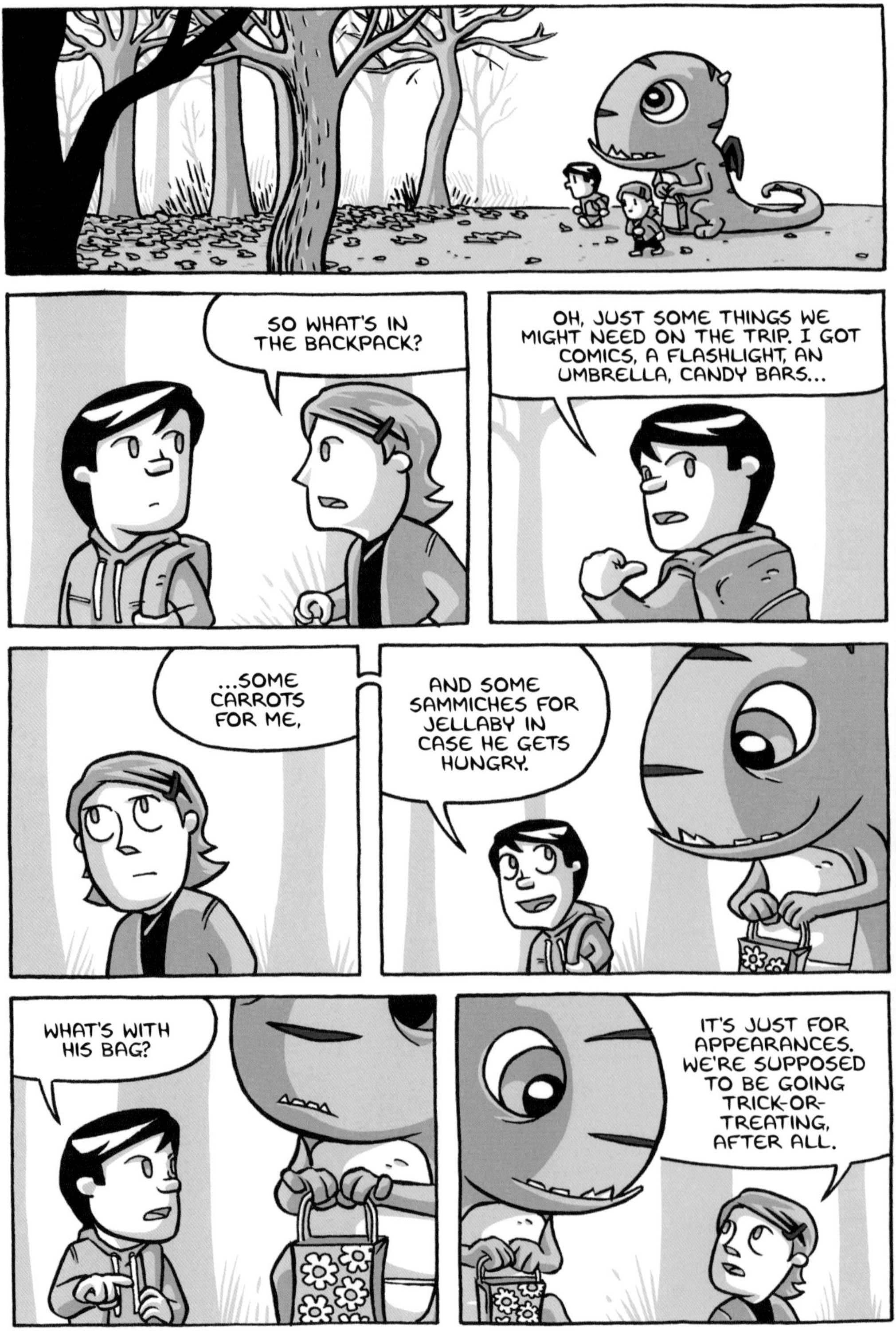
SO WHAT'S IN THE BACKPACK?
OH, JUST SOME THINGS WE MIGHT NEED ON THE TRIP. I GOT COMICS, A FLASHLIGHT, AN UMBRELLA, CANDY BARS...
...SOME CARROTS FOR ME,
AND SOME SAMMICHES FOR JELLABY IN CASE HE GETS HUNGRY.
WHAT'S WITH HIS BAG?
IT'S JUST FOR APPEARANCES. WE'RE SUPPOSED TO BE GOING TRICK-OR-TREATING, AFTER ALL.

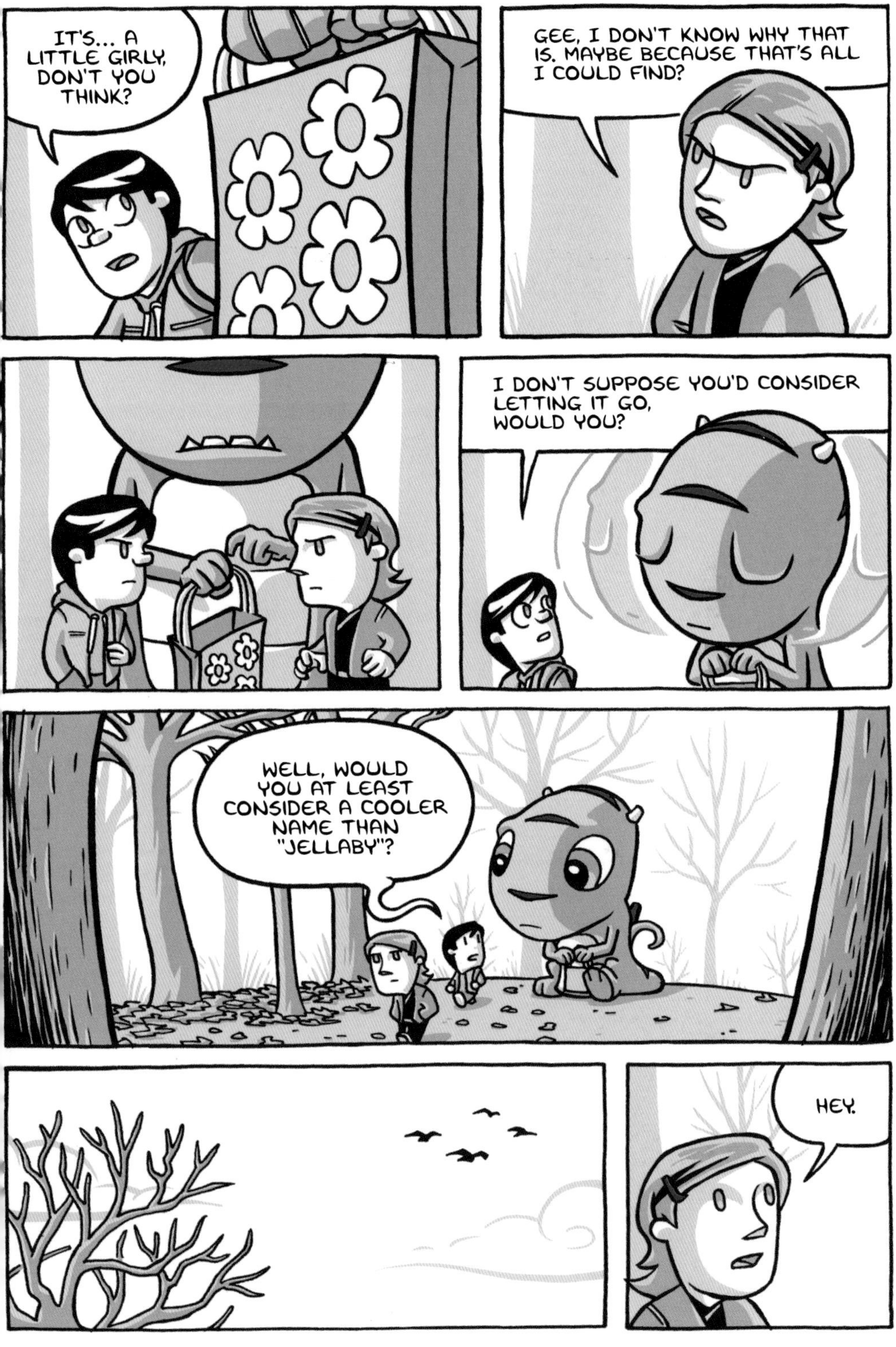
IT'S... A LITTLE GIRLY, DON'T YOU THINK?
GEE, I DON'T KNOW WHY THAT IS. MAYBE BECAUSE THAT'S ALL I COULD FIND?
I DON'T SUPPOSE YOU'D CONSIDER LETTING IT GO, WOULD YOU?
WELL, WOULD YOU AT LEAST CONSIDER A COOLER NAME THAN "JELLABY"?
HEY.

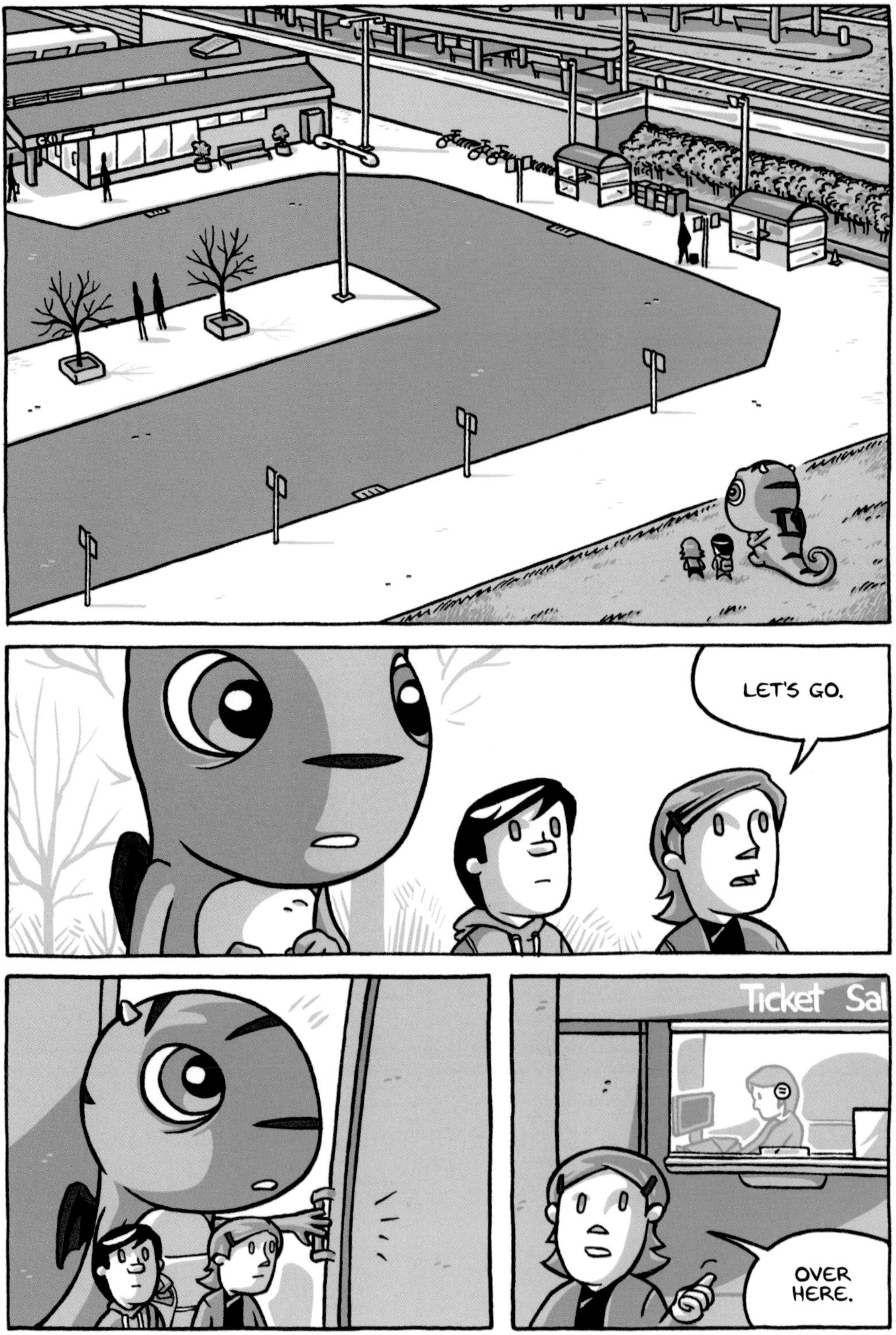
LET'S GO.
Ticket Sal
OVER HERE.

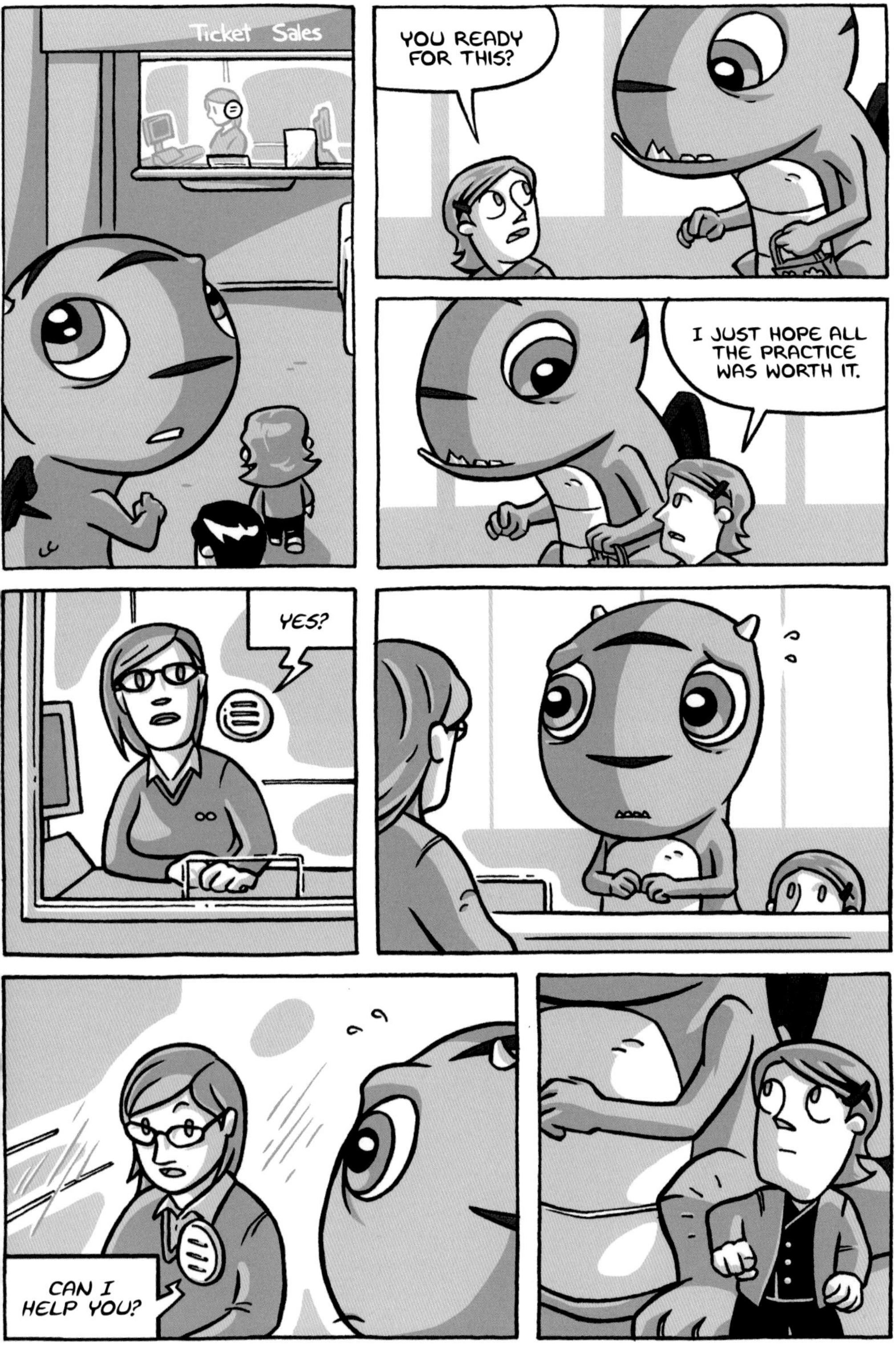

Ticket Sales
YOU READY FOR THIS?
I JUST HOPE ALL THE PRACTICE WAS WORTH IT.
YES?
CAN I HELP YOU?

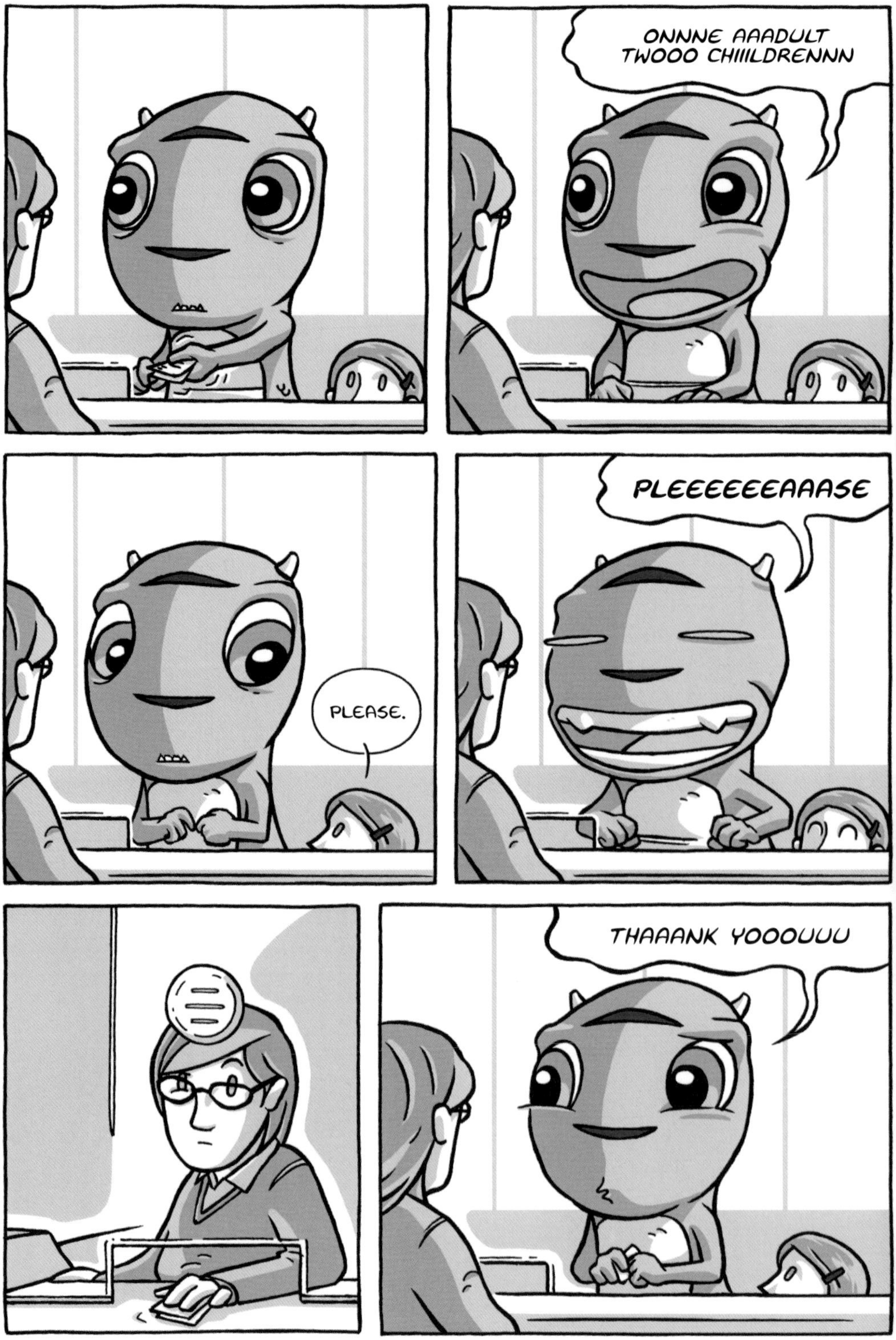
ONNNE AAADULT TWOOO CHIIILDRENNN
PLEASE.
PLEEEEEEEAAASE
THAAANK YOOOUUU

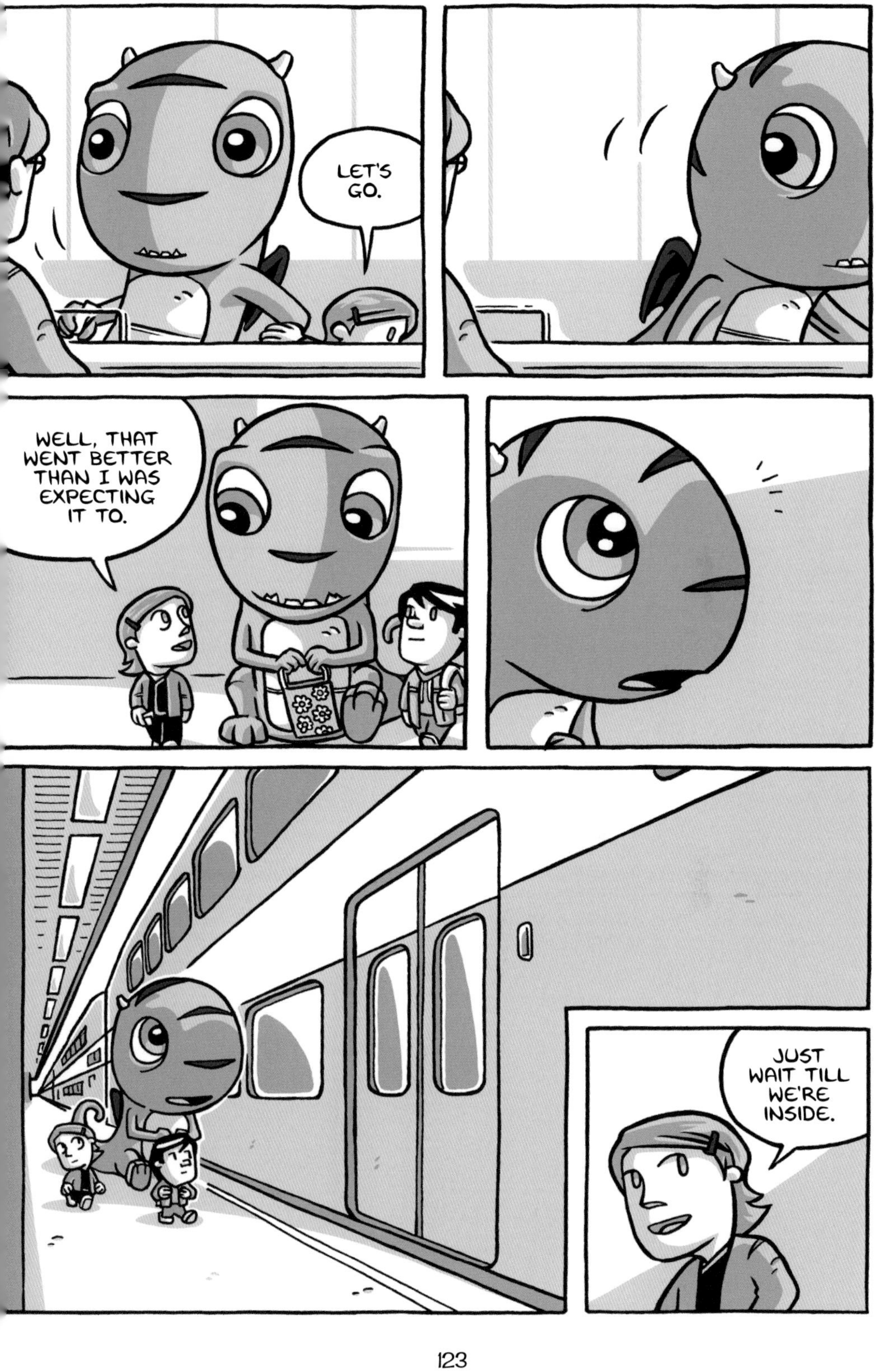
LET'S GO.
WELL, THAT WENT BETTER THAN I WAS EXPECTING IT TO.
JUST WAIT TILL WE'RE INSIDE.

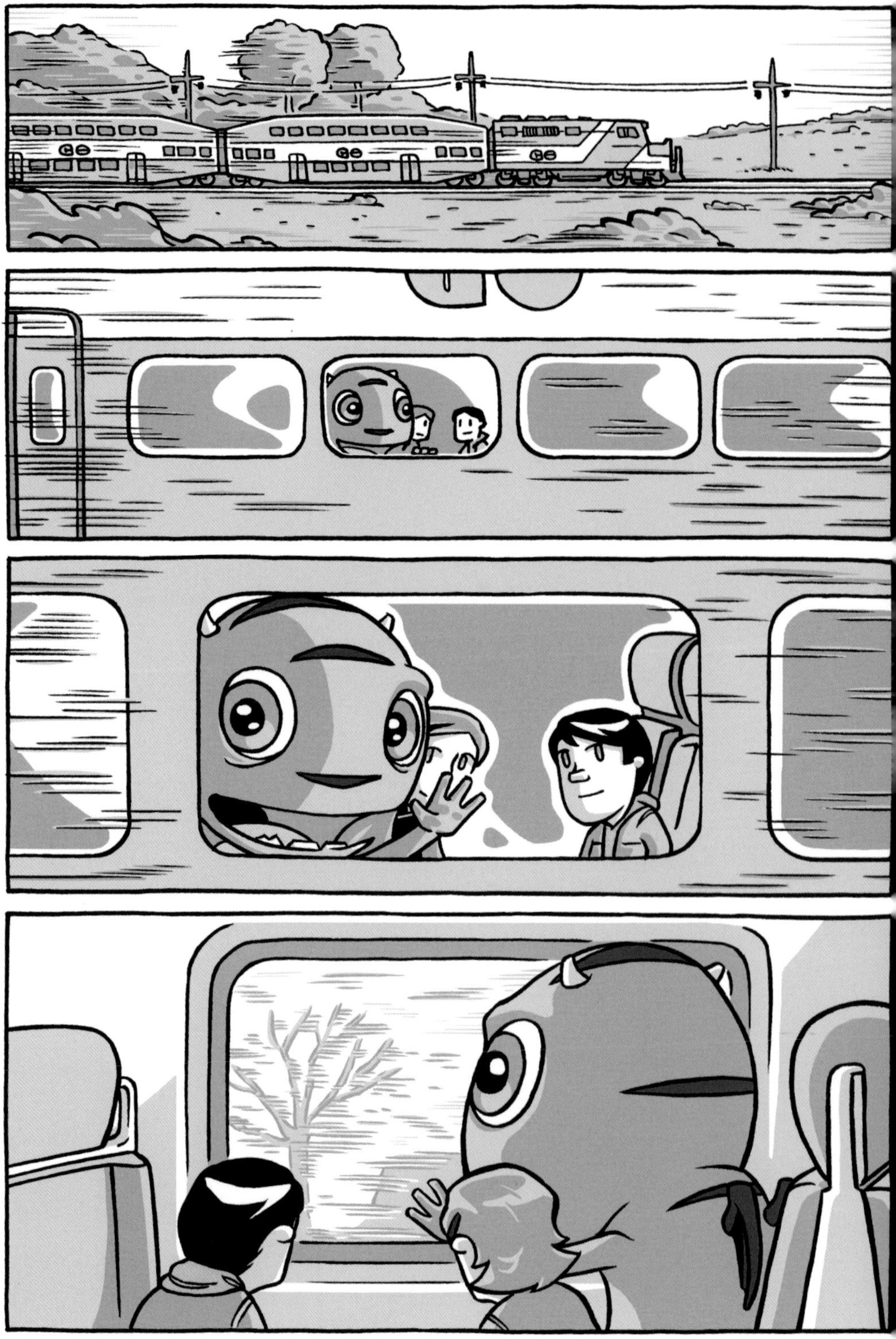

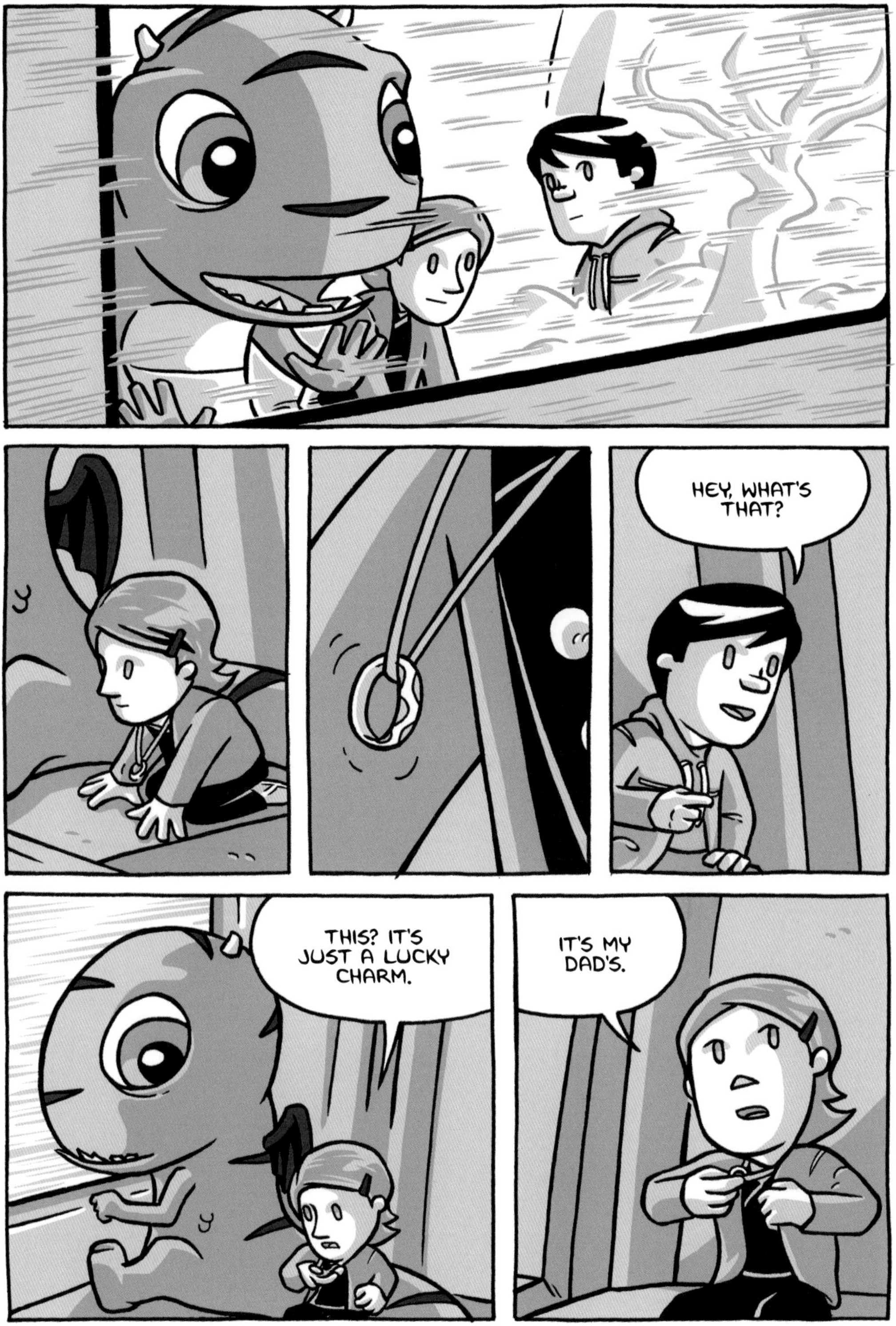
HEY, WHAT'S THAT?
THIS? IT'S JUST A LUCKY CHARM.
IT'S MY DAD'S.

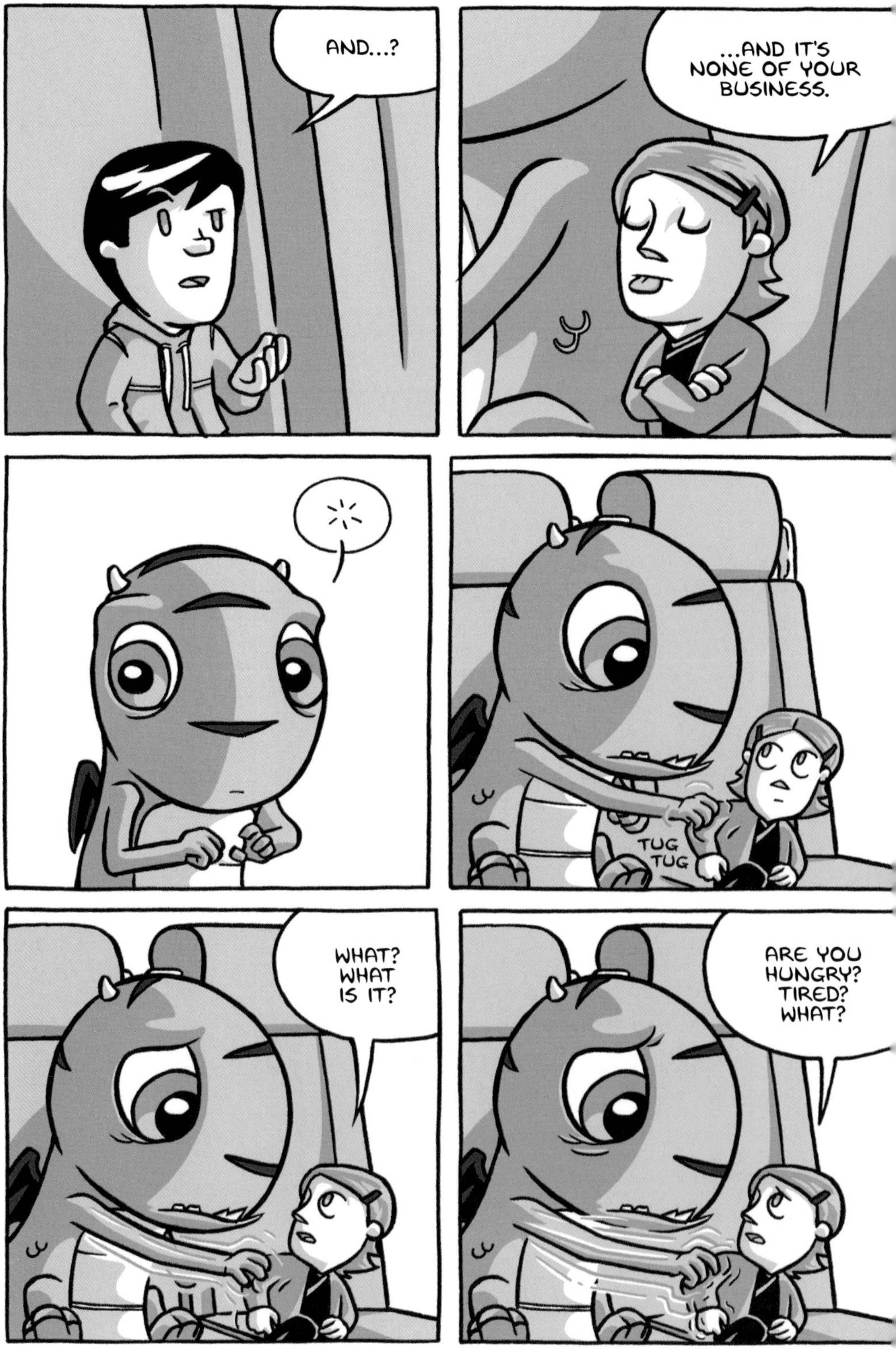
AND...?
...AND IT'S NONE OF YOUR BUSINESS.
TUG TUG
WHAT? WHAT IS IT?
ARE YOU HUNGRY? TIRED? WHAT?

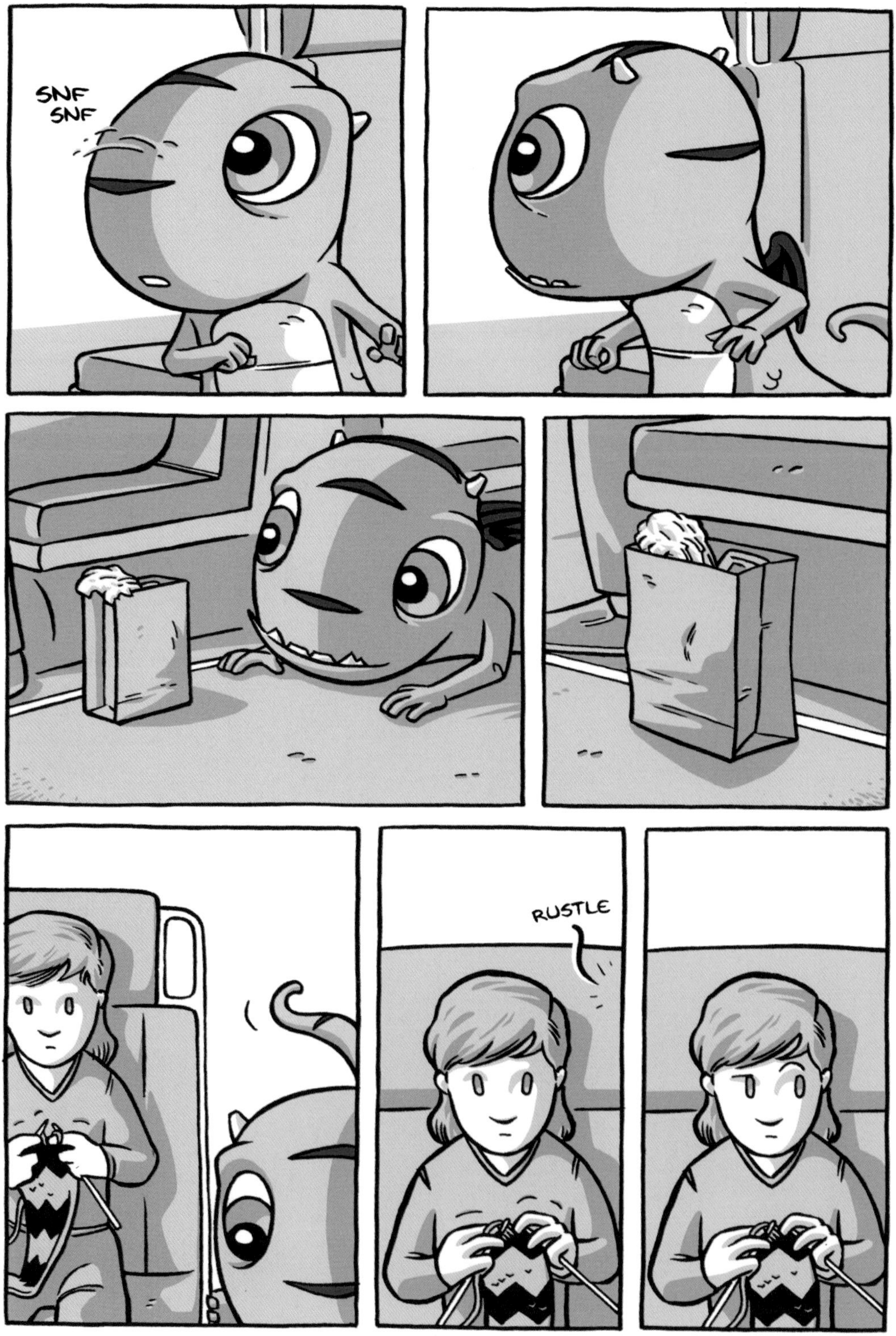
SNF
SNF
RUSTLE

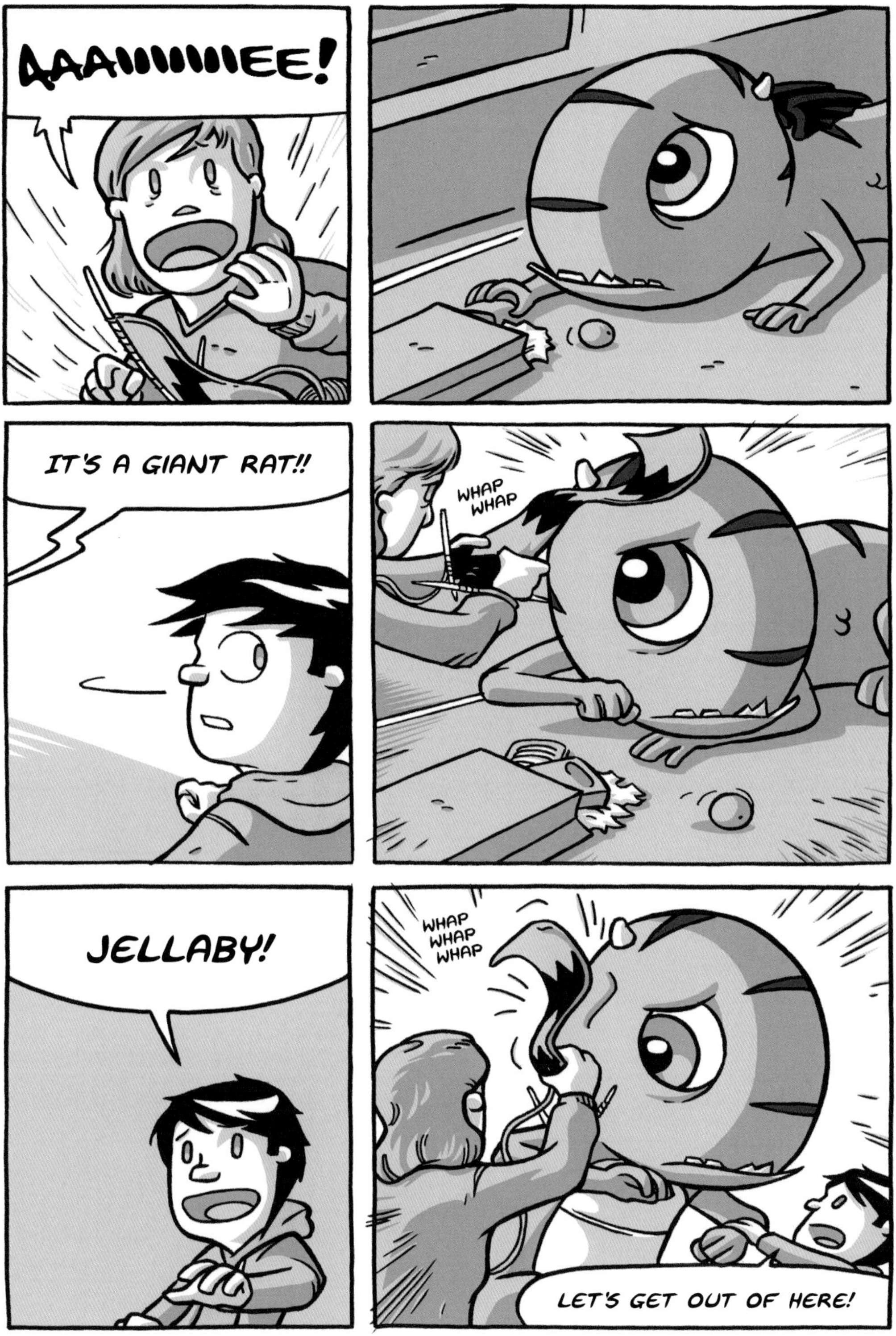

AAAIIIIIIIEE!
IT'S A GIANT RAT!!
WHAP
WHAP
JELLABY!
WHAP
WHAP
WHAP
LET'S GET OUT OF HERE!

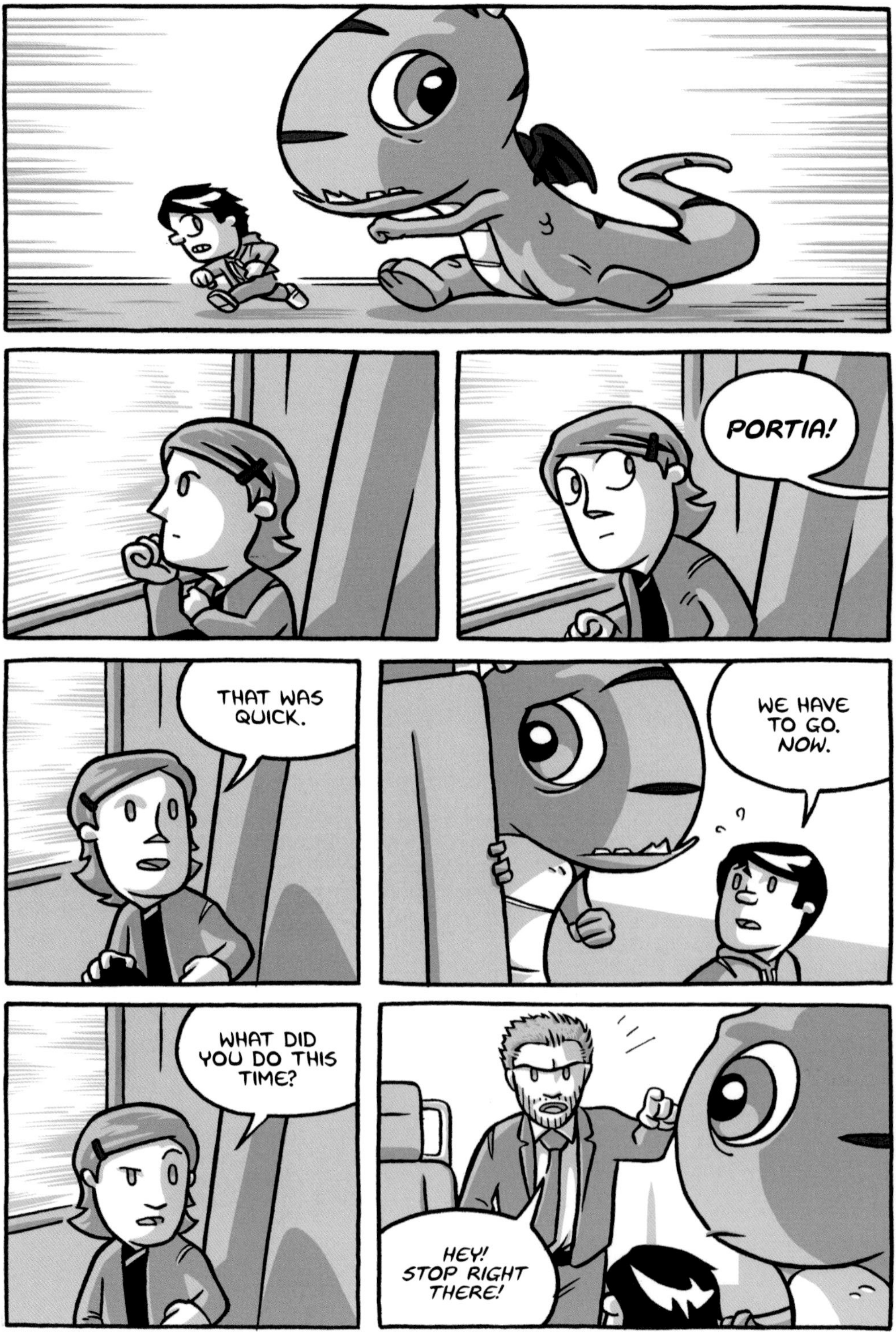
PORTIA!
THAT WAS QUICK.
WE HAVE TO GO. NOW.
WHAT DID YOU DO THIS TIME?
HEY! STOP RIGHT THERE!

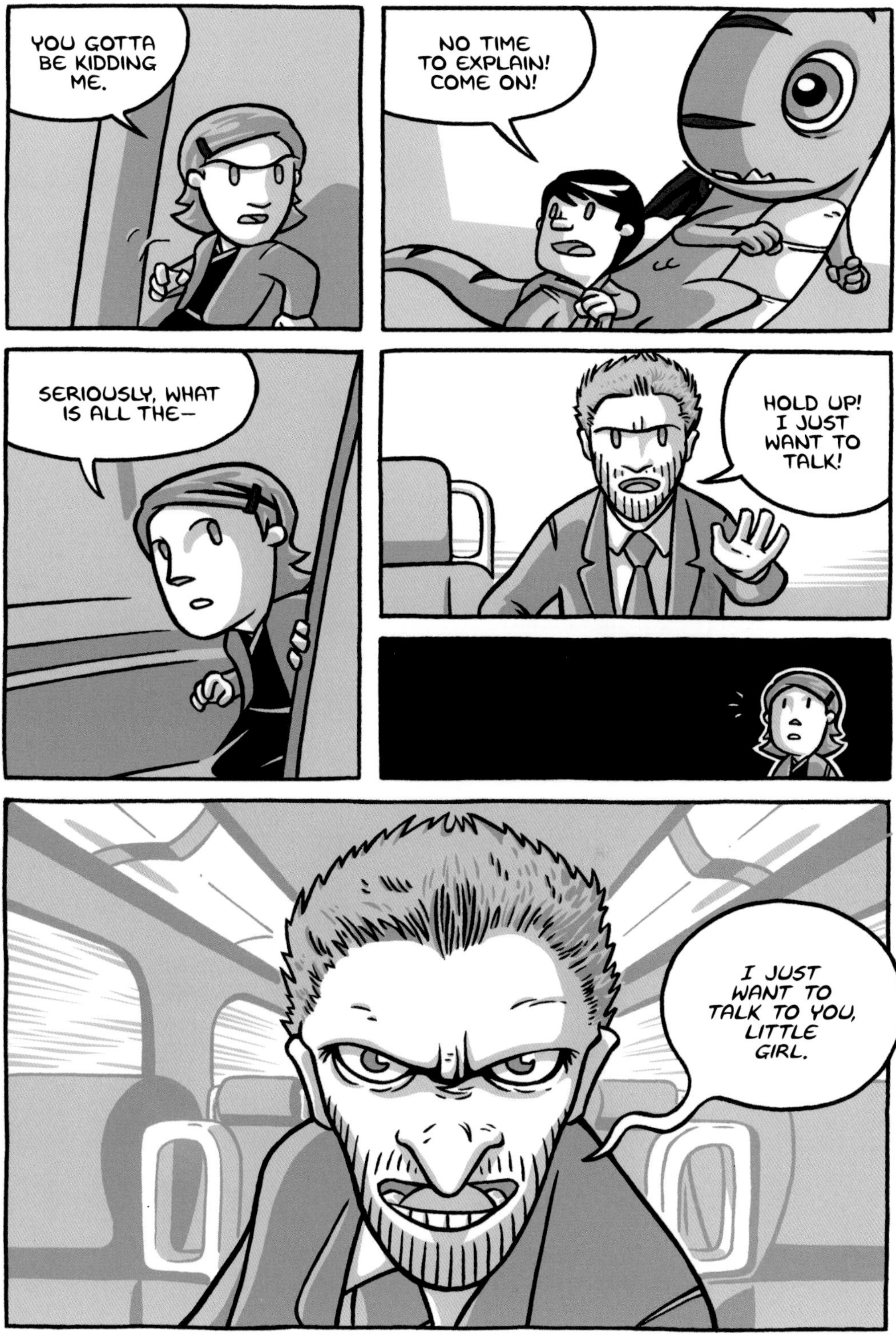
YOU GOTTA BE KIDDING ME.
NO TIME TO EXPLAIN! COME ON!
SERIOUSLY, WHAT IS ALL THE—
HOLD UP! I JUST WANT TO TALK!
I JUST WANT TO TALK TO YOU, LITTLE GIRL.

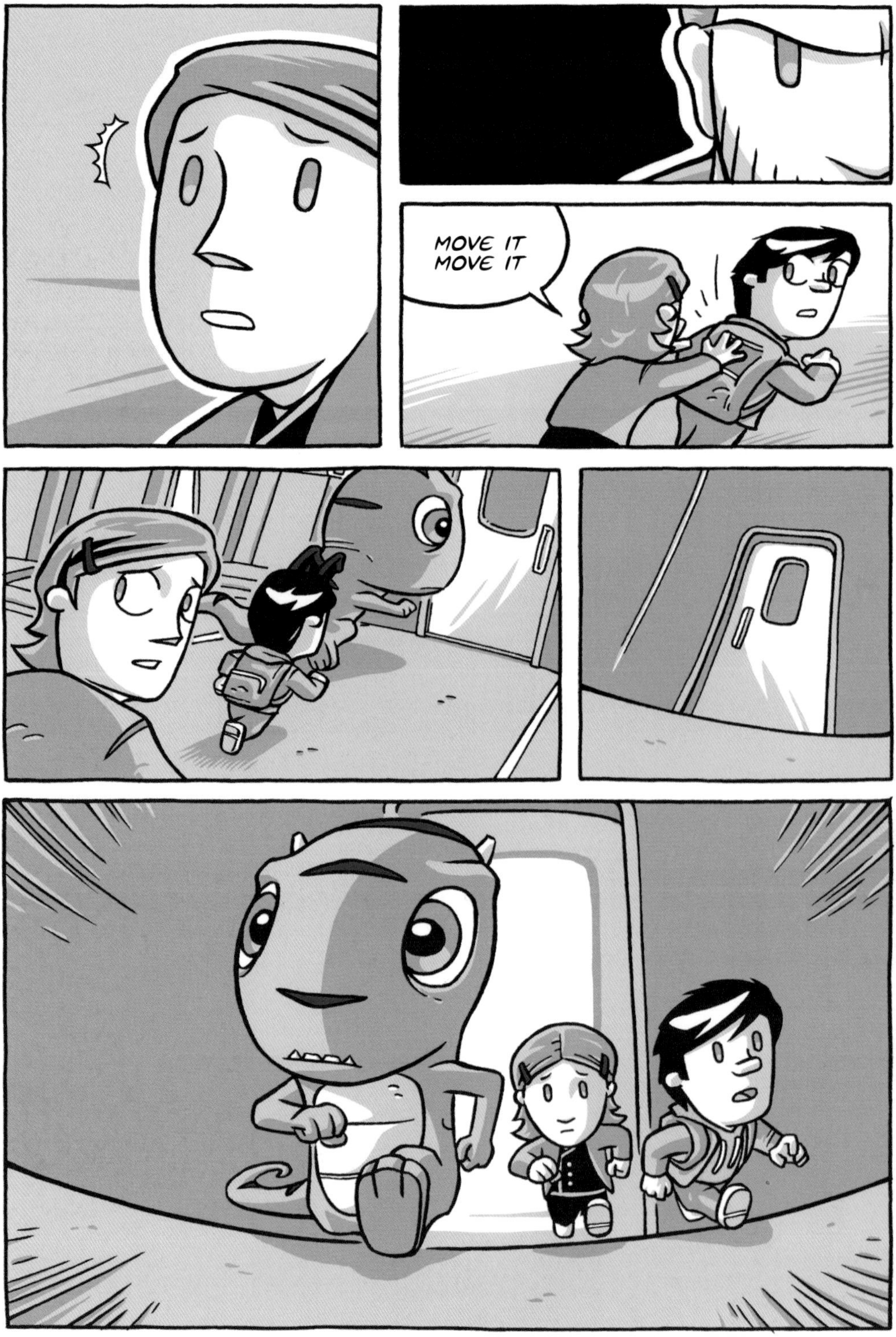
MOVE IT
MOVE IT

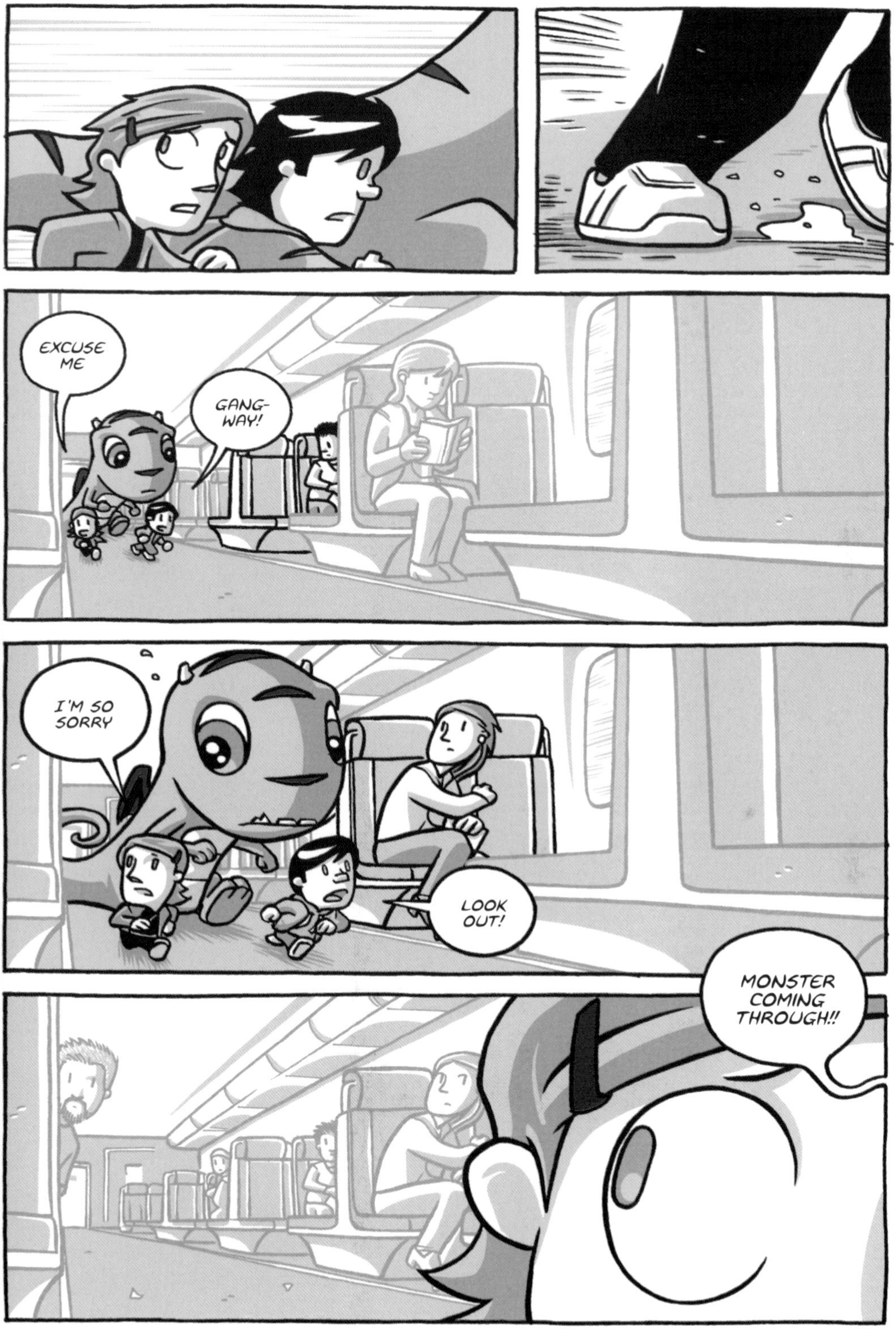
EXCUSE ME
GANG-WAY!
I'M SO SORRY
LOOK OUT!
MONSTER COMING THROUGH!!

137

138

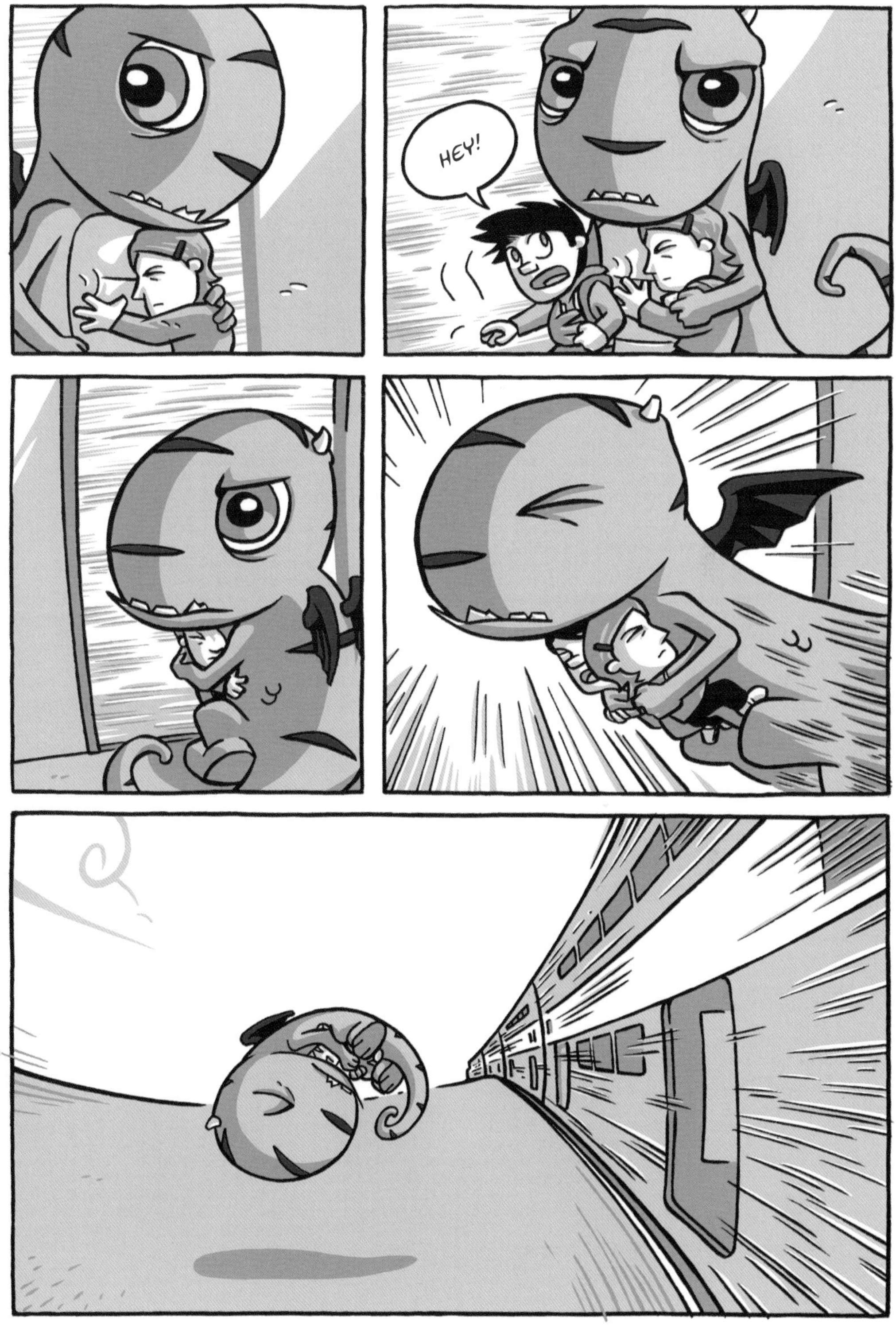
HEY!

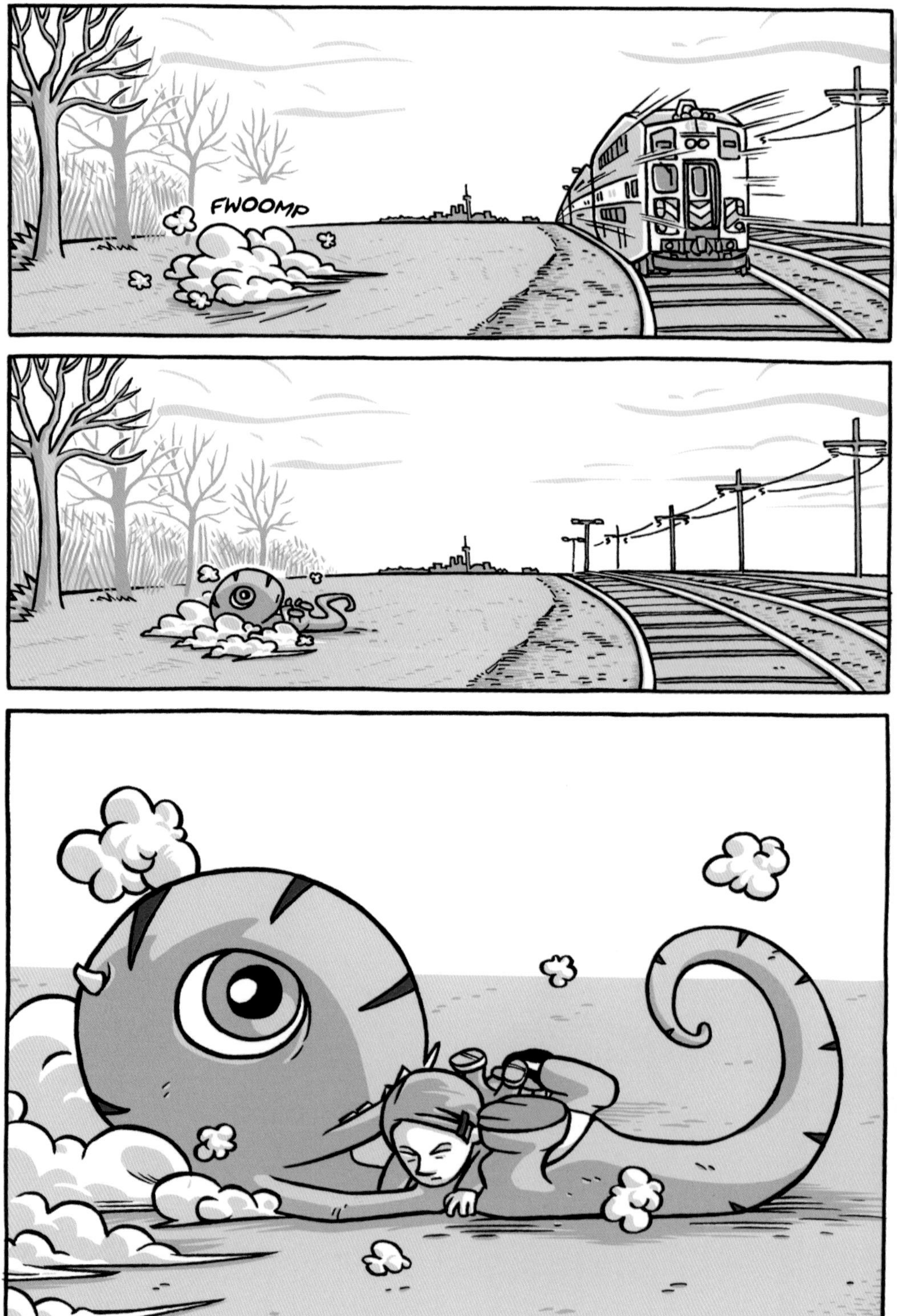
FWOOMP

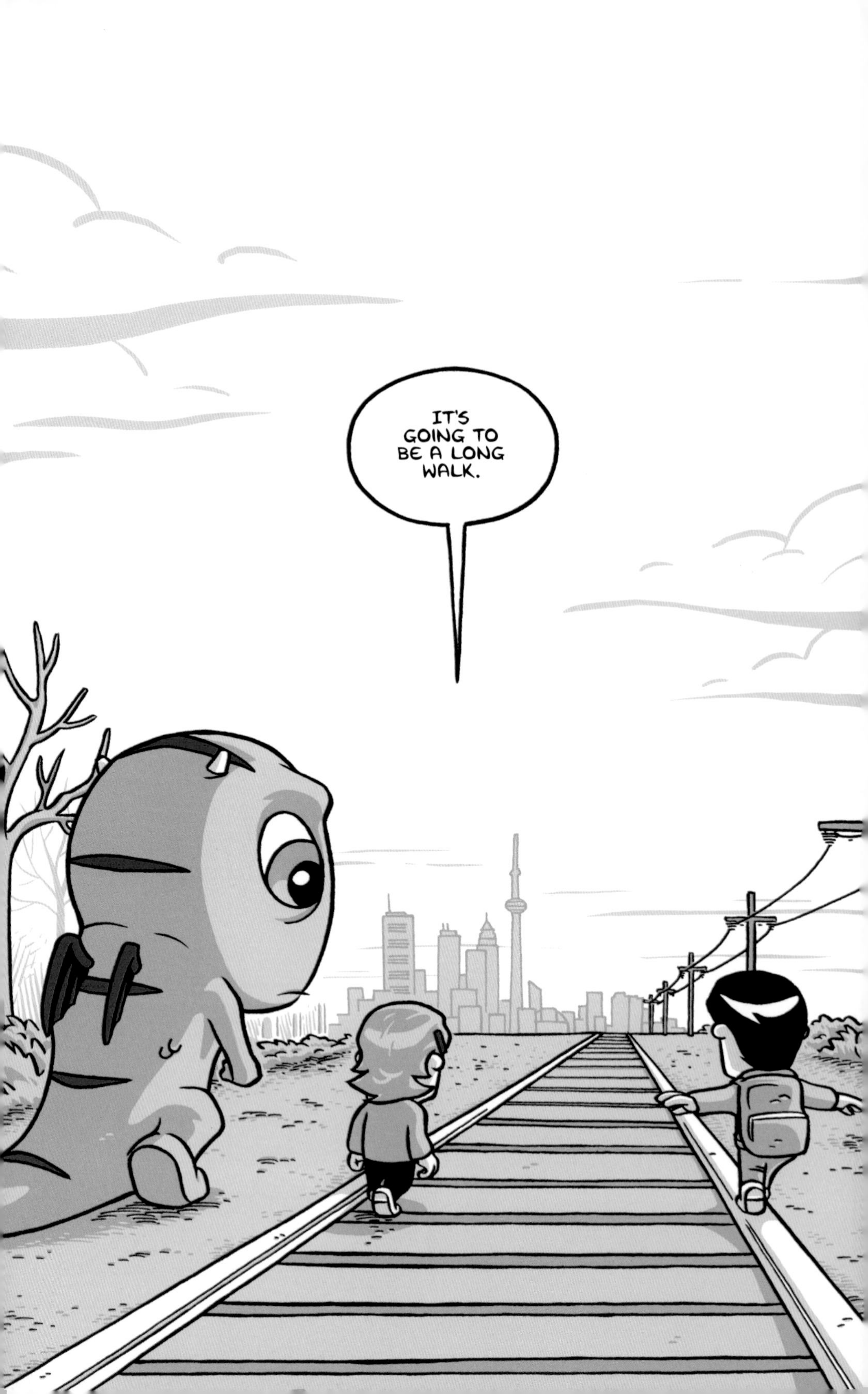
IT'S GOING TO BE A LONG WALK.

TO BE CONTINUED...

ABOUT THE AUTHOR

BORN IN ENGLAND AND RAISED IN HONG KONG, KEAN SOO
SETTLED IN CANADA, WHERE HE PLANNED TO EMBARK ON
A CAREER IN ELECTRICAL ENGINEERING. HOWEVER, HE
DISCOVERED THAT HE'D RATHER DRAW COMICS INSTEAD.
KEAN BEGAN POSTING HIS COMICS ON THE INTERNET IN
2002, AND LATER BECAME AN ASSISTANT EDITOR AND
REGULAR CONTRIBUTOR TO THE ALL-AGES FLIGHT
ANTHOLOGIES. HIS ONLINE WORK HAS BEEN NOMINATED
FOR SEVERAL AWARDS, INCLUDING AN EISNER AWARD
NOMINATION FOR *JELLABY*.

KEAN LIKES CARROTS, BUT NOT NEARLY AS MUCH AS HE
LIKES TUNA SANDWICHES, USUALLY WITH LOTS AND LOTS
OF WASABI MAYONNAISE.

PORTRAIT OF THE AUTHOR BY PHIL CRAVEN

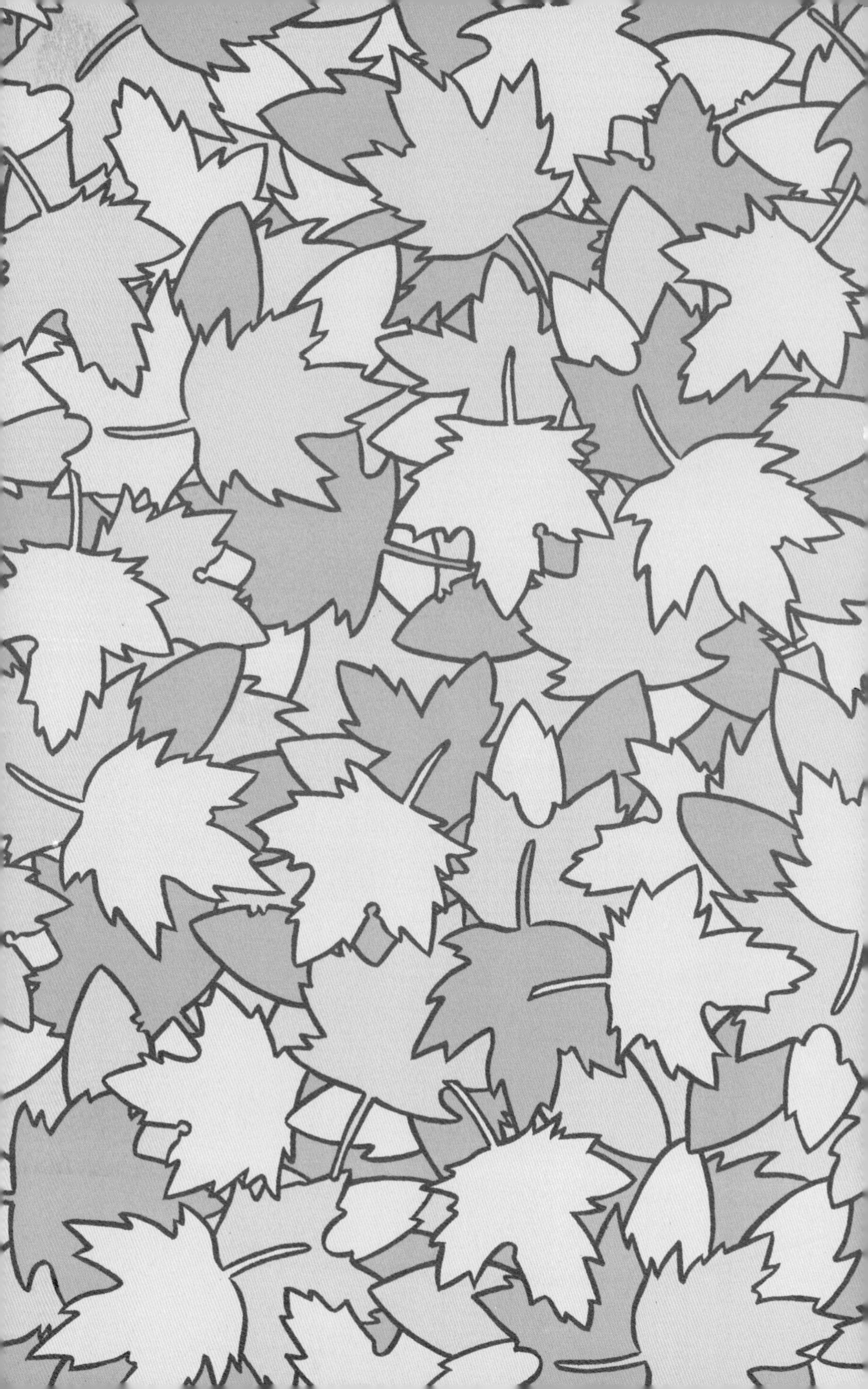